David Dominé

True Ghost Stories and Eerie Legends from

America's Most

HAUNTED

Neighborhood

David Dominé

David Dominé

ISBN: 1494289016
ISBN-13: 978-1494289010

Table of Contents

A historical marker on South Third Street in Louisville reminds visitors of the city's fame for beautiful homes, many of which are found just south of the downtown core, in the Old Louisville preservation district. Because of the high concentration of paranormal activity in these dwellings, Old Louisville has gained a reputation as "America's most haunted neighborhood."

Central Park

The green heart of Old Louisville is Central Park. A lovely mission-style building was constructed there shortly after the park's 1905 redesign by the firm of famed American landscape architect Frederick Law Olmsted. Call (502) 718-2764 to arrange a guided history and architecture walk of the neighborhood; or better yet, sign up for the evening's ghost walk and see many of the sites described in this book. Tours are offered year round.

COVER DESIGN

for

*True Ghost Stories and Eerie Legends from
America's Most
Haunted Neighborhood*

by

Carrie Sweet

Chapter 1 – A Poltergeist Named Lucy

Like many homes in Old Louisville, the unassuming residence at 1228 South Third Street has seen its share of history. Named for its first owners, the Widmer House has stood silently while more than a century's worth of untold events unfolded in front of – and behind – its ornate Flemish-arabesque façade. It sits about halfway between the downtown area and world-renowned Churchill Downs on a small plot of land measuring only thirty feet across and eighty feet deep. As you're leaving down the front walk, if you take a left on Third Street and walk due north for twenty minutes or so, you'll cross Broadway and enter the revitalized downtown entertainment district along Fourth Street. If you take a right and stroll a couple miles due south, you might just hear the starter's bugle at the famed racetrack for the spring and fall meets at Churchill Downs. Either way you chose, you'll see a stretch of antique residential design that experts have called one of the richest architectural experiences in the country, and you'll pass dozens and dozens of beautiful homes, each of them with a story.

Widmer House, for example, saw its first inhabitants around 1895 when it opened its doors for the business manager of the National Tobacco Works. His name was Joseph C. Widmer, and his wife was Kate Widmer. One of many tobacco houses in a city that produced half of the world's tobacco in its day, the National Tobacco Works employed some five hundred workers and produced more than six million pounds of burly a year. The house Joseph Widmer bought sat on a larger plot of land originally owned by a neighbor to the south, J.S. Bockee, who also worked in Louisville's thriving tobacco industry. Although he had already made a name and fortune for himself as an astute broker of Kentucky's most famous crop, Mr. Bockee realized more money could be made by the sale of land already in short supply at that time. He took his piece of land to the north, removed an older structure there, and then equally divided the plot into two smaller parcels where he built larger homes with identical floor plans.

Rather small compared to other dwellings along Third Street, its roughly four thousand square feet of living space include three floors, six bedrooms, eight fire places, four flights of stairs, one large linen closet and a poltergeist named Lucy. At least, that's how the house's previous owners always described it.

Although yet to be proven, Charles D. Meyer, Louisville's first and foremost architect of national acclaim, probably designed the spacious town home to make the most of the small plot of land where German,

Irish, African-American and Kentucky craftsmen would create a thoroughly modern and efficient home for its time. Erected at a cost of $12,500, the house boasts a unique façade that might be more at home in a medieval village in northern Europe or one of the many whimsical movie palaces built across this country in the late 1920s. Or perhaps in a Victorian notion of what a Moroccan-inspired palace in Spain might have looked like. Locals at one time did in fact refer to Widmer House as the "Moorish Palace" given its mosque-like finials and dramatic roofline, and it reputedly hosted several lavish parties in the late 1920s that played on the Lawrence-of-Arabia theme.

By this time the Widmers had already sold the house, and ownership had passed through several hands, most of them single females, by the time World War II ended. For most prosperous cities around the nation, the next several decades bore witness to a dark period in terms of urban development, and Louisville, like all the rest, suffered a period marked by neglect of – and flight from – its grandest neighborhoods. Many gracious homes fell victim to the wrecking ball, and mansions in Old Louisville became flophouses and bordellos, passed to absentee landlords or sat abandoned. A look through the *Caron's City Directories* of the mid 1900s shows that a large number of these stately residences served as boarding houses for single men and woman employed in the Louisville workforce.

Widmer House, for example, housed employees of the nearby L & N Railroad for many years, and it continued as a boarding house until the 1970s. Although it had not been totally stripped of its character like other dwellings in the area, the former residence of Joseph and Kate Widmer had seen better days when a small family bought it in the 1980s. Over the next fourteen years – and with no small amount of elbow grease – they patiently converted the former rooming house to a comfortable single-family residence.

Although it had been largely restored on the interior, many people in the neighborhood said it had always looked like a haunted house to them from the outside. The ornate façade had been painted a dingy battle-ship gray that always cast a gloomy pall, and a dramatic, steep-pitched gable soared menacingly overhead and warded off would-be visitors like the severe gaze of an unfriendly sentry. A pair of gargoyle-like chameleons bared their teeth and seemed to hiss at passersby from their perches twenty feet off the ground. Time had weathered the terra cotta garland adorning the arched window on the ground floor, and bits of broken stone and brick lying at the base of the house hinted at more damage overhead. Mortar had totally eroded from between the bricks in some spots, and bare tree branches rattled above. The house appeared to be little more than a solid slate of dark gray with numerous cracks and broken sculptural details.

Now the elaborate facade has been restored, repaired and brightly painted. So brightly painted, in fact, that many people in the neighborhood referred to it as the "Christmas House" because of the abundance of reds, greens, and gold leaf. When it was newly restored, details practically invisible to prior observers from the street leapt out and dazzled the eyes, and passersby frequently stopped dead in their tracks to admire the colorful collection of architectural adornment looming before them. With its colorful paint job, few suspected that the cheerful house at 1228 South Third Street might be haunted.

That's where I come in. I bought the house in 1999 and lived there for a number of years. In keeping with the home's original arabesque charm, I tried to incorporate a Victorian-inspired Moorish motif when redecorating the formal rooms in the house – the front parlor, reception hall and dining room. The small parlor has walls covered in gold anaglypta paper with patterned studs and a ceiling finished to look like gem-crusted Cordovan leather. A gold-leafed panel over the double doors leading into the foyer bears an inscription in Moroccan Arabic that says "Welcome." For the most part, all the changes I've made to the house have met with very positive feedback. Some alterations, on the other hand, did not receive the same approval. That's where the ghost comes in.

Although I've always considered myself a skeptic, I love ghost stories and have been intrigued by the paranormal since childhood. So, even if I didn't buy into the notion of chain-rattling spirits, the idea of living in a reportedly haunted house held a certain fascination for me. And Margaret, the previous owner, had just spent the previous fourteen years in the Widmer House, and if anyone knew of on-site ghosts or spirits, I figured she'd be it. When I first looked at the house, therefore, I asked Margaret if the premises happened to have a resident ghost. I said it more as a joke than a serious inquiry, something to keep the conversation going as we roamed from room to room in the house. But Margaret was totally serious when she said: "Just one. Lucy is her name, and she won't bother you too much." I followed her down the back set of stairs and chuckled as she continued the conversation. "She doesn't like it at all when you change things around, though." The way Margaret added this last comment as an afterthought made me a bit uneasy, but the excitement I felt as I summed up the house's potential in my mind quickly erased any misgivings I might have had about poltergeists. Several weeks later, on December 1st, I moved in, and quickly found myself with much more on my mind than ghosts. A chimney needed to be rebuilt before it collapsed and fell onto the neighbor's porch, the roof had three major leaks, and chunks of plaster kept falling from the ceiling in the parlor. During those first weeks, when pictures and prints kept falling from the walls in the kitchen and adjacent butler's pantry, I had no idea that anything other than a poor job of hanging them might have been the culprit. Even after they had been hung the third and forth times – with bigger nails and in different locations – most of them refused to stay put.

"Well, did you ask the ghost if it was OK to start hanging things on the wall?" a friend of mine asked as I swept up the broken glass from an antique lithograph of a huge pig that hung over the stove. It had just fallen for the third, and final, time. I decided it would look better sitting in the study on an old oak desk that I recently purchased at the Louisville Antique Mall. In the kitchen, my friend, Wendy, stood with hands planted firmly on her hips and stared at me while other people went to admire the newly decorated tree, a 13-foot one that took advantage of the high ceilings in the front parlor. Just the day before my housemate Ramon and I and some friends had spent a whole afternoon decorating the tree, only to have it tip over on us when we were out shopping, so people were curious to see the latest version. "Well, did you?" Wendy demanded. "A house this old has got to have a spook. My grandmother had a ghost in her house and she always said when you moved into a new place you needed to ask the spirits there if it was OK. Or else they'd cause trouble for you."

I had totally forgotten Margaret's comments about the resident ghost not liking things changed around too much in the house. I rolled my eyes and scoffed at Wendy as I took the dustpan and walked to the trashcan to deposit the last bits of broken glass I had collected. Just then, a loud crash echoed through the bottom floor and sent a thud reverberating through the walls. Convinced that yet another fully loaded Christmas tree had toppled over onto the hardwood floor, we both ran to the front of the house to survey the damage and destruction. But, the small group of friends gathered at the tree in the parlor had run into the foyer and awaited us with the same expectant look of dread, heads turning on crooked necks to see through the dining room and discover what had fallen in the kitchen. We all exchanged puzzled looks and wandered from room to room searching for the source of the loud commotion. From the sound of it, we all decided that a large chandelier must have fallen somewhere. In the parlor, however, the tree stood stock still, anchored in place by an invisible bit of wire that stretched between the crown molding and the top of the trunk.

A thorough search of the ground floor yielded absolutely nothing and we moved to the second and third floors – with the same result. We pulled down the steps to the attic and searched it to no avail and then made our way back down through the house and ended up in the basement. Nothing there seemed to explain the loud noise and shattering glass we had heard either. A quick run around the outside of the house in the frigid air resulted in the same puzzled looks and lack of explanation.

Back in the foyer, Wendy assumed the same hands-on-hips position and raised her eyebrows. "See? You have to OK it with the ghosts first!" Before I could shrug it off with another scoff, she went to the counter and picked up the hammer lying there and began waving it in the air. Punctuating her words, the hammer had been raised over her head and waved to and fro. "If you won't do it, I will!" Trying to look as imploring and respectful as a mad woman waving a hammer wildly about could, Wendy raised her eyes and shouted. "Dear Ghost Person, we just want to hang some nice pictures back here. You'll like them, so please don't knock them down anymore. We don't want to bother you and we understand it's your house. Thank you!" I flinched at the last comment, and Wendy started gathering nails so she could make better use of her hammer. Within five minutes she had managed to rehang all but one of the pictures that had fallen. The pig lithograph would still go to the study, but it needed to be reframed first.

A week later it proudly sat atop the old oak desk, and in the kitchen all the pictures had managed to stay where Wendy had hung them. Back in the kitchen, she had assumed her usual stance and slowly turned around to admire her handiwork, a smug grin painted on her face. "See? I *told* you so." She emptied her glass of wine in one gulp and opened another bottle. Once again, the same group of friends had gathered for our usual Thursday-night dinner, a weekly tradition for a number of us who used to work together in a downtown restaurant. Since we all loved to eat and drink, our weekly dinners tended to be long, drawn-out affairs where we would chat and tell stories late into the night. And since I had become a free-lance food and wine writer, it provided me with the perfect opportunity to try out new recipes for columns and cookbooks I was working on at the time. That night, even though I had been in the house only a couple of weeks, it already had a cozy, homey feel to it, and we sat down in the dining room for a dinner of Bibb lettuce salad with smoked trout, roasted pork tenderloin, mashed potatoes, and red cabbage. By the time we passed around generous helpings of bourbon gingerbread and whipped cream for dessert, little mention had been made of the ghost.

"So, what did the previous owner tell you about the spook in the attic?" Tim inquired in a nasally tone as he sloshed generous amounts of

Woodford Reserve into large snifters before passing them out to those assembled around the dinner table. Fondly named "Skippy" by his closest friends, he worked in Versailles at Brown Forman's Labrot & Graham Distillery, where they produced the small-batch Woodford Reserve bourbon. We took our whiskey and moved to the fire in the front parlor while I repeated what the previous owner had said about Lucy the poltergeist not liking to see things changed around too much.

"Maybe we should get out the Ouija board and see if we can contact her." Skippy looked around the room for approval after making the suggestion. But Ramon stood up hastily and bolted for the kitchen. "No way. I don't like those things. They're bad news!" He disappeared and left behind only a trailing epithet of curses in Spanish. A second or two later, something made of glass suddenly crashed to the floor in the kitchen and broke into pieces, causing us all to jump. We stared at each other and waited. "Ramon? Was that you – or the ghost?" Beth, a lawyer friend who had showed up just in time for dessert, stood up and sat her snifter on the mahogany mantelshelf and waited. A few seconds later, Ramon showed up at the parlor doors, a meek smile on his face. "Oops." He held up a piece of broken glass. "Sorry. I dropped one of the champagne flutes."

An hour later we had finished our drinks, and I closed the door as the last of the guests headed out into the wintry night. I tidied up a bit, made the rounds of the rooms to turn off the lights, and jumped into bed. Only after I had snuggled in under the warm covers with Rocky and Bess, our two miniature schnauzers, did I recall seeing that the pig print on the desk in the study had fallen or been turned over so it lay face down. I debated getting out of bed and standing it up again, but another sudden loud noise downstairs startled me. So I got out of bed to investigate that instead, Rocky and Bess trailing cautiously behind. It seemed to come from the small bathroom under the main stairs on the first floor, and the closer I got to it, the more it sounded like a hissing noise. Pushing the door all the way open, I turned on the light, and inside I could see the little black cat we had recently adopted. She stood on all fours with her back arched and hissed at something unseen. Then she ran into the tiny closet next to the toilet and refused to come out. This had become her new home as of late. Ever since we had moved into the new house, the previously mischievous troublemaker had turned into a literal scaredy cat. No amount of coaxing could make her leave the confines of the tiny bathroom, and she wouldn't even eat or drink unless someone brought her food and water. After several minutes of reassuring pats, I left her to the little closet and returned to my bedroom on the second floor, not paying too much attention the chandelier that appeared to swing back and forth ever-so-slightly in the hallway at the top of the servant's stairs. When the strong smell of coffee awoke me the next morning, I had all but forgotten about the disturbance with the cat and the swinging light fixture. I was more concerned with why there was such a persistent smell of coffee in the kitchen although nobody had made coffee that morning. Since the houses in Old Louisville tend to be very close together, I told myself the smell must have wafted in from one of the neighbor's kitchens, and that was that.

Christmas came, and it seemed that the house would burst with a steady stream of family, friends and out-of-town visitors that didn't abate until holiday decorations came down on the sixth of January. Since I was now living in a Victorian home I had been doing a good deal of research about period customs and such, and I had discovered that in many parts of the country, Epiphany on the sixth of January, or the twelfth day of Christmas, was the traditional day for taking down the tree. So we had a party on the sixth of January and down it came, and I congratulated myself on keeping Victorian customs alive.

The dreary weather that followed in the next two months provided ample opportunity for our small group to meet in front of the warm fire in the front parlor, and it seemed that I had effortlessly transplanted myself in a home that felt like a familiar friend. I looked forward to the warmer weather of spring just around the corner, not only for the pleasant temperatures, but also for the chance to do some major work around the house. Three rooms sat totally empty, in need of furniture, wallpaper and drapes, and I couldn't wait to tear up the outdated shag carpeting that covered the entire second floor and redo the hardwood underneath. The crumbling façade would have to wait until the following year, and in the meantime I would occupy myself with details like repairing plaster walls and searching antique shops and thrift stores for light fixtures and furnishings.

When April finally arrived, it seemed as if spring had come overnight, and the neighborhood just as quickly transformed itself into a fresh garden of greenery and branches of all sorts, heavily laden with buds ready to erupt. By the end of the month and the start of the annual Kentucky Derby festival, the early tendrils of summer had already taken hold, and the humidity and warmth in the air hinted at the sultry summer evenings to come. Azalea bushes danced with hundreds of animated blossoms in scarlet, crimson and fuchsia, and dogwood branches displayed delicate petals of pink and ivory at every turn. And tender sprigs of mint seemed to shoot up wherever a neglected patch of moist soil would permit – around the gas lamps on Saint James Court, where the wrought-iron legs of old benches dug into the damp earth of Central

Park, at foundations, and through the cracks in cobblestone and brick courtyards.

For most people in Louisville, fresh mint in April means that the Kentucky Derby is right around the corner – and that mint juleps are in store. All in anticipation of the one time of the year when even the strictest of teetotalers will allow themselves this one indulgence, people pull out rare silver cups and cocktail shakers, long-necked spoons passed down from one generation to the next, and secret family recipes. It seems that the two weeks before the actual races can barely contain all the parties, and at no time of year do the southern drawls sound as marked as they do in the time leading up to the Derby. From the grandest mansions to the most humble cottages, debates rage as to which bourbon makes the best julep, if indeed one should use crushed or shaved ice in the drink, and whether the sprigs of mint should remain in the cup after they have been bruised with a silver spoon to release their fragrant oils.

I had just returned from one of these parties the Sunday afternoon before the Derby when I found myself in the kitchen, at the back of the house. Puzzled once again by the strong smell of coffee that pervaded the room, I suddenly felt a chill run down my spine at the realization that, once again, no one had made coffee the entire day. As a matter of fact, no one had been in the house since I left that morning just before noon. And I had been totally alone the several times prior to that when the curious coffee aroma had awakened me in the mornings. I moved next to the stove, and it seemed that the smell intensified and I could almost feel the warmth of coffee brewing on a front burner. Although we had hired several men to redo the hardwood floors on the second story a couple of days before, they would not be back until the following Tuesday, and they had the only spare key to the house. I looked in the sink for any evidence of coffee making and found none. I told myself again the smell must be coming from one of the neighboring houses and set about testing a recipe for a book about Kentucky cooking I had just started writing. I had just finished the recipe and was cleaning up when the phone started ringing. I ran to the front of the house to answer it.

It was an old high-school friend, calling from her new home in Texas, and she was eager to hear more about my recent move. An archeologist, she couldn't get enough when I told her a bit about the layout of the house and the historic neighborhood I called home. "Do you have any ghosts?" she asked several minutes into the conversation. I chuckled and told her about the pictures falling, the strange noises when I first moved in and the several times I had come across the unexplained smell of freshly brewed coffee, but I carefully added that I considered myself a skeptic. She listened as I recounted some of the details, and I suddenly caught my breath when a door on the third floor slammed shut. "What is it?" From the other end, Mindy sounded somewhat alarmed. I told her to be quiet for a second, and I listened as distinctly audible footfall started down the stairs. Ramon was away visiting his family in Texas, so I knew it couldn't be him. "I think there's someone in the house," I whispered. The telephone stood on a small cigar table under the main stairs, and I stretched the cord to position myself to see up into the stairwell – but there was only darkness. I could hear the steps as they slowly made their way down the stairs, tread by tread – from the top floor, to the landing, and then down to the second floor.

"Someone is coming down the stairs," I said softly, then holding my breath as the steps continued down from the second floor to the landing just a few feet away from where I stood. The stairs from the first floor to the second floor doubled back midway at the landing, obscuring it from sight, and I expected someone to appear at any moment. It sounded like the invisible steps had reached the last landing and a pair of feet would materialize as they rounded the bend to come down the final section of stairs. I waited, but the steps simply stopped, the unknown source concealed in the shadows. I had the impression that someone had just walked all the way down the stairs and stopped on the very last step necessary to stay out of view.

I set the phone down and flipped on the light in the stairway. "Hey, what's going on?" Mindy's tense voice crackled from the other end of the line. "Are you OK?" I had already run up and down the stairs and found no one by the time I was able to give her an update. I had seen nothing at all, and I had no idea what caused the sound of feet coming down the stairs. In the end I just shrugged my shoulders and said it must have been the sound of wood expanding and contracting due to the warmer weather, perhaps aided by the sanding the workers had given the floors upstairs. "Hmmm, maybe your ghost doesn't like what you're doing to the house?" my friend said.

I chuckled and mentioned that she hadn't been the first one to think of that. We spoke for a couple minutes more, and then I said good night and hung up, careful to leave on the light in the stairwell. I walked into the kitchen and set the teakettle on the stove, relieved to notice that the strong smell of coffee had dissipated. However, whatever sense of uneasiness I had experienced quickly returned when I realized the temperature in the room had dropped to almost freezing. I checked the thermostat, and although it registered 68 degrees, it seemed that an icy wind had filled the small space. Pushing any negative thoughts out of my head, I waited for the water to boil, made my tea and ran up to the study on the top floor. After doing a bit of work on the computer, I watched a movie, and when the pot of tea ran out, I decided to turn in for the evening. I ran downstairs to set the teapot in the sink and then called the dogs to let them outside.

The back door propped open, I watched them run around the back yard a bit and then called them inside. Before I had the chance to close the door all the way, a black blur shot past me with a sharp hiss, ran out the door, and disappeared over the back fence. The nervous little black cat had abandoned its home under the stairs and it ran outside, something it had never done before. She had never even been outside, for all I knew, so I got in the car and drove around the neighborhood looking for her. After more than an hour and no luck, I decided to return home and resume the search the next morning if she hadn't come back by then. Once inside, I turned off the lights, gathered the dogs, and then we all headed for bed. The next morning I resumed the search and even put up signs throughout the neighborhood. Although I looked and looked, we never saw the little black cat again.

Even though spring had definitely arrived, the week the cat ran away it seemed that a bit of a chill still remained in the house. Several nights later, I settled in under the covers and quickly drifted off to sleep. I had slept for perhaps an hour or so when the uneasy stirring of the dogs on the bed roused me from my slumber. Despite the darkness, a small patch of light from the street illuminated the bed through the window, and I could see both dogs as they stood and looked towards the hallway, a low growl barely audible as Rocky lowered his head and stared. I pulled them both towards me and calmed them down, then listened. At first I could hear nothing, but then I heard a long, slow, wooden creak. I thought maybe a door had swung open by itself, and I waited to hear more. A minute or so passed, and I heard nothing, so I lay back down and waited to fall back asleep. Once again, a long, drawn-out creak resonated slowly in the hallway and sent chills down my spine. I thought someone had surely broken into the house, and I attempted to visualize his location in relation to my bedroom.

Another moment passed, and I heard another long groan from the floorboards in the hall, this time closer to the bedroom door in front of me. I could see both dogs as they cocked their heads in response to the noise, and I suddenly realized I was afraid. Almost paralyzed, I listened as something seemed to make its way up and down the hallway that ran from the large room at the front of the house, past the home's original nursery, my bedroom, the linen closet, and bathroom to the small bedroom in the rear of the building. After several minutes' hesitation, I finally mustered the courage to hurl all 220 pounds of me out of bed, grab the aluminum baseball bat propped against the wall, and switch on the light. Making as much noise as possible, I rushed out of the room to confront the unseen intruder, the bat wielded overhead as I cautiously ran the length of the corridor and turned on several other lights. Finding nothing, I searched the other two floors and even looked around the attic and basement before returning my bedroom. I told myself I was acting like a fool as I went back to bed.

I closed the bedroom door this time, and once tucked under the covers again, I tried to convince myself that I hadn't gone crazy and had just imagined the sounds of an intruder in the hallway. After several minutes, I started to relax, comforted by the thought that the closed door would offer some sort of protection in the unlikely event I started to hear the strange noises again. Even if they did start up again, I'd be fine, I told myself, as long as the weird noises did not bother me *inside* the bedroom. But another minute or two passed, and then a loud groan slowly reverberated from the floorboards from the left side of the bed, just inches from where I lay. My skin started to crawl at the realization that the noises had not only returned, but had entered the room. Fighting the sense of panic welling up inside me, I forced myself to take slow breaths and reassured myself all would be fine, as long as the noise stayed on the left side of the bed. Several tense moments of silence dragged on, and I dreaded the idea that the strange creaking would move around the bed to my right-hand side. Suddenly, the floor let out a long, moaning squeak that ended with a loud pop, and my eyes involuntarily squeezed themselves shut. The creepy, wooden groan had come from a spot at the foot of the bed. A shudder ran down my spine and set my heart to racing even faster. I kept telling myself it had to be the result of the wood expanding and contracting due to the warmer spring weather, but if the sound moved all the way around to the right side, I decided, I would be leaving.

I held my breath and waited. The dogs seemed to be holding their breaths as well. One minute passed, and then another, the lengthy silence compounding the tension that hung in the darkness. Another minute went by, and I exhaled as quietly as possible. I listened intently and squinted to better discern any movement in the darkness, all the while overcome with the uncomfortable sensation that something was watching me. Bess lowered her head and slowly stretched out on the bed, and I cautiously relaxed a bit, my ears still straining to hear the slightest noise. I turned my head to the right and struggled to make out any shapes in the blackness, but still I saw nothing. Then, the same long, drawn-out type of creak shot through the floorboards on the right side of the bed, almost as if an invisible visitor had taken a step or shifted his weight while standing there. The loud noise faded into a soft echo, and then I heard what sounded like a pluck and strum on the strings of a harp.

I flew out of bed, grabbed my cell phone and baseball bat, and – making sure the dogs followed – ran down the stairs as I pulled on my bathrobe. The door slamming shut behind us, we ran out the back way and piled into the car. The clock on the cell phone read 3:30 AM, and after turning the key in the ignition, I dialed Skippy's number to let him know I would be coming over. I looked back at the darkened house, almost expecting to see the windows all aglow with an eerie red, and when I saw nothing, I reconsidered the decision to leave. Before the phone started to ring on the other end, I hung up and decided to go back inside – but in a bit, after I came up with a perfectly logical explanation for the strange happenings. I finally decided that the creaks and groans were caused by the wooden floorboards expanding and contracting with the recent temperature changes and that the strange wire-plucking sound must have come from the old line leading to the gas fireplace in the bedroom. I got out of the car, and Rocky and Bess reluctantly followed me back to the house.

Once inside, I closed the door and listened. There was nothing but total silence. Not completely convinced that I had imagined everything, I gathered the dogs near and we sat in the small room between the kitchen and dining room and watched TV until the sun came up. Stifling a yawn, I finally trudged back up the stairs to the bedroom on the second floor and managed several hours' sleep, content at the fact that I was able to unwind, if only for a short while. After I woke up, I took the dogs for a walk and then decided to run some errands. As I collected my keys and wallet in the kitchen, I once again noticed the strong smell of freshly brewed coffee. The two workmen had arrived and could be heard on the floors above me, so I walked up to them and inquired if either of them had made coffee, or maybe brought any along. When they both answered in the negative, adding that they never drank coffee, I did my best to ignore the uneasy feeling that overcame me. I also asked them if the sanding and warmer weather might account for an increase in the creaks and groans that seemed to pervade the house. One of them shrugged his shoulders and said "It happens, I guess." But his coworker just gave him a skeptical look. "I never heard it happen before," he stated. Not reassured either way, I left the house to do my errands.

Later that afternoon I returned home, eager to check the progress on the hardwood floors. Although an entire week had passed since the work started, most of the time before had been spent pulling up the old carpeting and removing nails and staples imbedded in the boards. Curious to see if the workers had managed to sand more than just the front room, which they had begun several days prior, I walked into the house and followed the loud drone of a drum sander upstairs. The scent of fresh pine and sawdust permeated the air, and I made a room-to-room inspection while waiting for the noise to stop. Pleased with the progress they had made, I walked up behind them when they finally turned the sander off and said hello. They almost jumped out of their skins at the greeting. "Lord, you scared me to death!" the older of the two said with a sigh. He looked at his companion and then back at me, then laughed uneasily. "Were you in the house before, about an hour or so ago?" the other said. I told them that I had just arrived home minutes earlier and asked why. "We were positive someone was in the house." Both men looked down the hall towards the small room that sat at the back of the house. "They kept slamming the door shut back there." I assured them that I had not been in the house since they had last seen me and asked if they had seen anyone. The younger man scratched his head and scowled a bit. "No, but we sure got the feeling somebody was watching us."

I walked back to the room and stuck my head through the door. A small, plain room that sat directly above the kitchen, it was to be the last of the rooms the workers sanded. When they finished the three rooms at the front of the house, they would work their way down the hallway and then start on this, the smallest room. I looked around and saw nothing out of the ordinary, save for a thick layer of dust that had settled on the mantel and the dressing table, despite the sheets of plastic hung over the doorways to contain the fine sawdust stirred up by the sanders. I noticed a thin layer of dust in the hall leading up to the room I had just entered, but other than my own two footprints, nothing hinted at a possible explanation for the slamming sound. I closed the door and turned to go downstairs, but before I moved from the spot I heard what sounded like three knocks coming from the other side. Startled, I quickly opened the door and peered inside, not at all surprised to find nothing. I walked to a window in the room and looked out into the back yard, but nothing showed itself. Then I noticed what seemed to be the smell of a hot iron and freshly pressed laundry, although something about the odor didn't strike me as quite right. It had that starchy, burnt smell an iron gets at a very high setting when it threatens to burn delicate fabric or when build-up starts to collect on the bottom. Thoroughly unnerved, I left the room and ran downstairs, unable to shake the feeling that a pair of invisible eyes followed me. I convinced myself I was only getting psyched out because of what the workers had said about feeling watched.

Despite my trepidation, the next couple of days passed without event, except for the continued creaks and groans. During the daylight, it seemed, it was always easy to convince myself that my mind was playing tricks on me, but on several mornings I did happen to wake up to the pleasant aroma of fresh coffee downstairs. Once again, however, I let myself assume that a generous breeze had carried it on from a neighbor's kitchen. By the time Thursday evening rolled around, all the Derby-related festivities were catching up to me and I found myself looking forward to a little quiet time. That would have to wait, though, because I had my own Derby party to attend to, and guests had already started to arrive, many of them regulars from our weekly get-togethers.

A number of people had already heard about the strange sounds that had almost driven me from the house on the weekend, so talk naturally tended to gravitate towards Lucy and any part she might have played in the matter. "Maybe she was a guest here once and she starved to death, so she's come back to haunt you." It was Gregory, standing alongside the dining room table. He looked down at several empty silver trays and dabbed a moistened finger in the remaining crumbs.

A peal of laughter echoed from the doorway to the kitchen, and David, another friend, emerged with a large platter heaped with hors d'oeuvres from which he replenished the depleted trays. "I'll make sure I don't starve," he said. Not content with the small cocktail plates on the table, he ran back to the kitchen and returned with a large dinner plate stacked high with finger sandwiches, beaten biscuits with country ham, and chicken salad canapés. On a second dinner plate he had artfully arranged a large assortment of candied pecans, bourbon balls and chess tartlets for his own personalized dessert selection. Feigning irritation, he informed us he didn't want to be disturbed and walked into the parlor to eat.

"If you do have a ghost," someone said, "it was probably somebody who used to live here. That's the way is usually works." I had already done quite a bit of research about the house, including a retrieval of all the prior deeds to the property, and nowhere had I come across the name Lucy among the previous female owners and inhabitants. I shared this bit of information with my friends as I passed around a tray of modjeskas, a local candy that consists of a marshmallow covered in caramel.

"Well, maybe one of the previous owners had a visitor or a family member who died here in the house," someone said, popping one of the sweets into her mouth. "Even if no one died here, chances are they had the body laid out for the wake or funeral. That's what they used to do in the olden days."

"Yeah, back then, they had dead people lying around all over the place. Thank goodness we've got funeral homes nowadays." David had walked back into the dining room and fixed himself another mint julep. He grabbed the three modjeskas remaining on the tray and walked back to the front parlor. "Someone's at the door," he yelled, over his shoulder.

I ran to the door and let in another group of people, and before long talk had shifted to the incredible spring weather and the upcoming races. After another mint julep, Lucy was all but forgotten.

That would soon change, however. The next few nights I hardly got any rest at all since loud footsteps, creaks and groans had kept me from sleeping. Friday night was so bad that I called two friends and asked them to come and spend the night. Of course, when they arrived after 3:30 in the morning, the loud knocks at the back door that kept waking me up and the eerie sounds in the back room had all stopped. Although I hesitated at first, afraid they might think I had lost my mind, I told them the most frightening part had been after I had run down to the back door the third and final time. I had heard three distinct raps and had run to see who was at the back door. Each time I got there, the last time just seconds after hearing the knocks, I could see no one. I was climbing the back stairs when all of a sudden the curtains on the window in the stairwell billowed out in front of me, as if blown by gale-force winds. I became all the more unnerved when I remembered that the window had been sealed shut and painted over. Not so much as the tiniest draft of air could be felt when I examined it later. My friends just looked at me and shook their heads. "Uh…you really need to do something, and soon."

I had been keeping a journal of all the weird goings-on, and even though I chalked a lot of it up to an over-active imagination, there were lots of things that were hard to explain. Furniture being moved around in the middle of the night, and the dogs acting like they could see something I couldn't see, for example. There also had been a lot of odd people turning up at the front door at all hours of the night, but after a while I discovered that wasn't that uncommon, given our location near a busy intersection the locals referred to as "the corner of Fourth and Crazy." I found myself thinking about having a team of paranormal investigators come and check the place out, although most of the "experts" I had previously dealt with came across as overly eager to find something supernatural at best – and charlatans at worst.

The Derby came and went, leaving in its wake a spell of hot weather that brought locals out to their porches to enjoy the warm evenings. By the time the next week rolled around, people were glad to be done with parties and we looked forward to a return to the mundane. When I awoke Thursday morning, I was actually happy to have no plans for the entire week and I hardly gave a second thought to the overpowering smell of hot coffee in the kitchen. I decided to go to the Filson Historical Society and see if I could dig up anything new about the house, but I wanted to be back at noon when the men arrived to work on the hardwood floors upstairs.

Several hours later, the smell of coffee still pervaded the kitchen. "Whew! That sure is strong today." One of the workers walked through the back door and wrinkled his nose as he looked around the room. "Did you ever figure out where the smell is coming from?" I responded it must be coming from the neighbor's house, and the two made their way up the back stairs. "We'll start on the last room today and should be done in another day or two," said the older of the two men.

They headed upstairs to do their work, and I took some photographs for the cookbook I was working on. An hour later I left and ran out to the grocery store so I could get some things I needed for a new recipe. When I returned that afternoon, the strong coffee smell in the kitchen had faded, only to be replaced by the familiar smell of a hot iron and fresh laundry. I scratched my head and looked around, then walked into the next room. Upstairs, I could hear a loud scraping noise, the irritating sound of wood against wood. It appeared to come from the linen closet on the second floor, and from the loud footsteps running back and forth, it sounded like the workers had decided to concentrate on that room instead of the small room at the back of the house. I couldn't figure out exactly what they were doing, however. It sounded like they were pulling out the huge wooden drawers for sheets and pillows, and then pushing them back in again. *In, out, in, out.* The incessant scraping noise had really started to annoy me.

I was just about to run up for a look-see when the back door opened, and in walked the two workers. I just gaped at them and then bolted upstairs to the linen closet. Although the cupboard doors remained open, and the large storage bins and drawers pulled all the way out, no sound could be heard, except the two workmen as they trudged up the steps behind me.

"Let me guess," said the older gentleman as he reached the top of the stairs. "You heard all kinds of racket in this linen closet here, like someone was running around and pulling out those big wooden bins there."

"Yes," I said, "but how—?"

Before I had a chance to continue, the younger man cut me off. "Man, this place really is haunted! That's all there is to it. We kept hearing strange noises the whole time we were here, and it felt like someone was watching us, too." He looked at the other man.

"Yep. We took a break an hour ago because we couldn't stand it anymore and didn't want to be here alone. This here door kept slamming shut, too." He pointed at a door outside the linen closet that divided the long hallway on the second floor into two sections of equal length when it was closed. Although I had heard it slam shut many times, I assumed it had been the result of the breeze from an opened window.

"And come take a look at this," he said as he motioned for me to follow him to the small room at the back of the house. "Remember that iron smell you were always complaining about?" The room had been stripped of its outdated carpeting, exposing the beautiful century-old heart-of-pine flooring underneath. He stopped in front of the fireplace and pointed to a spot on the floor. Although the wood had lost its original luster due to years of neglect and layers of paint, the workers had sanded it clean, revealing the shape he was pointing to. I could easily make it out. It was about five inches long, and triangular, but the two longest sides were slightly rounded. A shiver ran along my spine as I realized I was staring at a burn mark on the floor left behind by an old-fashioned flat iron.

Is this burn mark in the former maid's room a clue to the reported haunting at Widmer House?

The former servant's room on the second floor of the Widmer House

I ran back to the dividing door in the middle of the hallway, and as I stood and stared at it, things slowly started to make sense. I closed it, and realized it divided the front half of the house from the back half. The front half included the original lady's day room now used as a study, the former nursery and another bedroom, all of which had interconnecting doors and doors that opened onto the front part of the hall. From the hall, one could mount the carved oak stairs to three bedrooms on the third floor, or take them down to the public rooms of the house – the parlor, foyer, dining room and small bathroom under the stairs.

I explained this all to my group of Thursday night friends when they arrived for our weekly dinner half an hour later. Opening the hall door, I ushered them through to the back half of the house and then closed it again. We stood in the dark rear corridor and studied the layout in silence. Doors granted entry to the large linen closet, several smaller closets, a bathroom and water closet, and the small bedroom at the very back of the house. The plain back stairs led down one flight to a small coat room and the cellar stairs, and then into the butler's pantry and the kitchen at the back of the residence. For the most part, I realized, all the strange activity had centered on the back part of the home.

"Oh, I see!" exclaimed my friend Laura. "The back part would have been where the servants worked and had access. That must have been the maid's or the housekeeper's room." Our heads slowly turned to the small room where at one time a hot flat iron had charred its mark on the floor. "Do you think Lucy could have been a former servant here?"

We all walked back downstairs and debated the possibilities over tall glasses of something called tobacco baron's punch, a potent concoction of bourbon, gin, sherry, lemon juice, and grenadine that Skippy had discovered while doing research at the distillery. Laura had volunteered for cooking detail, and around the table we soon passed rolls fresh from the oven and a large tray of grilled asparagus vinaigrette. After the roast chicken, corn pudding and scalloped potatoes, we were still talking about the ghost at the Widmer House. Before dessert, we knew what had to be done. Walking from room to room in the servants' area of the house, we all followed Wendy as she reassured Lucy that she was free to enjoy the house as she wanted. No one wanted to bother her, Wendy said, and we understood that she was just keeping watch over her part of the house. Afterward, we drank coffee and talked till the wee hours of the morning, and other than laughter and lively chatter in the front parlor, not a sound was heard that night at Widmer House.

After that, not much out of the ordinary happened as far as would-be ghostly activity was concerned. I had two different paranormal groups come and "investigate" the house, but after setting up their equipment and collecting their data, both groups said they found nothing unusual. Nonetheless, word got out that there was a ghost afoot in Widmer House and local newspapers began running stories about the place and the fact I had started delving into the haunted past of the neighborhood. I began working on a book that would chronicle the history and architecture of Old Louisville through its ghostly lore. Of course, it was hard to juggle my writing projects with the home restoration efforts, but little by little, the house on Third Street regained much of its former splendor. Each time I attempted a major project, however, I made sure to clear it with Lucy – even though the gesture was always very tongue in cheek. Once in a great while during for the remaining six or seven years we were in the house, something strange would happen, like at Christmas time when the stockings on the mantel in Lucy's room tended to disappear and then reappear in different parts of the house, but for the most part, I got the impression Lucy was content with the arrangements.

A couple of years before we moved out of Widmer House I had an unexpected visit one afternoon from an elderly lady who said her grandmother had been one of the first owners of the house. She asked to come in and see the place, and I was more than happy to oblige her. As I led her from room to room and listed to her comments about what changes had taken place and how much she approved of the decorating, I grew anxious to hear her comments when we reached Lucy's room at the back of the house. Sure enough, she confirmed that the housekeeper had indeed lived in that room, but other than that, she couldn't recall anything in particular about this person.

When I asked if the name Lucy rang a bell, the old lady shook her head and confessed to not remembering any Lucy who had lived in the house. One thing she did remember, she informed me, was that her grandmother's housekeeper had come to her as a young girl, and that even though everyone in the house was very fond of the girl, they always complained about her nosiness. With a chuckle, the old woman told how her grandmother was constantly scolding the girl for eavesdropping when she had visitors in the house. Instead of staying out of sight in the back part of the residence as servants were supposed to do, the young girl liked to sneak down the front staircase and listen to conversations in the parlor, making sure she stayed just out of sight in case someone exited the parlor and spotted her perched near the landing.

I thought about all the times I had heard footsteps on those stairs and wondered if the ghost of the mischievous young housekeeper had wanted to eavesdrop and nothing more. Each time I had the distinct impression that someone was trying very hard to stay out of sight. But then I reminded myself that I'm a skeptic and had never really seen anything that could remotely be considered a ghost. Instead, I had only heard and smelled things, and on occasion I had experienced what I considered unexplainable movements and eerie sensations. I had to wonder if all of it could have been attributed to nothing more than imagination and pure happenstance.

Whatever the reason for the strange occurrences at Widmer House, I never lost my fascination for unexplained phenomena and the paranormal. To the contrary, I went in search of the ghostly past around me and in the process of poring through old newspapers and talking to fellow homeowners and residents, I discovered a very haunted neighborhood. Old Louisville is one of the largest and best preserved Victorian districts in the country, so it's not surprising that spooky legends and tales of otherworldly visitors should abound. And since there are lots of people like me, individuals who love ghost stories, I decided to start writing down these tales and legends and share them in an effort to keep history and oral tradition alive. Whether or not you believe in the supernatural, ghost stories are the perfect way to entertain and educate. So who says you have to believe in ghosts to enjoy a good ghost story?

Widmer House, after the façade was restored in 2001

Rocky, Fritz and Bess – three of the four schnauzers at Widmer House

Not all, but some of the regulars for the Thursday Night Dinner Club -
From left to right: Beth, Tad, Laura, Skippy, Wendy, David

Chapter 2 – The Old Orphan's Home

A large, brick structure with white trim and an imposing tower looms over the 1100 block of South First Street. Small, dormered windows accented in burgundy-red peer down over the neighborhood from the pyramidal roof overhead. With its austere façade, four stories, and squat tower jutting skywards, it cuts a rather striking, albeit somewhat daunting, figure from the street level. And when the occasional fog swells up from the Ohio River and rolls in to blanket the neighborhood in a billowy shroud of milky white, it joins the ranks of church steeples and bell towers that rise like needles above the dense haze and pierce the low-hanging sky over Old Louisville. Although this impressive piece of architecture sits tucked away on a block seldom seen by visitors, it commands attention nonetheless and jealously guards its spot in local history. Like most old buildings in Old Louisville, 1135 South First Street has seen numerous past lives, and even though time has rubbed the slate of memory clean for many, the staid old structure harbors untold secrets and perhaps a disembodied spirit or two.

"The first time I saw the ghost, I almost fell over from shock," says Babette Philips. A graduate of Bellarmine University, the 30-something lived more than three years in the large building, which has been converted into condominiums. When she moved into the spacious apartment on the second floor, Philips never expected her quarters to come with its own ghost. "If anyone had told me that they had seen the strange things I saw in that building, I wouldn't have believed them. I've always considered myself *extremely* skeptical of things like this, so when you actually experience a paranormal occurrence, it's quite a shock. And, when the shoe's on the other foot, it really makes you stop and think. I'm a true believer now, but I don't expect people to believe it when I tell them I saw a ghost. And, I really don't care, to tell you the truth, because I know what I saw, and that's all I need."

Babette's friends, on the other hand, told her that what she really needed was an exorcist. It seems that once she saw the spirit, it grew attached to her and refused to leave the premises. "I had been there for about a half year when I saw the ghost for the first time, and I had pretty much settled in and had everything unpacked and in its place. But I kept misplacing things, and it was starting to get on my nerves," she recalls. "I just assumed it was because I wasn't used to the layout of the apartment and was being forgetful, but then little things started to happen that made me think that maybe I wasn't being so forgetful after all." For example, when she would go to bed at night and place her glasses on the nightstand next to her side of the bed, she would awake the next morning to find that they had been placed on the nightstand on the *other* side of the bed. "The first time it happened, I figured I must have put them there before I went to bed or something, because there's no way I would reach all the way across my king-size bed and put them on the table farthest away from me," Philips explains. "But when it kept happening over and over again, I knew something was up. Someone or *something* was moving my glasses to the other side of the bed while I slept. I always read before I fall asleep, and the last thing I do before turning out the light is put my glasses down next to my book on the nightstand. Why would I reach across and put them on the other table?"

Not only that, Philips claims an unseen force started to open and close doors in the various rooms of her unit. "One day, I had just come out of the bathroom and walked into my bedroom when I suddenly heard a loud *slam!* in the living room. I ran out to see what it was, and it turned out to be the door leading into the guest bedroom." Mesmerized by the sight unfolding before her, Philips says she stared as the door opened and then slammed shut with a loud bang three times in a row. "Now, when it happens over and over like that, you know it cannot be the wind," she explains. "Something had to actually pull the door open each time and then slam it shut. And I know I wasn't imagining that!"

On another occasion, loud noises drew the startled woman to the kitchen. "One day it sounded like someone was putting things away or something because I could hear the cupboard doors opening and closing, and it sounded like someone was pulling open the drawers and closing them. But they kept doing it over and over again. That's what made me nervous." Somewhat apprehensively, the young lady approached the entryway to the kitchen and careened her head around the corner, fearful of what she might actually see. "You'll never believe it," she says, "it was like an invisible person was in there opening and closing drawers and cupboards. It seemed like every single drawer and cabinet door was flying open and then closing again all on its own – it was one of the strangest sights I've ever beheld."

When pressed as to her course of action after experiencing these initial disturbances, Philips says, "What are you supposed to do in a situation like that? Call the police? I don't think so. They'd cart you off to the loony bin if you did something like that. I just told myself there had to be a rational explanation for it all and decided to grin and bear it. Besides, it wasn't like I was afraid or anything." For Babette Philips, fear would come later on, after she had her first sighting of the ghost at 1135 South First Street.

"So, this went on for the first five, six months that I was in the condo. Every few weeks something would happen. Doors would open by themselves and then slam shut before my very eyes," she recalls. "My glasses would keep moving around on their own, things like that. One evening I even thought I heard a young boy's voice coming from my bedroom, but I convinced myself that it had to be coming from a neighboring unit or something like that." Not too long after that, Philips said she could perceive a palpable change in the atmosphere in her home.

"It was like all of a sudden the air in the place got very oppressive, very dark and gloomy. And I noticed I started to get depressed all the time. It was like the rooms were giving off some kind of bad energy or something." In addition to the negative "vibes" Philips claimed the condo gave off, she claims she started to experience strange dreams as well. "I guess I dream like any normal person does, but I usually didn't remember most of the dreams I would have," she explains. "But, not too long after the strange energy took over in the place, I started having these really weird dreams – dreams like none I had ever had before." Although the dreams themselves contained no horrific images or frightening scenes, Philips claimed they filled her with a sense of foreboding and despair, and often left her mentally drained.

"Whenever I had these dreams, I'd wake up the next morning completely exhausted and depressed. And the dreams weren't really that strange, because all I would see were these crowds of little kids looking at me, nothing else. But, it was like they were so sad and lonely, and that's the dark impression that stayed with me. All that sadness." When asked to give more details about the children from her dreams, she could only say that "they appeared to be wearing old-fashioned clothing, and they had absolutely no expressions on their faces, just these blank faces with these blank stares." Philips also adds that she could recall very little color from these odd dreams, only differing shades of gray, black and white – and sad, pale faces.

When she finally saw the ghost at 1135 South First Street, she would remember these sad, pale faces from her dreams.

"I had just come back from a walk around the neighborhood," she recalls, "and I was sort of laughing to myself because on the street I had seen this old lady they all call the Stick Witch. She's always got this shopping cart full of branches and stuff that she pushes around all the time, and there are all kinds of different stories as to who she is – a homeless lady, a real witch, a crazy person who escaped from an asylum, whatever." Some residents in the neighborhood also claimed to have seen her for decades, if not longer. "Well, I was sort of smiling because she's always very friendly when I run into her, and she always has something nice to say to me. Although, I've heard from others that that's not always the case." Still enjoying the warmth of the spring weather she was leaving outdoors, Philips unlocked her door and walked into the living room. *Slam!* The door to her bedroom appeared to open and close on its own.

"It was a little creepy, I admit, but I had sort of grown used to it, so I just shrugged it off and headed into the bathroom." She never anticipated what waited for her in the hallway outside the room. "Right there, down the corridor a bit, was this little kid staring at me. Maybe about four feet tall, ten years old or so, I don't know, but he was just standing there looking at me." Philips says she initially assumed that the child belonged to her sister, who sometimes arrived unannounced with children she would babysit. However, something gave her the impression that she had just had an encounter with a ghost.

"First off, the poor thing was all pale and sickly. Now I see where they get the phrase 'white as a ghost' from. It looked like a dead child almost. Second – and this is the creepiest part – I realized as it was staring at me that it didn't have any eyes. Just these black, black holes where the eyes should have been. And it's not that he had dark-colored eyes. He didn't have any eyes at all, just these empty sockets."

According to Philips, she and the eerie apparition stood face to face in the hallway outside her bathroom for what seemed an eternity. "I was just hoping it would disappear or something, but it never did, and I didn't know if I should speak to it or what." Finally, she says, the ghostly figure of the little boy turned around and walked down the corridor. "When it got to my bedroom door – which was closed – it just walked right through it and vanished from sight." Understandably, Philips says she felt somewhat nervous about opening the door to her bedroom. "I half expected him to be inside waiting for me when I got up the courage to open the door and venture inside, but no one was there. I guess that's a good thing."

Philips claims she encountered the same apparition on four different occasions after the initial encounter. "Things kept moving around the house, and I would constantly hear slamming and footsteps, but the worst was when the little boy would show himself in the hallway," she recounts. "I realized he wasn't a malevolent spirit or anything, but I didn't exactly get a happy vibe from him, either. It was a real haunting, I guess, because I always had a 'haunted' feeling afterwards. Those dark slots where the eyes should have been were truly haunting." Although the ghostly manifestation had acquired a normal routine of appearing in the hallway and then turning around and walking through the door to Babette's bedroom, she does recall one instance in which the wraith deviated from its usual habit.

"It was the second-to-the-last time that I saw him," she explains, "and I had anticipated him because the door in the living room kept opening and shutting, more insistent than usual." Hesitantly, she turned the corner and entered the corridor to find the ghost there as she had on previous occasions. "There he was, as usual, just standing there and staring in my direction with those awful, empty eye sockets. I could feel the air charged with energy, too. The fuzz on the back of my neck was standing straight up, and an icy chill filled the room. You could even see my breath come out as I was breathing."

Despite the ominous signs, Philips claims she didn't feel threatened by the strange sight before her. "Like I said, I had started to feel sorry for the little guy, because I felt as if he wanted to tell me something or communicate with me in some form, and I decided to try and get a little closer to him. So, I decided to take a step towards him and see what would happen." According to Philips, the ghostly figure threw its hands up, as if in sheer terror, and bolted away from her. "He put his hands up over his face like he was covering his eyes, and then he ran away. That was the only time I actually tried to get close."

By this point in time, Philips' close friends had heard about the strange goings-on in the looming building at 1135 South First Street, and some urged her to consult a priest or medium who could help rid the premises of the phantom boy. "I didn't want to get rid of him, though. That's what they didn't understand. I wasn't afraid of him, and I didn't feel threatened, so I didn't think it was a big deal or anything." Although she readily admits that the eerie apparition had disconcerted her on more than one occasion, Philips says she had acquired a certain affinity for the young specter. "Yes, all that slamming and the noises spooked me, and, yes, when I saw those vacant sockets for eyes, it did give me the willies, but at no time did I feel frightened for my life or anything. I did get some negative vibes, but my gut instinct told me I would be fine."

Her friends, on the other hand, refused to buy this argument and insisted that she entail the services of someone qualified in parapsychological matters. "They were really afraid for me and basically made someone come over and check the place out. I refused to have a Catholic priest come over because I was afraid that he would scare the little boy away, so we settled on someone who claimed to have psychic powers." Philips knew of someone with purported extrasensory abilities through her mother and decided to go with him. "Since I hadn't even told my mother any details about my experiences – other than I had seen an apparition – I felt reasonably comfortable that this guy would come in with no prior knowledge of the situation. He wasn't a bona-fide medium or anything, as far as I knew, and he was very young, so I was a bit skeptical." But Philips says the amateur psychic quickly changed her mind.

"As soon as the guy entered my place and started walking around, I got the feeling that he was picking up on something," she recalls. "The first thing he did was to walk through the living room and to the hallway, where he stopped outside my bedroom." According to Philips, the sensitive immediately raised his hands to his eyes and held them there for a moment or two. "And the first thing he said was that he was getting a strong impression about something to do with eyes." Philips says her blood turned cold in an instant. "I hadn't told anyone about the little boy's eyes at all!" she explains. "I was the only one in the whole wide world who even knew that. I was totally amazed when he pointed that out after being in the apartment for not even a minute."

After that revelation, Philips says the psychic entered her bedroom and seemed to walk about in a trance-like state. "Jim – that was the guy's name – walked around in a wide circle and then told us he could sense the spirit of a young boy, and that he used to live in the area where my bedroom was." Intrigued, Philips decided to ask a question of the young medium. "I was just about to ask if he knew how old the little boy was, when all of a sudden, he just spun around as if he had read my mind and said 'He's young, very young, only eight or nine years old.' You can imagine my shock at that."

Jim then continued to make his way through the apartment and reported that he had received impressions from other children as well, but he couldn't give many details, other than "there used to be a lot of children in this house." Within ten minutes he had made the rounds and sat himself down on a sofa in the living room. "I was really eager to get more information from him, but he told me that he wasn't picking up as much as he usually would in that kind of situation. He said he knew there were children involved, but he wasn't getting many details for some reason. All he could say was that there was a lot of sadness." Grateful for the information she had received, Philips says the young psychic left after another half hour and some idle chitchat. "He offered to come back and try again sometime, saying that some days are better than others for this kind of thing, but I never got around to calling him back."

I received an email from Babette not too long after this visit from the psychic named Jim, and about six months before she moved to California. It was late 2005. By that point, the book I had been working on was in the bookstores and I was amazed at the amount of publicity it had generated for the neighborhood. "I hope you don't mind me getting in touch with you," she wrote, "but I just read your book *Ghosts of Old*

Louisville and was wondering if you knew anything about 1135 South First Street. I've experienced unexplained sounds there, and also had several sightings of a young boy who I believe is a ghost. A psychic recently informed me that he could sense the presence of a young child here as well. Have you heard about the place being haunted at all? Any information you have would be greatly appreciated."

I hadn't heard anything about 1135 South First Street, so – as I usually do – I got the dogs leashed and took a stroll over to identify the building. As I made my way down the block toward 1135, a wide smile spread as I spied the building that I had seen so many times before. Although I didn't recognize the street number per se, I had always admired the stately Italianate building for the squat tower that soared over all the other roofs in the neighborhood. Like other buildings in Old Louisville, this brick structure looked like the kind to have a ghost story, and I was happy to hear that someone had made it official.

Before I responded to the email, I decided to do some research and see what secrets I could dig up about the past lives of the brick giant. Although I had come across an interesting old photo of the building – with an intriguing identifying caption underneath – while doing research one day at the Filson Historical Society, I decided to verify what I knew about the current residence of Babette Philips. I made my way down to the Jefferson County courthouse and began rummaging around in the deed room to see what I could find.

As very often happens, tracking the deeds of the property back to the original owners of the land proved to be a bit of a challenge, so I decided to enlist the help of John Schuler, a friend and fellow writer who also happened to be a title examiner. After poring through aging documents and deciphering the perplexing connections from one deed to the next, he was able to confirm my original hunch: the building at 1135 South First Street at one time had been an orphanage. The caption I had read at the Filson Historical Society identified it simply as "the Old Orphans' Home," but I had suspected that this wasn't the official name of the institution. With John Schuler's help, I discovered that the original deeds identified the property as belonging to the Jewish Welfare Federation. After consulting the *Encyclopedia of Louisville* I learned that the old orphanage on First Street had been known as the Jewish Children's Home at one time.

I shared this information with Babette over lunch at the Third Avenue Café at the Corner of Third and Oak, just half a block from my house, on a blustery autumn day. The original Jewish Children's Home had been established on December 4, 1910, at 223 Jacob Street and then moved to 1233 Garvin in 1912, and remained there till 1922. In that year,

Property deeds suggest the imposing Italianate structure at 1135 South First Street served as an orphanage for the Jewish Welfare Federation in the 1920s and 30s. Does a former ward haunt a second-floor condo in the building today?

it moved to the First Street location and stayed there until 1933. What was hard to discern from the deeds is whether the building had been built expressly as an orphanage or whether the structure already occupied that plot of land. Although the architectural style clearly suggests an older structure, the deed implies that two plots had been acquired with the express intent of providing for an orphanage for Jewish children in the neighborhood in 1922. Whether the building actually went up before that year is inconsequential, I suppose, since Babette at least had a possible source for the haunting in her condo. Not only that, I had also gleaned from the *Encyclopedia of Louisville* that the old orphanage had also served as a convalescent home for children after it shut its doors in 1933. For more than forty years, till it closed in 1975, the stately brick building at 1135 South First Street harbored numbers of sickly children under its roof.

"That has to be why I was having all those weird dreams about the kids just standing around looking at me, with all those sickly faces and all that negative energy," she said as I divulged this information between bites of fried portobello mushroom dipped in horseradish sauce. "I'm sure being an orphanage all those years and then a hospital for sick kids left some negative energy in that space. There must have been a lot of sad kids around there." Satisfied with the history of the old red-brick building at 1135 South First Street, Babette finished her meal, and we said our good-byes.

After our meeting at the café, I didn't really expect to hear from her again. But, several days before Christmas, as a blanket of powdery white carpeted the entire neighborhood, I got a call from her. "You'll never guess what," she said. "I've got a picture with the apparition of the little boy in it," she gushed. "My cousin was here the other day and she took some pictures here, and there, in one of them where you can see the hallway in the background, is a cloudy figure in the shape of a boy. It looks just like the apparition I've been seeing." She wanted me to see it, and we agreed that we'd meet sometime after New Year's, once the holiday hubbub had subsided.

Christmas came and went. New Year's was very uneventful, and on January 6 – Epiphany – I went and paid Philips a visit in her First Street condominium. She greeted me at the door with a crestfallen expression. "Come on in," she said half-heartedly. "You're never going to believe what happened. I don't have the picture anymore." I walked inside, and Babette explained what had transpired.

"My cousin's sort of religious," she said. "And the day she was here and took that picture with her digital camera, she got really freaked out when we saw that form in the photo – and it was obvious right away that there was a little boy standing there. But her church teaches that anything like that is associated with the Devil and is wrong, so she got really nervous. I told her not to worry about it and asked her for a copy, and she told me she'd get one to me the following day, so I thought everything was going to be hunky dory." From the tone in Babette's voice, I could tell that her cousin had had a change in heart about the picture and refused to let her have a copy.

"So, she doesn't get in touch the next day, or the day after that, so I call and see what's going on, and then she tells me she's not going to give me the photograph. In fact, she had already deleted it from her camera." When I prodded as to the actual reason for not handing over the picture, Babette explained. "She went and spoke with her pastor, and he told her it was an evil photograph that needed to be destroyed, so she deleted it from the memory card and tore up the one copy she had. She told me – all smug-like and everything – that she was going to have no part in promoting the dark side. She knew I wanted to show you the picture for your book, too." The distressed woman shrugged her shoulders and sat down. "My cousin never was the brightest bulb on the Christmas tree," she exclaimed with a sigh.

"It was such a cool picture, too," she added. "The image was pretty clear and looked just like a little boy standing there – just like the little boy I had seen. And as with the little boy I had seen, you couldn't see his eyes. It was so creepy. All you could see in the picture were these big black holes where his eyes should have been. I can't believe that even showed up on the camera."

Babette and I chatted about random things for the next half hour or so, and then I left to go and prepare dinner for the Thursday Night Dinner Club. Several hours later, we all sat by the fire in the front parlor, nursing mugs of mulled wine and hot cider as an icy wind roared outside. Soon we were passing around steaming bowls of turkey and sweet potato dumplings, and the frigid temperatures outside were all but forgotten. For dessert, there were bourbon balls and cups of strong, black coffee for fortification, and just before the stroke of midnight everyone said their goodbyes, gathered their things, and left. As I watched the last of them leave in the bitter night wind, my mind raced back to that afternoon's meeting with Babette, and the goose flesh on my bare arms wasn't provoked by the freezing darkness outside. I was thinking about the apparition of the ghostly little boy with the empty eyes.

Just then, the phone rang. It was Babette Philips. "You won't believe the visit I just had," she said, apparently unaware that it was midnight. "This old woman came and talked to me, and she identified the little boy I've been seeing." I sat on the bottom step of the stairs in the foyer and waited for her to continue.

"I was out on a date tonight and got back around 10:30," she explained. "I got out of the car and was coming up the front walk when I noticed someone standing on the sidewalk looking up at the building. At first, I couldn't tell if it was a man or woman, someone young or old, whatever; I just assumed it was a homeless person and ignored it." Philips said she then ran the flight of stairs up to her condo, discarded her coat and hat and made ready for bed.

"I went to close the curtains in the living room," she said, "when I noticed this person was still out on the sidewalk, looking up at my window. It made me a bit nervous, so I kept an eye out for five or ten minutes, and it became apparent that this person was not going to budge from that spot on the sidewalk." Philips then got dressed, put on her coat, and ran down to face the stranger.

"I went down the steps to the sidewalk, and it was like the person didn't even notice me coming as I approached. When I got close enough, I could see it was an elderly woman, and she didn't appear to be homeless at all. She looked nicely dressed and everything, so I said 'Excuse me, is there something I can help you with?' Well, this startled her because she wasn't expecting me." According to Philips, the woman jumped a bit and gathered her coat tighter around her. "She told me she was sorry for staring, and she explained that she used to live in my building and pointed up at my window. This intrigued me, so I invited her inside, and she readily accepted."

When Philips asked why the lady was out so late by herself, she responded that she had lost track of time and must have been standing there for two or three hours. "It wasn't that late when she got there, I guess, but she had just lost track of time. She must have been daydreaming." Babette made the woman, a New Jersey resident named Mrs. Weinberg, a cup of tea and sat down next to her as the visitor shared an interesting story.

"Mrs. Weinberg told me that she and her twin brother had both been wards of the state under the auspices of the Jewish Welfare Federation, and that they had ended up in the orphanage in 1930, the year after the big stock market crash. She didn't know for sure, but I think her father lost everything and died because of it, leaving them all on their own. The father had a sister out west, supposedly, but they couldn't find her, so that's how they ended up in the orphanage." According to Mrs. Weinberg, their mother had died of tuberculosis just two years after they were born.

"She said they were five years old when they arrived at the orphanage, and things were fine – at first. They were treated very well, and – all things considered – they were relatively happy. The only problem was that they couldn't find anyone to adopt the both of them and keep them together, so they stayed on in the orphanage for another three years, until a terrible accident would separate them forever.

"I felt so sorry for Mrs. Weinberg as she was telling me all this," said Babette, "because I could tell it was painful for her to relieve the past, and she must have been eighty years old or so. There were a couple of times when she was on the verge of tears as she told me this. That poor woman."

According to Babette, Sarah Weinberg and her twin brother, Harold, had discovered various nooks and crannies around the orphanage in the years they called it home. "She says they used to sneak up to the tower room and that they had a secret way to get down to the cellar, as well. And they used to hide out in a janitorial closet that was somewhere in the vicinity of my condo. I tried to find out where the closet was exactly, but Mrs. Weinberg said she couldn't be sure, but she thought it was in the hallway area somewhere, or maybe where my bedroom was. I guess they had made some changes to the layout since the time she had been here. She did remember it was close to the window that looks out over the street from my living room, though."

With tears in her eyes, the old woman went on to tell of the tragic mishap that would claim the life of her twin brother. "So, she told me her brother had this awful accident and ended up dying from it. But when she told me the exact details, my blood ran cold," explained Philips. I hugged the phone closer to my ear and used a free hand to rub away the goose bumps along my arm. "They supposedly liked to play hide-and-seek around this old janitor's closet they had discovered, and it got to be their own special little spot, where they would come to when they were upset, or to share secrets and things like that. Well, one day, they both ran into the closet, but they didn't know that the custodian had left a large pail of undiluted bleach in the middle of the floor. The little boy tripped and landed headfirst in the bucket of bleach." All of a sudden, the goose bumps were back in full force and I could feel them spreading to my back.

"The bleach blinded him," said Babette. "That's why he didn't have eyes whenever I saw him! He was blind."

According to Mrs. Weinberg, her brother – although blinded for life – most likely would have made a speedy recovery were it not for one thing: the orphanage made plans to institutionalize him in a special school for the visually impaired. "That meant that he and his sister would have to be separated," said Philips. "Isn't that awful? When he found that out, the poor thing took a turn for the worse and just lay in bed and wasted away till he died a week or two later. He didn't want to live without his sister and just decided to die instead. Now I've got his ghost in my condominium to prove it."

According to Babette, Sarah Weinberg eventually found an adoptive family in New Jersey and grew to be a happy young girl, although sad memories of her twin brother would haunt her for the rest of her life. After she went to college and married, she made a vow to return to Louisville every five years to visit the old orphanage where she and Harold had known a time of relative contentment and security together. I was never able to talk to Sarah Weinberg in person, so I had to accept Babette Philips at her word before she left Kentucky for California, but I hope they both make it back to Old Louisville for another visit to the Old Orphan's Home.

David Dominé

Chapter 3 – The Campion House

The Old Orphan's Home is not the only place in Old Louisville reputedly haunted by the spirits of children. On South Third Street, another structure stands just three doors down from my former residence, the Widmer House. For those who don't know much about South Third Street, this is one of the most impressive stretches of antique architecture in the entire United States, and for over a mile, there are well-preserved examples of most styles representative of the late Victorian era. The lineup includes beautiful specimens of Châteauesque, Italianate, Richardsonian Romanesque, Queen Anne, Beaux Arts, and more. Many of these houses were built by people associated with Kentucky's famous thoroughbred racing industry, hardly a surprising fact given that Churchill Downs is situated just a mile from the southernmost boundary of Old Louisville today. The owners of Azra, the winner of the 1892 Kentucky Derby, resided in a beautiful château-inspired townhouse at 1366 South Third Street, and that address would later be home to Daniel E. O'Sullivan, the manager of Churchill Downs in the 1920s. The treasurer of Churchill Downs, Hamilton Applegate, lived in an imposing redbrick Richardsonian-Romanesque structure at 1334 South Third Street. Applegate would become majority owner of Old Rosebud, the winner of the 1914 Kentucky Derby and – according to *Blood-Horse* magazine – one of the top 100 U.S. thoroughbred champions for the 20th century. Anne and Alan Bird currently live in the large home that belonged to Applegate, and they were my neighbors for the eight years I lived at Widmer House. Right before I moved, they acquired the neighboring property to the south, at 1238 South Third Street, and announced their plans to renovate it for use as a bed and breakfast. Known as the Campion House, the beige brick residence has its own connection to the neighborhood's equine past, but this connection is a ghostly one – and one that involves children.

Given the home's history, it's not that surprising that there might be a ghost associated with the property. The reclusive former owner boarded up most of the windows and doors, and for years locals referred to it as "the haunted house." What the Birds acquired was an old residence that had been sealed off from the rest of the world for decades. Old pieces of furniture and antiques decorated the musty rooms, many of which must have looked much the same as they did around 1920 when the former owner's family, the Campions, bought the home and moved in. In some areas, walls had crumbled and decayed, but throughout the

Constructed in the 1880s, the Campion House sits on the stretch of Third Street known as Millionaires Row.

spacious mansion details such as delicate ceiling ornamentation and elegant stained glass hinted at a lavish past.

The Birds began restoring the residence to its former grandeur so they could share it with overnight guests, but these projects require patience. Although the main house isn't finished yet, renovations on the spacious carriage house to the rear of the property have been completed and the Birds welcome company for overnight retreats at their cozy alley getaway. Although the accommodations will ensure a comfortable stay, visitors might get a startle if they chance upon an unexpected encounter with a ghostly apparition that allegedly haunts the alleyway in back of the main house. Guests need not worry, however, for it seems to be a benign spirit, that of a young stable hand who is unaware that years have passed since the last horse clip-clopped its way through the lanes of Old Louisville.

"I saw him," says Anne Bird of the boy specter, "one day out back, leaning against the carriage house." According to her and other eyewitnesses, the phantom appears to be a lad in short pants with a light vest and dark cap. Hundreds of these youngsters would have been found throughout the neighborhood during Old Louisville's heyday when they were employed to run errands, do odd jobs, and, more often than not, attend to the horses stabled in the carriage houses. Although no documentation has been located to substantiate it, a neighborhood story claims that a young stable hand died in the alley behind the Campion House sometime in the 1880s.

This oral tradition is borne out by one man who claims to have first-hand knowledge of the event. "Supposedly, my great uncle died as a little boy in that alley running behind the 1200 block of Third," says Manfred Keppler, a resident of Sixth Street whose family has lived in the neighborhood since the late 1800s. "I don't know the exact details of it all, but we were all told as kids about my grandmother's elder brother who was killed one day when a team of horses got loose and trampled him. He was a stable boy for one of those homes on Third Street. I don't remember the date, but I know it happened when the world's fair [the Southern Exposition] was going on over at Central Park." The Southern Exposition was held every year from 1883 to 1887.

As if one ghost weren't enough, there seems to be other specters afoot on the grounds of the old Campion house, which neighborhood records suggest was built around 1884. These two spirits, on the other hand, allegedly haunt the dim interior of the mansion, occasionally allowing fleeting glimpses of themselves from behind the handrail on the staircase to the upper floors. Like the stable hand spotted by Anne Bird, the haunting in this instance seems to involve a younger ghost, or ghosts, as it were. Over the years, a number of reports have surfaced from the Campion House, and they all have one thing in common: the sighting of two fair-haired little girls in simple white dresses. And for many years, local residents have speculated about the reasons for why this pair of young spirits might haunt the Campion House.

According to most accounts, news of the hauntings started to spread in the 1960s, when the first in a series of employees was hired to help Mr. Campion with work around the house. One night he had come home and startled a man trying to steal one of the stain glass windows from the front of the house; in the confrontation that ensued he was attacked and sustained injuries that provoked a case of something akin to agoraphobia. He boarded up the windows and from then on he rarely left the house. "I was his neighbor for almost eight years," says Randy Hughes, a teacher who lived several doors down in the 1970s. "In that whole time I only saw him twice. Once, he was getting into a cab out in front of his house. The other time, I was walking in the back alley one night and saw him coming down the stairs of his carriage house. He actually greeted me when he saw me and we chatted for a few minutes. Said he had lived in the house his whole life, but didn't say anything about ghosts."

The people hired to work in the house, on the other hand, had no qualms about sharing their experiences with the paranormal during their time there. The first woman who came to clean the house, for example, supposedly left after just two weeks because she couldn't handle the ghostly activity she encountered. "The lady who replaced her didn't last very long, either," says Sherlissa Dawson, a former caretaker who spent many evenings in the old home with the elderly Mr. Campion. "She just up and left one night, saying she didn't want to work in a house with ghosts in it." When asked what she saw, Dawson claims the cleaning woman refused to give any details before leaving, insisting only that she "had seen something creepy on the front stairs." And that would have been enough for Dawson, had she not had a strange experience herself several weeks later.

"One night I was coming from the back of the house to the front, to go up the stairs, when something flashed in the corner of my eye," she recalls. "So I looked up and, all of a sudden, I saw a little girl crouched down behind the railing, looking at me." According to Dawson, the child spirit appeared lifelike and real, despite the pallor of its skin and dark circles under its eyes. "It like to scared the life out of me. She had her hands grabbing hold of the bars and just stared at me. I was scared at first, but then I saw she had started giggling. Two seconds later, she was gone."

Or so she thought. A little farther up the stairway, another movement caught her eye and she noticed another apparition. Hands clutching the railing spindles, a little girl with blonde hair stared down at her. Once again, Dawson was struck by the milky paleness of the wraith's skin and the dark, sunken eyes. "At first I thought the little girl had just moved up a couple steps, but I was wrong. After a second or two, I saw that it was not the same child at all. She looked a bit different, although it was obvious to me that they were related. But, it was two different girls, that's what I realized. This one had a grin on her face, too."

According to Dawson, that initial sighting of the two apparitions signaled the advent of several months' worth of disembodied laughter in the foyer of the once grand mansion. "I kept hearing those little girls giggling all the time after that. Like they were running around and playing on the steps or something. I thought I must have been going crazy, but then one night out of the blue Mr. Camp looked at me and asked if I had ever heard about the girls who haunted the house," she says. "When I told him I was hearing them quite often he was not surprised in the least. When I told them I had even seen them once, he was not shocked, either. He told me they didn't show themselves very much, and that they were part of the family lore. I gathered from what he said that he had seen them himself." Although Dawson never had any additional sightings of the apparitions while she worked at the house, she says the sounds of children in play often echoed from the stairwell at the front of the house. In addition, she often got the impression that someone was watching her as she moved from one part of the house to another. "But I did not let it worry me very much. Mr. Camp did not seem to be too concerned and if he was okay with it, then so was I."

Although another helper on the premises claimed to have seen the spectral children on several other occasions, Dawson says the supernatural incidents gradually subsided and stopped all together. "It was like the more used to them we got, the less we would hear from them. Maybe they just got tired of playing with me and found someone else to joke around with. I didn't mind them going away, because to tell you the truth, it was a little creepy. But, it was just two little girls, so I suppose they were harmless. I always wondered why they were there, but I never did find out."

Over the following years, the house started showing signs of neglect, and many people in the vicinity assumed nobody lived there. Once in a while, a passerby would see the porch bulb flicker on and off, but other than that not a light could be seen in the dwelling, whose boarded-up windows gave it the appearance of being abandoned. The fact that its sole resident never left the premises added to the allure and little by little its reputation as a haunted house grew. From the back alley, just a couple doors down from my house, it looked even worse. The small yard was unkempt and overgrown, dotted with several piles of dirt and rubbish, and the rear portion of the house seemed to be in an extreme state of disrepair. Bricks had come loose and dislodged themselves in certain areas, and the structure seemed to sag under its own weight.

The first and only time I ever met Mr. Campion was in 2001, just two years after we bought Widmer House and moved in. Like most of the people I talked to, I assumed that his place was abandoned – until one night when I returned from a late stroll with the dogs around the neighborhood. I was coming down the back alley when Rocky and Bess lifted their noses and began to sniff something in the air. As we came near the carriage house at the rear of the Campion House, I realized it was cigar smoke they had scented and they tugged on the leash and began pulling me to the side. That's when I spotted a small circle of glowing orange suspended in the shadows of the carriage house and realized that someone stood there and was smoking. My first reaction was to pull the dogs in the other direction and avoid a potentially dangerous situation, but before I could tug on the leash a friendly enough voice called out a greeting and said he was sorry if he had startled me. I returned the greeting and we exchanged some small talk before I urged the dogs forward so we could get home. It was only later that I discovered it was Mr. Campion and that he actually lived in the house. Had I known, I'm sure I would have stayed out in the back alley all night so I could pick his brain about the things he had seen during his many decades in Old Louisville. As it was, Mr. Campion's health began to deteriorate not too long after our chance encounter in the alley that night and I never got the chance to visit with him again. By that point, I had heard some of the strange stories associated with the house and I really was hoping to pay him a call, but he died before I ever had the chance.

When Alan and Anne Bird entered the Campion House the first time after acquiring it, they hadn't heard about the girl ghosts on the stairs, although they had heard a number of interesting stories about the house and its past lives. What interested them most was the condition of the house and the amount of work that needed to be done, so they made their way from room to room, taking stock of the most important projects ahead of them. Ceilings and walls throughout the house were in serious need of care, and some of the rooms looked like they had been shut off and forgotten for decades. But since the entire back of the structure was in such sorry shape, it would have to be stabilized before the brick could be tuckpointed and any cosmetic work could be done.

I paid the Birds a visit one day not too long after restoration work began on the Campion House, and Anne took me inside and showed me their progress. They hadn't gotten around to any major changes on the interior by that point and I was able to behold the interior much as it was when Mr. Campion had lived there. In many of the rooms, family furnishings remained, most likely in the same spots where they were placed in the 20s and 30s. Dusty and decaying chifferobes, lamps with fragile and cracking celluloid shades, old carpets, and artwork on the walls – it seemed that every step took us deeper into a time capsule from eighty years before. As Anne led me from room to room, she pointed out interesting discoveries she and Alan had made, including the fact that the man who built the residence hadn't gotten around to completing several interior projects such as the ornamentation on one of the railings on the front stairs.

Anne also recounted how an interesting find awaited them on their first real foray through the house after Mr. Campion's death. "We wanted to see how many of the stained glass windows were still here, so we went from room to room and took down the boards so we could see what we had," she explained, pointing to a lovely pane of stained glass in the front parlor. "Some of the windows had plain old clear glass, but there were also some really nice ones with colored glass." She stepped into the dining room and motioned for me to follow so she could show me their most prized discovery. Then she lifted her hand and pointed a finger. At first I couldn't see what Anne was indicating because it was somewhat dark in the room, but then I realized she was pointing at the solid fireplace surround in the southern wall. More exact, she was pointing at the large window above the mantelshelf. At that very a moment, a shaft of sunlight worked its way into the narrow space separating the Campion House and its neighbor to the south and the window lit up, revealing a view hidden to the outside world for decades. I caught my breath and smiled to see a beautiful painted glass panel, iridescent and multi-hued, that hinted at the earliest days of the Campion House. But a slow shiver ran up my spine as my eyes adjusted to the bright colors and gradually took in the image before us. Staring down were the delicately crafted likenesses of two young girls. Both of them had fair hair and wore simple white dresses.

I filled Anne in on the stories about the two girls that supposedly haunted the Campion House and after some investigating, she discovered that the beautiful glass window traced its origins back to the first occupant of the house, a Mr. Thomas Batman. Although they uncovered little else about the Batman family, the Birds heard that Mr. Batman resided in the house at a time when the neighborhood was experiencing tremendous growth, and he took in as boarders local craftsmen employed to construct the mansions springing up practically overnight. In return, they helped Batman complete many of the interior finishing projects on the newly constructed mansion. According to the Birds, however, some of the smaller jobs apparently remain undone today, as is evidenced in random patches of coarse woodwork and incomplete detailing in parts of the home.

I thought the discovery of the stained glass window on its own was interesting enough in its own right, but a year later I happened across another bit of information that added a poignant note to the story. I had taken some out-of-towners on an architectural tour of Old Louisville and after saying good-bye, I stopped at Buck's for a drink before heading home. Sitting at the bar with its trademark vases filled with white flowers, I sipped a bourbon on the rocks and struck up a conversation with an older gentleman who had returned to Louisville for his 50th high school reunion. We got to talking about the neighborhood, and as it turns out, his family knew the Campion family quite well and they had been to the house on Third Street many times, especially in the 30s and 40s. On the off chance that he might know something about the stained glass window with the images of the two little girls, I brought it up. Before I could even go into much detail, his eyes lit up and he said he knew exactly which window I was talking about. When I asked who the girls were, he said the Campions had always told his family the children in the window were the daughters of the man who built the house. "Supposedly the little girls died in one of the typhoid or yellow fever epidemics that swept Louisville in the 1880s, when their father was building the house on Third Street," he went on to say. "And this happened before the family had the chance to move into the new place. The parents had the window commissioned as a sort of memorial, a way to immortalize the two girls in a stained-glass work of art that would survive as long as the house." We chatted for another half hour or so and then I said good-bye before heading home.

The next week I spent some time trying to find out more about the Thomas Batman family, the first occupants of the Campion House, but I wasn't able to dredge up any documentation that might substantiate claims that the children in the stained glass window were his daughters. As is sometimes the case, I stumble across answers to these kinds of questions years after researching a story, often when I least expect it, so I'll just put it on the back burner and hope that I'll find out more someday. Oral accounts are nice, but I find it's always better to have written historical information when piecing together a ghost story. For now, Anne and Alan Bird will just have to add these unanswered questions to their to-do list as the old Campion House continues to come back to life. Someday soon it may be ready to lodge guests in the same Victorian style as it did in the past. If anyone spots the two little girls on the front stairs, I hope they get in touch with me.

Old Louisville resident Susan Coleman believes this photo from 2010 captured the image of the two little girls that haunt the Campion House. This photograph of the front door was taken from the sidewalk after nightfall.

David Dominé

Chapter 4 – Shrieks at the St. Ives

Although large, stately mansions and comfortable single-family dwellings dominated the residential scene in Old Louisville, a smattering of apartment buildings and flats still remains from a time when wealthy locals viewed high-rise tenants as little more than residential mavericks with neither the resources nor the common sense to secure proper accommodations. Upper crust Victorians entertained the strict, albeit somewhat naïve, notion that *respectable* families lived exclusively in large, sprawling mansions with their own grounds and staffs of servants, and anyone who did not adhere to this rigid mold invited the disdain of neighbors and society alike. In the 1890s when the king of St. James Court, Theophilus Conrad, proposed the construction of an elegant apartment building at the mouth of Fountain Court that would reach an unheard of *five* stories, his neighbors balked and insisted that no self-respecting family would even consider living, packed like sardines, in "that can" of a building. "Living life on a shelf" they mockingly called it, and they dubbed the elegant St. James Flats *Conrad's Folly* and waited for its imminent demise. Their derision soon subsided, however, when it became shockingly apparent that not everyone shared their same stilted point of view. Around the country, innovative apartment buildings provided alternative lodging for those in search of convenience and adventure, and they offered the additional allure of picture-perfect vistas from over the rooftops. Apartment dwellers came to be viewed as daring, ground-breaking pioneers, and apartment houses offered trendy, even sophisticated, accommodations for both the prosperous middle class and the socially elite. By the 1900s, Old Louisville apartments had arrived en vogue.

One of these early 20th-century apartment buildings stands at the corner of Oak Street and South Second Street in Old Louisville. It is a solid, squat building with four floors that failed to reach the heights of many of the city's snazzier apartment houses, but it cuts a striking figure nonetheless. Rust-colored roof tiles, interior balconies and staid exterior tiles with colorful mosaic inlay paint a cohesive picture of the façade on the old structure while hinting at the ghosts of its former existence. Perched soundly on the corner of an active intersection, it has a good vantage point for much of the activity in the neighborhood, and two arched entryways – ornamented with multihued tile surrounds – provide access from Oak Street and Second Street. Unless one stops to study the unique façade, one can very easily pass by without ever even knowing that this building has a name. There, above the entrance and imbedded in a greenish coat of arms, one can spot a handful of cobalt blue mosaic tiles that spell out the name *St. Ives.*

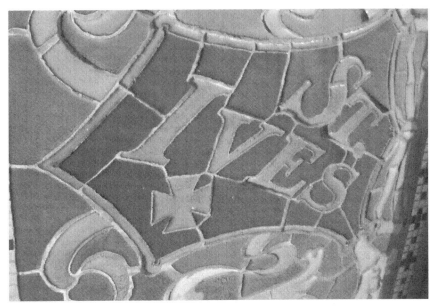

The St. Ives – a haunted apartment building at the corner of Second and Oak?

In Old Louisville, many phantoms of the past refuse to leave the confines of the opulent mansions they once called home in a former life, preferring the comforts and safety afforded by rambling architecture and sprawling floor plans. However, some blithe spirits have been known to haunt apartments as well. Many consider the St. Ives, for example, a hotbed of paranormal activity, and stories abound about the wailing ghost in unlucky apartment 13.

"When I lived there, there wasn't really an apartment 13 *per se*, but everyone talked about the apartment that used to be apartment 13 when the place was originally built in the 1920s," recalls Cap Sorrensen, a bank teller who rented from the St. Ives in the 1980s. "Some said it was on the ground floor, but others claimed it was on the top floor. In any case, different people in different apartments claimed that they lived in the original apartment 13, and that was why they would experience odd things and have bad luck. I never really believed it until I started going out with a girl who said she lived in number 13."

According to Sorrensen, he first got the inkling that there might be something to his girlfriend's insistence that she lived in a haunted apartment one cool spring day as they prepared to go to the track. "It was Derby Day, and my bank had a box at the track, so we planned on getting there bright and early in the morning before the crowds. Even though it was only 10 in the morning, we decided to make mint juleps to get us in the mood. I went to the kitchen, and that's when I noticed something very strange."

Walking through the doorway into the kitchen, Sorrensen claims he saw a bottle of bourbon slide slowly across the counter. "It was like someone gently slid it from one side of the counter to the other, a total of five or six feet, but there was no one there. At first, I thought Becky had to be playing tricks on me, so I just laughed and told her I wasn't buying it, but when she looked at me like she didn't know what I was talking about, I realized something weird was going on." When confronted with the moving bourbon bottle, the girlfriend replied with a smug "I told you so." It seems she had told her skeptical boyfriend about various items in the kitchen that had the odd tendency to move about of their own accord, and the bottle of Maker's Mark happened to be one of them.

"When I finally saw it with my own eyes, I felt really bad because I had been giving her such a hard time," Cap explains. "But, it was really happening, and I saw other things move around after that as well." For example, he remembers a strange incident that occurred several days after he witnessed the sliding bourbon bottle on the counter. "I walked into the kitchen, and before I had even taken two or three steps, one of the chairs at the kitchen table just slid out from under the table and sailed across the floor and came to a stop right in front of me." Looking for a rational explanation, Sorrensen says he pulled out a level and checked the pitch of the floor to make sure it was even. "Even if it had been off a bit, which it wasn't, it wouldn't have explained how a chair could go sailing such a distance at such a speed. *Something* besides sheer gravity had to make that thing move the way it did."

When liquor bottles continued to move across the counter on their own, Sorrensen says he tried to look for a logical explanation there as well, but he could fine none. "I saw the same bottle of Maker's Mark slide across the counter a couple of days after that, and I was convinced that the counter had to be crooked or something, so I took my level and checked it, but it was perfectly even." The puzzled man says he even turned the bottle upside down to check for wetness on the bottom that might account for the easy glide. "But, it was totally dry. There had to be some force propelling those objects in the kitchen. To this day, I have no reasonable explanation for how those things would move around by themselves."

Sorrensen says he has no explanation, either, for the other strange events he and his girlfriend experienced in their apartment at the St. Ives. "After I started seeing the things move around on their own, other weird things started happening, too. For instance, we started having strange smells that we couldn't explain. Smoke, very often, for example. Once we were convinced that the building was burning and we even called the fire department, but when they got here, you couldn't smell it anymore, and – of course – there wasn't a fire here or anyplace else on the block for that matter." Cap Sorrensen says he and his girlfriend grew accustomed to the unexplained odors and assumed they ensued from a neighboring apartment. "When the strange shrieks started, though, that was harder to explain away."

One fall evening, Sorrensen says he found himself on the couch watching movies in the living room when a piercing scream filled the room. "It was Friday night, and we were just laying on the sofa while a movie played on TV," he recalls, "and we had just commented to each other that the smell of something burning was especially strong that night. All of a sudden, we hear this God-awful scream behind us, like it's coming from the wall or something." The couple jumped up in fright and cautiously examined the area behind the sofa against the wall. "It sounded like it came from the wall right there behind us, but we couldn't find anything. I wondered if maybe a rat or some type of animal or something had got in the wall and had made that noise, but we never found out. I don't think it could've come from another apartment, either, because it sounded like it was right there next to us. It sounded just like a woman shrieking – shrieking in pain. It was awful."

Sorrensen and his girlfriend had moved out of the apartment by year's end – not because of the unexplainable disturbances, but because Cap received a promotion that required him to transfer to Pittsburgh – and they both feel relatively certain that the purported paranormal activity would have escalated to an unpleasant climax. "It wasn't like it was horrifying or anything," he explains, "but you could tell it was going to get worse. When we left, I made sure to tell the manager about the strange things we had witnessed, but he just laughed it off and didn't say a word about it. I told him he needed to warn the next tenants, but he didn't want to scare them off – for obvious reasons."

Although the manager refused to share the information about the alleged haunting with the next set of tenants, Cap Sorrensen had the opportunity to do so himself. "It turns out that a coworker of mine ended up taking over the lease for the apartment at the St. Ives," he says. "I made sure to tell him about the weird stuff going on there right away, but it didn't seem to bother him it all. He just shrugged his shoulders and said he didn't believe in ghosts or anything associated with the occult."

After moving into unlucky apartment 13 at the St. Ives, the new tenant wouldn't be saying that any longer.

"I was always a staunch nonbeliever in ghosts and goblins," says Mike Cunningham, the new tenant who took the apartment over from Cap Sorrensen's girlfriend, "so when I heard that I was moving into a supposedly 'haunted' apartment, I just rolled my eyes and chuckled to myself. 'There is no such thing as ghosts!' is what I had always been taught." But maybe Mike Cunningham had been taught wrong. I called him while I was working on my second book about Old Louisville hauntings and he agreed to meet and talk more about his odd experiences in the St. Ives. It was a cold day, but the sun was shining intently as we sat down at a table in the Granville Inn, a popular hangout with students from the University of Louisville.

"The first sign I had that something odd was going on in my apartment happened right as soon as I moved in. My animals acted really strangely in the living room. I have two tabby cats, and they just started acting crazy as soon as we moved in. They were okay in other parts of the apartment, but they got wired up every time they went into the living room – that is when I could get them to come into the living room." Cunningham says his cats gravitated to the kitchen and dining room area, where their food bowls and litter boxes were, and rarely ventured past the threshold into the living room. "My cats always used to sleep with me, but after we moved into the St. Ives that pretty much stopped because it required them to walk through the living room to get to my bedroom, and they just wouldn't do it. Even when I picked them up and carried them through to the bedroom, they'd hiss and spit the whole time we were walking through the living room. It just drove them nuts."

From the safety of the kitchen, says Cunningham, the two cats would often peer into the dark recesses of the living room, oftentimes moving their heads in unison as if following an invisible figure. "It always looked like they were watching something that I couldn't see, and sometimes they'd lower their heads at the same time like they were going to pounce on something. But instead of jumping, they'd usually hiss and growl at something and then run back into their corner in the kitchen. It was crazy."

On other occasions, Cunningham recounts how he would find the two animals perched on the kitchen counter as they faced the doorway to the living room, their backs arched and their tales all bushy, as they bared their fangs at some unseen force and made the most bloodcurdling wailing, hissing sounds. "It sounded like someone was killing them," he explains. "I had *never* heard them make such awful noises before. That's what really made me stop and think."

Cunningham recalls how some of these encounters resulted in what appeared to be attacks the cats attempted on the invisible force. "I remember how – on a couple of occasions – the cats actually jumped from the counter in the direction of the doorway into the living room and looked like they were trying to attack something – or someone – that had just entered the kitchen. They'd scream and hiss and jump up in the air and claw and bite at something that I could not see. Then they'd run and hide in the corner."

From that point on, things only got worse in his apartment at the St. Ives, reports Cunningham. "The cats got so they'd only stay in the kitchen – in the corner farthest away from the door to the living room. And then all the other things started happening."

The "other things" Cunningham refers to included cries and shrieks in the middle of the night, unexplainable olfactory sensations, pushes and shoves by unseen hands and shadowy visions out of the corner of his eyes. The most unsettling of these disturbances concerned an eerie stain that kept appearing on the wall over the couch in the living room. "It started showing up the first time I heard the scream," he recalls. "Some friends had come over for cocktails and had just left when I was making my way around the place shutting off lights and stuff, when I heard this God-awful wailing. Sort of like a woman screaming or a banshee or something – I'm not quite sure what it was, but it was terrible. It made the hair stand up on the back of my neck."

Cunningham says he checked the apartment and couldn't find any reasonable source for the sound. "I just assumed it had come from the street or something." He got himself ready for bed, and that's when he noticed a slight discoloration on the wall near the sofa. "I could see this grayish stain there, almost like it was water damage or something that I hadn't noticed before. I decided to call the manager the next day, and let him deal with it and went to bed." He crawled under the covers and had just started to doze when "I heard that same awful scream again!" Convinced someone had to be in his living room, he ran there and looked around.

"There was nobody there – of course – so I just tried to shrug it off, but that's when I noticed the stain on the wall had gotten larger and darker. I moved the couch and could see that it went pretty much all the way down to the floor. I'd say it was about five feet tall in all, and a couple of feet across." Although he didn't voice his opinion at the time, Cunningham claims the odd shape had a distinctly *human* form. "It was like the shape of a person, but around the edges, it looked all fuzzy and spiky, like rays were shooting off of it. I don't know how else to describe it."

The next day, as the manager of the building stooped and examined the large spot, he scratched his head and looked perplexed. The stain, he told Cunningham, wasn't the result of a water leak or anything, but an oddity that came along with the apartment. "He told me he thought that it had been taken care of already, but apparently not. Other people had supposedly had the same stain in the apartment, in the exact same location, and every time they thought they had it taken care of with paint and primer, it would reappear. I thought it was a new stain or something, but they had been having problems with it for years." According to the superintendent, no amount of paint could keep the odd form from mysteriously reappearing at will. "He said it might take a year or two for it to come back, but it always worked its way through the top layer to the surface. He said it could happen in a couple of months or even weeks, as well."

Deciding the living room needed a new color scheme anyway, Cunningham bought two gallons of paint and had the entire room repainted by the next day. "I bought the good stuff, too, and made sure I gave it three coats. I was sure that would take care of the problem – for a while at least." He was wrong. The stain reappeared within a week. "I was stunned," he says. "I had even painted the walls a dark blue color just in case it decided to come back, so it would hide it if it did, but it stood out more than ever!"

Convinced that faulty plumbing or a strange mold had to account for the odd stain, he had a plumber come and look at. "The guy came and took a look and told me it couldn't be water damage. Told me it was a solid brick wall and there were no pipes anywhere near it. I checked the apartment above me, and they didn't seem to have any plumbing problems, either. All their pipes were on the totally opposite side of the building, anyway."

When a mold expert ran some tests and told him the apartment had not the slightest trace of mold in it, Cunningham said he was dumbfounded. Although the number of strange incidents in the apartment had dramatically increased since the initial stain appeared, he says he failed to make any connection between the events.

"All this time, I'm hearing strange noises and whispers here and there. Things kept moving all over the apartment," he recalls. "And I'd keep finding wine glasses I'd put in the kitchen sink back on the table in front of the couch; I'd turn around because I had the weird feeling that someone was watching me, and the nearest door would slam shut; the windows would slide open on their own." On one occasion, Cunningham remembers how he turned and saw his cell phone shoot across the living room and smash against the wall in the kitchen. "It seemed like whatever it was, was getting mad at me or something. That's when I started suspecting that the stain had something to do with all the weird stuff going on there."

Not one to let a discoloration on the wall daunt him, Cunningham says he painted the wall a total of five times, and each time the stain would reappear within a week or two. "It was wild," he says, "and it was like I was getting possessed or something. I'd paint and paint and paint, and then I'd wait and see what would happen. When the stain reappeared, I'd paint, paint, paint once more, and then it would come back all over again. I was obsessed with this thing and wanted to win." On one occasion Cunningham – a devout Catholic – says he even walked over to the St. Louis Bertrand church on Sixth Street and "prayed" for the reoccurring stain to not reappear.

But Cunningham finally gave up and decided to leave the apartment. "It was really taking a toll on my cats," he explains, "and it wasn't fair for me to put them through it. We moved to an apartment over in the Highlands, and the cats returned to their normal selves. They were so happy to get out of there. When I saw that, I realized that apartment had to be haunted. Or else it had some kind of negative energy or something, I don't know, but there was something definitely not right in that place. I'm glad I didn't stay there." Since then, Mike Cunningham hasn't had any paranormal encounters in the other places he has called home, and he suspects that "there might be such a thing as ghosts after all." He admitted this, albeit somewhat begrudgingly, after I reported a curious bit of information to him I had uncovered about the St. Ives several months after our initial meeting. It was a bright spring day and we had decided to me at the Granville again. As chance would have it, we ended up at the same table as on our first meeting. The air was heavy with the smell of stale beer, hamburgers, and fried onions.

I hadn't actually uncovered the information I went on to share with Mike Cunningham – stumbled across it by chance might be more appropriate. The week before, I explained, I had been out to dinner with Kelly Atkins, a friend with some paranormal knowhow I had approached about writing a foreword to one of my books. Over a dinner of fried green tomatoes and roast chicken with country ham and red-eye gravy, talk soon turned to the supernatural, and I brought Kelly up to speed on some of the more interesting stories I had come across in Old Louisville.

When I started in about the story at the St. Ives, I told Mike Cunningham, Kelly's eyes had grown wide and he immediately cut me off. "The St. Ives? Brother, why didn't you tell me you were researching that place before?" He fairly crowed with indignation. "I can tell you all you need to know about that place! If there's anything haunting that joint, it's my great-aunt Katie Nugent. She died in that place back in 1937!" I sat back in my chair, ordered another Woodford Reserve on the rocks, and listened to what Kelly Atkins had to say. Several points in the narration caused a fine layer of goose flesh to break out over my arms despite the warm temperatures inside the restaurant.

In early 1937 a terrible flood – the worst in Louisville history – rose from the Ohio River and inundated the city in a wet blanket of murky water, mud and silt. Even though more than a mile removed from the banks of the river, the Old Louisville neighborhood saw almost total flooding as well. The majority of the houses, however, escaped serious damage since most of them rest on limestone foundations well above the street level. In other parts of the city, nevertheless, tens of thousands of people lost their homes, and many more were displaced as the flood waters slowly subsided. Kelly's great-aunt, Katie Nugent, counted as one of these. In response to the dire need for shelter, the city supposedly commandeered area apartment buildings to house many of the homeless. The St. Ives was one such place.

"They put Katie Nugent and a whole bunch of others up there," explained Kelly over mouthfuls of rhubarb crisp. "She wasn't supposed to stay more than a couple of months there, but she ended up dying there before they moved her out," he concluded.

When I asked how she had died and what had happened, he put his drink down and gave me a dastardly grin. "That's the part I'm getting to, see—" He paused dramatically and looked around the dining room before redirecting his gaze back at me. "She burnt to death, that's what happened, see?" When he filled me in on the awful details surrounding the poor woman's death, my blood ran cold, because I realized there might indeed be a reason for the strange occurrences in unlucky apartment 13.

"Old Katie liked to sit by the kerosene heater at night with her glass of Madeira, and she'd usually drink till she got tired or passed out. One night, she got too close to the heater and caught her skirts on fire and ended up burning to death. The neighbors said it must have been pretty awful, because they heard her shrieking and wailing, and by the time they got to her it was too late."

The next part really made me shudder.

"And they said she had knocked things over and had fallen all over the place trying to put the fire out, but she finally collapsed and fell against the wall and gave up. They said you could see an exact outline of her body that had been made as the fire consumed her and left its mark on the wall." Fortunately, Kelly and I had both finished our desserts long before the story came to its gruesome climax. Otherwise, I don't think I would have been able to stomach another bite.

When I finished the story, Mike Cunningham sat there and didn't say a thing for the next moment or two. Then, he slowly shook his head and wriggled his shoulders as if he were trying to ward off a shudder. "That had to be my apartment," he finally said. "It all fits so perfectly. I'm sure the stain that kept reappearing had to be the spot where that poor old woman burnt to death." We chatted for another half hour, then finished our beers and headed outside.

The next year, Mike Cunningham followed his coworker to Pittsburgh, where he received a promotion as well. I included the story about their experiences at the St. Ives in my second book, and I sent a copy to both Mike Cunningham and Cap Sorrensen shortly after it was released. They both contacted me to say how much they enjoyed the book and when I asked if they had been back to Old Louisville, they both responded that they hadn't. Neither of them was sure if he wanted to return to the St. Ives for a visit.

Chapter 5 – The Phantom of Brook Street

Brook Street in the late 1800s counted as one of the most respectable upper-middle-class streets in Louisville. Lined with shade trees and large, unassuming, two-and three-story homes, many considered it the prime location for the town's merchants, bookkeepers and business managers, and even the odd lawyer or schoolmaster. As early developers sold off prime plots of land on Saint James Court and up and down Third and Fourth, the desirability of land in the area increased and extended the boundaries of the Derby City's most exclusive neighborhood. Although some of the Old Louisville elite may have felt that it had a definite *working-class* air about it, the residents of Brook Street certainly enjoyed a comfortable existence during Louisville's Gilded Age.

Victorians in the River City's upper class lived in a time when the influx of river trade and train travel inundated the city with an unprecedented degree of wealth and sophistication. This prosperity showed itself in an overabundance of impressive residential architecture that made Louisville a city famous for its comfortable and elegant homes. In 1909 *The Louisville Times* of December 31 reflected on the town's self-proclaimed title as the "City of Homes" in an end-of-the-year article describing national acclaim for her impressive residences. "Those who come to Louisville from afar return whence they came with an abiding admiration for the instinct that teaches men and women of Louisville to make the home the paramount interest of their lives. Proportionately to its size Louisville owns more handsome and livable homes than any other city in this country; and the instinct is still fully alive."

Within a matter of fifty years Louisville had transformed itself from wilderness outpost to a bustling river town, and by the time it reached its centennial in 1892, it had all the trappings of a modern-day American city. From newspapers and the arts, to luxury hotels and restaurants, science and industry, Louisville could compete with any town its size – or larger – in the nation. As industry prospered and generated wealth, the number of affluent families dramatically increased, and as a result, so did the attention paid to social standing and perceptions of good taste and etiquette.

Just like its snootier neighbors in the residential core, Brook Street strictly adhered to Victorian custom, and female residents observed "calling days," certain days of the week when ladies of the house on a particular street would stay home to receive visits from other ladies in the neighborhood. And even if they couldn't afford to keep a whole household staff like their neighbors in the mansions on Millionaires Row, people on Brook Street enjoyed their domestic help as well. If a butler, maid *and* housekeeper couldn't be afforded, a respectable family had to have at least a live-in maid to take care of the most menial chores.

Today's residents of Brook Street have long thought their street to be haunted by the ghost of one of these Victorian housemaids. A shadowy figure that appears just after nightfall, she has come to be known as *the Phantom of Brook Street*. Although actual descriptions of the ghost vary, they all have one thing in common: her clothing, said to be reminiscent of a maid's uniform in the 1800s. Observers have described seeing a young woman in a light gray, long-sleeved dress with a white lace apron and matching bonnet. Most can easily identify her as a maid or some type of servant girl from a foregone time. Witnesses also say she seems to float along the sidewalks at night, usually with her face turned away from the viewers, and they almost always hear a long, piercing scream before she vanishes into thin air.

Hattie Sullivan lived in a second-floor apartment near the corner of Brook and Oak Streets for many years, and she recalls a very similar scene on one summer evening as she gazed out of the window. Looking down at nothing in particular with her chin resting in her hands while her elbows rested on the windowsill, she couldn't sleep that night for some reason.

"I had gone to bed early, about 10, since I had worked late, and I was really tired," she explains. "But after I had dozed off, I woke with a sudden jolt because I heard someone scream. It was a woman, and it seemed to be a painful, blood-curdling scream. I lay there awake at first, not sure if I had dreamed it or really heard it. I was so riled up, that I couldn't sleep, so I got up out of bed and turned on the radio." With soft tunes floating from the AM channel, Hattie walked over to the window where she had a good view of the intersection below and decided to take a look. She saw nothing unusual, just the occasional car or bus driving by, and maybe a college student or two returning home after night classes, but she enjoyed her little corner and what excitement it offered every now and then. Besides, she didn't have a TV, so other than books and the radio, this provided her main form of entertainment when at home.

"I just propped my elbows up on the window ledge like I always did," she explains, "and I just started to watch. I wasn't hoping to see anything in particular, just people walking by, neighbors coming and going, stuff like that. It was a really warm night, I remember. It was right after the Derby, and it was one of the first really warm nights we had that spring. I had been there for about ten or fifteen minutes when all of a sudden I got this really strange feeling. I was looking down Brook Street, towards downtown, and I noticed some of the streetlights had gone out. All I could see was our intersection and then sort of like a dark cave under the tree branches where the rest of the street disappeared. It was like the street just sort of disappeared into blackness. As I was looking down, trying to see how many streetlights had gone out, a cool breeze suddenly swept up the street, rustling all the leaves in the trees. It was like a really hot summer day, when a storm sneaks up on you and the first indication you get is when the wind turns cold."

Hattie says she expected to see rain fall soon, so she lowered the window a bit and pulled her housecoat tight around her. "I pulled it up under my chin and leaned over against the side of the window, waiting for the rain to come, but nothing happened. Instead, all I saw was this eerie glow coming from under the trees on my side of Brook Street. As I watched, it seemed to get brighter, and all the while the hair was standing up on the back of my neck, and the wind was still blowing hard. Then, like out of nowhere, I saw this figure come out of the darkness."

As a first reaction Hattie wanted to retreat back into the safety of her apartment, out of view of whatever walked the street, but she seemed glued to the spot, transfixed by what she saw. "Out of the corner of my eye I could see the fireplace mantel on the wall next to me, and I just wanted to run over there and start a fire for some reason," she reports. "I don't know why, but I just wanted to go and light a fire. I just felt *so cold*. And I got such a bad case of goose bumps!" Even if she had managed to muster herself from her perch at the window and make it over to the fireplace, Hattie wouldn't have been able to start a fire anyway, since the flues had been closed up years before that. Nonetheless, she had a large, ornately carved fireplace mantel of maple and oak in her small bedroom, and she liked it because it reminded her that she lived in a house where rich people used to live.

"This figure I saw looked like a maid that might have worked in one of these houses way back when," she reports. "I knew right away I was definitely looking at a maid girl or servant because of her uniform. The dress was sort of plain and gray, but she had on a white apron with lace trim and a frilly bonnet like they used to wear in the 1800s. I couldn't see her hair or anything, but I had the impression that she was white, maybe with darker hair and eyes. And she was short. She just seemed to float out of the dark under the trees, surrounded by a strange, hazy yellow glow. I just watched her come down the sidewalk for what seemed like an eternity, but it probably lasted more like thirty or forty seconds. Then all of a sudden, she raised her hands to her face, and I heard the same terrible shriek that woke me up before that, and she just disappeared. The wind stopped blowing, and the street lamps came back on, and it was like nothing ever happened. It was nice and warm outside, but I still had goose bumps all over me."

Many witnesses to the Brook Street phantom report the same chilly wind, eerie glow and sense of longing that accompanied Hattie's sighting. Some even claim that the haunt, forlornly sobbing for some unknown reason and with her face in her hands, has seemingly hovered along the sidewalks of Brook Street. Many have suggested that these sightings involve the ghost of a young maid in search of a house to clean. Joe Grayson, an active member of the Louisville Paranormal Society and native Louisvillian, claims his grandmother, a longtime resident of Brook Street, referred to this ghost as "the Old Maid," although most agree that they get the distinct impression of a very *young* woman.

Charlie Hutchins thinks that people are seeing the spirit of a young woman who used to work in one of the homes that no longer stands on Brook Street. A spry octogenarian who has lived his entire life in the Old Louisville neighborhood, Charlie can recall references to the Brook Street phantom from his days as a student at the old Male High School in the 1920s. He even claims to have seen an apparition that fits the description of a young Victorian housemaid.

Although the local school board almost demolished the structure in the mid 1990s, preservationists and neighborhood activists teamed up to save the significant landmark and today it serves a community center. When Charlie Hutchins attended in the 1920s, Male High School had just barely completed its first decade of existence. "Back then," he explains, "that was the place to go. If you lived downtown, you usually went to Male. The location was terrific. During our lunch break or after school let out, we'd head over to Fourth Street and hang out. Back then, that's where everyone went." Up until the 1950s and 1960s, Fourth Street served as the city's premier entertainment artery, offering locals and visitors alike a wide variety of theaters, clubs, cafes, restaurants, and shops.

"We'd spend the whole afternoon walking up and down Fourth Street," Charlie recollects, "just window shopping and watching the girls and swapping stories. Saturdays were the best there, though. I'd get up early, do my chores at home, and then meet my friends in front of the Seelbach Hotel, and then we'd just walk up and down the street. The Great Depression had just started, but to see Fourth Street back then, you'd never think there were any problems in the country. Everyone seemed happy."

During one of these Saturday walks up and down Fourth Street, a friend told him the story about the ghost of Brook Street. "I don't know if I really believed in spirits and haunts and such, but it was getting close to Halloween and we were making plans to sneak into the cemetery at night, so talk turned to witches and spooks." A classmate, Eddie, told him that a servant had been murdered in one of the houses near the school, and that her ghost supposedly walked the halls late at night.

"Other kids talked about this ghost, but I don't know that I ever believed any of it at that point. As for the story of the girl getting killed in one of the houses, that was something I had heard before, too. My dad had told me about that, so I pretty much believed it." Charlie says he became a believer in ghosts not too much longer after he had heard the stories that his friend Eddie had told him. "It was the middle of November, and some of us had stayed after school to help the teacher get ready for the upcoming Christmas play. A bunch of guys were in the auditorium putting up decorations, and I had to get some stuff from a storage room down the hall."

His arms full of rolls of green and red streamers, an uneasy feeling suddenly overcame him as he walked alone down the corridor. "I looked up, and right in front of me I saw this *figure* or something. It was all white and looked to be a servant girl with an apron and bonnet. I stopped dead in my tracks, and she just seemed to stare straight ahead, almost looking right through me. And then she just started to fade away, and soon there was nothing at all. I ran back to the others and made sure I was never alone in those halls again."

Others have had even closer, and more unsettling, encounters with the ghost on Brook Street. One of them, Louisville native Rhonda Buckman, now lives on the East Coast. As a U of L dental student, she rented an apartment on Brook Street for five years in the early 1980s when in her late twenties. Although she had grown up in that part of town, she had never heard anyone talk about a phantom on Brook Street. "My family was very Baptist and very conservative, so ghosts were out of the question for us," she explains.

Nonetheless, she cannot explain a strange series of events that happened to her while she lived in her Brook Street apartment during her student days. "I decided to get this apartment because, number one, the rent was cheap, and, number two, it was right down the road from school. Some people thought me foolish for living in this part of town, but it didn't bother me at all." A tall, athletic girl, Rhonda played volleyball and loved to cycle when she had the time. She usually tried to get in a good jog around the neighborhood before it got dark, and before she had to crack the books for her classes the next day. When she needed a break, she liked to walk the several blocks to nearby Fort George on Floyd Street and relax on the solitary park bench in the middle of the small memorial garden.

"One day I got home after 5 that afternoon, after a quick jog over to Fort George and that neighborhood. Since it was fall, it was just getting dark. I had been in the apartment for about two months, and I pretty much had established a routine. I'd get home from class around 3, take a nap for an hour or so, do stuff around the house, jog for half an hour, come home, shower, fix something to eat, and then start to study. I'd usually go to bed around 2 in the morning. It was my second year of school, and I was really enjoying myself. I usually had lots of free time on the weekends, and I had a great apartment."

Although Rhonda's family had lived in a large, modern condominium in the city center, she had grown especially fond of her first-floor apartment in a large, three-story mansion on Brook Street. Although it had been divided into three spacious apartments, the hundred-year-old building had belonged to a well-to-do family until the 1930s, when the last member had sold it and moved to Florida for the warmer climate. From the abundance of rich woodwork, gleaming hardwood floors with inlay and elaborate fireplace mantels, the family obviously had spared no expense when building the house. Even though the plain, brick façade would never have betrayed its secrets, many considered the interior to be a bit ostentatious, at the least. The house also had an impressive grand stairway, an abundance of stained glass and polished brass, and even the maid reputedly enjoyed more than average comfort in her two-room quarters on the third floor.

"In my kitchen, which was the original kitchen of the house, there's a back stairway that leads straight up to where the servant lived on the third floor. Even though it was blocked off at the top of the stairs and no one could enter the stairs except from my kitchen, I never liked being on those steps. I always got a very strange feeling on those stairs." She had never experienced anything more than an uncomfortable feeling when she opened the door to the back stairway, but other renters had claimed to hear strange noises and sobs coming from that part of the house. "I never considered myself superstitious or anything, but I had heard stories that the third floor was haunted. Since I was on the first floor, I tried not to think about it too much. But, when I did have to get on the stairs, it did creep me out sometimes."

On the night in question, Rhonda had just opened the door to the servant's access stairs when she had the distinct feeling of someone watching her. "I kind of used the steps for extra storage because there weren't a lot of closets in the apartment, and I needed some clean dishtowels I usually kept in a basket on one of the lowest steps. As I opened the door and reached down for a towel, I froze. I could feel someone's eyes on my back, and it gave me chicken skin." Not sure of what she should do, she slowly closed the door and straightened up. "I wanted to turn around and look, but I knew if I did, I'd see someone."

Before she could muster her next thought, she heard a series of taps on the small window over the kitchen sink, and she couldn't help but spin around. "I was surprised that there was no one behind me, since the feeling I had was so strong, but my heart was still beating a hundred miles a minute. Sometimes people stop by unexpectedly, so I walked over to the sink and looked out the window, and there was no one there at all." She stopped to think for a minute, and wondered if maybe a friend was playing a trick on her, but then remembered that the small window over the kitchen sink had to be at least ten feet off the ground. Like many of the homes in the neighborhood, the house sat on stone foundations that raised the ground floor four or five feet above street level.

"At first, I was really spooked, but then I just convinced myself that I had imagined someone rapping at that window. I went ahead and made dinner and ate, and then cleaned up a bit before going into the living room to study for a couple hours. I had pretty much forgotten the whole episode." That is, until she walked into the living room and turned on the lights. In front of the fireplace, on the floor in the middle of the room, someone had taken two fireplace pokers and laid them out in the shape of a cross.

"It felt so strange when I saw that!" she recalls. "It was like someone punched me in the stomach and knocked the wind out of me. I just gasped for air and ran out of the room. After a couple minutes I was finally able to pull myself together, and it was then that I realized that I was terrified!" She ran to a friend's house a couple of blocks away and brought him back to her apartment, where everything looked fine, except for the pokers that still rested on the floor in the living room. "I thought that somebody had broken in, but we looked around and couldn't find anything. It was then that my friend told me the story about the ghost on Brook Street."

It seems that Rhonda's friend, Tom, had lived on Brook Street most of his life, and he had grown up hearing stories about the Brook Street haunt. "When I brought him back to the apartment," explains Rhonda, "he tried to convince me that I was imagining things or that someone I know had been in the apartment, but when he saw how scared I was, he started to take me seriously. He didn't really want to tell me anything, but when I pressed him, he gave in and told me what he had heard."

According to neighborhood lore, the lost spirit of a young girl still walks up and down the street. Perhaps she worked as a maid in one of the Brook Street residences in the late 1800s and hasn't found her employer's house yet. Tom's grandmother had told him that a woman servant in the late 1880s had been alone in the house and startled two burglars at the fireplace. They attacked her and savagely beat her, and a couple days later she died. Ever since then, people on the street have reportedly heard terrible moans and shrieks late at night, and some even claimed to have seen the apparition of a young female in a maid's uniform. Neighbors had also given accounts of strange occurrences in people's homes, and these reports almost always involved ghostly activity around the fireplace.

"When I heard about the fireplace, my blood turned cold!" confides Rhonda. "I really started to wonder about the place where I was living." Sensing her uneasiness, her friend offered to spend the night and make sure that nothing bad happened, an offer she quickly accepted. He needed to run home and get a change of clothes, and Rhonda said she would be fine for the five or ten minutes he'd be gone, however, when Tom returned he found a pale and visibly shaken Rhonda waiting at the front door.

"Listen!" She pointed back towards the kitchen, her hand shaking violently. Loud footsteps could be heard running up and down the stairs at the back of the house. "It started right after you left," she explained anxiously. "There must be someone in the back stairway." Cautiously, they both made their way to the kitchen and stopped in front of the door that opened onto the servant's stairs. They listened closely as what sounded like a pair of bare feet ran quickly up and then down the stairs before starting all over again.

"We just looked at each other and stared. I was shaking all over, and I could tell that Tom was freaked out, too, but he was trying to hide it." After what seemed like an eternity to her, and after she had convinced her male friend that no one could have entered the back stairs other than through her kitchen, he reached out and quickly yanked open the door.

"The second he opened the door, the footsteps stopped – just like that! It sounded sort of like they reached the top of the stair, and then just vanished." Standing at the bottom of the steps, the two looked up and into the empty stairwell as a rush of icy air quickly enveloped them. Only a dim 40-watt bulb hanging over the second floor landing lit the gloomy interior, casting long shadows on the outdated wallpaper as it slowly swung back and forth. Rhonda still can't find the words to describe the uneasy sensation that overcame her at the sight of the light fixture gently swaying in the empty stairwell. "It was so creepy that I almost fainted," she recalls.

Even after her friend had ascended the full two flights of stairs to make certain that the doors to both the second and third floors could not be opened, Rhonda couldn't rid herself of the apprehension that plagued her. "We left the apartment right after all the noise on the stairs, and I didn't come back for two days. When I finally did come back, I brought two girlfriends along and they stayed over the first night." Although she had calmed down a bit, Rhonda still had doubts about being alone in the apartment after dark.

"As long as I had people around, it didn't bother me as much. I guess it made me feel better knowing that I had witnesses to whatever strange stuff went on there." She hoped that the running noises on the steps turned out to be a one-night affair, even if her skeptical friends didn't receive the proof they needed to convince them that she hadn't imagined the whole event. However, they too would soon become reluctant witnesses to the ghostly activity playing out in Rhonda's kitchen, no matter how hard she tried to keep them away from the back stairs that night.

"The minute I walked back into the apartment," she recalls, "I got that same awful feeling again, and I was sort of expecting something to happen again. We ordered pizza, so we really didn't need to be in the kitchen." The more skeptical of her friends insisted on checking out the servant's stairs for herself, so she made a beeline to the kitchen as soon as they entered the apartment, ran up the steps and tried to open the two doors that went to the other floors. "I told her they were nailed shut, but she had to check for herself. She wouldn't rule out the possibility that someone could have come through from the other side until I convinced her that I had been in the other apartments and seen it with my own eyes." Rhonda remembers that a new wall covered the door to the back stairs on the second floor and that the landlord had built a large set of shelves to cover the entrance on the top story. "I had thought of that possibility as well, so before I went back into the apartment, I talked with both of my neighbors and asked if they had heard anything strange that night." Neither of the tenants had heard anything that evening.

"Everything seemed fine and we ate our pizza, played cards and watched a little TV. It was a Friday night, and we didn't have to worry about classes the next day, so we also had a couple bottles of wine. We were all feeling pretty good when we stumbled to bed around 2 that morning." Rhonda remembers showing her friends to the large guest room that adjoined the living room next to hers and then falling fast asleep as soon as her head hit the pillow in her own bed. "I was in a very deep sleep, and I usually am a very light sleeper. I guess it was the combination of the wine and the stress from the two days before. I was out like a light."

She doesn't remember what woke her, but Rhonda recalls suddenly sitting upright in bed, staring out the door towards the kitchen. She could hear both her friends yelling, the panic in their voices very evident. "I shot out of bed and bolted for the kitchen, not really sure what to expect. I was so groggy and out of it, I couldn't even remember where I was." As she ran past the open door to the guest bedroom, she saw one of the girls sitting upright in the bed, a look of bewilderment and fear painted on her face. The large patchwork quilt lay on the floor. Her other friend stood in front of the door to the back stairs and stared down at the doorknob as it slowly turned around and around.

"I saw that door and the handle going around and around, and then I remembered where I was. It all came back to me and then I could hear the same steps as someone or something ran up and down the steps." Her friend just stared, her eyes wide in amazement as the brass knob kept rotating in the same direction. The woman in the other bedroom slowly emerged, the quilt tightly around her body. Hair matted over to one side, it looked like she had just awoken from a very long sleep. "I asked what had happened, and she just shook her head and shrugged her shoulders. I could tell she was still half asleep."

Rhonda later learned that the two had been fast asleep when someone yanked the large comforter off the bed they shared. They then heard the footsteps coming from the kitchen, and something that sounded like laughter. A woman's laughter. "I didn't hear anyone laughing," confides Rhonda, "but I did hear those footsteps again, that's for certain. The same creepy footsteps." Her friend at the door still had her eyes transfixed on the spinning doorknob when she slowly reached out and took it in her hand. Taking a deep breath, she paused and then pulled the door open without effort. Rhonda says, "I told her not to open it, but she went ahead and did it anyway. I was afraid we might actually see something this time." They could see only the dark interior of the stairwell and then the wicker basket Rhonda normally kept the towels in, as it tumbled slowly down the steps and landed upright on the tiled kitchen floor.

"It was like someone at the top of the stairs threw the basket down at us. We just kept staring at it on the floor, not knowing what to do." Trying to mask her fear, her friend grabbed a flashlight from one of the cupboards and then ran up the stairs. "She was convinced that somebody had run up, even when she reached the top and saw that both doors couldn't be opened. I could tell she was upset, but she just didn't want to admit that something strange had just transpired. She's the kind that thinks there has to be a logical explanation for everything." However, they could come up with no plausible explanation for the happenings in the kitchen of the old house on Brook Street. Nor could they rationalize the sight that awaited them in the living room when they returned to the comforting glare of the TV. Once again, the fireplace pokers lay in the shape of a cross in the middle of the floor. "Both my friends turned white when they saw the pokers crossed on the rug," recalls Rhonda. "We turned on the television and stayed up all night. They left the next morning and didn't want to come back."

For the next two weeks Rhonda stayed in the apartment off and on, always making sure that she had at least one other person with her at all times. "I was still scared," she readily admits. "It was bad enough when people were with me, and I didn't want to risk it all alone. Besides, my friends wouldn't have let me go back alone anyway. They were pretty concerned, especially when we started to hear the screams." The next Monday night, Rhonda, not able to sleep in spite of her exhausted physical and mental states, lay in bed. Tom and another friend slept soundly in the adjacent guestroom. "I was just starting to get drowsy when we heard this horrible scream all of a sudden. It sounded like it came from the kitchen, a woman's horrible, painful scream." By the time she ran to the kitchen, the two men had already turned on the lights and waited in front of the closed door to the back stairs. They all heard the same set of feet race quickly up and down the wooden steps, however, this time the footsteps sounded much louder and angrier, almost deliberately so.

"It sounded like *she* – or whatever it was – was really angry. The steps just kept getting louder and louder, like she was pounding her feet on purpose to let us know she wasn't happy. It eventually got so loud and violent that the girl on the floor above me heard it and came down to see what all the commotion was." Rhonda quickly explained the situation and escorted the other woman to the back of the house and showed her the stairwell. Angry feet still stomped up the steps behind the closed door, and the four individuals gathered there could discern the barely audible moans of someone at the top of the stair, faintly sobbing. "Of course, we opened the door again, and like before, there was no one there at all. Even though we had replaced the light bulb from the time before, it was burnt out again, and the two guys had to use a flashlight to see their way to the third story." Unlike the previous disturbances, however, no one hurled the basket at them or set the light to swinging on its chain. The two men did report a spot of icy air at the top landing and a strange mist-like fog that materialized and hung over the spot for a minute or two before vanishing. They noted a strange scent lingering in the air as well, a sickly sweet floral aroma reminiscent of the orchids and lilies sent for funerals. "I just took them at their word," says Rhonda. "There was no way at all I was going up those steps!"

Suddenly, they all jumped and turned around, startled by several loud knocks on the window over the kitchen sink behind them. Much louder and more violent than the soft taps Rhonda had heard that first night, these raps threatened to shatter the glass pane. Rhonda's friend Tom bolted to the sink, followed by the other man. A bright outdoor floodlight illuminated the small back yard, and at the window, the two men could see nothing at all out of the ordinary. Dry leaves over the patch of ground beneath the window lay undisturbed, and an old brick carriage house with weathered gingerbread trim offered no way of escape since a rusty old padlock secured the solitary door that opened onto the back yard. "The four of us ended up in the back garden, and it was easy to see that if someone had been there, they would have had a very hard time leaving. The back door into my apartment and the door to the old carriage house are the only two ways to get out. The other two sides are bounded by very high – and dense – holly hedges with chain link running through them."

Clustered around the moss-covered stone fountain, the small group stood in the middle of the back garden while the men debated the practicality of a return to the apartment. As she pulled the blanket closer around her, Rhonda listened only half-heartedly, her eyes drawn to the small window over the sink that looked into her kitchen. Her skin prickled with nervousness and the first signs of fall in the chilly air, she let her eyes wander up and across the towering back façade of the building and then let her gaze rest on one of the second floor windows. Her eyes slowly focused and she quickly inhaled a long gasp of air. She could discern a vague form standing at the window and it seemed to be looking down at them.

"It looked like the shape of a young girl or a child with a frilly bonnet, but I couldn't really make anything else out," she recalls. "It was definitely a person, that's for sure, but it looked very one-dimensional, as if I was looking at a sheet of fog or mist. It kind of hovered there and flickered or shimmered. It's very hard to describe."

Her startled gasp drew the attention of the others, and they all found themselves staring up at the strange figure in the window. The diaphanous form of a woman in light gray seemed to float in the darkness of the windowpane, keeping close watch over the four individuals below. She appeared to lift her hands and cover her face, and then vanished.

"We just figured that we had experienced yet another strange phenomenon – one of many that week – and I guess we didn't know what to do. We were just going to wait and see, I suppose, but then, all of a sudden my friend Tom turned completely pale. He was staring up at the window and he was white as a sheet." According to Rhonda, Tom had figured out what it was about that window that had been bothering him. "At first he, just like the rest of us, assumed the window belonged to the apartment on the second floor. But the more he stared at it and went over things in his head, the more he realized that it couldn't be a window to the second-floor apartment." Tom had figured out that the window had to be in the same spot as the second-floor landing in the back stairway, the servant's stairs. He also recalled that he had seen no windows whatsoever along the back steps leading up from Rhonda's kitchen.

The next five or ten minutes seemed to float by, as Rhonda recalls, and every minute has been indelibly etched in her memory. "It almost felt like I was in a movie, but watching everything from the outside." When they all realized that the window had to lead somewhere, the small group ran back to the kitchen and then up the stairs to the small landing on the second story. The sound of feet running up and down the steps had ceased, and the lone bare bulb that hung overhead had not burned out this time. "We all stood there, crammed together on the landing, and tried to figure out where that window could have been," she explains, "but it was obvious that there were no windows in the stairwell." Finally, they started to run their hands over the tattered wallpaper in the hopes of feeling something hidden underneath. In older dwellings such as this one, property owners often boarded up or otherwise obscured unnecessary or cumbersome interior windows, so they decided to at least try and find something. Rhonda found a small indentation in the wall about four feet off the ground and started to work her fingers through the moldy paper until her index finger hooked a small latch lying flat in a vertical recess. "I pulled on it, and a section of wallpaper started to tear away as a small door came open a bit. We ripped off all the paper that was covering it, and then yanked on the door some more, but it was really hard to open. It must have been years since it was last opened, so it had lost its square and the bottom really scraped against the floor."

Three of them managed to heave and pull till the door had cracked wide enough for someone to slide through the opening. Inside, by the light of a flashlight, they discovered a small room probably used as a cleaning closet or utility room at one time when the original family occupied the house. Although squirrels and pigeons had definitely felt at home there, it seemed that people hadn't used the space for seventy or eighty years. Old mops and brooms still rested against the wall, and soap and cleanser in their original boxes sat on bare wooden shelves. Local newspapers spanning two decades lay in a heap on the floor, the most recent of which gave details about the "Great Loss of Life" and "Immeasurable Human Suffering" after the sinking of the Titanic in 1912. Several tattered items of clothing, rendered almost unrecognizable after years of neglect and decay, hung on a wooden peg next to the small window that looked out over the back garden. One appeared to be a shapeless gray smock or tunic, the other was a small white apron, its lace trim still crisp and neat.

After that night, Rhonda says the strange activity in her old apartment on Brook Street stopped completely. She and her friends heard no more footsteps up and down the back stairs, and they heard no raps at the window. The fireplace pokers stayed put in their stand to the left of the mantel in the living room, and Rhonda never again experienced that uneasy feeling she sometimes had in the kitchen near the back stairs. "After we discovered that secret little closet off the landing, all the weird stuff stopped. It was like she wanted us to find that room for some reason. Was she a maid in search of her next assignment? Did a servant really die a tragic death on this street long ago? I don't know. But I do hope she, or whatever it was we saw that night in the window, is at peace now."

Although Rhonda claims that research about that specific house yielded no evidence of foul play or tragedy in its past, I did dig up accounts from city newspapers in 1887 that give some credibility to the notion that the spirit of a young servant girl might haunt Brook Street. On April 21st, 1887, a twenty-three-year-old housemaid living in the home of the Mr. A. Y. Johnson family at 1522 South Brook startled two burglars as she came down the stairs into the dining room. Described as "a stout, healthy young woman of impeccable reputation," Jennie Bowman had been left in charge of the house that morning while Mrs. Johnson and her children paid nearby relatives a visit. Thinking the residence empty, Albert Turner and William Patterson, two local men, had entered and started searching for valuables when Jennie Bowman startled them. Although she did put up a brave fight, the two criminals attacked her and beat her terribly.

A short time later, the Johnson's son returned home to retrieve something his mother had forgotten. Seeing the door was locked, he crawled through a window and saw that the place was a "ghastly shambles." He quickly scrambled out and returned with his mother and neighbors, who found "pools of blood all over the floor, glass broken, furniture much displaced and rugs scattered about." Upstairs they found Jennie Bowman lying on a bed, where her attackers had left her, just barely clinging to life.

The two doctors attending her, W.O. Roberts and J.S. Haskins, reported shock at the extent and savagery of the young girl's injuries. She had "three skull fractures, with her face and features completely disfigured, and finger prints on her neck." Most disturbing of all were reports that the two criminals had beat her around the head and shoulder with fireplace pokers, and that one of them struck her such a powerful blow to the cranium that it dislodged an eyeball from its socket. Even though she did succumb to her injuries a couple of weeks later, she reportedly had several lucid moments when she was able to give a remarkably accurate description of her attackers. In an ironic turn of fate, she was able to mar the face and seal the doom of one of her assailants, just as he had done to her. In her last act of bravery before losing consciousness, she had grabbed a broken wine goblet and raked it across the face of William Patterson, permanently branding him a killer.

With this information to go on, police soon apprehended the man and his accomplice, and took them to the old Jefferson Street jail to await trial. Louisvillians became so incensed as word and details of the horrible crime spread that a vicious mob soon formed and tried to storm the gates of the old city jail. Newspapers carried daily updates on the girl's progress and sensational accounts of the search for the killers, and Governor Proctor Knott and city authorities became so alarmed at the situation that they had the men moved to Frankfort to await trial. Within a year the alleged killers were tried, convicted and hanged, and Louisville eventually returned to normal after one of its most brutal crimes and worse cases of civil unrest. It was one of the most sensational stories covered by Kentucky newspapers in decades.

Today little remains concerning the tragic story of Jennie Bowman, other than several weeks' worth of newspaper articles and various accounts of the Brook Street phantom. Although the residence at the time had the address of 1522 South Brook Street, it doesn't pay to go looking to 1522 South Brook Street today for answers. In an effort to deal with the city's massive expansion and keep up with the influx of new homes in its first suburb, Old Louisville, the local government passed an ordinance in 1906 that changed the street-numbering system. The original house where the crime occurred occupied a spot not too far from Broadway and has long since been demolished. A stretch of I-65 covers that entire block, which – curiously enough – sits directly across from the old Male High School.

David Dominé

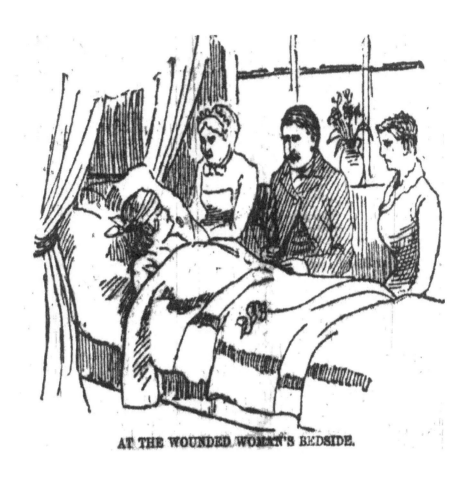

An illustration from the 1880s depicts the wounded Jennie Bowman with family members. She would die several days later.

A BRUTAL CRIME.

Bloody Work With a Poker In the Hands of a Desperate Negro Burglar.

Jennie Bowman, a Domestic, Murderously Attacked In the Residence of Her Employer.

A Lucid Interval, After a Lapse of Seven Hours, During Which She Described the Assailant

Number of Arrests Made, But the Right Man Not Yet In Custody.

MARION JONES BADLY WANTED.

Jennie Bowman, a domestic at the residence of Mr. A. Y. Johnson, Jr., No. 1522 Brook street, was brutally assaulted in her employer's house, yesterday morning, and beaten into insensibility. Her injuries are pronounced necessarily fatal. At 12 o'clock last night she was barely alive.

There are only three residences on the block where stands the house in which the murderous deed was done—between Caldwell and Kentucky. Immediately across the street from the Johnson place is an alley, and to the south of this is located the warehouse of the Pictet Artificial Ice Company. On either side of the residence are commons, frequently used for base-ball games and circus exhibitions.

About 10 A. M. yesterday Mrs. Johnson and her children left Miss Jennie Bowman in charge of the house while they went to spend

On Saturday morning, April 23, 1887, Louisville awoke to news of the terrible attack at 1522 Brook Street. Daily updates on the case were given over the next two weeks.

THE WOUNDED WOMAN.

SCENE OF THE TRAGEDY.

CONDITION OF THE VICTIM.

Miss Bowman Passes a Terrible Day and But Little Hope is Left.

MISS BOWMAN AT EIGHTEEN.

Miss Bowman grew considerably weaker during the day than she has ever been, and

Chapter 6 – The Demon Leaper

Old Louisville is a neighborhood full of many picturesque views throughout the year. A glimpse of multihued stained glass sparkling in the late afternoon sun. A colorful bit of painted detail on a porch behind the delicate scrim of branches covered in dogwood blossoms. A wintry blanket of white draped over a small front yard enclosed in ornate curlicues of wrought iron fencing. Vistas like these come to mind when I think about the seasons in Old Louisville. But, as can be imagined, my favorite scenes tend to occur in autumn when the threat of frost has mercilessly scared the green from the shade trees along the sidewalks and pedestrian courts.

Fleeting and melancholic, fall weather predisposes one to the meditative side of things, and it can turn a simple walk into an evocative stroll in Old Louisville. One October, during such a stroll along Third Street, I had the chance to study the façade of a building that had always captured my imagination. Later I returned home and started to do some research on the place, and like so many of the structures in Old Louisville, it turned out to have an interesting story to tell. It's an immense Gothic church, a veritable masterpiece of stone and mortar that looms at the corner with St. Catherine Street, and when the towering trees that shield the three west-facing entryways put on their fall finery, it is a spectacular sight to behold. Brilliant yellow leaves form a dazzling canopy for the wooden doors in their intricate lancet arches, and when offset by a sharp blue sky, the ivory structure radiates grandeur and permanence. It is the Walnut Street Baptist Church, and its flock – one of the most active in the community – has a storied history in the state, making it a proud congregation in the midst of many proud residents.

Given the fierce sense of pride that Old Louisvillians feel about their style of living, it would then come as little surprise to discover that this hubris extends back to the early days of the neighborhood. The beginning of the 20th century in Louisville was a time of unbridled opulence that culminated an almost two-decade surge in residential construction and public architecture. During the heyday of the famous Southern Exposition, it seemed that new mansions sprang up practically overnight, and they would dramatically alter the view along Third and Fourth Avenues. These counted as two of the most popular thoroughfares for the city's elite – for those of established, old-money wealth and up-and-coming incomes alike – and it was reported that in 1885 alone some 260 elegant homes went up in that area, signaling, as it were, the advent of prosperity and easy living for a growing upper-middle class.

Correspondents from national publications such as *Harper's Weekly* poured in and, notebooks in hand, they scoured the new neighborhood in search of stories and sketches to send back to their readerships. Illustrations of spacious Louisville residences with solid construction and innovative design painted the city with a very complimentary brush, and word soon spread that a Kentucky city – in less than a century since its inception no less – had carved out an enviable slice of living for itself on the frontier. Local press ran with the accolades, and the Derby City soon became the standard bearer for the notion of the "house beautiful." In an article that reflected on this incredible building boom, *The Louisville Times* of December 31, 1909, touted the local sentiment when it claimed that "nothing can rob Louisville of the distinction of being the real home center of the country."

As if to bolster this assertion, it added: "The stranger within our gates has ever remarked that Louisville homes far outclass those of other cities. Those who have enjoyed the privilege to enter many of them regard that privilege highly, and take good care that nothing may jeopardize it. Those who own them may realize the truth of these words, and those who do not, may doubt; but the Louisville home stands for itself regardless of the spoken or written word – it is the Louisville home."

In 1900, the readers of *The New York Times* got an idea of how protective these homeowners actually were when a September article proclaimed: "TO BOYCOTT LOUISVILLE CHURCH: Fashionable Third Avenue Church Indignant at Baptist Congregation's Action!" The Walnut Street Baptist Church, it reported, "the richest and largest congregation of the South," had recently sold its downtown location and had plans to build a magnificent $150,000 structure on "a fine lot on Third Avenue, the best resident street in Louisville." However, instead of adhering to the accepted property line of some thirty feet back from the thoroughfare, "the building line will be ignored and the edifice will go up from the sidewalk."

The article then went on to declare that "residents are greatly excited over the matter, but the church will not yield." When John Gathright, an adjacent property owner, confronted Dr. Eaton, the pastor of the church, with the allegation that disregarding the property line would devalue neighboring homes, the latter replied "that the church would buy the land when it got cheap." The article then concluded: "The church will be boycotted by the mansion owners."

The church demolished two homes on the site and went ahead with its plans to construct the grandest church on Millionaires Row. Today, the lovely front doors open right onto the sidewalk, silent and graceful reminders of the church's disregard for its Old Louisville neighbors. This might explain the unspoken animosity towards the beautiful Gothic structure on the corner of Third and St. Catherine that still lingers on in the vicinity to this day.

TO BOYCOTT LOUISVILLE CHURCH

Fashionable Third Avenue Residents Indignant at Baptist Congregation's Action.

Special to The New York Times.

LOUISVILLE, Ky., Sept. 11.—The Walnut Street Baptist Church, the richest and largest congregation in the South, recently sold its old church in the business part of the city on Fourth Street and bought a fine lot on Third Avenue, the best residence street in Louisville.

It has begun the erection of a church which is to cost $150,000, but to the amazement of the residents the building line will be ignored and the edifice will go up from the sidewalk. As Third Avenue contains the finest homes in Louisville, and as they have been built back over thirty feet from the sidewalk, the plans for the church will destroy a beautiful view.

The residents are greatly excited over the matter, but the church will not yield. To-day John T. Gathright, whose property adjoins the church, took out a permit for a sixty-foot fence, with which he will cut off the church from his property and also from the sight of the avenue. Mr. Gathright says that when he asked the pastor of the church, Dr. Eaton, not to disregard the building line, as it would depreciate the value of residence property, the minister replied that the church would buy the land when it got cheap.

The church will be boycotted by the mansion owners.

The New York Times

Published: September 12, 1900
Copyright © The New York Times

An article from The New York Times *details a long-forgotten feud between residents of Old Louisville and the Walnut Street Baptist Church. According to local legend, a strange winged creature known as the Demon Leaper haunts the spires and rooftop of impressive Gothic structure.*

Or else, it could have something to do with the eyewitness reports of a strange, winged creature that supposedly haunts the ornate towers and steep rooftops of Old Louisville's grandest house of worship. Described as half human and half demon, it has become known in local lore as *the Demon Leaper*, and the many theories as to its origins only serve to muddy the waters of legend and ensure its position among the most bizarre stories the Bluegrass has to offer.

"My great-grandmother saw this thing several times when the church was under construction, and she always said it had the appearance of a large, bat-like creature. And she said it was jet black, too. That's how she always described it: like a huge, black human bat." Rose Hardy, a former resident of Louisville who now calls Brooklyn home, has repeated this eyewitness description of Old Louisville's Demon Leaper many times since she first heard it from the family matriarch many years ago. "When I was a young girl in the 30s, we lived in a row house on St. Catherine Street, which, I'm told, was torn down in the 60s," says the retired nurse. "It was my father's grandmother's house, and we lived with her for a time. It wasn't too far from the big church on the corner, and we had a good view of the towers from our room on the top floor."

Although Hardy never witnessed the creature for herself, a vivid image nonetheless remains in her memory. But, given the many detailed accounts passed down by her great-grandmother, this is hardly surprising. "In my mind, this creature was always a frightening, gargoyle-type thing with dark wings and a hooked beak. That's how it was described to me. It terrified me as a kid," she recalls, "and I can still see it as an actual living thing, although, I must admit now, that it most likely never existed."

That doesn't mean, however, that Hardy discounts the alleged sightings of the strange creature witnessed by her great-grandmother. "I'm convinced she saw something, because she never came across as the flighty type to any of us, but maybe she exaggerated what she saw, or else, maybe she saw something that had a perfectly normal explanation. Maybe it was a big bird or something. I don't know, but I can still see those images in my head of a big, bat-like man hopping around the roof of the church."

Could a human gargoyle or a so-called Demon Leaper frequent the steep-pitched roofs of the Gilded-Age structures in Old Louisville today? Hardy's reservations aside, tales of strange winged creatures in this part of the country go back to Native American legend, and early European settlers supposedly reported unnerving encounters with beings of a similar description as well. In addition, it seems that Louisville encounters with frightening flying oddities that began in the past have continued up to the present and seem to now focus on the Old Louisville neighborhood. There are also those who claim to have seen this creature face to face – and recently.

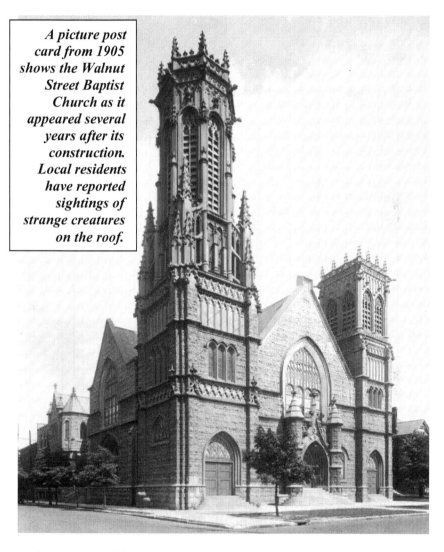

A picture post card from 1905 shows the Walnut Street Baptist Church as it appeared several years after its construction. Local residents have reported sightings of strange creatures on the roof.

Jonas Cartwright, a transplant from Florida who moved here in the late 1990s, rented a third-floor apartment in a large 1880s house not more than two blocks from the Walnut Street Baptist Church. It was there that he had an unnerving nighttime encounter in 2005. "I have a little roof deck at the back of the house where I like to sit out when it gets hot in the summer. I was out there one night in August, my friend who was visiting having just gone home, and I decided to enjoy another beer and then go inside and call it a night. I had to work early the next morning." Cartwright, in his late 30s, works in a local factory and usually has to be in for a shift at 7 a.m. "I had just put my empty beer bottle down on the table and was getting ready to stand up," he recalls, "when all of a sudden I heard this really strange *whoosh* sound, like a big bird coming in for a dive. Right then, a shadow comes down out of nowhere and lands on the edge of the roof, just two or three yards away from me!"

Although the startled onlooker says the strange apparition lingered for just a fraction of a second before it bounded over to the neighboring rooftop in a single leap and then sprang into the air and vanished, he says the image that presented itself will haunt him. "I love ghosts and things like that, but this was something entirely different," he explains. "That sight will stay in my head till the day I die. It was something demonic, maybe a mutant or something, I don't know. But it was totally unnatural."

When pressed for a more detailed description of the creature, Cartwright says: "It was as tall as me, but completely black. It had wings that look webbed, like a bat's, and its legs were very powerful. When it landed in front of me, it kept the wings raised most of the time, so I didn't get a good look at its face, but it did seem to have sharp features from what I could tell. Maybe a pointed chin, something like that. I'm not sure, but it could have had a tail. I don't know." Cartwright also remembers one other detail that makes the chance encounter all the more chilling: "When the thing landed and then took off again, I could hear the scrape of claws or talons on the tarpaper of the roof." Talons seem to be a common theme when examining descriptions of Old Louisville's Demon Leaper.

"I'll tell you straight off that I don't believe in ghosts and things like that," confesses Marc McConnell, another witness to the strange creature, "but I saw something in Old Louisville that defies explanation. It had big wings and claws, and it scared the life out of me!" McConnell currently practices law in eastern Kentucky, but he can still recall his days studying at the University of Louisville and the time he almost came face to face with the so-called Demon Leaper. Like Jonas Cartwright, he agreed to share his experiences, even though he was afraid of being ridiculed once the story came out.

"I lived closer to campus, but it was a night I was staying over at my girl friend's place. She had a gorgeous apartment in one of those huge mansions on Third Street, and her apartment took up half of the second story. She also had a little balcony that jutted out from her side of the house. It wasn't very big, but there was just enough room for two tiny lawn chairs out there."

On the night in question, McConnell claims to have seen a strange form on this very bedroom balcony. "It was pretty late, and my girl friend was in the bathroom taking a shower. I had just come from the shower and was drying myself off as I walked over to the window that opened up onto the balcony. It was the only window in the bedroom, so I was just going to take a peak outside and see if anything was going on."

As with most of the residences in Old Louisville, there is usually not much to see when looking out a side window because the homes have been built so closely together. "But even though you couldn't see that much, you could still look down and see the sidewalk that ran between the two houses. There was a very bright outdoor light, and you could look sideways and see what was going on out in the street."

As he approached the window, McConnell says he heard scratching overhead. "It sounded like something was up in the attic or maybe on the roof, and that's when something caught my attention on the balcony." At first he thought it might be a raccoon or a possum, but then he saw that a huge form had perched itself on the low railing of the balcony. "I hadn't actually gotten there yet and must have been just a foot or two away from the window when something swooped down and landed right outside the window. At first I thought it was just a big bird or something, but then I got a better look at it."

McConnell then saw something he can't classify to this day. "Even though there were some very flimsy lace curtains over the window, I got close enough where I could actually see through some of the larger holes in the pattern of the fabric, and whatever landed on the balcony was not a bird." Fully illuminated in the bright exterior light, the creature then fell into a crouching position and folded in a pair of massive, prehistoric-looking wings. "I'd estimate the wingspan at seven or eight feet before he brought them down, and they were black, like the rest of his body, and he was all leathery. And it didn't look like there was hair or fur anywhere."

When asked how tall he figured the creature to be, McConnell says it must have stood about six feet when fully erect. "When I first saw it, my heart just skipped a beat, and my first reaction was that one of the gargoyles from the big church on the corner had come to life. But before I had any more time to study the thing, it jumped up into the air and was gone. As it jumped, I noticed that it had feet like a bird's. I could see curved talons as well." McConnell says that when he checked the railing the next morning, he could see scratchy imprints left on the mossy stone surface that were about twice the size of his hands.

Although I was highly doubtful when the first rumors of a strange flying creature in the Old Louisville neighborhood surfaced – it had all the trappings of an urban legend to me – I have to admit that the eyewitnesses interviewed came across as highly credible. In a worst-case scenario, I concluded, they had seen something perfectly explainable that had been misconstrued by the cloudy view of rushed judgment or else they had just imagined it. In any case, the strange reports piqued my curiosity, and even though I normally shy away from the stories of cryptid creatures and UFO sightings, I decided to snoop around to see what I could find. The strange apples I discovered did not fall very far from the large and twisted tree of peculiar Louisville history. As it turned out, an interesting story unfolded over the next two weeks, showing that mysterious airborne objects and strange creatures have populated the skies over Louisville since the late 1800s.

After no small amount of time searching on the Internet, I came across an interesting article in the archives of *The New York Times* that would prove invaluable in my efforts to track down sightings of Louisville's obscure Demon Leaper. Entitled "An Aerial Mystery", the piece had been published on September 12, 1880, and it described "a marvelous apparition" seen near Coney Island the previous week. "At the height of at least a thousand feet in the air a strange object was in the act of flying toward the New Jersey coast. It was apparently a man with bat's wings and improved frog's legs. The face of the man could be distinctly seen, and it wore a cruel and determined expression. The movements made by the object closely resembled those of a frog in the act of swimming with hind legs and flying with his front legs." The author astutely pointed out that "[o]f course, no respectable frog has ever been known to conduct himself in precisely that way, but were a frog to wear bat's wings, and to attempt to swim and fly at the same time, he would correctly imitate the conduct of the Coney Island monster. When we add that the monster waved his wings in answer to the whistle of a locomotive, and was of a deep black color, the alarming nature of the apparition can be imagined."

Although fascinating, the article appeared to deal exclusively with the East Coast. I was about to stop reading when another bit caught my eye: "About a month ago an object of precisely the same nature was seen in the air over St. Louis by a number of citizens who happened to be sober and who are believed to be trustworthy. A little later it was seen by various Kentucky persons as it flew across the State." Could this be the same creature spotted in Louisville? With the exception of the "frog's legs," the description seemed very similar to those of recent eyewitnesses. The article then went on to say: "In no instance has it been known to alight, and no one has seen it at a lower elevation of a thousand feet above the surface of the earth. It is without a doubt the most extraordinary and wonderful object that has ever been seen, and there should be no time lost in ascertaining its precise nature, habits, and probable mission."

But instead of attributing the mysterious aerial phenomenon to superstition or diabolical forces, the analytic mind responsible for the article opined that "either the flying man or some Scientific Person at present unknown has invented the bat's wings and frog's legs with which the flying man now sails through the air." And given the fact that the inventor of the flying equipment had not chosen to reveal himself, the author surmised that the flyer must therefore be "engaged in some undertaking which he cannot safely proclaim. In other words, he is an aerial criminal, a fact which explains the cruelty and determination visible on his countenance..." Therefore, claimed the reporter, "the flying villain must have an object, and we have a right to assume that only a peculiarly nefarious object could induce a man to fly to St. Louis or New Jersey in hot weather and without an umbrella or mosquito net."

The author even went so far as to venture a guess as to the identity of the individual who had devised the flying get-up and for what purpose. His conclusion: it must have been the notorious American preacher, Dr. Talmage, who "equipped himself with wings in order to study the interesting types of immorality from the lofty height of a thousand feet." And the best part of all: "He has flown over St. Louis and Kentucky – precisely the places which might be expected to yield a rich reward to an investigator of crime; and he is now flying to and fro over Coney Island, preparatory to preaching a scathing sermon on the wickedness and indecencies of our bathing resorts."

Intrigued and amused by this bit of information, I made my way to the Louisville Free Public Library and began the arduous task of scrolling through archived volumes of old Louisville papers on microfilm. I figured if such a creature had trolled the skies over Kentucky, the state's largest paper would surely have mentioned it somewhere in the weeks preceding the September piece from *The New York Times*. Starting with the first weeks of September, I worked my way back, entertained by the many reports of local and national news, but increasingly disappointed as no reports of winged creatures surfaced. After two fruitless weeks I had made it to the beginning of the August issues of *the Courier-Journal* and was about to give up when an article caught my attention.

On August 6, 1880 *the Courier-Journal* had run a curious piece about "The Flying Machine." After scanning it, I realized that it followed up on a previous article and I traced it back to the original article, which had been written on Thursday morning, July 29. Tucked away back on page 5, it appeared in the "More Monkeying" section "With Other Edifying Morsels of News." The headline ran: "A FLYING MACHINE – WHAT TWO LOUISVILLIANS SAW LAST EVENING," and the body told an unusual story:

Between 6 and 7 o'clock last evening while Messers. C. A. Youngman and Ben Flexner were standing at a side window of Haddart's drug store, at Second and Chestnut Streets, looking skyward, they discovered an object high up in the air, apparently immediately above the Ohio river bridge, which they at first thought was the wreck of a toy balloon. As it got nearer they observed that it had the appearance of a man surrounded by machinery, which he seemed to be working with his feet and hands. He worked his feet as though he was running a treadle, and his arms seemed to be swinging to and fro above his head, though the latter movement sometimes appeared to be executed with wings or fans. The gazers became considerably worked up by the apparition, and inspected it very closely. They could see the delicate outlines of machinery, but the object was too high up to make out its exact construction. At times it would seem to be descending, and then the man appeared to exert himself considerably, and ran the machine faster, when it would ascend and assume a horizontal position. It did not travel as fast as a paper balloon, and its course seemed to be entirely under the control of the aeronaut. At first it was traveling a southeastward direction, but it reached a point just over the city, and it turned and went due south, until it had passed nearly over the city, when it tacked to the southwest, in which direction it was going when it passed out of sight in the twilight of the evening. The gentlemen who saw it are confident that it was a man navigating the air on a flying machine. His movements were regular and the machine was under the most perfect control. If he belonged to this mundane sphere he should have dropped his card as he passed over, to enlighten those who saw him, and that his friends, if he has any, might be informed of his whereabouts.

The August 6 piece that I initially discovered had corroborated a similar sighting reported by a D.F. Dempsey in the *Madisonville Times*, and an additional article on July 30 had described the hullabaloo created the day after the original sighting when throngs of visitors appeared at the drug store to hear more about the strange flying object. With this information in hand, I searched the Internet for reports of odd aerial activity or other anomalies in the skies of Kentucky in the 19th century and was amazed to find a citation from the book *Weird America* that described a strange encounter around the time the Coney Island monster had been spotted:

> A tall and thin weirdo, agile as a monkey and with a long nose, pointed ears, and long fingers, appeared in this vicinity [Louisville] around July 28, 1880. He wore a sort of uniform, made of shiny fabric, and with a long cape and metallic helmet. On his chest under the cape was a large, bright light. His big thing seemed to be scaring people – particularly women – sometimes getting so familiar as to pull their clothing off. His favorite method of escape was by springing smoothly over high objects like haystacks or wagons, then vanishing on the other side.

Since this report varies somewhat from descriptions of Old Louisville's Demon Leaper, it appears that the Louisville area in the 1880s also harbored potential sightings of UFOs, alien visitors, flying human beings and/or any combination of the three. Because of the time frame, my first reaction compelled me to conclude that all these reports somehow centered on the same phenomenon. I assumed that reports of whatever Louisvillians had spotted in the skies on August of 1880, although apparently distinct from those of the Coney Island monster, must have been erroneously identified and misconstrued as the same thing seen flying toward the New Jersey coast. In any case, the probability of an unidentified flying machine, a strange uniformed prankster with superhuman abilities and an airborne bat-like creature all in the vicinity of Louisville – and all around the same time – seemed highly unlikely to me.

When I returned to the archived versions of Kentucky papers to find actual articles written about the leaping "weirdo, agile as a monkey" on or around July 28, 1880, I came up empty handed. That's not to say, the reports don't exist; it's just that I didn't find any mention of them. It's very easy to overlook things when you're going through reels and reels of microfilm with tiny print, so there could still indeed be articles written about this strange creature that I just haven't uncovered yet.

Once again, I decided to return to the Internet to see if I could get any assistance in tracking down verification of the cape-wearing invader that had allegedly been spotted in Louisville. That's when I made some very interesting discoveries. It seems that the Louisville sightings tie into English folklore and reports of an odd apparition known for its terrorizing antics and inhuman jumping abilities. This miscreant first surfaced in the early 1800s and intimidated locals with its menacing, subhuman appearance and astonishing ability to elude capture with animal-like leaps and bounds. Many early versions of the unearthly being included descriptions of sharp talons, powerful legs, and pointed facial features with bulging eyes that often glowed red. Most witnesses also claimed the odd being appeared to be cloaked in black, at times with something akin to bird-like appendages or wings.

This menacing creature was known as *Spring Heeled Jack*, and long before Jack the Ripper began terrorizing the dark lanes and back alleys of foggy London, Spring Heeled Jack held Victorian England in the grip of hysteria. Although his antics never reached the level of gore and brutality associated with those of his infamous successor, this allegedly half-demon, half-human creature managed to frighten both villagers and city dwellers alike for more than four decades before he extended his appearance to other parts of the globe.

First documented in 1837, when a London businessman returning home for the evening reported an unsettling encounter with an outlandish being who leapt a high cemetery fence in a single bound, he was described as a muscular man of diabolic appearance with large, pointed ears and nose, and bulging, glowing eyes. Later in that same year, his alleged encounters became more violent when he sexually assaulted a young servant girl and not too long thereafter caused a coachman to overturn his carriage and seriously injure himself. In both cases, witness commented on the being's devilish, high-pitched laughter and his apparent superhuman ability to leap great distances. As the press gradually publicized details of the frightful accounts, the strange character came to be known as Spring Heeled Jack or the Terror of London.

Over the next several years the attacks escalated, and descriptions of the perpetrator grew to include a metallic helmet of sorts, and cold, clammy hands with claw-like appendages. Some females experienced serious injuries during these occurrences, and some correspondents claimed that others had literally been scared to death or had been frightened into fits of madness. During separate incidents involving assaults on two teenage girls, reports had it that the spectral being had spewed forth flames as well. One victim alleged that "[h]is face was hideous; his eyes were like balls of fire. His hands had claws of some metallic substance, and he vomited blue and white flames." The other claimed that the monster had breathed fire into her face, causing her to experience violent spasms for several hours after.

In November 1845 the agile assailant became a murderer when he suddenly appeared in the dingy tenements of Jacob's Island and attacked a young prostitute named Maria Davis on a wooden bridge over an open sewer. After reportedly exhaling flames into the petrified girl's face, the mysterious attacker seized her in his talons, lifted the victim above his head and hurled her to a certain death in the putrid waters below.

These incidents catapulted the crazed entity to local stardom when Spring Heeled Jack became the subject of several plays and penny dreadfuls, the serialized fiction publications in 19th-century Britain that cost one cent per installment. As the century came to a close, his appearances became less and less frequent, and the once loathsome figure experienced somewhat of a transformation. Ironically enough, some eventually came to view him as a Robin-Hood-type character as the memories of his early, albeit somewhat more depraved, antics faded.

The covers of two 19th-century penny dreadfuls depict the antics of Spring-Heeled Jack. Is this Victorian mischief-maker an early cousin to Old Louisville's Demon Leaper?

In her on-line article, "The Legend of Spring Heeled Jack," Sharon McGovern writes that "Spring Heeled Jack was seen leaping up and down the streets and rooftops of Liverpool in 1904, then disappeared from England for close to seventy years." She then goes on to say that "[b]y that time, however, he had become notorious in the U.S. Jack's American visits were first reported in Louisville, KY in July of 1880. There, he was described as tall, having pointed ears, long nose and fingers, and was clad in a cape, helmet, and shiny uniform. He accosted women, tore at their clothing, and emitted flames from a blue light on his chest." In those respects, Spring Heeled Jack would seem to be a British ancestor of Kentucky's monster-like Demon Leaper. In other respects – namely the mention of intelligible spoken English and modified garb with mask, helmet and claw-like attachments on the hands – the descriptions would suggest an entity of human design.

Other sources report that from Louisville, Spring Heeled Jack traveled on to terrorize other parts of Kentucky and the nation. On June 18, 1953, a figure bearing similarities to previous descriptions of Spring Heeled Jack was allegedly sighted in a pecan tree in the yard of an apartment building in Houston, Texas. Three witnesses described a man in a black cape, skin-tight pants, quarter-length boots, and dark form-fitting clothing.

According to a wealth of information about the legend of Spring Heeled Jack provided by the online encyclopedia *Wikipedia,* his most recent appearance took place some twenty years ago. "In South Herefordshire, not far from the Welsh border, a travelling salesman named Marshall claimed. . . to have had an encounter with a Spring Heeled Jack–like entity in 1986. The man leaped in enormous, inhuman bounds, passed Marshall on the road, and slapped his cheek. He wore what the salesman described as a black ski-suit, and Marshall noted that he had an elongated chin."

Today, many theories abound as to the origins of this strange creature that supposedly crossed the pond and lurked in the streets of Gilded Age Louisville – and perhaps lurks here still. Some believe the being arose as a non-human entity of demonic beginnings, a bounding boogeyman, as it were, hell-bent on terrorizing the simple folk of England's secluded hamlets and back roads. Others, however, have argued that sightings dealt with a flying humanoid of extraterrestrial nature, an early Martian visitor to the Britain of the 1800s. But London writer Mike Dash, for many years a contributing editor to *Fortean Times,* has thoroughly researched the case of Spring Heeled Jack since 1982, and he thinks otherwise: "Jack should be classified not, as he generally is, with UFO occupant reports, but alongside other 'phantom attackers' and with reference to 'urban terrors' and other social panics."

In a well-researched paper that sheds light on the fact and fiction surrounding the legend of Spring Heeled Jack, Dash reveals that many of the initial reports dealing with the mysterious figure proved to be unfounded or had been exaggerated or misconstrued, something not altogether implausible given the excitable nature of the subjects involved. "Nevertheless, most of the newspapers were prepared to concede that something must have caused the panic," he writes, "and several reported the rumor that a gang of noblemen was carrying out the attacks as part of a wager," a specially appointed investigatory committee contending that "the Spring-heeled Jack 'gang' was made up of 'rascals connected with high families, and that bets to the amount of £5,000 are at stake upon the success or failure of the abominable proceedings.'"

Although many more accounts and variations of subsequent attacks by the Spring Heeled Terror abound, as do possible explanations for their causes, it seems therefore that a more practical allegation involves the notion that the original Spring Heeled Jack incidents might have arisen as nothing more than failed sexual assaults or misguided practical jokes that escalated into copy-cat pranks and eventually devolved to the stuff of urban legend. Given that 19th-century America often looked to Victorian London for the latest in news and fashions, it would come as little surprise that reports of a fleet-footed freak abroad could inspire frontier versions of the same phenomena.

So, what, if anything, has been seen perched on the rooftop and steeples of the Walnut Street Baptist Church? An errant gargoyle brought to life by the chance encounter of imagination, light and shadow? A demonic aberration brought on by past misdeeds and neighborly disregard? An alien visitor intrigued by Gothic architecture? A costumed jokester hoping to liven up a dull evening? I'll leave it up to readers to decide. Be he a Gilded-Age ghost, alien visitor or nothing more than a practical jokester, Old Louisville's Demon Leaper has nevertheless joined the ranks of spectral beings that pepper the haunted past of this grand Victorian neighborhood. The next time I pass the majestic façade of the Walnut Street Baptist Church in October, I'll be making sure to look up at the roof and the towering spires.

AN AERIAL MYSTERY.

One day last week a marvelous apparition was seen near Coney Island. At the height of at least a thousand feet in the air a strange object was in the act of flying toward the New-Jersey coast. It was apparently a man with bat's wings and improved frog's legs. The face of the man could be distinctly seen, and it wore a cruel and determined expression. The movements made by the object closely resembled those of a frog in the act of swimming with his hind legs and flying with his front legs. Of course, no respectable frog has ever been known to conduct himself in precisely that way; but were a frog to wear bat's wings, and to attempt to swim and fly at the same time, he would correctly imitate the conduct of the Coney Island monster. When we add that this monster waved his wings in answer to the whistle of a locomotive, and was of a deep black color, the alarming nature of the apparition can be imagined. The object was seen by many reputable persons, and they all agree that it was a man engaged in flying toward New-Jersey.

About a month ago an object of precisely the same nature was seen in the air over St. Louis by a number of citizens who happened to be sober and are believed to be trustworthy. A little later it was seen by various Kentucky persons as it flew across the State. In no instance has it been known to alight, and no one has seen it at a lower elevation than a thousand feet above the surface of the earth. It is without doubt the most extraordinary and wonderful object that has ever been seen, and there should be no time lost in ascertaining its precise nature, habits, and probable mission.

That this aerial apparition is a man fitted with practicable wings there is no reason to doubt. Some one has solved the problem of aerial navigation by inventing wings with which a man can sustain himself in the air and direct his flight to any desired point. Who is this adventurous flyer and what is his object? are questions of immediate and enormous importance. Of course, the first impulse of the unreflecting mind will be to exclaim that the mysterious flyer is an aeronaut who has invented practicable wings, and is secretly experimenting with them before making his invention public. This is fore making his invention public. This is directly at variance with the known habits and customs of aeronauts. Had any aeronaut invented a pair of wings he would have advertised, long before his invention was perfected, that he was in possession of a machine wherewith to make an aerial voyage to Europe in twenty-four hours, and that he was prepared to exhibit it for a few weeks to every one who would pay 50 cents to see it. A little later he would have taken up a subscription to pay the expenses of his proposed voyage in the interests of science, and would probably have published a book on, the science of aeronautics. Then he would have suddenly disappeared, taking his wings with him, or accidentally burning them, and after the first outburst of indignation on the part of a swindled public would have been totally forgotten. This has been the invariable practice of these ingenious aeronauts who have claimed to be the inventors of balloons or other apparatus capable of navigating the air. That the mysterious flying man has not followed this custom makes it perfectly clear that he is not a professional aeronaut.

Beyond any question, either the flying man or some Scientific Person at present unknown has invented the bat's wings and frog's legs with which the flying man now sails through the air. Why has not the inventor patented his invention and had himself duly written up by the press? The reason is obvious. The flying man is engaged in some undertaking which he cannot safely proclaim. In other words, he is an aerial criminal, a fact which explains the cruelty and determination visible on his countenance, and what can be the nefarious object which this probable wretch has in view? It cannot be simply theft and robbery, for it would manifestly be impossible for him, in his flying costume, to perpetrate burglary or highway robbery, or to pick pockets. It cannot be plumbing, for obvious reasons, neither can it be the sale of books published by subscription only. Yet the flying villain must have an object, and we have a right to assume that only a peculiarly nefarious object could induce a man to fly to New-Jersey or St. Louis in hot weather and without an umbrella or mosquito net.

It has not escaped notice that of late Mr. TALMAGE has been wandering in the West in search of entertaining varieties of crime wherewith to embellish his sermons. It is also known that he returned to this City just before the flying man of Coney Island was seen. Now, if there is a man in this country whose arms and legs are fitted to endure the muscular strain inseparable from the act of flying, that man is Mr. TALMAGE. He has preached for years with those graceful limbs, and must have developed and hardened their muscles to an extent which would fill every other professional acrobat with envy. What is more probable than that Mr. TALMAGE has equipped himself with wings in order to study interesting types of immorality from the lofty height of a thousand feet? He has flown over St. Louis and Kentucky—precisely the places which might be expected to yield a rich reward to an investigator of crime; and he is now flying to and fro over Coney Island, preparatory to preaching a scathing sermon on the wickedness and indecencies of our bathing resorts. Here we have a natural and probable explanation of the flying man, and it is earnestly to be hoped that no one, with mistaken zeal for field sports, will attempt to shoot the preacher on the wing with a shot-gun. There is not a shot-gun in existence which will do any good at a distance of a thousand feet.

An article published in The New York Times *on September 12, 1880 speculates the origins of the strange winged creature spotted recently over different parts of the country, including Kentucky. Is this related to the flying object that made an appearance over the Ohio River or the leaping "weirdo" spotted in downtown Louisville around the same time? Are these strange incidents related to the creature known as the Demon Leaper in Old Louisville?*

Chapter 7 – The Ghost of the Old Lady in the Rocking Chair

Sheltered by towering shade trees, a unique building sits on the 1300 block of South Third Street, about two blocks south of the Walnut Street Baptist Church. I used to walk by it every day with my dogs, and it is another of those unusual buildings that always piqued my curiosity. Like so many of the homes in Old Louisville, red brick figures prominently in the construction, something that hearkens back to a day when only the well-to-do could afford residences built of brick and stone. A brightly painted turret juts out from the corner to the north, and two neat porches trimmed in ginger bread – one set back slightly from the other – flank the front of the building. Parallel walkways lead from the street and end at twin sets of steps that go up to the porches, where strange things have been known to happen when the sun goes down and the gas lamps bathe the streets of Old Louisville in a warm glow.

And like so many of the historic structures in Old Louisville, the building at 1324 and 1326 South Third Street harbors a secret. It's not one of those dark, menacing secrets that hides a long lost murder or covers up evil deeds, but rather one of a more mundane nature. It's the kind of secret that involves nothing more than the all-too-common themes of family intrigue and sibling rivalry.

The story has it that construction on the spacious home began sometime around 1890, when Mr. Bowen, a well-to-do merchant decided to build something known as a "semi-detached" home on Third Avenue's emerging Millionaires Row. Although one might still hear that term used in England today, "semi-detached" has fallen out of style in this country, and most opt for the more accepted "duplex" when referring to a two-family home here. As can be imagined, this reportedly caused more than a little consternation among the well-heeled residents of Third Avenue, who balked at anything other than the notion of a three-story, single-family mansion joining their ranks. The respectable, albeit nouveau riche, families of the area had to have their own homes and grounds, and people who didn't meet these rigid standards lived "beneath" them. God forbid anyone in the late 1800s should talk of apartment living, a maverick lifestyle for those off-kilter dwellers content with "living life on a shelf" or "packed in the sardine can." And on Millionaires Row at least, residing in semi-detached homes was only one notch above apartment living.

When word got out about Mr. Bowen's plans to build a duplex, it seemed that resistance – if not in the neighborhood, along Third Avenue

A vintage post card of the stretch of Third Street known as Millionaires Row in Old Louisville shows the penchant for sprawling, single-family residences.

– would foil his plans for the structure. It was rumored that some of his prospective neighbors had even threatened to take Mr. Bowen to court in an effort the thwart the addition of the two-family home to the burgeoning single-family streetscape of Millionaires Row. That was, until the reason for Mr. Bowen's building the duplex came to light. Mr. Bowen, it would seem, was burdened with two daughters who had entered their 30s with the misfortune of being single. Given their extreme degree of singleness, the two ladies were relegated to the annals of spinsterhood, and their father had no choice but to provide them with a comfortable abode in which to live out their remaining years as old maids.

Whether it was this revelation that softened the steely resolve of the Third Avenue residents or the fact that Bowen's financial situation had recently revealed him to be wealthier than most of his Old Louisville neighbors, nobody can say, but a wave of charity nonetheless swept the barren lot at what would become 1324 and 1326 South Third Street, and the community welcomed the Bowen sisters with open arms. Mr. Bowen had the home built, and the sisters moved in, each taking up residence in her half of the dwelling. And for many years, so the story has it, the sisters lived in their comfortable home on what is now South Third Street. After the last sister died, with the Great Depression looming on the horizon, new owners moved in. Soon, the Bowen sisters were all but

Another post card from the early 1900s illustrates the size and scale of the comfortable residences built along Millionaires Row. The houses seen here are still standing, just a small fraction of the 1,400 structures that survive in Old Louisville today.

forgotten.

About that time the first reports of strange occurrences on the front porches started circulating throughout the neighborhood. Unexplained apparitions and odd, bouncing balls of orange light had begun manifesting themselves on the front porch, usually in the warm evenings of the spring and summer. According to various eyewitnesses, they were eerie, glowing orbs of light that would dance back and forth between one porch to the other.

"It was about 8:00 in the evening," says Norbert Samuels, an Old Louisville resident who recalls a particular evening in the late 1930s as he strolled along Third Street with his mother, "and we were passing by the old Bowen place." Samuels and his mother lived in a small apartment on nearby Kentucky Street, and they – like many in the area – had acquired the habit of taking regular after-dinner strolls. This, no doubt, hearkened back to the early days when Third Street, once named Third Avenue, counted as the main promenade thoroughfare in the city. Clad in the latest fashions, Old Louisvillians of the Gilded Age considered a stroll down its wide sidewalks an essential part of every Sunday afternoon. And an evening walk or "constitutional" down what the locals simply referred to as the "Street" would become a tradition that lasted until the years after World War II when city dwellers started fleeing to the suburbs.

"It was a beautiful spring evening," says Samuels, "and the light was just beginning to fade, when all of a sudden my mother stopped abruptly." Samuels, who would have been no more than five at the time, recalls that her grip on his hand tightened as she turned and stared at the porch. "I wasn't really paying attention at first, so I just stood there, but after I realized that she was looking at something, I looked up and followed her gaze to the porch on the old Bowen place."

The young Samuels drew in close to his mother as his eyes squinted to make out the activity on the porch. "There was a bouncing light or something there, and that's what had caught her attention," the now 85-year-old recalls. "Today I know it would have been called a light orb, but back then it just looked like a shiny dot bouncing around. It was kind of yellowish orange and very bright. I've never seen anything like it." Samuels says that he and his mother stood for several minutes and observed as the orb darted back and forth across the porch. "It just kept bouncing back and forth, and then it sort of grew into a see-through cloud." Samuels says he then heard a gasp from his mother, something that caused him to turn and look. "She raised the other hand to her mouth, and when I turned back to look at the porch, I saw why."

According to Samuels, the cloud had assumed the shape of what appeared to be an old woman sitting in a rocking chair. "She looked like she had white hair done up in a bun in the back, and she was just sitting in that chair, rocking back and forth," he says. "My mother and I talked about it for years afterwards, and we eventually discovered that other people had seen the same thing." The ghost of *the old lady in the rocking chair*, as she came to be known, had apparently become a permanent fixture on Third Street.

"As children, our parents always used to tell us about the ghosts in the neighborhood," recalls Annabel Jordan, a Fourth Street resident who grew up in the very house her grandparents had built in the late 1800s. "And of all the stories we would hear, I always loved hearing about the old lady in the rocking chair. It wasn't a scary story at all, that's what I liked about it. It was just a nice old lady people would see every now and then." Little did Annabel Jordan know that she would one day be one of those people to witness the apparition of the old dame in the rocking chair.

"I remember the night quite well," recalls the retired math teacher "because I had just left my best friend's birthday party and was on my way home from the corner of Third and Gaulbert. She had just turned ten, and it was May 5th, 1949." Jordan says nothing seemed out of the ordinary as she walked down the brick sidewalk and approached the house to her left. "That's what I thought at first," she recalls, "but then something caught my eye. There was some kind of form on the porch. It was gray and cloudy." Once she reached the first walkway leading up to the front steps, Jordan says she stopped and tried to focus on the vague shape before her. "I wanted to go up the walkway and get closer to the porch, but something in the back of my head told me to stay put. Maybe it was because the hair was standing up on the back of my arms."

The young girl stood there for a full minute and tried to make sense of what she was seeing. "It was very faint, but there was a definite shape on the stoop. I knew right away I had to be seeing the ghost of the old lady in the rocking chair because I could see right through the apparition to the brick wall on the other side of her. In all my life I had never seen such a thing." After a moment or two studying the strange sight, Jordan says she could even make out distinguishing features on the ghost. "It looked like it was sitting in an old-fashioned, high-back rocker, and I could see her hair in a bun on the back of her head. There also appeared to be a white, long-sleeved blouse with a cameo brooch at the collar and high-top, black leather boots. I could even see that she had on a pair of small, wire-framed spectacles."

Not too long after the realization that she had come across the apparition of the famed old lady in the rocking chair, Annabel Jordan says the ghostly form simply disappeared. "Just like that," she explains, "it vanished! There one second and gone the next! In all my life I had never experienced such an odd encounter. I won't forget it until the day I die."

Others who have experienced firsthand the ghost of the old lady in the rocking chair share this sentiment. "I never saw her myself," says Richard Oswald, a former resident of Old Louisville who now resides in San Diego, "but I can vividly recall both my grandmother and grandfather talking about her. Both of them claimed to have seen her in the 40s when they were both kids, and the thing that I recall most is them saying that they could see that she was wearing glasses, the old-fashioned kind that looked like little round spectacles."

Ruth Gibson remembers the same kind of glasses on the nose of the specter she spied in the 1950s, when she and her older brother would spend summers with their grandparents in a palatial home on Ormsby Avenue. "They had the most amazing house, and I'm pretty sure it's still in good shape, even though it was divided into apartments in the 1960s. The grand staircase was the most striking feature of the home, and I have many fond memories playing on it as child. There was an absolutely huge landing between the second and first floors with an incredible stained-glass window. It was gorgeous."

Gibson says it was on this same landing with the large stained-glass window where she first heard tell of the old lady in the rocking chair. "My brother and I used to go up there at night and tell ghost stories. We'd wait until right after the sun went down, we'd grab a flashlight and blanket and go up there after dinner to see who could scare the other more. Rance, my brother, usually won." Years later, Ruth Gibson says the story that she remembers most vividly is that of the lady in the rocking chair.

"The way my brother told it was that an old woman was sitting out on her porch one night and an escaped convict found her and murdered her, and that's why her ghost still haunts the spot. But it turns out that he was really exaggerating the story. There wasn't a murder at all. Leave it to my brother to try and make the story gorier than it actually was." However, Gibson didn't discover this fact till many years later, many years after she had a strange encounter with the apparition herself one day.

"It was the summer of 1955, and we had only a week left at my grandparents," she recalls. "It was the Thursday before Labor Day weekend, and the last thing on my mind was ghosts. I had spent the day with a friend at her house down by the university and I was just walking home down Third when I looked up and saw a strange light out of the corner of my eye." At that moment, Gibson came to the realization that she found herself in front of the mysterious porches at 1324 and 1326 South Third Street.

"I swear, just a couple nights before, my brother had been telling me about the ghost of the old woman in the rocking chair, and all of a sudden, there I was in front of the porch he had been telling me about. And there was this strange little ball of light, just sort of dancing around." According to Gibson, the orb seemed to float in the air, bouncing back and forth between the two porches that flanked the front of the house.

"At first I thought it was a reflection from somewhere," she explains, "but after studying it for a bit, I realized it couldn't have been a reflection. I could see that it had some dimension to it. It was spherical in shape." After what seemed to be a minute or two, Gibson says that the point of light exploded before her eyes.

"It all of a sudden erupted into a little cloud of sparkling light with all these little shimmering bits. It's very hard to explain, but that's what happened. All of a sudden there was this cloud hanging there, and the light sort of faded away. At first I couldn't believe my eyes and thought I had to be imagining it or something. Or that there had to be some explanation for it." But Ruth Gibson didn't have an explanation for what happened next.

"Believe it or not, the cloud started to increase in size, and it gradually began changing shape. People think I'm crazy when I tell them this story, but it eventually assumed the shape of what looked like an old woman sitting in a rocking chair. I swear it. You could even see her rocking back and forth." Ruth Gibson says she stood there, arms dangling at her sides, for another half minute or so. Then the mysterious figure faded from sight and vanished.

"It was as if she had never been there at all. I looked around to see if there was anybody in the vicinity to corroborate what I had just seen, but I was alone. No one was on the porch. It was just me and my chill bumps." She scratched her head and reluctantly made her way home.

"Of course, I wanted to tell my brother," she explains, "but I had the sneaking suspicion that he wouldn't believe me." Although he enjoyed telling ghost stories, it appears that her older brother didn't necessarily believe in specters himself. "Rance loved scaring me and all, but he was very much the scientific kind," says Gibson. "For him, there had to be a rational explanation for everything, or else it didn't count. The only explanation for ghosts in his mind came from the paranormal, so he dismissed the idea of ghosts as reality. It was just fun and games in the end, and that's what he enjoyed."

It turns out her suspicions weren't entirely unfounded. When she arrived at her grandparent's large home on Ormsby Avenue, she rushed upstairs to tell her brother what she had just witnessed. "He just sort of looked at me like I was crazy," she confides. "He didn't accuse me of lying or anything, but I could tell he didn't believe what I was telling him. He said I must have seen an odd reflection or something, or that someone had to be playing a prank on me. He still says that to this day. Even though he has talked to other people who claim to have seen the very same thing, he remains the eternal skeptic."

But, when it comes to the ghost of the old lady in the rocking chair, there are skeptics who have been swayed. One of them goes by the name of Madeline Hecht. She has become a firm believer in the specter that haunts the porches at the late Victorian duplex in the heart of Old Louisville. She is also the person who shared some very interesting information that might explain the reason for the purported haunting.

"I used to live in that building," she explains. "I'm related to the Armstrongs, who at one time lived there. They were real bigwigs in the neighborhood and had quite a lot of money at one time. They got involved with the telephone when it first came out in Louisville and made a killing from it." John Armstrong, president of the Louisville Home Telephone Company, would eventually move out of the home and purchase a much grander residence just a half block down the street. "I think most of the strange stuff with ghosts on the porch started way after they moved out," says Hecht, "so I doubt that they ever heard any of the weird stories, but when I lived there some forty years ago, most of the people I knew in the neighborhood had heard about the little old lady who would return from the grave every now and then to rock a spell on her front porch."

An amateur historian who has lived most her life in the Old Louisville neighborhood, Hecht says she considered herself a skeptic when she first heard the accounts of odd specters in rocking chairs plaguing the front porch of the duplex at 1324 and 1326 South Third Street. "I'm pretty straight-laced," she explains, "and I had always been told there were no such things as ghosts. My father was a science teacher, and my mother was an atheist, so neither of them believed in the eventuality of an afterlife. For them, specters were nothing more than the result of an over-active imagination."

But Hecht says she always had a fascination with old homes and ghost stories. "I didn't believe in ghosts since I had never seen anything, but I still loved to read about ghosts and hear other people's stories about encounters with them. I don't know what it was, but I really loved ghost stories." And when she heard the odd tale about the old lady in the rocking chair that supposedly haunted the front porch where she lived, it quickly became one of her favorite ghost stories.

"When I lived there, there was an Irish woman who would come in from Butchertown once a week and clean the place for us," she explains. "Her name was Mary, and she was highly superstitious, so it didn't surprise me at all that she believed in ghosts and would tell me stories all the time. In fact, I think she got a rise out of telling me those stories and trying to scare me." Mary, as it turns out, would also be the first individual to give Madeline Hecht a first-hand account of the strange activity that frequented her front stoop.

"One day, Mary came in from a bad storm outside. She was sort of flustered as she shook the water from her umbrella and asked me if I had seen her. When I asked her who she was talking about she just sort of looked at me like I was crazy and shook her head. *The old woman in the rocking chair, that's who'* was her answer. This time I was the one who looked at her like she was crazy."

According to the older woman, a foggy shape resembling that of a woman in a rocking chair had just vanished from the porch. "She told me she had just walked up the front steps and was collapsing her umbrella when she looked up and saw the form to her right." Although the apparition had a somewhat hazy cast to it, the startled woman claims she could still make out enough features on the specter to identify it as an elderly woman with grayish hair done up in a bun in the back. "And she even said it was wearing glasses – the old-fashioned round spectacle type – and a high-wasted skirt to boot. Now, I don't know if she was telling the truth or not, but she did seem sincere at the time of recounting. Like I said, she was always making things up to scare me, so she could have been inventing this time, too, but I found it strange that she was reporting the types of things on the ghost that people had been talking about before. Who knows? Maybe she was just repeating what she had heard from other people."

But there would be no such explanation for the sight that greeted Hecht's eyes one morning in April as she knelt in the front yard and pulled weeds from the flower bed while her mother prepared lunch inside. "It was just your average cool spring morning, and I was enjoying myself among the jonquils and pansies, praying that my mother wasn't preparing chipped beef on toast for me. To this day, that is something I simply cannot abide."

Hecht says she heard something stir on the porch and averted her gaze there, mesmerized by what she saw. "I looked up, and there she was! Just as plain as the nose on your face. It was an old lady in a rocking chair, gently rocking back and forth, and it didn't even look like she noticed I was there. She did seem a bit one-dimensional to me – sort of like an old black-and-white newspaper photograph – but it was clearly the ghost I had heard talk about." As with other sightings, Hecht says the apparition sported a bun in the back, small wire-framed spectacles, and a long-sleeved, old-fashioned blouse with a cameo and lace at the throat.

"But that's all I was able to make out," she explains, "because as soon as I saw her, I yelled for my mother and ran inside. And you would have thought someone had gotten themselves killed by the way I was screaming! My mother almost had a heart attack when I ran back to the kitchen. I was just all over the place, trying to grab her hand to get her to come back with me to the front porch.

"But, of course, by the time I finally dragged her out there, there was nothing to be seen. When I was able to get my wits about me and tell her what I had seen, she just gave me that kind of look that all kids hate getting from their parents: a pitying stare that said she didn't believe me and might have even been disappointed in me. No amount of pleading could convince her that I was telling the truth. It really bothered me, too, because my mother knew I was not the kind of child to make things up.

According to local reports, the ghost of an old woman in a rocking chair haunts the front porches at 1324 and 1326 South Third Street.

"Fortunately, my mother finally gave in and conceded that I must have seen something, however, she would never admit that I saw a ghost, always claiming that I had to have seen something that was a strange reflection or else some kind of hallucination. That was my mother for you. Till the day she died, she would not entertain the notion of anything possible in the afterlife."

Hecht says that this was the case even after she came up with a plausible explanation for the haunting on the porch. "We ended up moving out of there several years after I saw the ghost, but from that point on, I was obsessed with finding out who the ghost was. My mother being the rational being that she was, I figured I needed proof of some sort, so I started talking to people and tracking down different reports of ghostly sightings on the porch. I was sure if I could prove that someone fitting that description lived there, my mother would be more prone to accept it.

"I talked to two other people who had seen the ghost, and they described the exact same thing I had seen, so that wasn't really of any help, other than in the sense that it turned out to be something that corroborated my initial sighting. When I asked them if they knew anything about who or what the ghost was, none of them had an answer.

"That's when I decided to start talking to the old-timers in the neighborhood and see what people knew about the house and all the different families who had lived there. At first, it was slow going, and it didn't seem that I would find anyone who knew anything. I talked to several elderly people who had spent their entire lives in this area, and one of them said he knew of two older women who had lived in the house at one time, but he said he didn't remember either of them wearing their hair up in a bun like that. From what he said, it seems they were both pretty big women and had darker hair – not thin like the specter I had seen, and not having gray or white hair. That's when I sort of gave up and stopped asking people so many questions.

"But then one day – out of the blue – I met someone who had an interesting story to tell. It was in October, the cold weather was just around the corner, and my parents had hired a painter to come and touch up the wood trim on the porch and the windows. I guess I've always been a talker, because I spent most of the day outside watching the painter and chewing his ear off. Looking back, I'm sure he must have been extremely annoyed by all my questions, but if he was, he never showed it. He was a nice old guy and patiently answered all my questions, never giving the impression that he was bored.

"In any case, I ended up asking him a ton of questions about painting and the kind of paint and tools he was using, and the conversation eventually took a turn to talking about the house and the kind of architecture it had. It seems that back then people didn't appreciate the old Victorian homes as much as they do now, and a lot of people thought the houses in Old Louisville were old-fashioned, dark and gloomy, nothing special, but you could tell that this old guy really loved the old homes. He started telling me how hard it was to find nice homes with that quality of construction, and then he started talking about the front porches on the place.

"He told me that ours and the neighboring porch were wonderful examples of Victorian craftsmanship. He started using different terms for the patterns and told me the different names of the various pieces, and, they were, of course, words I had never heard before. And, of course, I don't remember any of them today. But that's when a question came to me. Since he knew so much, I asked him why the porches on the house were the way they were – why one was offset and set farther back than the other. That's when he gave me an answer that took my breath away.

"He stopped what he was doing for a moment and turned to me and said 'Oh. Haven't you heard that story? There used to be two old sisters who lived here – one on this side and the other one on the other side – and they didn't get along well. They supposedly refused to live next to each other; that's how much they disliked each other.' So, then the old guy goes on to say that their father built them each a separate porch so they would be able to sit outside in their rocking chairs and not have to look at each other." At this point in the interview, Madeline Hecht started laughing and didn't stop for a good 30 seconds.

"Then he just turned around and went back to painting, not understanding the shock he had just delivered. The hair just stood up on my arms and the back of my neck. I didn't know what to say, so I just went back inside and sat on my bed, thinking about it all for a while. That was the connection I needed to explain the haunting, but when I eventually told my mother, she didn't pay me no never-mind, although I did notice the strange look she got on her face when I told her what I had learned. To this day, I think deep down she must have wondered a bit if my story couldn't have been true after all."

The many individuals who have had personal encounters with the specter known as the old lady in the rocking chair no doubt believe the story to be true. But, as is so often the case with these kinds of tales, no concrete proof exists that two feuding elderly sisters inhabited the red brick duplex at 1324 and 1326 South Third Street. I had my friend John Schuler pull up the deeds to the property, and he was able to confirm that a family by the name of Bowen owned the property early on. Belle Booker Bowen, the wife of E.H. Bowen, can be found on one of the early deeds, but other than that, no mention is made of other Bowen family members. When she died, her widower husband inherited the residence, so if there were any children, it is very plausible that they could have lived on in the property while it was still in their father's name. After my second book came out, I was contacted by two readers, Dr. Deborah Yarrow and "Rita", who graciously shared findings of the 1910 and 1920

Census with me via email. The records clearly show that Mr. Bowen had a daughter named Bertha, but no mention is made of another daughter. So, until some proof emerges that substantiates the existence of a second Bowen sister, aficionados of Old Louisville ghost stories will have to wonder if the story of the old lady in the rocking chair draws more heavily on fact or fiction. In all likelihood, the tale has evolved as a combination of both, making it a colorful legend with a basis in history. In the research I've done, I did find one mention of this story in an old walking tour brochure of the neighborhood, but other than that, no written evidence exists.

One day, as I was walking the dogs past the old Bowen place, I couldn't resist, so I tied up the dogs and snuck up to the front porch at 1326. I stood where I imagined an old rocker most likely would have been placed and looked out toward the street. I glanced to the side and then ran over to the porch at 1324 and did the same thing. Staring out at the traffic making its way south on Third Street, I glanced back over at the porch where I had just been, and sure enough, I could see it was true: when you were on one porch, you had no view of what was happening on the other porch. If two quarrelsome siblings had indeed lived at this address, it would have been very possible to sit out at night and have no contact with the other.

VIEW ON THIRD AVENUE, LOUISVILLE, KY.

Another postcard view shows the type of large residences built along Third Street, which for a time was known as Third Avenue. Architectural experts have claimed that the surviving stretch of old homes along Third Street constitutes one of the richest collections of Victorian architecture in the entire country.

David Dominé

Chapter 8 – Two Royal Specters

Old Louisville, like much of Kentucky, has become aware of the many negative stereotypes surrounding the state. Ever since East Coast reporters unfairly, and incorrectly, portrayed Kentuckians as little more than backwoods savages while national attention focused on the notorious feud between the Hatfields and McCoys in the 1890s, it seems that the Bluegrass has had to fight an uphill battle to maintain its good name. However, in true southern fashion, Old Louisvillians don't lend much credence to outsiders' opinions, as long as they're free to enjoy the generous slice of gentility they cut for themselves over a hundred years ago. A tumbler of mellow bourbon in hand, many sit in front parlors, surrounded by damask draperies and green velvet cushions, hardwood oak floors inlaid with cherry and walnut, patisseried ceilings, crystal chandeliers and elegant fireplaces, while thumbing their noses at those who don't love the neighborhood as much as they do. For many, isolation is a small price to pay for refinement that money can't buy.

After all, as any Old Louisvillian will tell you, this was among the first neighborhoods in the nation to make widespread use of electric lights, and for decades it enjoyed one of the best public transit systems around. In addition, no residential neighborhood in the country could boast the high number of comfortable, elegant homes or the same impressive standard of living that characterized day-to-day existence in Old Louisville. A *Courier-Journal* reporter touted these virtues in an article from September, 1888, saying, "As a residence city…Louisville enjoys many remarkable advantages, not the least of which is the taste which has been characteristic, from the first, in the beautifying of and building of homes." People in the 1800s even talked about how well inhabitants of Louisville ate, compared to other cities across the country. By the time the city had barely completed its second decade of existence, the state's thriving commercial wineries – the largest in the nation – provided a steady and generous supply of fine spirits to local dinner tables. Old Louisvillians, as a consequence, have always prided themselves on their homes and knowing how to live well.

"The stranger within our gates has ever remarked that Louisville homes far outclass those of other cities," proclaimed the *Louisville Times* in 1909, commenting on an astounding two-decade explosion in local home construction. This sense of residential well-being and contentment caught the attention of more than one visitor to Louisville. Famed director Walter Damrosch, for example, made the following observation after he brought the New York Symphony Orchestra to delight Louisville audiences during two seasons of the Southern Exposition in 1885 and 1886: "I shall always look back on those two summers with delight and gratitude...Louisville at that time was a small community, but with an old civilization which manifested itself in a circle of charming people of established culture and social relations."

An interior shot shows the level of comfort typical of many Old Louisville homes. Elegant paneling and coffered ceilings round out a room that has all the trappings of Gilded Age domesticity: comfortable furniture, fine porcelain, stained glass, and artwork on the walls. The room is the study in the Third Street mansion of C.C. Mengel, Jr., which still stands today. (Courtesy of Raymond Morgan)

It's little wonder, then, in a time when a man's home was his castle, that Old Louisvillians felt somewhat like royalty. During the Gilded Age, residents of Old Louisville, like most of wealthy Victorian America, paid extra special attention to taste and good manners. And true to fashion, they were obsessed with all things noble and aristocratic. In 1895, the country was titillated when *two* American heiresses bagged royal husbands from European nobility. For weeks, newspapers ran accounts of the courtships and marriages of Consuelo Vanderbilt to Charles Richard John Spencer Churchill, ninth Duke of Marlborough, and Anna Gould to Count Paul Ernest Boniface de Castellane.

In 1901 Louisville buzzed with the news that one of its own would join the ranks of European nobility. In a quiet ceremony at 1438 South Fourth Street, Patricia Burnley Ellison married Sir Charles Henry Augustus Lockhart Ross, ninth Baronet of Balnagown. Patricia, the daughter of an Old Louisville family of modest means, had met and fallen in love with Sir Charles on an Atlantic crossing, having been invited to take a trip abroad by a wealthy friend and her family. Only a small wedding took place since Sir Charles had been married once before, the marriage ending in divorce in1897. The "People and Pleasant Events" section of *The Louisville Times* reported that only a few people attended the ceremony and that the bride wore a lovely tailored gown of gray cloth with a matching hat. Andrew Ellison Jr., and General and Mrs. J. B. Castleman gave a dinner following the ceremony. After the exchange of the marriage vows in Louisville, the couple traveled to Scotland, where a wedding party was held at Balnagown Castle, part of Sir Charles' family's estate since 1672. Recording her impressions upon arriving at the castle for the first time, Lady Ross wrote: "The castle was surrounded by the straight tall stems of the Scotch firs, let to pink by the winter sun, the great splashes of vivid green moss on the Beech trees, the men's ruddy faces, their brawny knees displayed below their kilt, the softness of the voices, and the harshness of the bagpipes." Later, the newlyweds took up residence in Quebec, Canada.

Given the storybook circumstances surrounding the engagement, most of Old Louisville assumed the marriage would be a happy one – especially since this seemed to be a marriage for love, unlike the marriages of Anna Gould and Consuelo Vanderbilt. Whereas both the heiresses who had married to obtain royal titles came from the wealthiest families in the US, Patricia Burnley Ellison came from a modest family. She had the added good fortune that her husband counted as the largest landowner in the British Isles. By all accounts, they were to have a life of wedded bliss. However, within several years, the new Lady Ross realized hers would not be a happy marriage. True, she had the advantage of living a life of luxury in Europe; nonetheless, she could not count a faithful husband as one of her gains. People close to the couple described him as a womanizer, and an unkind one to boot. In the various divorce documents that were eventually filed, Ross seemed to be petty and stingy as well. Although Patricia remained married to Sir Charles Ross for more than two decades, her life proved to be one full of sadness. Sir Ross spent much of his time residing in Canada, Washington, D.C., and St. Petersburg, Florida, while Lady Ross lived primarily in London, with a few months of each year spent in New York.

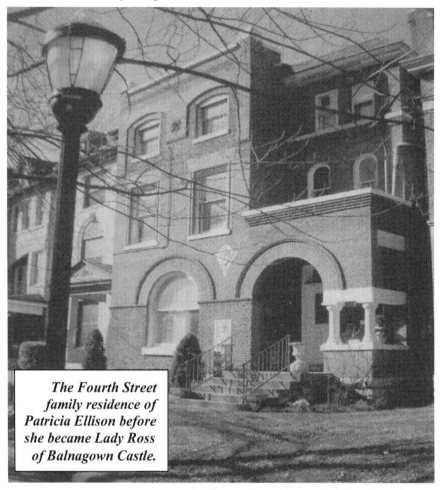

The Fourth Street family residence of Patricia Ellison before she became Lady Ross of Balnagown Castle.

Whenever possible, however, Lady Ross returned to Louisville to visit family and friends. Although infrequent, her trips home always left a mark on her, as can be seen when she wrote that "I have just had three divine weeks in Kentucky and I would like to see the demon that could take them from me. They are mine and the people who gave me those weeks are tucked away in a little compartment of the inner shrine of my memory where no others will ever be." On February 17, 1929, she wrote, "For myself, I am suffering a queer sort of homesickness. I long to see America again. I have a longing for the old days, Southern days, for old scenes and colors, smells and sounds."

Perhaps it is these feelings of nostalgia that account for the strange apparitions that have manifested themselves at Lady Ross's family home on Fourth Street in Old Louisville. Since she left over a hundred years ago, some believe her spirit has returned to search out the happiness she once knew there. Several prior residents of the house at 1438 South Fourth Street claim they have seen the apparition of an elegant woman in attire from the Edwardian era, the period when Lady Ross first realized she would not have a happy life. On several occasions people have sighted a spectral form with pearls around her neck, sadly making her way down the very same stairs she used to make her wedding-day entrance over a hundred years ago.

Sandy Carter told several friends about "the regal-looking woman on the stairs" she had seen many times before discovering that the former Lady Ross had lived in the house where she rented an apartment in the 1990s. "The first time I saw her was right before Thanksgiving, and it had just snowed outside," she recalls. "I got up early one morning, before the sun had even come up, and while I was in the kitchen I saw this woman walking by the stairs, just as plain as the nose on your face." Sandy remembers that the woman had a "matronly, kind appearance, and she was very well-kempt." Carter, a single mother of two at the time, claims the woman's elegant bearing struck her as out of the ordinary. "I thought to myself that it must have been someone from the '20s or '30s, since she was so classy and was wearing that kind of stuff. Then I realized I had to be seeing a ghost of someone who had lived there." As soon as the apparition appeared, Carter says it vanished. Although she remembers seeing the same apparition on several different occasions, Sandy claims she never felt frightened or experienced apprehension. Several other former residents of the house at 1438 South Fourth Street claim they have witnessed the same apparition, and like Sandy Carter, none of them were bothered by it. They also made special note of the fact that "she looked like a real lady" and had an air of sadness about her. James Pearce lived in an apartment at the top of the stairs from 1999 to 2001 and he claims he saw the ghost of Lady Ross one evening after returning from a party. In addition to her regal bearing, he commented on the fact that "she wore a light gray dress with an old-fashioned, lacy headpiece."

Lady Ross finally divorced her husband in 1928, and when she died on February 5, 1947, she had become a bit of a local icon. Although she never returned to her hometown, other than for brief visits, she served as a sort of correspondent for the *Courier-Journal*, commenting in her columns on British politics and society. She always wrote under the byline of "Lady Ross of Balnagown Castle" although she never really spent very much time there. On one occasion shortly after her death, a former colleague of Lady Ross claims to have seen her apparition in his offices at the *Courier-Journal*. He, like the others, reported no fear at the encounter, "only a tinge of sadness and bit of admiration for the courageous lady who was dressed to the nines." Oddly enough, all these occurrences seem to happen in November, the month when Patricia Ellison wed Sir Charles in her family's Fourth Street residence.

Postmarked 1907, this post card of Balnagown Castle was sent by Lady Ross to a friend in Louisville. After Sir Charles divorced her, he married for a third time, in 1938. The new Lady Ross was his American secretary, Dorothy Mercado. Sir Charles died in St. Petersburg, Florida in 1942, and his widow inherited the estate, which was heavily in debt at the time. After she remarried, Lady Dorothy Ross attempted to operate a sporting venture at Balnagown Castle, but it was unsuccessful. Much of the estate had to be sold, and the castle itself fell into a state of disrepair. In 1972, Mohamed Al-Fayed purchased the castle and restored it to its former grandeur. Al-Fayed, the Egyptian magnate and owner of Harrods Department Store in London, is the father of Dodi Al-Fayed, who died in the August 1997 car crash with Diana, Princess of Wales.

Opposite page: The wedding gown worn by Particia Ellison, as seen in this family portrait provided by Gladys Schneider, her niece.

THE Lady Ross of Bal-
nagown formerly was
Miss Patty Ellison of Louisville.

LADY ROSS.

Lady Ross, as she appeared in the 1920s

Lady Ross is not the only royal specter to haunt the neighborhood, however. Another regal spirit is said to haunt one of the local inns. Historic neighborhoods like Old Louisville lend themselves to bed and breakfast inns, and with such an impressive collection of old houses, it's only natural that innkeepers would throw open their doors to welcome visitors in search of an up-close-and-personal experience. Apart from the Samuel Culbertson Mansion and the Columbine, several other grand mansions along the old Millionaires Row have been converted to cozy B & Bs where guests can enjoy a relaxing sojourn in the heart of this grand neighborhood. One of them, a beautifully restored stone mansion in the Richardsonian-Romanesque style built around 1888, can be found at 1022 South Third Street. Today locals know it as the Rocking Horse Manor.

Like so many of the structures in Old Louisville, the interior of this home retains many of the typical features that defined life in the late 19th century. Ceilings soar almost thirteen feet over beautiful hardwood floors, intricate hand-carved fireplace mantels, and original hand stenciled walls with pocket doors and ornate millwork. Lovely stained glass, such as the colorful panes in the wainscoted wall next to the grand stairway in the foyer and in the elegant transoms in the second-floor windows, hints at the Old-World charm enjoyed by the home's first residents.

Max Selliger, a prominent local distiller, built the home, and his family occupied it until the 1930s. Most recently, John Lysaght and Ricardo Bermudez have called it home, and during their tenure they've made thousands of overnight visitors feel at home. Given the large number of guests to the mansion, it's somewhat surprising that only a few people have reported ghostly encounters.

Does the former residence of Max Selliger host a royal ghost?
(Photo by F&E Schmidt)

"As far as ghost stories, we haven't heard of any around here," say John and Ricardo, "but we're ready to hear any from previous guests with interesting encounters." Fortunately, two former visitors to the Rocking Horse Manor contacted me after reading my first book and shared with me their accounts of strange occurrences there.

Joe Leslie, a native of Cleveland, Ohio, spent a weekend at John and Ricardo's bed and breakfast in early 2007. Despite the comfortable bed, the then 45-year-old claims he had trouble falling asleep. "I don't know if I was all wired up from the trip or if I had eaten something that didn't agree with me, but I just couldn't fall asleep at first. I would start to get tired, but then I'd have the feeling of being watched. I got used to it after the first hour, but then the light on the bedside table flickered on and off several times. I turned it off, and it flashed on and off twice more after that, even though it wasn't on."

Leslie claims that a faint noise could be heard in his room as well. "Several times, when the light went out, I could hear this soft rustling noise. It was like someone had shaken heavy curtains. Or like I could hear a woman's heavy dress swishing back and forth. It is really hard to describe the sound, but rustling fabric came to mind when I heard it. At one point I even thought I caught a glimpse of a woman in a big fancy dress out of the corner of my eye."

Marty Green, a Kansas City businessman who spent a weekend at the Rocking Horse Manor in 2006, also reports a strange encounter with an elegantly dressed woman. "I have to tell you, I don't normally believe in this kind of stuff, but something very strange happened to me at that inn. I guess it was around two o'clock in the early morning and I was sleeping like a log. And I was having this really weird dream. There was this old woman standing at the foot of my bed, just staring at me. But, she was almost smiling. She wasn't scary or anything."

According to Green, the thing that struck him about the vision was the woman's attire. "She was wearing some sort of sash across her upper body and had a tiara or something like that on the top of her head. She was wearing a big, old-fashioned dress, too, sort of like a ball gown. All I know is that she looked like an important woman from the Victorian times."

Green woke up a short time later and had a hard time falling back to sleep. "I kept thinking about that dream and couldn't get tired again. It was a really strange dream, one of those that seemed so real. So I just lay there in bed and decided to see what was on TV. Before I did that, though, I ran to the bathroom." On the way back to his bed, Green paused to take a look from one of the windows looking out onto Third Street. "Don't ask me why, I just wanted to see if anything was going on out there. So, I leaned up against the window and was looking out, when I saw someone coming down the sidewalk."

In an instant, Green realized that the vision from his dream stood before him. "Crazy, right? I had to pinch myself to make sure I wasn't still dreaming. I rubbed my eyes, and there she was, out on the street, the older woman in the ball gown I had dreamed about. She was just casually making her way down the sidewalk, going south. She didn't look up at me or anything, she just kept on walking like she was the only one in the world."

Despite the estimated 50 yards that separated him from the apparition, Green claims he could nonetheless make out details on the ghost such as the sparkling tiara. "I could see the banner or ribbon across her chest, and she had one of those old-time skirts that kind of billowed out around her. I could see her as plain as day. That lasted for maybe ten seconds. Then, as she reached the end of the block, she disappeared. I know it sounds crazy, but that's what happened."

I shared this last account with several paranormal experts who live in Old Louisville and asked for their thoughts on the matter. They suggested two possible scenarios that might explain away this alleged case of haunting. Assuming that what Mr. Green described is accurate, they feel he might have experienced a waking dream. In fact, he might have only dreamed that he awoke and got out of the bed, and witnessed the subsequent apparition.

The other theory involves the coincidental notion that he could have actually seen a woman wearing a tiara walking down Third Street in the wee hours of the morning. Old Louisville is a neighborhood known for its Bohemian characters, and, suffice it say, stranger things have been seen here. When I was living in the house on Third Street, I looked out my third-floor window one January afternoon and saw a young man, probably a student at U of L, sailing down the sidewalk on a skateboard, in nothing more than a Speedo. Not only that, he had a surfboard strapped to his back and was playing guitar at the same time.

Could the rustling of the invisible fabric heard on the previous occasion be the swaying of the apparition's dress as she skulked about in Joe Leslie's room at the Rocking Horse Manor? It could be. Personally, I like to think that the apparition spotted in front of John and Ricardo's bed and breakfast is none other than the ghost of Lucinda, a famed character from Old Louisville's Gilded Age who made frequent appearances up and down Millionaires Row.

As is already known, the Old Louisville of the Gilded Age counted as a bastion of elegance and refinement. In its lavish parlors and drawing rooms, emphasis was placed on manners and the correct way of doing things, and, over time, a tight-knit community with its own customs and caste system evolved. Manual laborers such as bricklayers and deliverymen occupied the lower rungs of the social ladder and right above them fell household servants and day workers. In the middle came those with professions like teachers, bookkeepers and clerks, and at the very top fell a substantial echelon with the more moneyed classes. Some of its members came from old Kentucky families of wealth, but many of them were merchants who derived their fortunes from the booming industries that had sprouted up to supply city residents with the necessities. Shoe manufacturer, oil refiner, furniture producer, hardware merchant, carriage maker, wholesale saddler – these are just some of the professions listed for early residents of Old Louisville. An examination of early city directories, however, shows that a large number of distillers, tobacco executives, and – later on – racetrack associates populated the neighborhood. It was these, the kings of industry, who would shape the cultural landscape of the neighborhood, and it's only natural that the very wealthiest residents would come to be seen as local royalty.

As it turns out, a substantial number of Louisvillians other than Patricia Ellison would actually achieve regal status through marriage to members of the European nobility. In early November 1900 Miss Grace Carr married Lord Newborough, "head of one of the oldest Welsh families in existence," in the Savoy Chapel in London, and at the end of that same month *The New York Times* announced: "Another Louisville girl will marry a member of the Continental nobility." The wedding, between Miss Lillian May Langham and Baron Herman Speck von Sternburg, took place on December 5 in London. In 1903 papers across the country buzzed with the news that Lady Newborough's sister, Mrs. Alice Carr Chauncey, was set to become a peeress with her marriage to Lord Rosebery, the ex-Premier of England. In addition, *The New York Times* reported in 1912 that heirs had settled the six-million-dollar estate of the late Baroness von Zedtwitz, "formerly Miss Mary Elizabeth Caldwell of Louisville." It would seem that her sister, the Marquis Monstiers-Merinville, had also done well for herself in the marriage business.

Given the number of royal women from the area, would anyone wonder that the ghost of an elderly dame in regal attire has been seen promenading along Old Louisville's Millionaires Row? The historical record shows that there was indeed such an eccentric individual and without a doubt she counts as one of the most colorful characters in the Louisville of the late 1800s. She called herself Lucinda, and she was a regular sight on the streets of Old Louisville when the neighborhood teamed with visitors to the famous Southern Exposition. Although not much is known about her personal life, people such as Max Selliger had always considered her a somewhat eccentric character, and several newspaper accounts from the 1880s documented her antics as she promenaded up and down the street. There seems to be no evidence that she counted as true-blooded royalty, but she was seen downtown frequently, where she would make weekly "proclamations" from a street corner near the courthouse. Sadly, as her eccentricity increased, her grasp on reality loosened and somewhere along the line, Lucinda proclaimed herself the "Queen of America."

The New York Times picked up on Lucinda's antics in 1885 and reported the details of an incident that played out on October 30. "An old lady, with a remarkable appearance and bearing, swept into the Circuit Court this morning with queenly grace. She was under the escort of a couple of policemen, and was given a seat in front of the jury. This was a celebrated crank, Lucinda, Queen of America," it wrote. "For several years, she has been a conspicuous character, and she was in the habit of appearing in public places in regal attire. She would go to the Galt House and ask for the King and everywhere she was the same queenly personage."

It appeared, however, that Queen Lucinda had some problems in her kingdom. She feared a plot to assassinate her and became convinced that someone wanted to usurp her throne. When she engaged a local attorney to bar the would-be usurper, he jokingly informed her that "the Attorney-General of the United States was the proper person to take steps. The next thing heard of her she was in Washington besieging President Arthur...Since that time, she has issued long weekly proclamations, sending them to all the newspaper offices."

But things took a turn for the worse when the 74-year-old barricaded herself in her rooms on Sixth Street, terrified that the assassins had come to do their dirty work. After a minor scuffle, the authorities hauled her off to jail and then to a courtroom to discuss the issue of her sanity. According to the reports in *The New York Times,* the regent reported to all assembled that the country was well governed and that the threat of assassination had passed. "Her son was Emperor and Bob Ingersoll was King. Mr. McDonald, of Texas, was President... She was of course adjudged a lunatic."

When I first stumbled across this story while doing some research in late 2007, I failed to make a connection with an old newspaper article I read several years prior, a piece I hadn't taken notes on because it hadn't seemed relevant at the time. It wasn't till after my third book of ghost stories came out and a reader contacted me with some questions that I recalled a potential link to the Lucinda story. I had been spooling through reels of microfilmed editions of old Louisville newspapers at the library one day and happened across the brief account of a woman named Lucinda, whose son and husband were killed in an accident on Third Street. The woman, the reporter said, was not able to bear the grief and was often seen roaming the streets in an unhinged frame of mind after that. He also made mention of the woman's outlandish costumes and even mentioned that she carried a scepter at times. Of course, now when I go back to look for that story, it's impossible to locate, but I hope to stumble across it again in the near future.

Even without the substantiation that Lucinda, Queen of America, went insane because of the tragic loss of her son and husband, it's enough for many that her existence has been documented, as well as the fact that she often strolled the street in front of the bed and breakfast inn where guests have reported an apparition matching her description. What happened to Lucinda after the courts committed her to the insane asylum has yet to be learned, but it is somewhat comforting to entertain the notion that her ghost might be one of two royal spirits that are alive and well in Old Louisville.

THE QUEEN OF AMERICA.

A REMARKABLE OLD LADY ADJUDGED TO BE A LUNATIC.

LOUISVILLE, Ky., Oct. 30.—An old lady, with a remarkable appearance and bearing, swept into the Circuit Court this morning with queenly grace. She was under the escort of a couple of policemen and was given a seat in front of the jury. This was a celebrated crank, Lucinda, Queen of America, and she was to be tried for lunacy. For several years she has been a conspicuous character in this city, and she was in the habit of appearing in public places in regal attire. She would go to the Galt House and ask for the King and everywhere she was the same queenly personage. Upon one occasion by her presence she created something of a sensation at McCauly's Theatre. She was not, however, always happy. Her throne was being usurped. About two years ago she called at the office of a leading lawyer to engage his services for the purpose of removing Arthur the usurper. He told her jestingly that the Attorney-General of the United States was the proper person to take steps. The next thing heard of her she was in Washington besieging President Arthur, and was arrested as a crank meditating assassination and sent home. Since that time she has issued long weekly proclamations, sending them to all the newspaper offices. The circumstances which led to the inquest of this morning are these: A short time since she engaged a furnished room on Sixth-street, between Grayson and Walnut. For the past three or four days she remained barricaded in her room, and acted in such a manner as to attract more than the usual attention of other lodgers. Her insanity had taken another turn, and she was laboring under the fear that she was to be assassinated. The police were informed of the old lady's situation, and last night she was removed to jail. The officers were compelled to force the door, as she refused to let them in. She had a club with which she threatened them, but was too feeble to use it. This morning she was the reigning queen and the jury were her obedient subjects. Arthur had retired and Cleveland was banished. Her son was Emperor and Bob Ingersoll was King. Mr. McDonald, of Texas, was President, and the country was well governed.

"If you are Queen and Ingersoll King, then you are husband and wife."

"No, we are not married" was her reply.

She said she was 74 years of age. She was of course adjudged a lunatic.

Chapter 9 – Avery, the Ghost of the Pink Palace

Majestically rising from the middle of Belgravia Court and towering over the south end of St. James Court, the Pink Palace boasts a history as colorful and storied as any of the hundreds of grand mansions that dot the Old Louisville historic district. Its most striking feature, a spire-like turret at its western end, hints at the Châteauesque design that guided its construction around 1891, a year that saw the addition of many elegant residences to the burgeoning St. James Court neighborhood. Word had spread that Louisville's movers and shakers would be calling the newly developed suburb home, and by the turn of the century land in the city's trendiest neighborhood commanded premium prices. St. James Court with its would-be aristocrats and devoted Anglophiles had become an elite neighborhood. Bankers lived next door to well-to-do merchants, distillers, and tobacco barons, and newspapermen resided amongst local business magnates and city dignitaries. A smattering of well-known writers, artists, and poets added a bit of respected sophistication to the mix. These men of influence would need a place to congregate, and this place would be the Pink Palace.

Although people in the area have called this magnificent home the "Pink Palace" for ages, it originally began its life on St. James Court as the "Casino." Long before Las Vegas branded this innocuous Italian word for a small country home with its current gambling connotation, *casinos* often served as relaxing country getaways where the affluent could unwind and pursue those pastimes typically pursued by the affluent. In Victorian America, prestigious neighborhoods sometimes had their own casinos where families could meet for day outings and wind down as much as allowed by rigid societal norms. In 19th-century Kentucky, well-to-do residents of its largest city added their own twist to the local casino, and it became a haven for an exclusively male clientele. Also known as the Gentlemen's Club of St. James Court, it served as a crony-ridden escape where local bigwigs could sit at ease while enjoying bourbon and cigars, diverting themselves with an occasional hand of poker and plenty of neighborhood gossip.

For them, the surroundings would have seemed comfortable and luxurious without being ostentatious. A spacious foyer invited the gentlemen inside, where an attendant usually stood at the ready in case members needed to dispose of their coats and hats. Enveloped in the warm glow of polished parquet floors and oaken trimmings, a grand staircase framed with double arches and gleaming columns twisted its way to the upper floors where gentlemen could conduct their business. On either side of the entry hall, plush chairs, comfortable divans, and card tables completed the two main clubrooms where waiters in starched collars served drinks and provided the most recent copies of the various city newspapers. During the day, sunlight filtered its way through the impressive art glass windows encased in the stairwell and littered the lobby with random jewels of multicolored light. During the evening, after long shadows made their way down the brick sidewalks and faded into darkness, the gas lanterns clicked on with a hiss and bathed the stylish interior with a warm glow that highlighted the burgundy draperies and embossed wall coverings. Tucked away in the contented confines of their respectable dwellings, most of the residents of St. James Court pulled their curtains to and politely ignored the palatial structure that dominated the south end of the court. It seems that – by night – the Gentlemen's Club of St. James Court took on another life, one that catered to the more carnal nature of its members.

That's what Kent Thompson and Jeff Perry, then owners of the Pink Palace, told me as we sat around the dining table at my Third Street house one evening in January 2005 and listened to an icy winter wind roaring outside. By the fire in the front parlor, we had sipped cups of mulled cider spiked with bourbon as I passed around a tray of hors d'oeuvres, before moving to the dining room, where I planned to show off several recipes from my new cookbook. We had just started with bowls of squash bisque and glasses of a nice Riesling from a local vineyard, when Kent alluded to this seedier side of the Pink Palace. "The upstairs rooms have closets that are *exceptionally* large," he explained, "and this was always a bit puzzling, because many homes back in the late 1800s didn't have a lot of closets. It seems that early tax assessors considered closets actual rooms in a home and charged the property owners accordingly." We switched to the next course – broiled salmon with beurre rouge and pureed potatoes – and Jeff couldn't resist interjecting, "It turns out that their female counterparts *conducted their business* in these little rooms."

We dug into the next course, coq au vin with homemade spätzle and pearl onions, and between bites Kent and Jeff finished the interesting yarn about how their house became known as the Pink Palace. By the time I served chocolate gingerbread and thick cream flavored with nutmeg and Galliano for dessert, everyone at the table had become quite familiar with the history of this local landmark.

It seems that the storied past of the Gentlemen's Club of St. James Court would be a short-lived one, and not too long after it opened its doors to the wealthy male residents of the neighborhood, it passed to a local family who called it home until 1910 or thereabouts. Sometime thereafter, it became the headquarters for a national organization that is still in existence today. By an ironic turn of fate, the new tenant of the lovely, red-brick structure at 1473 St. James Court would be none other than the local chapter of the WCTU, that largest of all women's organizations in the Gilded Age known as the Women's Christian Temperance Union. Although the organization founded in 1874 can claim many admirable achievements in the areas of voting rights for women and labor law, most people today remember it for its spirited campaigns against the sale and consumption of alcohol. In fact, many doubt that the Volstead Act of 1919 would have passed without their well organized 'pray-ins' at local saloons and their fierce abstinence rallies across the nation, events that ushered in the bleak period from 1920 to 1933 known as Prohibition.

At least many "thirsty" citizens considered it a bleak period; teetotalers, on the other hand, considered it a triumph, and the aristocrats of the Kentucky prohibitionist movement now had a palace in which to gloat. The only problem was that the WCTU's new building had the reputation as a hotbed of drinking activity in its early days, not to mention it was also a place where men partook of the pleasures of tobacco, gambling and prostitution – all the things condemned by the WCTU. Supposedly, the first thing the Women's Christian Temperance Union did then was to paint the former gentlemen's club pink as a means of distancing themselves from the building's sordid past. In addition to wiping the slate clean, as it were, the dazzling shade of pink would illuminate the path for wayward drinkers in the neighborhood, and the color remained long after the WCTU vacated the premises and after Congress finally repealed the Volstead Act, much to the delight of many Depression-weary Americans in search of a good – and legal – drink.

Considering the colorful past of the Pink Palace, would anyone be surprised to learn that at least one spirit lingers on in the comfortable home at the southern end of the expansive urban green known as St. James Court? Although the current owners have yet to see the resident ghost they acquired with their purchase of the former casino and gentlemen's club, previous owners have had unsettling encounters with him, and they say his name is Avery. Although he heard mostly positive things about Avery, Jeff Perry never felt that he needed to verify the existence of his ghost. "I didn't want a ghost in my house," he said. "I was afraid if I talked about him too much, he'd show up and never go away!"

Jeff's reservations aside, it seems as if most residents of the Pink Palace have always appreciated the ghostly presence there. According to

Locals believe the helpful spirit of a former owner lingers on to watch over new tenants at the Pink Palace, one of the most recognizable structures on St. James Court. This photo shows it after its most recent paint job.

several paranormal investigators I consulted about this case, Avery's appearance has been attributed to that of a "crisis apparition" or a kind of haunting where the ghost in question only shows up at moments of crisis. Some parapsychological experts claim that these types of manifestations usually take place when an individual finds him or herself in imminent danger and sends the body's spirit on as a type of emissary to warn loved ones or to prepare them for news of the individual's passing. Others claim that crisis apparitions can occur when ghosts sense danger and make an appearance so as to warn certain individuals of possible harm. People who have experienced Avery at the Pink Palace suggest that his sightings involve the latter, because he usually makes an appearance when something bad threatens to happen.

Strange experiences with Avery in the former gentlemen's club have convinced Jenny Dickerson that the ghostly sightings involve a friendly spirit, a sort of harbinger or portend, if you will, who still lingers on in the splendid environs as a way of watching out and protecting those who inhabit his home. Decades ago, Dickerson sublet a basement apartment in the Pink Palace when she did her graduate work in library science at the nearby University of Louisville, and she claims to be the person who "discovered" and named Avery. If truth in fact has any bearing on the curious incidents that transpired during her residency, it would appear that Avery, indeed, has stayed on at the Pink Palace to guard the place from danger.

"Back in the 60s and 70s when I was studying at U of L," she explains, "I rented out an apartment in the basement of the old gentlemen's club on St. James Court. And if anyone had told me back then that I would see a ghost one day, I would have said they were crazy – because I never believed in ghosts and such. That is, until I saw one for myself one day. I don't care if people believe me or not! It happened, and I know it happened, even though I cannot explain why such things happen. People can take it or leave, but I always tell my story to those interested in hearing it."

Jenny's story began one evening as she stood at a counter in her tiny kitchen chopping vegetables for a soup she had just put on the stove. As if to foreshadow the appearance of the strange vision, a fierce wind roared outside and caused the windows to rattle in their casements. When the soup started to boil and fill the small space with an inviting aroma, Jenny tossed in the chopped vegetables and turned around to deposit the cutting board in the sink. "I had this strange feeling someone was there, watching me, but when I turned around to check, there was nothing there," she said. "It was a Saturday night in December, and I had been invited to a Christmas party down the block, so I decided to bake a batch of cookies to take along. I was going to let the soup sit overnight so it would taste better the next day, but as it simmered I figured I could use the time to bake the cookies." Jenny started in on her baking and soon she was ready to pull the last tray of cookies from the oven. "But as I opened the door and bent over to remove the last batch, I got that weird feeling again, like someone was watching me," she said. "And this time, as I stood there, with the hot air from the oven blasting up in my face, I felt a chill run down my spine." Dickerson said she hesitated a moment before slowly straightening herself and setting the tray of the cookies on the counter. Then she turned and looked in the direction of the strange sensation.

"I froze," she said. "There, standing right before me, in front of the cupboards, was a man. He wasn't real, though, because I could see right through him. I could see the cupboards on the other side of him. He was relatively tall – about 6 feet, I'd say – and he was wearing an old-fashioned duck suit, sort of like the one Colonel Sanders always wore. And like Mr. Sanders, he had on a black string tie. His hair was white, too, but his face didn't look like the Colonel's at all. He was clean shaven and very aristocratic-looking, and he had an incredible mane of wavy hair. It was white, I think, but it could have been any color, I guess, because the way the thing presented itself; it was all in black and white."

Dickerson says she just stared at the apparition and didn't know what to do next. "I wasn't really afraid, but I still couldn't believe what was happening. I thought for sure I was imagining the whole thing and I rubbed my eyes a couple of times, and he was still there, just looking at me, no expression on his face at all. I'm not even sure if he could see me, because his face didn't register any emotion. It was so odd. Then, all of a sudden, he was gone."

Never having seen a ghost before, Dickerson says she wasn't certain how to react when the apparition showed itself. Scream? Faint? Run away? What does protocol dictate when you have your first ghostly encounter? "Well, I didn't know what to do, but my heart was racing a hundred miles a minute, so I just sat down at the kitchen table and tried to figure out what I had just seen. I wasn't tired and I wasn't under stress or anything, so I knew I had seen something real. I concluded, therefore, that I had seen a ghost, which, of course, seemed the most logical explanation under the circumstance. It was quite an earth-shattering moment for me, because I had never believed in that kind of thing, and now I had seen one for myself, and *had* to believe. I'll never forget that first vision as long as I live."

Despite the strange encounter, Dickerson decided not to tell anyone about her experience that night, for fear of being ridiculed. "I didn't want anyone to make fun of me, so I decided to keep it secret. But the curious thing is that when I regained my composure and got back to cleaning up the kitchen, I jokingly wondered to myself if I'd have any more run-ins with 'Avery' in the future. I decided he wasn't there to harm me, so it really didn't bother me one way or the other. But then I stopped for a minute. Why did I call him 'Avery?' I realized that nobody had told me his name. It just had come out of the blue that his name was Avery. I guess I sort of sensed it, that's all, but after that, everyone always called him 'Avery.'

As it turned out, Dickerson did have another encounter with Avery. "It happened to be that very same night! I turned off the soup, cleaned up the mess from the cookies and looked at my watch. There was another hour to go before the party started, so I decided to take a bath." The bathroom in her apartment was in the small space immediately under the turret on the west side of the building, and the bathtub was an old-fashioned one with claw feet and made of cast iron. "So I put in some bubbles and got in so I could soak for half an hour or so." But then Jenny did something I wouldn't have done, had I just had a ghostly encounter: she lit a solitary candle on the table next to the tub and turned off the light. "It was nice," she said, "and I just lay there and unwound and relaxed in the warm, soapy water. But I had just started to doze off when I had a strange sensation – sort of like someone was staring at me. A cool breeze blew across the surface of the bathwater, and I opened my eyes, and there he was again."

By "he" of course, she meant Avery, the ghost in the white duck suit and black string tie she had just seen an hour or so before. "He was standing in the doorway to the bathroom again, just staring at me, no expression on his face, nothing. Wearing the same clothes and all. Like before, he didn't scare me or anything, but for some reason, I was afraid all of a sudden. Not of him, but of *something*. I panicked a bit and looked around the bathroom, and when I directed my eyes back to the doorway, Avery had vanished into thin air. He was gone, but I still had the same uneasy feeling, so I jumped up and out of the tub, and grabbed a towel and my bathrobe and ran through the doorway."

Seconds after pulling her foot from the hot water, Dickerson heard a terrible crash, the sound of breaking glass and splashing water. "I turned around, and there was water all over the place and one of the windows was broken out. I was filled with a terrible dread and had no idea what had just happened, so I picked up the phone and called the police. They were there a minute later, and then we were able to figure out what had happened." As it turns out, Avery had apparently foiled a dangerous visit by two would-be intruders, and just in the nick of time.

"Two burglars were trying to break into my apartment – that's what happened." According to details later discovered by Dickerson, the two thieves had been hiding behind a boxwood hedge outside, casing the joint as it were. It was a Saturday night, and they had been watching as, one by one, tenants in the different apartments left to go out and have their fun of a Saturday evening. As each one left, they turned off the light to the apartment. When Dickerson lit her candle and turned off the light in her bathroom, the burglars thought the Pink Palace was empty. "So they took a big cement block and threw it through the window that was right *above* the bathtub. It landed right in the tub – right where my head would have been – and smashed the whole thing to pieces, four or five pieces. It would have killed me, without a doubt because afterward I found the part where the cement block made contact, and it was right where my head was resting. I guess the wannabe crooks got scared when they realized someone was still inside. And then when they heard the police coming, they decided against coming inside."

Dickerson believes that if Avery hadn't warned her, she "would have stayed in the bathtub, and who knows what awful things would have happened that night?" She's convinced he showed up that night to warn her of impending danger. "He saved my life," she says.

According to Dickerson, she finished her degree the next year, in the spring, and moved out to the West Coast, where she got a job at a state library. A young married couple who were friends of hers at the university took over the lease to the basement apartment in the Pink Palace and moved in. But, afraid of being ridiculed, Dickerson never told them about her strange encounters in the apartment. Nonetheless, she wasn't exactly surprised when the new tenants called just a couple of weeks after moving in, wanting to know if Dickerson had "experienced anything strange in the apartment" when she lived there. Immediately, Dickerson had to wonder if her friends had encountered the same aristocratic southern gentleman with the wavy white hair, linen suit, and black string tie. "I asked them what had happened," says Dickerson, "and I found out that he had appeared to them just the night before, in the kitchen."

Dickerson listened as the woman told how she and her husband had just finished cooking and were getting ready to sit down to dinner at their small dining room table. "So, he was in the kitchen, and she was sitting at the table, waiting for him to bring in the roast from the oven. But, her husband didn't come, even after she kept calling to him. Finally, she got up from the table and went into the little kitchen to see what was taking him so long." There, she found her spouse, transfixed by an apparition standing next to the stove. "My friend said her husband was just glued to the spot, serving platter in hand, staring at a tall man in an old-fashioned duck suit. He was there one minute, and gone the next." The next instant, a wall of flame shot up along the wall behind the stove and a smoke alarm went off; the fire, they later discovered, was a result of faulty wiring. "Since they were right there, they were able to put it out right away using baking soda and dishtowels, but she said it would have been a real disaster if Avery hadn't shown up." As they were cleaning up the mess, the woman realized that had she not come into the kitchen just a minute sooner, she would have been trapped in the small dining area, which had no separate exit, when the fire broke out. True to form, Avery only made appearances when danger threatened the occupants of 1473 St. James Court.

"The really funny thing about the story is something interesting I discovered years later, after I moved back to Louisville to teach at the schools here," Jenny explains. "It was at least twenty years later, and I found myself back in Louisville. I had pretty much forgotten about Avery and the Pink Palace, because I lived in another part of town and didn't get down to Old Louisville much." One day, though, she was nearby, helping a friend with a grant proposal that required some research at the Louisville Free Public Library. "It's a beautiful old building from the early 1900s, and I always love going there to do research. Well, anyway, one day I was down there, digging through some old newspaper clippings, and the topic of investigation was totally unrelated to Old Louisville or the Pink Palace. I had pretty much found what I needed and was getting ready to leave, but as I put the clippings back in their box, I noticed one of them that I hadn't read because it had a familiar picture on it." It was a photograph of 1473 St. James Court.

"I decided to read the article, and it turned out to be a story about the old gentlemen's club and casino and how they were moving to a new location. They gave some descriptions of the interior and all the wonderful furnishings inside, and told how a family had recently acquired it and were planning on living there." Not only did the new owners have to undertake some renovations to make the old gentlemen's club habitable as a family residence, they also had to deal with the public perception that they were moving into a former house of ill repute. "It was very interesting reading about their efforts rehabbing the place, but the big shock came when I got to the end of the article, because there, at the bottom of the page, was another photograph." This time, it was a smaller picture, a portrait of a man. Staring out at her, like he had all those years before, was the photo of a distinctive-looking gentleman with a white suit, black string tie, and wild, wavy hair. "And the strangest thing of all? The caption underneath said something to the effect that

'Mr. *Avery* and his family have recently acquired the former casino and gentlemen's club and will be calling it home from now on.' I was absolutely dumbfounded! It turns out there was an actual Avery, and his picture matched the apparition I had seen to a tee!"

Not too long after making this discovery, Dickerson contacted me and shared her story. She had read my first book about Old Louisville hauntings and figured that I might be interested in her paranormal experiences, so I was all ears when we met on St. James Court one day as the autumn leaves gently fell from the trees. It dealt with a well-known landmark, so of course I was interested and I listened intently as we strolled from the Pink Palace, down to the park and back. The next day I did some research to see what background I could dig up about the old gentlemen's club and although I failed to locate the newspaper article Dickerson claimed to have read, I did manage to locate all the deeds for the property at 1473 St. James Court. They proved that a Mr. Avery was indeed the first man to call the old casino and gentlemen's club home. A wealthy merchant, his family owned the B.F. Avery Company, a manufacturer of farm equipment and machinery that survived long after his death. I eventually made contact with some of his descendants, and they told me that Avery indeed cut a dignified figure on the court and had the reputation of being a typical Kentucky Colonel. People who remembered him said he was a wonderful neighbor, a man who was not only proud of his neighborhood, but also proud of his house. He usually managed an evening stroll around the court, and in the warmer months, he was most often seen in his cotton duck, a shiny walking stick in hand. By all accounts, he was a loyal resident of Old Louisville and one who was very protective of his home and family, so it would be very much in keeping with his past life that his spirit would linger on after his death to keep watch over his former residence.

Avery, it seems, counted as just one of many colorful tenants that called the Pink Palace home. Another early tenant, Dr. George H. Wilson – or Dr. "Eardrum" Wilson, as he was known – made a name and fortune for himself after inventing the Wilson Eardrum in 1913, a dubious precursor to today's hearing aids, and he reportedly owned the first automobile to motor its way around St. James Court. In the 1990s, a reportedly cantankerous artist took up residence in the old casino and became embroiled in somewhat of a local scandal when he threatened to change the color scheme of the lovely Pink Palace. After numerous battles and stop-work orders from the Louisville Landmarks Commission, a compromise was reached and the characteristic pink color was retained, albeit in a rather more bedazzling shade of pink and with the addition of lavender trim that has caused more than a few eyebrows to arch in bewilderment. A couple years after I published the story about Avery, Kent Thompson and Jeff Perry moved out of the Pink Palace, and a new family calls it home today. As far as I know, they haven't had any strange encounters with the ghost known as Avery, but they've become aware of the storied past surrounding their current digs and have settled nicely into life on St. James Court.

Previous page: The helpful apparition known as Avery is not the only spirit rumored to haunt the Pink Palace. Previous residents reported several sightings of a ghostly woman in a white dress, always seen in the turret room on the second floor; in addition, a number of passersby have reported similar sightings from the street, always in the same room and always when the house was supposedly empty. In October 2009, Amy Almes of San Diego took this photograph of the Pink Palace while visiting the St. James Court Art Show. She believes she captured the face of a disembodied female spirit in the far left window of the turret room on the second floor. When shown the image, Jeff Perry had no explanation for what could have caused it.

Chapter 10 – The Ghost of Annie Whipple

Although many of Old Louisville's most impressive mansions of the Gilded Age can be found along the stretch of South Third Street known as Millionaires Row, splendid homes can be found throughout the entire neighborhood. Given that it at one time marked the southernmost extension of the original city, Ormsby Avenue has some of the earliest and largest residences in the area. The comfortable upper-middle-class enclaves of First and Second Streets both have impressive dwellings known for their innovative architectural styles, and St. James and Belgravia Court mansions and town homes have come to epitomize the charm and elegance of Old Louisville's Victorian past. But, if one street in Old Louisville can rival South Third Street for the size and grandeur of its Gilded-Age masterpieces, it would be Fourth Street.

Once an exclusive address for the city's merchants, downtown Fourth Street transformed itself from a pastoral residential district to a bustling center of commerce and entertainment by the end of the 19th century. Although no visible reminders of the once-vibrant housing scene that characterized the street north of Broadway remain, the southern stretch that passes through Old Louisville boasts quite a number of spacious and elegant mansions from the city's golden age. One of these sits at the corner of Fourth and Park in the heart of Old Louisville. Known by many as the Russell Houston Mansion, 1332 South Fourth Street counts as one of the most inviting and elegant Victorian queens in the neighborhood, and like so many homes in Old Louisville, it has its share of stories and legends.

Construction on the 7,400-square-foot residence started in the mid 1880s, a heady time for Louisville because of the excitement and national publicity generated by the famous Southern Exposition. Russell Houston, a judge and president of the L&N Railroad, was the first owner and prominent Kentucky architect Maury Mason designed the eye-catching redbrick masterpiece with elements of the popular Richardsonian Romanesque style on the exterior. Historians William Morgan and Samuel H. Thomas have described its appearance as "a picturesque massing of brick into a powerful composition of tremendous originality," making special note of the highly decorative red stone trim, sills, quoining, belt courses, lintels and columns that unify the lovely façade. A jaunty turret juts from the south-facing corner and a lone dormer perches on the steep-pitched roof over a graceful third-floor balcony.

Does the ghost of a former nanny known as Annie Whipple haunt the former residence of Russell Houston?

In the spacious foyer, arriving guests notice inviting coffered ceilings and an impressive stairway that gently wraps its way around to the second floor. The one-of-a-kind fireplace in the dining room features an embedded window in a double-flue chimney with an enviable view of the green heart of Old Louisville – the Olmsted-designed Central Park that replaced old DuPont Square in 1905. And in addition to the many charming details and antique furnishings that fill the interior spaces, rumor has it that a resident haunt adds her own special character to the home of Russell Houston. Known as Annie Whipple, she is a tall and school-marmly specter that has been seen ascending and descending the lovely, curving staircase in the residence. And those who have seen the ghost believe her sad disposition is due to something that happened over a hundred years ago, when Annie Whipple worked in the lovely brick mansion across from Central Park.

According to local lore, Annie Whipple was a mysterious widow who arrived from New England in the late 1800s, after her husband, a whaling captain, had been lost at sea. She had a teaching background and eventually became a live-in nanny at the Houston home, where she enjoyed a position of authority and respect. "That is, until one day, when she started to dabble in the practice of the black arts." At least, that's what Mae Ferrell told me one day over coffee in the front parlor. It was during my last month there, at the Widmer House, and I had been packing boxes on the third floor, when the doorbell rang. When I went down to answer it, I found a spry woman in her 80s, smiling and telling me she had just bought one of my books. As if to prove her story, she pulled out a copy and asked if I wouldn't mind signing it for her. Glad for a break from my moving chores, I asked her to come inside and I had her sit while I autographed and dedicated the book for her. She was a very chatty lady, and before I knew it, I was offering her coffee and cake and listening to her tale about Annie Whipple. It was a story that had intrigued me before, but no matter how much I researched, I was never able to pull up any real corroboration with historical events or actual places in Old Louisville, so I just assumed it was a legend and decided to treat it as such. At least with Mae Ferrell I would have another version of the story to compare my notes with. The story she told me not only confirmed a great deal of the particulars I had already heard, it also added some new and interesting details.

Annie Whipple, it seems, had only been with the family for a couple of years when yellow fever struck the household. She helped nurse them back to health, however, one of the children, a girl she had grown quite attached to, wasn't getting any better and the doctor finally said he could do nothing more for her and told the family to prepare for her imminent death. Annie Whipple, nonetheless, refused to give up and stayed at the girl's bedside day and night. Other than use cold compresses and weak tea to make the girl feel comfortable in her fits of delirium, there was little Annie Whipple could do. So, she leafed through the local newspapers, catching up on the day's events as she kept watch at the girl's side. Often, the reports consisted of stories about local mediums and psychics and updates from the spiritualist movement, but Annie Whipple, by all accounts, didn't subscribe to such notions. One day, however, one story caught her eye and Annie Whipple read with interest about a local doctor known to cure not only "bewitched" people, but also patients with all sorts of ailments. When she read about his miraculous powers, Annie Whipple immediately had the idea to contact him and see if he couldn't help cure the sick girl under her care. "So, she rushed down the stairs, hitched up the horse and buggy, and drove over to see

Dr. Anderson the next day," said Mae Ferrell. Although the previous versions of the legend I had heard always included reference to a doctor with strange powers, Mae Ferrell was the first person to put a name with the man: Dr. Anderson. "But when poor Annie Whipple got there, she noticed that the front doors of his house and adjacent practice were all decked out in black bunting. Someone had died." As fate would have it, Dr. Anderson himself had died just the day before, and Annie Whipple was forced to return home without the help she so desperately sought.

There, she resumed her post at the ailing girl's bedside, in a room next to her own at the top of the stairs on the second floor. As before, the nanny occupied herself with reading the newspaper between attempts to make the girl comfortable. "But the next day when Annie Whipple was reading the *Louisville Times* or one of the other dailies, she started to pay more attention to the spiritualist news," said Mae Ferrell. "She read how many individuals believed they could actually commune with the dead, and how respected scientists were reporting success in their attempts to correspond with the long departed. That's how she came up with her idea." The idea was to attempt to contact the spirit of the recently departed Dr. Anderson, in the hopes that he could still offer assistance, but from the other side of the grave. "So, under advisement from an old African woman who knew of such things and witchery, Annie Whipple learned the secrets of séance and was given over to finding a cure for the dear girl's misery."

According to local sources, the old woman in question was a former slave by the name of Josephine. Some reports say she was from Kentucky, others say she was from Louisiana, which might better explain her knowledge of voodoo, which was usually referred to as "hoodoo" in this part of the country. "On a night, when the moon was full, and when frost tipped the breeze with cold, Annie ran down the stairs and out the side door to meet the old woman at the Witches' Tree, just a block away from where she was living," said Mae Ferrell. When Mae asked if I had ever heard of the witches' tree before, I told her I had indeed heard about the gnarled old tree that supposedly was a favorite meeting spot for local witches, but I didn't tell her that I was working on a story about this tree for a new book because I didn't want to distract her from the task at hand. Mae had gone off on several tangents immediately after starting the story, and we had already downed many cups of coffee, and I encouraged her to finish.

"Annie Whipple explained to Josephine that she needed to contact the spirit of Dr. Anderson. Then she gave the old woman some money and listened to her instructions. Afterwards, Annie went home, rushed up the stairs to her room and did as she had been told." If the story is to be believed, Annie Whipple then engaged in an act referred to as automatic writing. Also known as *psychography*, it is an alleged psychic ability that enables an individual to produce written words that arise from the subconscious or a supernatural source. Many parapsychologists believe this can occur when spirits possess an individual and use the individual's own hands to write out the messages they want to deliver. In this case, Annie Whipple lit a solitary white candle, gathered paper and writing utensils, and sat at the table in her paneled room. "She sprinkled over its surface a strange kind of powder given by the old African woman and then intoned a prayer that had been written out for her, a summons to conjure up the spirit of Dr. Anderson." An eerie hush soon fell over the room, and although Annie Whipple could see nothing, it seemed a presence hovered at her side. Right before her head slumped and a deep trance took over, she requested Dr. Anderson's advice on how to help the sick girl. Barely aware, Annie Whipple lifted her hand and dipped the pen in ink before scrawling something across the paper on the desk. When she came to and beheld the message, it seemed that a medical prescription had magically appeared before her.

Early the next morning, hopeful that a cure was at hand, Annie Whipple ran to a nearby apothecary and had the prescription filled. Once home, she ran swiftly up the stairs to the sick girl and administered the potion. As the nanny waited at the bedside, and as the minutes turned to hours, it became apparent that the medicine had not served its purpose. To the contrary, the girl's condition only worsened and she fell into a deep coma-like sleep. The doctor was summoned and explained that the girl would surely expire by the coming dawn.

This must have come as a terrible shock to the woman who tried harder than anyone to save the poor girl. Annie Whipple ran to the table in her room, lit the candle, and sprinkled the magic powder over another piece of writing paper before once again summoning assistance from the other side. As before, a hush came upon the room, and although entranced, the nanny remained aware of the surroundings, her limp hand seizing the pen as if to scrawl out a message. But instead of writing, her arm started flailing and then her hand clutched the pen tightly and began to stab and slash at the wooden top of the desk. Over and over again, some force caused her pen to mar and gouge the writing surface, and then it turned its fury on the paper and started tearing and ripping at the sheet. Soon, the paper was torn to shreds, but there remained one piece large enough upon which to scribble a quick message. When she awakened fully, Annie Whipple was no doubt horrified to read the chilling words: *You fool! I am not Dr. Anderson!*

Annie Whipple reportedly fell to the floor in a heap, insensitive to all external consciousness, and they laid her limp body on the bed, where she lay in fitful slumber till daybreak. When she finally came to, it was only for a moment, as fever wracked her body with pain and restlessness, but it was enough time to for the nanny to make a confession of the strange things that had transpired the night before. As it turns out, it was a kind of deathbed confession because Annie Whipple died by the time the sun came up. Before she closed her eyes forever, though, she was able to see one last happy sight. There, by her bedside, stood the girl Annie had been caring for. Flushed and glowing, the girl had finally recovered from her illness, perhaps because of the delayed effect of the cure her nanny had procured for her.

A recent photo taken from the second floor shows the entry hall in the former residence of Russell Houston. Over the years, residents and visitors have reported a female apparition ascending and descending the steps. (Photo by Robert Pieroni)

Was Annie Whipple's life forfeited in exchange for saving the young girl? Was it a cruel spirit from beyond who found a portal to this world and decided to wreak havoc on the person who opened that portal?

Nobody can ever know, but since that day, legend holds that Annie Whipple's specter is fated to tread the lovely curved stairway in the mansion where the Houstons once lived, and where she tutored and cared for their children, no doubt reminiscing the day she dabbled in the black arts and surrendered the life she enjoyed on earth. "I think it was just a mean spirit who took it upon himself to teach Annie Whipple a lesson," said Mae Ferrell as I thanked her for sharing the story and showed her to the door. "That Annie Whipple should have left well enough alone."

Although initial research on the legend of Annie Whipple turned up little hard substantiation for this haunting, I did make some interesting discoveries concerning the history of spiritualism and what some might consider the 'black arts' in this area. Although the concept of communing with the deceased undoubtedly extends back to the beginnings of mankind and receives no small amount of comment in the Bible, most agree that modern-day spiritualism traces its roots to 1848, when the Fox sisters reportedly made contact with a ghost in their home in upstate New York. Word of the phenomenon soon spread, and within a decade or two it had taken hold on the imaginations of those in this country and abroad.

Among the early cases of spiritualist activity in the Louisville area is a tongue-in-cheek story in the *Courier-Journal* of 1869 about the "Very Latest in Spiritual Sensation." It reported: "The latest wonder in Jeffersonville spiritualism is the furnishing of money for shows and buggy riding by spirits to mortals." The specter of Mr. Bud Morgan, deceased several years prior, it explained, had made "its headquarters at the residence of Mr. Keigwin, and, it is alleged, that he is daily and almost hourly engaged in conversation with the different members of the family, who converse with him as freely and familiarly as if he were in the flesh." Not only was the deceased generous in his otherworldly correspondence, the piece also reported that members of the Keigwin family enjoyed the good fortune of communing with a spirit who often provided them with money to buy circus tickets and carriage rides.

The skepticism many displayed toward spiritualism often included scathing rebukes by the established clergy and warnings against the evils of "divining and sorcery." *The New York Times* of March 31, 1872 picked up on a sensational report about "The Lady of Louisville," against whom "a Presbyterian Church in Louisville, Ky. has instituted proceedings" for being "understood to be a believer in 'spiritualism'." After making the assertion that forbidden intercourse with the dead stemmed from Jewish law – and as such, the Christians of Louisville were not bound by "the multitudinous provisions of the Mosaic code" – the writer offered a somewhat liberal piece of advice for the times:

Let the Jewish law, which is supposed to forbid intercourse with the dead – though it is by no means certain that such is its true meaning – be treated in the same spirit in which we treat the Jewish prohibition of pork. We hold it wrong to eat measly pork, but right to eat wholesome and tender corn-fed pork. In like manner, let association with wicked and morally measly spirits be deprecated, but let us concede the right of any good man to converse with good spirits – if he can.

In conclusion, the commentator argued that most good spirits, as a rule, preoccupied themselves with rather mundane communications anyway, so any influence they could exert on the lady would most likely "be to provoke in her that meditative calmness immediately preceding healthy and innocent sleep."

I also came across an interesting article in *The New York Times* of July 30, 1871 that circulated a story first reported in the *New Albany Ledger*, which told the strange tale of a supposedly possessed woman in Indiana, just across the river from Louisville. What really caught my attention when I quickly scanned the report about "the bewitched woman" was the mention of a "witch doctor" by the name of Dr. Anderson who "lived in the city." It seems, therefore, that a Dr. Anderson did indeed exist, lending some degree of credence to the story about Annie Whipple and her ill-fated attempts at communication with the dead. Nonetheless some might argue that Annie Whipple was successful in that she accomplished her main objective, that of saving the sick girl. I've also come across written accounts of an "old hoodoo woman" named Josephine and her associations with the Old Louisville neighborhood. Like so many of the legends and unsubstantiated stories in Old Louisville, reports of these ghostly encounters suggest at least a tenuous connection with the past, a correlation borne out in neighborhood folklore and modern oral traditions.

If anyone needs convincing that the specter of Annie Whipple haunts the grand stairway at the Russell Houston home, don't fret. The redbrick mansion at the corner of Park and South Fourth was converted to a comfortable bed & breakfast a number of years ago, and owners Herb and Gayle Warren welcome overnight guests to come and check it out for themselves. Known as the Inn at the Park, the old Houston place now counts as one of the most popular B&Bs in the neighborhood. Although there haven't been any very recent sightings of a willowy wraith in a high-wasted skirt and lacy white blouse on the graceful, curving stairway in the foyer, believers claim it's just a matter of time before she reappears for another round of lessons.

A Bewitched Woman.

From the New Albany (Ind.) Ledger.

For several days past that part of the city situated in the gore made|by the Louisville, New-Albany and Chicago Railroad and the Charlestown road has been in a feverish state of excitement at the announcement that a bewitched woman resided in that neighborhood. Hundreds of persons have visited the house, and all kinds of stories and rumors were set afloat in regard to the actions of the woman said to be bewitched. Having heard many rumors in regard to the woman, we seized the opportunity of paying her a visit yesterday afternoon, to ascertain for ourself a correct statement of the case. Reaching a small house fronting on the railroad, several hundred yards beyond BRAENTIGAM'S, we tremulously rapped at the door. An old lady answered our call, and we were ushered into a room scantily provided with furniture. Upon a bed in one corner of the room we saw a woman, apparently about thirty years of age, who was evidently suffering from a dropsical disease in her lower limbs. We essayed to ask the nature of her illness, when she replied: "They say that I am bewitched."

"Bewitched!" we exclaimed, "who says so?"

"The doctor," replied the sick woman.

"What doctor?" we asked.

"Why, Dr. ANDERSON, the witch doctor."

"Who is Dr. ANDERSON?" we asked.

"Why, he is a man that lives in the city, and is called a witch doctor. If you get bewitched just send for him and he will cure you."

"How do you know you are bewitched?"

"If you had seen the things he got out of the pillows of my bed you would think I was bewitched. Why, he got some beautiful little fans, some of the feathers were sewed up in knots, several cloth cats, just as perfect as live animals, and bunches of hair sewed together in different forms."

"Where are these wonderful things?"

"Why, we burned them up," exclaimed the old lady, who proved to be the mother of the bewitched. "Hundreds of people came here to see them," she continued.

"Do you believe that the doctor took them out of the pillow? Might not he have taken them out of something else?"

"Oh! no. They came out of the pillow, sure."

We stated that we did not believe in witches, which caused the old lady to marvel greatly. She related to us a wonderful story of a negro woman and her child, living in an adjoining house, who were bewitched some time ago, but Dr. ANDERSON had cured them. She said the child would crawl on the floor like a snake, and snap at its mother like a reptile of the most venomous species, while the mother would gyrate about the roof of the house, climb to the topmost limbs of trees, and cut up all kinds of shines. She then wondered if we had ever read the Bible, especially that part relating to the witch of Endor, whom she declared had never died, and that she had ample opportunity to teach her vile arts to others.

"Who do you think bewitched you?"

"The Lord only knows. I know that I am be-witched."

We then attempted to argue the point with her, that witchcraft in this enlightened age was a humbug, but our efforts in that direction were of no avail. She is fully convinced that she is bewitched, and nothing will change her mind. The woman is married, and the mother of a girl about ten years of age, and her husband is a well-known citizen. She has been ill about four months, she informed us, and one of the physicians in the city was treating her for rheumatism for some time previous to the advent of the witch doctor. Under the treatment of the latter she assured us that she was getting better fast. Such is the effect of ignorance and superstition in this age. We would not believe that any person could be impressed with such an idea had we not heard it with our own ears.

David Dominé

Chapter 11 – The Witches' Tree

Visitors to Old Louisville often comment on the abundance of rich woodwork found throughout the interiors of the dwellings here. In addition to ornate staircases and parquet floors, there are coffered ceilings, paneled walls, fireplace mantels, and many other examples of fine millwork and wood carving. By the time construction was in full swing in Old Louisville, mills in exotic lands were providing a steady stream of ebony, mahogany, teak, and other valuable woods with which to trim out these houses, but early on, the lush areas surrounding the city yielded a steady supply of luxurious and sturdy native woods like cherry, oak, and walnut that appeared in the first homes. Today when visitors walk through the neighborhood, towering trees hint at the abundance the local countryside must have presented to early settlers and builders. Though many of the largest trees here figured as part of the early landscaping plans, a number of them were already standing when the neighborhood sprang up. Now, during the warm spring and summer months, the dappled shade of their canopies provide welcome relief from the sun, but when the chill winds of winter and fall rob them of their leaves, these trees and their bare branches can take on a more sinister appearance. At times, some of them can look downright spooky.

At the northwest corner of Park and Sixth in Old Louisville stands a gnarled old tree known by locals as *the Spooky Tree*. Others call it *the Witches' Tree*. A jagged canopy of dead branches juts out to the north, and large, barky warts cover the twisted trunk, adding to its scary appearance. Known as burls, these rounded growths often appear on tree trunks or branches, and they appear when a deformity arises in the wood grain. According to most experts, burls usually occur when trees undergo some form of stress induced by either environmental or human agents. In Old Louisville, however, most don't subscribe to this notion; the strange growths on the spooky old tree came about as the result of witchcraft.

Despite the scientific and technological advances of the 19th century, many parts of Louisville's largest city held on to old superstitions, and belief in curses, black magic and witches was commonplace. Given that the riverboat and rail connections to New Orleans and other points in the South ensured a constant stream of followers of the voodoo arts, these voodoo (also known as 'hoodoo' in some parts) practioners would keep the Old Louisville neighborhood hopping with supernatural action. The Witches' Tree would emerge as a meeting point for many of these dabblers in the so-called black arts.

According to Old Louisville legends, this spooky-looking tree was – and still is – a favored meeting spot for witches.

According to local legend, the tree known as the Witches' Tree started its life as a majestic, towering maple and strange circumstances would account for its altered appearance later on. The original tree supposedly sprang up practically overnight in the late 1800s when the Dumesnil family still owned the land. Famed for the lovely flower beds and hedgerows that graced the grounds of their estate, the Dumesnils once maintained an adjacent tract of land dedicated to the cultivation of ornamental shrubs, myriad rose bushes, and a wide variety of flowers. Known as the Dumesnil Botanical Gardens, it became a popular destination for visitors in search of a bit of rest and relaxation from the hustle and bustle of life in a 19th-century metropolis. During the warm months of the great Southern Exposition from 1883 to 1887 the shady pathways and fragrant blooms provided welcome relief from the Kentucky sun to many thousands of visitors.

When word later got out that the Dumesnils planned on selling their beautiful gardens to the city and that planners would develop the land to construct houses, many people in the neighborhood were heartbroken to think they would lose their treasured botanical gardens. The most distraught of all, however, was a coven of local witches. The remarkable tree, once with its perfectly straight trunk, but now with its gnarled twisted appearance, had become the preferred gathering spot for nightly rituals where they would mix potions and cast spells on those who had incurred their wrath or curried their favor. A terrible travesty had almost cost them their favorite tree fifteen years before, and they were not ready to lose it again.

By most accounts, problems began in the spring of 1889 as locals began preparations for their annual May Day celebrations. Although few people still celebrate May 1st as the advent of spring today, Victorian America saw it as a symbolic banishment of the cold winter weather, and, as such, a great cause for festivities. And, integral to any traditional May Day celebration was a dance around the maypole. Early Americans, following the traditions of their European ancestors, usually erected maypoles of maple, hawthorn, or birch, and then festooned the tall pole with flowers, greenery and large wreaths with long colored ribbons suspended from the top. Children would then perform dances around the maypole, their rehearsed steps resulting in the weave of elaborate patterns in the ribbons.

Given their connection to the lumber industry, it often fell to members of the Mengel family to organize the neighborhood May Day celebrations every year. Known as "the Mahogany Kings" among the locals, brothers Charles and Clarence Mengel oversaw a hardwood empire that channeled tons of millwork into the Old Louisville construction boom, so it's not surprising that they frequently headed the planning committee. In the early spring of 1889, the Mengels announced that they had selected the tree to be felled for the upcoming celebration, and their choice was the beautiful maple at the corner of Sixth and Park.

Naturally, the witches were less than thrilled to learn that their beloved maple had been singled out for its flawless shape and impressive height. And when they learned that it would be cut down, shorn of its branches, and then decorated for the festivities, they got together at the beginning of April and posted a parchment note of warning on their tree. Addressed to the Mengels, it not only advised against cutting down the tree, it promised revenge on the city in eleven months if their warning went unheeded. The notice hung on the majestic maple for almost a month and became tattered and torn as the elements battered and blew. Although the Mengels were informed of the warning, no one paid much attention to it, and the parchment eventually disintegrated and faded away altogether. It seems people didn't take witches as seriously as they had in the olden days after all.

On the last day of April, when two woodsmen from the Mengel factory sawed down the great tree, it was said that a mournful wail could be heard ensuing from the forests to the west of town, where the witches had fled for refuge. By the next day, the lovely maple had been resurrected in a different location, decorated with fresh flowers, colorful ribbons and boughs of greenery. A ceremony took place and the celebrations went off without a hitch. After the May Day festivities, the trunk was dried, cut, and then burned in a great Whitsuntide bonfire. And by the time the heat of summer arrived, most had forgotten about the witches' warning and the beautiful maple tree. When the winds of fall and winter starting whipping through the neighborhood, rumors had it that the coven had relocated to the nearby forest and that they had resumed their nightly gatherings and castings of spells. When townspeople began planning for the next year's May Day celebration, the witches' curse had slipped from memory. Not a soul had an inkling of the tragedy that lay ahead when the eleventh month neared its end.

On the evening of March 28, 1890 the most destructive tornado in the history of Louisville roared in from the west, along Maple Street no less, and destroyed a large portion of the city. Within five minutes, more than 600 buildings – including some 500 homes, 10 tobacco warehouses, 3 schools and the main train station – had been shattered like kindling. After obliterating half of the downtown area, the twister did a strange thing according to eye-witness, who said it made an abrupt turn to the south and headed into the area known as Old Louisville today. It was reported that the winds wreaked havoc at the Mengels largest lumber works, as well as a number of other businesses in the neighborhood, and that dead bodies, including horses, cattle, and humans, littered the streets.

In the end, more than a hundred people died – several of the victims were supposedly members of the Mengel clan – and weeks would pass before the city was back up and on its feet. Sympathy and support poured in from around the country and when the end of April rolled around, hardly a soul had thought about that year's May Day festivities. That's when residents near the Dumesnil Botanical Gardens reported another strange thing about the cyclone as it sped by. Supposedly, as the tornado roared past the corner where the witches' maple had once stood, a fierce bolt of lightning shot out and struck the stump of the shorn tree. When the winds of the storm had subsided, they noticed that a gnarled and twisted tree had magically sprouted up on the spot formerly occupied by the majestic old maple. With its scary warts and burls, the new tree (an Osage orange, actually) seemed to be an apt replacement for a coven of witches.

A close up of the trunk shows the gnarled surface of Old Louisville's famed Witches' Tree. Visitors often leave charms or amulets on the tree.

As word about the strange tree got out, the citizenry finally recalled the witches and their warning not to cut down their beloved maple. Most speculated that they had conjured up the terrible twister in their new forest home west of town and had sent it into Louisville to exact their revenge. When rumors spread that the witches had returned to their old spot to conduct their nocturnal rituals, nobody said a word, and from that point forward, locals refused to use maples for their annual maypole. Around 1905, when the Dumesnils sold their land to developers and many of the trees were felled to make room for the houses built in the new Floral Terrace neighborhood, they made sure to leave the Witches' Tree standing. People in Old Louisville claim witches still frequent the corner of Park and Sixth today, although they only cast evil spells on very rare occasions, and no one dares cut down any more trees of any kind in fear of incurring their wrath. To this day, people say the gnarled old tree violently rattles its brittle and twisted branches in warning whenever a tornado threatens the neighborhood.

Tornado damage, seen at the W.E. Caldwell Company, not too far from the Witches' Tree (Photo courtesy of the Caldwell family)

Below: One of hundreds, a **New York Times** *article from March 1890 updates the nation on the destruction in Louisville. According to popular local lore, witchcraft caused the terrible storm.*

LOUISVILLE'S BRAVE HEART.

BURYING HER DEAD AND CARING FOR HER AFFLICTED.

LOUISVILLE, March 30.—Snow began falling here about 4 P. M. It melts as fast as it falls, and has the effect of a gentle rain. But there has been nothing like a heavy storm, and no prospect of one. The flakes settle gently, and in five hours, though the snow has been continuous, not more than two inches has fallen.

Nearly everywhere some measures have been taken to protect property in the roofless territory. In many places temporary roofs of long plank have been put on and in a few instances permanent work has been nearly finished. Tarpaulins and whatever else will turn water have been pressed into service, and the damage will be greatly lessened. At the tobacco warehouses nearly everything is under tarpaulins or other protection. Crowds of men were set to work in them when it was plain that snow or rain would fall, and farmers' consignments, along with manufacturers' purchases, were made as secure as possible. In spite of all, however, the loss will be considerable and may reach well toward $100,000.

No work has been done on the ruins to-day
except by individuals, and no bodies are reported taken out anywhere during the day.

Funeral processions have followed each other
in quick succession to Cave Hill, St. Louis,
Bertrand, and the other cemeteries, and the
city has been all day in mourning. Many of
the funerals have been with military, Masonic,
or other honors, and some of the scenes have
been very impressive. Masses have been said
at the Catholic churches and sermons preached
at the Protestant. Hearts have been touched
that had long forgotten sentiment in battling
with the world.

Offers of help continue to come in. Liberal
contributions to the fund are reported from
citizens here, and several from outside. Among
others J. H. Kemble of Philadelphia sends a
check for $1,000 to the Hon. Henry Watter-
son at Jacksonville, Fla., to be used here. Mr.
Watterson will arrive here Tuesday.

Miss Clara Barton, President of the American National Association of the Red Cross,
with J. D. Hubbell, General Field, agent of the
association, and J. H. Moreland, foreman of
their work at Johnstown, arrived here to-night.
Miss Barton said:

"I find the calamity in Louisville has been
met with admirable courage and good sense.
In a large experience I have never seen any
disaster so efficiently handled. I have never
known efforts of relief to be better directed.
Where the débris has been removed here it has
been piled away regularly, so that it will not be
more trouble to handle the second time than it
was the first, as is often the case. When I see
how carefully and well everything has been
done I am quite ready to believe your authorities when they tell me you do not now need
assistance, and that they will almost certainly
be able to take care of your wounded. I understand you have a training school for nurses,
with a number of graduates, and these will be
able to supply all wants. If by any chance
there should be need of our aid it will certainly
not be withheld."

Chapter 12 – The Man at the Hanging Tree

The Witches' Tree isn't the only tree with spooky associations in Old Louisville. As mentioned before, during the heyday of Louisville's grand Southern Exposition in the 1880s, the area that now comprises Old Louisville also attracted large numbers of visitors to its immensely popular botanical gardens. The Dumesnil family flower beds, known for many years as just the *Floral Gardens*, sat catty-corner to Central Park, near the northwest corner of Sixth Street and Weissinger Avenue (which became Park Avenue after 1888). During the warm-weather months, people flocked in droves to the cool shade of those gardens and wandered among the rows and rows of rare ornamental shrubs and flowers on display. The area was later transformed into *Floral Terrace*, one of Old Louisville's famed walking courts. Pedestrian-only lanes that you sometimes find instead of streets in Old Louisville, walking courts were designed to replace the noise and bustle of traffic with a park-like setting. So when residents of walking courts such as Belgravia or Ouerbacker look out their front windows what they get is a beautiful view of their neighbor's façade across a landscaped green space.

A lovely view along Belgravia Court, Old Louisville's oldest walking court

Floral Terrace, on the site of the old botanical gardens, is another of these walking courts. But it's largely a hidden oasis whose secluded, charming gardens and quaint homes haven't been discovered by many area residents yet. On the west side of Sixth Street, about halfway down the block between Park and Ormsby, a small brass plaque in the sidewalk marks the entrance to the tranquil court. If you happen to stroll down the narrow brick pathway and then cross the alley, it seems that the small front yards suddenly explode in a brilliant green shower of shrubbery, grasses and flowers. At the center, a small fountain splashes peacefully, and if you sit at one of the little wrought iron benches and pause for a minute, you realize that you hear only the cool splash of water and the pleasant rustling of leaves in a soft breeze. Sometimes, as you're sitting there lost in thought, a fellow interloper might wander by and remark with a pleased sigh that she "had no idea this lovely space even existed." Such is the nature of Floral Terrace.

Some residents of this quaint neighborhood, however, believe that the tranquil gardens and tidy facades hide a more sinister history. According to local rumor, a large tree that stood in the center of the court served at one time as a hanging tree for various lynchings in the 1800s. A charming little fountain now occupies this site, and late at night, residents have reported sad moans and sobs coming from that area, and some even claim to have seen the disembodied ghost of a man swinging from the end of a rope in mid-air.

"It looked to be a young man, from what I could tell," says Homer Waite of an eerie apparition he claims materialized before him one summer evening at the fountain. "I was just sitting there, enjoying the warm summer night all by my lonesome," the lifelong resident of Old Louisville recalls, "when this thing just started to take shape in front of my eyes. In a minute or two it was clear enough to recognize, and I was able to see it was a man hanging from a rope. And he was still swinging back and forth, ever so slightly." Homer claims the scene reminded him of a lynching, although the only lynchings he ever saw happened on television or in photographs in the newspapers. "Well, I'm not one to get scared off too easy-like, but I decided right then and there it was time to get off my keester and find somewhere else to sit myself down. So I left."

Homer says he had heard plenty of odd stories about his neighborhood, but never had he heard ghost stories concerning a lynching tree on Floral Terrace. "No one ever told me a thing about a hanging tree on that path when I was growing up," he explains. "But after I saw that thing swinging from the rope that one night, I started asking around, and sure enough, quite a few people started saying that they had always heard there was a tree used for lynchings there at one time." Homer claims an uncle told him that an unfortunate man had been left hanging there for days in the 1870s after a mob unceremoniously executed him for looking improperly at a white woman. Marylyn Davies, an Oregon resident who spent the first three decades of her life in Old Louisville, remembers her mother telling her a similar story in the 1940s. "We lived on the far side of the park," she explains, "but my sister and I often went over to play with friends on Sixth Street. Our mother always told us to be careful and not to be on Floral Terrace after dark, or else the man from the killing tree would get us. He was like the neighborhood boogeyman, I guess." As far as lynchings are concerned, no written records can be found to substantiate these claims; however, as Homer Waite explains, "it wasn't too hard to cover up stuff like that way back when."

According to many historians, Louisville – to a large extent – was spared the lynchings and mob violence so typical of other larger cities in the South; nonetheless, some feel it would be quite a stretch to assert that outsiders viewed Louisville as an overly tolerant locale as regards racial issues in the late 1800s and early 1900s. Compared to other cities in the southern states, Louisville stood at the forefront in many issues of racial importance; unfortunately, though, large numbers of the population adhered to the institutionalized forms of discrimination that cast a pall on the southern landscape of the first postbellum century. Although Kentucky itself bore shameful witness to many lynchings from the1860s through the1920s, many seem to hold the notion that Louisville managed to escape the sight of these atrocities.

In his excellent book *Life behind a Veil: Blacks in Louisville, Kentucky 1865-1930* George C. Wright explores the complex history of black/white relations in the Derby City, attesting that "Louisville was spared the lynchings of other cities in the deep south." His thorough record of individual social injustices and police violence nonetheless points an accusing finger at a society rife with intolerance, one that could have easily bred a culture of vigilantism.

Wright relates a well-known incident, for example, from the late 1880s involving the only black player on the Toledo baseball team when they played in Louisville. Moses Fleet Wood Walker had tried to play once in Louisville before that, but the team manager caved in to public uproar and benched him when Louisville fans protested the presence of a "negro" on their all white-pitch. The second time Toledo played at Louisville, the manager stood his ground, however, and allowed Walker to play. Despite his normal talent on the field, Walker gave a dismal performance due to the constant barrage of boos, hisses, and derogatory comments during the game. The enraged home fans had reportedly gone so far as to hurl various items from their perches in the stand at the lone black player in their midst.

Wright also makes mention of the notorious Lieutenant Kinnarny, a rogue policeman known for his "unconventional" ways of dealing with blacks in late 19th-century Louisville. Kinnarny had an unfortunate penchant for shooting at innocent blacks who happened to be running away from him. When asked why he did this, he usually replied that "they were acting suspicious." In his book, Wright makes it painfully clear that black Kentuckians of the late 1800s and early 1900s enjoyed very little security in Louisville.

Although hard to find documented accounts of lynchings in Louisville and its surroundings, it is not entirely implausible that legends of lynchings have some actual basis in fact. Given that some local authorities often supported vigilantes, covered up their actions, or even participated in the crimes themselves, no one can really say with certainty that a lynch mob *never* in fact paid a visit to the massive cottonwood tree that used to stand at the center of Floral Terrace.

"I looked for hangings and such in the Louisville papers from the time after the Civil War to the early 1900s, and I never came across any accounts of lynchings," says Roscoe Tuttle, a native of Louisville whose family owned a home in the Floral Terrace neighborhood for many years. "I did read articles about lynch mobs and what they did in other parts of the state, but I couldn't find any about Louisville." Despite his lack of success finding reports to substantiate the rumors of lynchings, Roscoe claims he believes local lore nonetheless. "Both of my granddaddies told me they personally knew of a hanging there in the late 1800s, so that's good enough for me, I guess."

Not only that, but Roscoe had an "experience" in the 1970s that he claims made him realize the area had a sinister past. "What I saw made a believer out of me," he explains. "It was so awful a sight to behold that only something terrible like a lynching must have produced it." Like other individuals in the quiet neighborhood surrounding Floral Terrace, Roscoe Tuttle believes he saw the apparition of an unfortunate man who died there long ago.

"You have got to understand that I come from a family where spooks and spirits ain't anything out of the ordinary," he explains. "Part of my family is city people and the other part is country folk, that I'll grant you, but we all was raised believing in ghosts and haints and that spirits from another place was all normal and fine." Although he never used the word, it seems that Roscoe's family had quite a few superstitions as well. "My granny said never to give bananas to a baby, or else it would die, so we didn't. They also said not to be out running around after dark, or else the gypsies would get us and take us away. I figure now, it wasn't always right, what they told us, but when you're young you believe your elders." For this reason, the young Roscoe always tried to stay away from the center of Floral Terrace after dark. "They told us we'd be found dead the next day if the man from the killing tree got us. So we always stayed away from there."

Little did Roscoe Tuttle imagine that the ghost from the hanging tree would pay him a visit one day in person, years after Tuttle had matured and grown out of the family superstitions. "I still lived in the family house," he explains, "but both my parents had long since passed. And my grandparents had all been dead for ages." Roscoe lived around the corner from Floral Terrace in a small shotgun house on Park Street, and although he was just steps from the quiet gardens and neat homes of the terrace, he didn't venture out from his house as much as he used to.

"One night I decided to go out for a stroll because it was such nice weather, and I ended up at the center of Floral Terrace," he explains. "I sat down on one of the benches there. The air was nice and warm, and I was just sitting there, looking at the houses and how they had been fixing things up, when all of I sudden I could hear this strange creaking sound." In the dark Tuttle couldn't see where the sound came from, but he waited there for five or ten minutes, listening to the rhythmic sound of straining wood. "The sound never stopped. I'd hear a loud creak and then a softer creak, a loud one, then a soft one, and it just went on like that for what seemed like forever," he says. "At first I thought it was a big tree branch knocking about in the wind, but when I really paid attention, I noticed that there wasn't so much as the slightest breeze that night." Then he claims a strange feeling of loneliness overcame him.

"I was just about ready to get up and walk back to my house," Tuttle recalls, "when I noticed something out of the ordinary in the air in front of me." The elderly gentleman says that the figure of a man materialized before him, suspended in midair with a rope around his neck. "He looked like he was dead, like they had just hanged him maybe, and I couldn't believe my eyes. I knew it had to be the dead man from the tree people used to talk about!" Frozen in place, Roscoe could do little more than stare while the scene before him etched itself in his memory.

"It was a dark-complected man, I reckon, and it was just an awful sight, with his head off to the side at an unnatural angle," says Roscoe Tuttle. "His eyes was all bugged out, and I realized that the weird creaking matched up with his swinging back and forth. I couldn't see an actual tree branch or anything, but that must have been it. It sounded like a tree branch creaking under the weight as his body swung back and forth." Roscoe says he had seen enough and returned home.

"I was really spooked," he admits, "even though I grew up hearing about stuff like that. I only half believed it, though, and never thought I'd actually see something for myself one day. I didn't know what to do. What do you do in a case like this?" After a couple of hours in front of the television that night, Roscoe had relaxed enough to retire for the evening, and he went to bed. But he didn't get much rest.

"I had fallen asleep and must have been that way for two or three hours," he remembers. "I suddenly opened my eyes and was wide awake for some reason, though. I was just laying there on my back, staring at the ceiling, when I realized I was not alone in the bedroom." Roscoe saw something standing to the side of his bed that sent chills down his spine. As his eyes focused on the dark figure standing there, he realized it was the man he had seen earlier that evening. "He was just standing there, not moving at all, like he was watching me or something. Unlike when I had seen him before, he seemed almost alive, not dead!"

Although he admits to feeling terrified, Roscoe claims that he didn't feel threatened by the strange figure at his bedside. "I had the feeling he wanted something, that's all. Maybe he wanted us to know they had lynched him and he was innocent," he says. "A lot of the black men who were lynched back in the olden days were innocent, isn't that so?"

Roscoe Tuttle thinks about two minutes passed before he closed his eyes and "willed" the ghostly figure to leave. "I just put my head under the covers and prayed for that thing to go away!" When he finally opened his eyes, the dark figure had vanished, much to his relief. "When something like that happens, you start to second guess yourself," he confesses. "I had to stop and think whether or not I hadn't been dreaming or hallucinating. Just like with the hanging ghost I had seen earlier that night, it seemed so real as I was seeing it, but then afterwards, when it had disappeared, it seemed that it couldn't have really happened." Mr. Tuttle says he got up and made himself a cup of hot milk with honey, and a half hour later he drifted off to sleep again.

However, that would not be the last of his encounters with the ghost of the man from the hanging tree on Floral Terrace. Several nights later, while brushing his teeth in the bathroom, Tuttle received another unanticipated visit from the forlorn spirit. This encounter left him even more "spooked" than the first two. "I had just had my supper and was brushing my teeth over the bathroom sink," he recalls. "The sun had just gone down, and I planned on watching a little television before I hit the sack."

He finished brushing his teeth, rinsed out the toothbrush and then put it back in the medicine cabinet over the sink, not prepared for the sight that awaited him when he closed the door and saw his reflection in the mirrored front. "It was just like in one of them horror movies," he recalls, "because someone else was standing right behind me in the mirror! It was the man from the hanging tree, only this time he was a lot closer than the other times. He was standing right behind me and I could see his entire face, with those red, bloodshot eyes bugging out at me." Roscoe says he gasped and then spun around, but he found nothing whatsoever behind him in the bathroom. "When I looked back in the mirror, the reflection was gone, too."

Tuttle claims the restless soul returned to haunt him several nights after that, each time appearing by the side of his bed, or caught in brief glances in the various mirrors around the house. "Finally, I couldn't take it anymore," he says. "I went and saw a friend who lives nearby and who used to be a Presbyterian minister. He studied at the old seminary down on Broadway way back when, and he always used to love to talk about ghosts and stuff. So I asked if he could help me." The ex-clergyman came the next day, and the two men walked together to Floral Terrace and sat till the sun went down. Tuttle says his friend lit a candle and then said a short prayer designed to release an earthbound spirit. After another five minutes passed, they returned to his house on Park and had several cups of coffee. The clergyman performed a cleansing ritual before returning home. After that, Roscoe Tuttle says he received no more visits from the dead man on the hanging tree.

Perhaps someone will find documentation to substantiate claims that the cottonwood that once stood at the center of Floral Terrace served as a lynching tree, but for now, neighborhood residents will have to content themselves with local legend and lore. And it seems that legend indeed abounds on Floral Terrace. In my own research, I wasn't able to uncover any proof of the lynchings that supposedly took place there, but I did make another rather disturbing discovery. Although corroboration of vigilante killings at the tree were hard to come by, it wasn't too hard to find out that the tree that once stood at the center of Floral Terrace had been a favored spot for suicides. In 1933, a May 9 article from the *Your Street and Mine* column of the *Neighborhood Reporter* picked up on these legends of a killing tree. One report had it that that a distraught young man shot himself under the branches of the tree after losing his life's savings at nearby Churchill Downs. As a reminder against the evils of gambling, residents supposedly buried the body where they found it – just steps from the infamous killing tree of Floral Terrace.

I've talked to residents of the neighborhood who were present when the old cottonwood was cut down and the current fountain installed in its place, and they said if a body had been buried anywhere in the immediate

Random views of Floral Terrace today, including the fountain installed where the old "Killing Tree" used to stand. Residents claim the spirit of a man who died there still haunts the site today. (Photos courtesy of Franklin and Esther Schmidt)

vicinity, they would have discovered it during their excavations. According to them, not much was uncovered other than some pieces of rotting wood and a number of broken bottles and an old horseshoe. So even though there is written substantiation for the self-inflicted shooting death that took place there, the part about the body being buried there was probably something invented and added later on to the story for dramatic effect. It seems in any case that by the 1930s already the tree had an eerie association with suicides though, if not actual lynchings, and this is confirmed by a number or earlier reports of suicides taking place at the tree. Perhaps the most famous of these was reported by several local newspapers in the summer of 1901. On June 28, a reporter from the *Louisville Times* wrote, a young man by the name of Sam Turner decided to end his life. Under cover of darkness, he climbed the tall cottonwood, rope in hand, and found the highest and sturdiest branch he could find. Then, he shinned out to the end and tied one end around the branch and the other end around his neck, and jumped. The next morning an early riser spotted his body swinging 40 feet up in the air, and a crowd of more than 500 turned out to watch as his corpse was lowered and taken away to the morgue. Some who knew him said the excessive heat the night before had driven him to it; others said it was because of his recent arrest for a lottery he was running. It was reported that people feared a lynching at first, so that goes to show that it wasn't an unknown phenomenon in the area.

Did Sam Turner's ghost appear to people such as Homer Waite and Roscoe Tuttle, or was it one of the other known suicides that took place at Old Louisville's famed Hanging Tree on Floral Terrace? Or was it perhaps the spirit of an unfortunate man who met his demise at the hands of an angry lynch mob? As with so many of the ghost stories and eerie legends in Old Louisville, I can only piece together eyewitness accounts and cobble them together with scant pieces of historical research, letting people decide for themselves what is fact and what is fiction in the end. In the meantime, Floral Terrace remains one of Old Louisville's hidden gems, and most nights there's usually a free spot on the wrought iron bench next to the fountain where the old tree once stood.

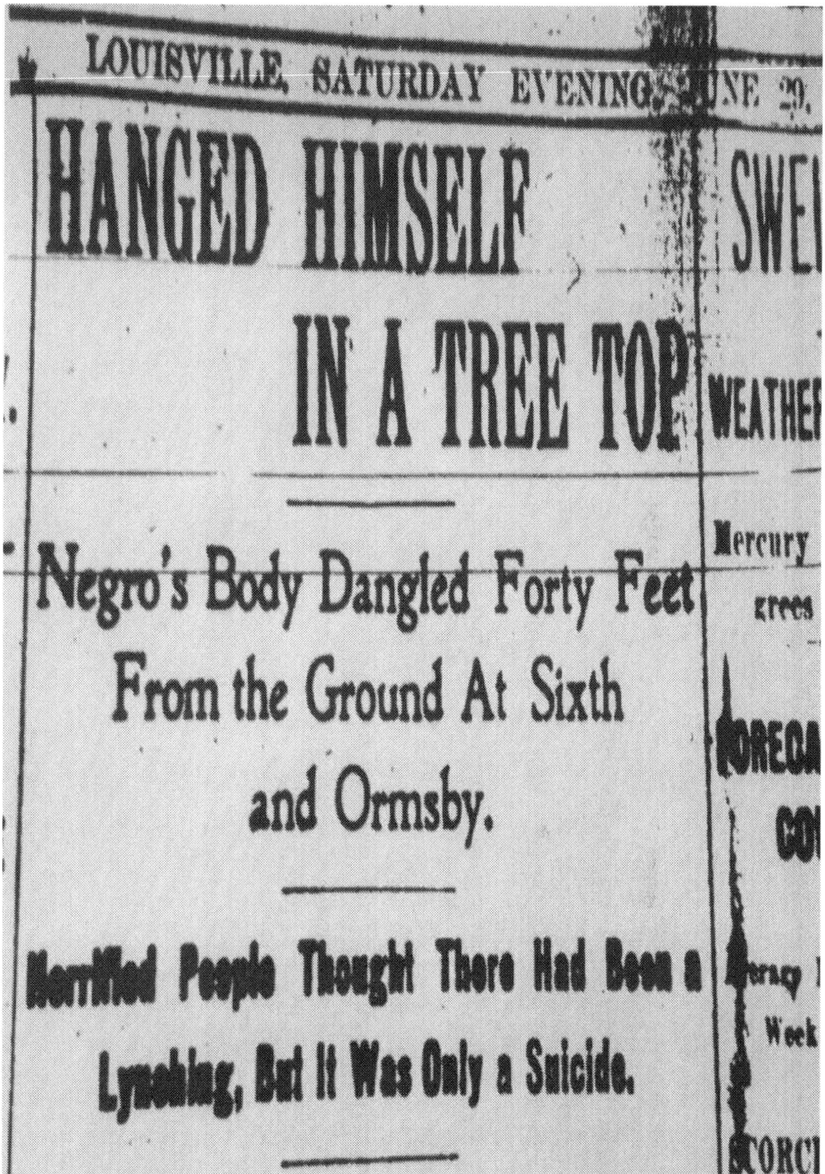

LOUISVILLE, SATURDAY EVENING, JUNE 29,

HANGED HIMSELF
IN A TREE TOP

SWE

WEATHER

Negro's Body Dangled Forty Feet
From the Ground At Sixth
and Ormsby.

Mercury

grees

FORECA

CO

Horrified People Thought There Had Been a
Lynching, But It Was Only a Suicide.

Mercury

Week

FORC

SAM TURNER'S SUICIDE IN A TREE TOP.

Chapter 13 – The Jennie Casseday Infirmary for Women

A block and a half away from Floral Terrace is another famously haunted location. The house at 1412 South Sixth Street doesn't quite fit in with the rest of the houses in Old Louisville. While the vast majority of neighborhood homes are of brick construction set back on a small plot of land, this one is not. Sheltered beneath the leafy shade of towering oak trees, it sits back from the street behind an ancient wrought-iron fence, far removed from the everyday activity of Old Louisville as the days silently pass by. Strangely out of place, but nonetheless grand and imposing, it has whitewashed trim and weathered gray clapboard shingles that might seem more at home in a quaint seaside village in New England. In all of Old Louisville, not a single building bears the slightest resemblance to it. Almost in its shadows, a smaller outbuilding in the same style sits next to it and a little farther back. If you pause and study the two buildings from the sidewalk, you get the distinct impression that something more than just architectural style alone makes them unique. Dark and foreboding, 1412 South Sixth Street has a secret to tell.

Unlike other stories in this book, I had to hunt down the secret of 1412 South Sixth Street. In most cases, people came to me with their stories, or referred me to other witnesses of paranormal activity in the neighborhood. I interviewed the various individuals and then did research to see if any corroborating evidence could be found to verify the substance of the stories before compiling them and putting pen to paper. In the case of 1412 South Sixth Street, I started with the assumption that a story would pop up somewhere along the line, and I set out to see what I could find. It was as if something about the old structure spoke to me, beckoned me to go and find out more about its past lives. Although it required a lot of time and patience, I was not disappointed.

My first line of investigation involved the usual poking around to see if people in the neighborhood had heard anything or knew anything useful about 1412 South Sixth Street. When told the street number alone, most had no idea which building I meant, however, when I added a description of the weathered shingles and mansard roof covered in gray slate, all set behind two stone gate posts, they knew at once which house I inquired about. Although no one knew anything in particular about the house, they all came to the same conclusion: if there wasn't a story there, there ought to be, because 1412 South Sixth Street looked like a haunted house.

Established in 1892, the Jennie Casseday Free Infirmary for Women provided badly needed services for individuals inside and outside of Old Louisville. According to local lore, it counts as one of the most haunted locations in the neighborhood.

Next, I did a title search to learn something about the past owners of the property. Unsuccessful every time I had knocked at the door in hopes of finding someone to talk to in person, I decided to uncover the year of construction and see what I could dig up regarding previous residents. Due to problems at the courthouse and mistakes made when recording the titles, this proved to be a time-consuming endeavor as well, so I decided to do what I usually do in cases such as this: wait and hope that something would show up.

And that's precisely what happened several months later as I found myself rummaging through books about Louisville history at the Free Public Library. I returned to scan the shelves in a section I usually patronize and managed to come across a book that had somehow escaped my attention before: Clyde F. Crews' *Spirited City: Essays in Louisville History.* I grabbed it from its perch and began perusing the pages, making notes here and there when I found any useful information. Several minutes later I found myself staring at an old black-and-white picture that captured my attention, on page 21. It showed an elegant Old Louisville residence, or so I thought, with several younger women standing before the spacious front stoop, all of them in starched, white Victorian dresses with high, ruffled collars. It looked oddly familiar, but for some reason, I couldn't place the building and thought it must have been one of the unfortunate many in Louisville to fall victim to the wrecking ball. Below the picture, the caption read: "(1895 photo) Jennie Casseday's Free Infirmary for Women." I stared at the large shingled building again, and then it dawned on me. This was an early picture of 1412 South Sixth Street.

A postcard image from 1897 shows the nursing staff in front of the Jennie Casseday Free Infirmary for Women. Many locals also refer to this structure as the Slate House.

Eagerly, I read on and learned what little I could about this early Old Louisville hospital and its founder, Miss Jennie Casseday. It seems that at one time quite a few hospitals dotted the city of Louisville in general, and Old Louisville in particular, a fact attributed to its unenviable geographic position along the somewhat stagnant waters of the Ohio River. As the author explained on page 17, "As the young town matured into its second generation, disease became the greatest stalker of human life. Abetted by the area's large amount of swampland, epidemics decimated the area, providing Louisville's earliest and least desirable nickname: *The Graveyard of the West.*"

In addition to the problems with tuberculosis and cholera, Louisville had to deal with the normal big-city health problems associated with poverty and poor sanitation as well. Like most American cities of the late 1800s, Louisville had started to recognize the plight of the poor in its midst, and one of the main concerns became the deplorable conditions for those living in the city's slums and tenements. The Cabbage Patch Settlement House, a place of refuge and aid for many of Louisville's poor in the early 1900s, still exists today, just steps from the elegant mansions and graceful homes along tree-lined Saint James Court. Although first founded in 1910, the Cabbage Patch relocated in 1929 to a part of Old Louisville still considered the outskirts of the neighborhood, a section of the district where comfortable two and three-story homes start giving way to more modest bungalows and shotgun structures before completely disappearing a couple blocks over on Seventh Street.

When friends of Jennie Casseday built her Free Infirmary for Women in the late 1800s, right across the street from today's Cabbage Patch Settlement House, the area still had pigs running around in fenced-in yards, and even scores of fowl and the occasional cow. Recognizing the added burdens of pregnancy and child care placed on many women of the lower class, Jennie Casseday hoped to provide free health care to the women who needed it most. Casseday, a devout Methodist and member of the Holiness Movement, also saw it as her Christian and human duty to help those less-fortunate members of her community. When associates constructed the state-of-the-art facility in the 1890s they saw Casseday as a sort of champion for the rights of the down-trodden, and especially the everyday working girl. Not surprising, unwed mothers, worn-out housewives of the lower class, and abandoned women of all ages comprised the majority of her clientele. With this knowledge in hand, I knew there had to be a story somewhere. All I had to do was find it.

A year passed, and I had found nothing about the old infirmary, other than it later became known as McMurtry's Infirmary, but that took me to dead ends as well. In addition, an old-timer from the neighbourhood informed me that the slate used on its roof had come originally from the main pavilion of the Southern Exposition, supposedly the largest wooden building in the world when the event ended in 1887. It seems that much of the disassembled building was recycled and its materials incorporated in the many mansions being built in the area. I had also hunted down several inhabitants of the building after it ceased its functions as hospital and clinic, but no one had experienced anything unusual on the premises or had heard of anyone else who had. The closest I got was a chance encounter with an elderly gentleman at the Saint James Art Show whose father had been born at Casseday's Clinic, as he called it, in 1898. His father had died long since, and the gentleman lived in Louisiana now, so he couldn't offer much more than a few recollections and a heavy southern drawl. I got my break a couple of weeks later when I got an urge for a double latte as I was walking my two schnauzers down Belgravia Court.

A new coffee house had just opened up at the corner of Fourth and

Hill Streets, and as Rocky and Bess led me through the east gate and out onto Fourth Street, I realized some caffeine would hit the spot. Right across the street was the Old Louisville Coffee House. Realizing I had a dilemma on my hands, I crossed the street and puzzled as to what I should do with the dogs. There weren't many people at the counter inside, so I looped the end of the leash around one of the dull spikes of the wrought-iron fence surrounding the neighboring lawn and ran inside to place my order, making sure to keep an eye out for the dogs through the window. When I returned several minutes later, latte in hand, I discovered my canine friends had made a new acquaintance: a little old man with white hair and bright blue eyes who had stooped to pet them and who – much to their delight – was feeding them sugar cookies.

I approached and said hello, to which the elderly gentleman straightened up and said he hoped I didn't mind his feeding the dogs. When I responded that it didn't bother me (or the dogs) at all, he remarked that he "used to have a little schnauzer over at "the old infirmary" on Sixth Street, and she used to love sugar cookies." Rocky, hearing the magic word, barked a stubborn little growl on cue that let us know he was waiting for the rest of the cookies. Bess, not one to bother with formalities, pushed herself up on her hind legs and started pawing the air around the remaining sugar cookies. I, on the other hand, had started to tremble at the thought that I might be getting my first big break in the story. "You don't mean the *Jennie Casseday Free Infirmary for Women*, do you?" I asked, trying to sound nonchalant. "Yes, that's what they called it way before they converted it to apartments," he responded. I held my breath and tried not to look excited. "Say," I ventured, "did you ever experience anything *strange* when you were living there?"

He had gone back down on his haunches and let the dogs finish the treats in his hand. When I asked the question he looked up and thought for a second. "Well, I lived there for almost two years when I was much younger, and I did see some *strange* things. This is a kooky neighborhood, you know," he said. "There are some strange characters out there, that's for sure." He studied me for a moment or two, and it seemed that his eyes had a certain mischievous sparkle to them. He patted Bess on the head and stood up again. "Yes," he laughed, "I witnessed many a strange thing over there, and just in case you were wondering, that place is haunted as the dickens." I invited him to some coffee, and we sat down at one of the ornate metal tables in front of the cafe while he told me his story.

Jack Conger rented a couple of rooms at 1412 South Sixth Street after he returned from duty in World War II in the late 1940s. Just twenty-five years old, he had a year of studies left, and hoped to finish them at the nearby University of Louisville. He recalls it as a carefree period in his life that afforded him a certain amount of leisure time and comfort, although his existence was far from a luxurious one. Unlike many young men at that time, Jack didn't have to work because his parents could afford to give him a modest monthly allowance to pay for food and rent. He spent most of his days reading or strolling around the neighborhood, where he'd make frequent stops at his favorite cafes and bars. In the evenings he liked to take in a movie or listen to the radio in his comfortable, yet sparsely furnished living room. That is, if he found himself at home after dark. Jack Conger says strange things happened at 1412 South Sixth Street when the sun went down.

The first incident he recalls happened one evening after returning from a night out with some friends on Fourth Avenue. "I had moved in about three months before, and to my knowledge, there was nothing unusual about my place," he remembers. "It was sort of boring to be there alone by myself all the time, so I spent as much time out and about as I could. We had been to a movie downtown, and after stopping for a bite to eat, I came home." Jack says he turned the radio on and listened to some classical music while leafing through a magazine. An hour or so later, he became tired and decided that he wanted to go to bed. He stood up, turned off the radio and went to the bathroom to brush his teeth before hitting the sack.

"I was cleaning my teeth," he explains, "standing there at the sink in front of the mirror when I realized music was still coming from the radio. I figured I must have forgotten to turn it off, so I went out there to turn it off, and lo and behold, it was turned off already! But I could still hear classical piano music plain as day." He turned the knobs off again, but music could still be heard, so he reached down and pulled the plug from the wall. A steady stream of classical tunes still seemed to emanate from the radio, and he could even hear the hiss and crackle of static. "I just stood there and stared at the radio, and it just kept going on and on," he says, "till it finally just sort of faded away about five minutes later. I finished brushing my teeth and then went to bed as if nothing had happened. I thought if I ignored it, it wouldn't happen again."

But it did happen again, only a week or so after the first incident, and in much the same way as the time before. He had turned off the radio, or so he thought, and returned to the living room to shut it off again. As happened the time before, he stood there staring at the unplugged device while various melodies poured out, until they eventually faded away. He resumed his nightly routine and prepared for bed, hoping he would be able to ignore the radio's odd behavior. As he walked to the bedroom, however, he realized he could still hear the music. When he returned to the living room, it became apparent that the radio had started up again. He waited, and it eventually started to fade, so he turned off the floor lamp that stood next to it and hopped into bed.

Once in bed, he turned off the small light on his bedside table and rolled over to go to sleep. The little schnauzer at his side didn't seem to be bothered, though. As Jack lay on his side and looked through his bedroom door to the living room, however, he noticed a bright light filled the space.

He returned to the living room, relieved to hear nothing coming from the radio, but strangely puzzled about the light. He reached down and slid the switch on the cord, but the lamp would not go off. As with the radio, when he pulled the plug out of its socket on the wall, the bulb refused to go out. He just stared at it, and in a few minutes it started to fade and then went out all together. Still convinced he could ignore it, he went into his bedroom, shut the door and slept facing the other direction so he wouldn't notice any light if it came back on again. From then on he tried to avoid the living room altogether, and entered only when necessity dictated. The strange force in the living room, however, would not be ignored.

After several weeks of doing his best to disregard the strange antics of the radio and floor lamp in the living room, Jack awoke one night from a deep sleep, startled out of his slumber by a strange noise outside his bedroom. As he lay there and listened, he discerned what sounded like a long, mournful moan – perhaps female – coming from the living room. It started out soft and quiet, and then slowly crescendoed to a higher, more intense pitch before fading to what seemed to be gentle sobs. Once it faded to almost inaudible weeping, there would be a moment or two of silence, and then the strange cries would start all over again. This went on and on for almost two hours according to the alarm clock on his night table, yet he refused to get out of bed and check for the source of the odd moans. Although the little dog's ears perked up at the sounds, he didn't seem too bothered, so Jack felt somewhat reassured. In another half hour the sounds stopped altogether and the living room grew deathly quiet, leaving him with nothing more than a rash of goose bumps to prove that he had not imagined the whole event.

For the next several nights, the same scenario played out in his living room at 1412 South Sixth Street. Loud sobs and moaning would wake him from his sleep, and he would lie there for hours as he listened to what amounted to mournful pleas and pained groans. Sometimes he could hear the radio as it rapidly switched from station to station, its volume fluctuating between high and low, or the frequency cutting in and out as the light from the floor lamp flashed on and off. Although Jack

179

The former Jennie Casseday Infirmary for Women by night

admits that it was very unnerving, he says he never really felt afraid or concerned for his safety. Rather, he felt sorry for whatever being made the pitiful noises. He had the impression that a woman in distress or great sorrow had invaded his living room, a sorrowful and disembodied voice the only tangible proof of her existence.

It seemed the more he tried to ignore the sad groans, the more insistent and frequent they became. After another week of the nocturnal sobbing, the moans started to take on an almost fevered, hysterical pitch and within a fortnight they had erupted into obvious screams. When this finally happened, Jack realized he couldn't take it any longer and jumped out of bed to confront the invisible intruder. He ran into the living room and found himself totally alone, save for the radio, the floor lamp, and some other furnishings, not surprised to see that radio and lamp were working overtime. A loud stream of static mixed with a whirr of voices crackled from the transmitter, and the light bulb seemed to pulsate and glow with energy surges of varying strengths.

He was a little more than shocked, however, when first the radio and then the lamp slowly lifted off the ground and levitated in front of him.

The hair on his arms and the back of his neck stood on end as he froze and stared at the objects floating in front of him. The air about him seemed charged with electricity, and he felt a faint tremble in the floorboards beneath. After what seemed an eternity, the lamp and the radio settled back down in their places and then slowly started their levitations again. The whole time he stood and watched, says Jack, he could hear the sorrowful moans and hysterical screams of a woman in pain, apparently emanating from the same spot as the two floating pieces of furniture. Completely overwhelmed by the sights and sounds around him, the only reaction he could muster was to flee the house and search for calm out of doors. He decided to take the dog for a prolonged walk around the neighborhood.

The next day Jack Conger decided he needed to do something. Granted, the various items randomly floating around his living room had at last settled down by the time he returned from his walk, but he knew that the daylight offered only a temporary respite from the supernatural activity plaguing his small apartment. He couldn't shake the feeling that he had more in store than just weird sounds and anti-gravitational phenomena. He knew quite a few people who believed in ghosts and spirits, but he didn't really know of anyone who could help him get rid of them. He decided therefore to pay a visit to his local priest.

Father Joe, as Jack called him, had known the Congers as long as they could recall and he had served in the same nearby church for years. An eternally cheerful man with ruddy cheeks and a kind disposition, the priest had a difficult time nonetheless believing in ghosts, so he did little to mask his scepticism as he listened to Jack's account of the unexplained phenomena. "But, Jack," he insisted, "I'm telling, you there *is no such thing* as ghosts! There has to be a logical explanation for what you've seen." Although he refused to accept the possibility of earth-bound spirits or any type of supernatural activity in Jack's apartment, he agreed to call the young man the next day and set up a time when he could stop by and officially bless the apartment. Relieved that he had at least shared his strange secret with someone else, Jack returned home and kept himself busy till darkness fell. He met some friends at a nearby bowling alley and didn't make his way back home until the wee hours of the morning. Fortunately, he fell fast asleep as soon as his head hit the pillow, and any would-be happenings in the next room failed to rouse him. The next morning he awoke, had coffee and donuts at a diner around the corner and then called Father Joe.

"You live *where*?" the priest repeated when Jack give his address as 1412 South Sixth Street. From the tone in his voice, the young man could tell that the priest had been taken by surprise. "You mean the *old infirmary*?" he demanded after Jack repeated the address. "They took that place and turned it into apartments?" He sounded somewhat incredulous. Before the younger man had a chance to respond, the priest said he'd be right over and hung up the phone.

An hour later, both men stood in Jack's living room and surveyed the field of supernatural activity. The radio and the floor lamp rested in their spots next to the wall and didn't so much as move an inch. The little schnauzer was curled up in its usual spot on the floor. Although he refused to divulge any information on the matter, Father Joe appeared to be a bit unnerved, and Jack felt sure the priest knew something that he chose not to share about the apartment at 1412 South Sixth Street. The priest placed a small leather valise on the table and unpacked several items including a small vile of holy water, a Bible and a brass crucifix. He draped a stole around his neck and quickly made his way from room to room, cross held out in front as he flicked holy water and recited a rapid succession of prayers in Latin. When he had finished, he packed his things and said his good-byes, refusing Jack's invitation to stay for a glass of wine or cup of coffee.

That very evening Jack found himself in the kitchen off of the living room preparing a light dinner before he headed to a friend's house for a game night. He had just scrambled three large eggs and watched them slowly cook and sizzle in a cast iron skillet laden with butter, when a strange sensation suddenly overcame him. A chill ran down his spine, and he found it very difficult to breathe, almost as if a heavy weight had been placed on his chest. He looked towards the living room and realized that dusk had fallen. As if forced and prodded by a pair of invisible hands, he reluctantly walked into the parlor as a sense of dread settled over him. His throat constricted for a moment, and he thought he might choke to death.

As he had feared, the radio and the lamp levitated inches above the surfaces that normally held them, and they both started to rotate before his eyes. The dial on the radio started spinning around and a blur of static and unidentifiable voices punctuated the air at the same time the light bulb flashed on and off. He could also hear the plaintive cries and sobbing screams that had filled the room before, but this time they seemed more distressed and pained than before. Immobilized, he stared at the objects in the air and gulped for breath, afraid he might suffocate if not able to rally himself from that spot. His head started to spin, and he grew faint, but whatever appeared to have a hold over him suddenly released itself and allowed him to breathe freely. At that very same moment a strange white mist started to fill the room, and the space seemed to experience a drastic drop in temperature.

Jack also noted a rapid rise in the humidity level about him, and he realized beads of moisture had started to accumulate on the wall behind the radio and floor lamp. In a matter of seconds, it seemed that a dense, white fog had blanketed the room and he could just barely make out the shapes of the two floating items as they settled back down to their original locations. Then he heard an almost muted pitter-patter and felt something soft hit his head. He looked up and realized that it had started to rain in his own living room. When he heard the water droplets start falling at a more rapid pace, he shook himself, scooped up the dog, and then bolted for the street. Once outside, he quickly sought out a pay phone and called Father Joe.

An assistant at the parish house answered and informed him that the priest had gone to St. Louis for personal reasons and didn't plan on returning for several days. At a loss, Jack Conger hung up the phone and checked into the nearby Marquette Terrace Hotel. He decided at that moment that he would not set foot in his apartment again unless someone else accompanied him or until the strange powers in his living room vacated the premises. That night he slept his first dreamless sleep in months, and when he rose the next morning he actually felt invigorated and refreshed. He called a cousin, and together they went to the apartment at 1412 South Sixth Street and retrieved some of his clothes. Jack decided to leave the dog at his cousin's until he figured out what was going on at his own apartment. As the two men entered the living room, Jack noticed pools of water - unevaporated despite the soaring summer temperatures outside - from the day before that had collected on the floor and on the tabletops. Pushing it out of his mind, he quickly wiped up the mess and returned to his room at the hotel and waited for Father Joe's return.

More than a week passed, and although the priest had indeed arrived safely back in town, he neglected to return any of Jack's calls. Puzzled, the young man decided to wait another day or two and then find the priest himself if he didn't hear back from him. Granted, he received a comfortable allowance from his parents, but it by no means meant he could afford to spend weeks at a time in a hotel. He needed to get back into his apartment, and he saw Father Joe as his only remedy for the situation at hand. And after the last weird occurrences in the living room, he definitely had no intention of being there on his own. As a matter of fact, he had gone so far as to call the landlord and see about getting out of his lease, but the old woman had refused, calling his sanity into question when he mentioned the strange things he had witnessed.

When Sunday rolled around without a call back from the priest, Jack Conger decided he needed to go to mass. He sat through the service and made sure to be one of the last to leave the church; that way Father Joe would have to talk to him. When the old man saw him approach, the look in his eyes betrayed the fact that he had been avoiding further contact with Jack. "Oh, shoot, I was afraid you'd hunt me down," the priest confessed. "I was hoping my little prayers had taken care of your problems." Embarrassed, he wrung his hands and looked down at his feet.

"Taken *care* of my problems?" Jack repeated sarcastically. "It got *worse* after you left." He studied the man in front of him for a moment, and then softened his tone. "Father Joe," he said gently, "it's *me*. Jack Conger. You've known my family for ages, and I've got a real problem here, and I need your help. I don't know what else to do." He stopped for a second and waited for the priest to react. Seeing that no response was forthcoming, he shrugged his shoulders and sighed. "I don't want to cause any trouble for you, I swear, but I just don't know what to do. I'm sorry."

At that, the priest looked up and took the young man by the shoulders. "No," he said with a gentle shake of the head, "I'm the one who should be sorry." He led Jack to the front of the church and told him to stay put; the priest had a couple of matters to attend to, but he told Jack he'd be back shortly. They would talk more then.

Twenty minutes later, the priest emerged through a small wooden door and found Jack sitting in the first row of pews, somewhat lost in thought. He approached the young man and sat down next to him, his leather valise still tucked under one arm. "Now, then," the older man chuckled, "I've got a confession for you." He slid in a little closer and handed Jack a small, leather-bound book emblazoned with golden letters across the front. "Remember how I said there is no such thing as ghosts and stuff?" he asked. "Well, I am not so sure of that."

More confused than ever, Jack just held the book and stared. "I don't get it," he said. "What's this all about? Does this have something to do with the strange things going on in my apartment?" He used his index finger to point at the book in the priest's hand. "I got the impression that you knew something and weren't telling me, but now I'm totally in the dark." He watched the priest slowly stand up and motion for him to follow. They walked outside into the bright sunshine and started off in the direction of 1412 South Sixth Street. By the time they reached their destination a half hour later, Jack Conger would get an earful about the haunting at his Sixth Street apartment.

Father Joe initially had not revealed to him that he had already paid several visits to the gray-shingled building on Sixth Street by the time Jack contacted him. The first times, he related, had been some fifty years before when they still used it as an infirmary. Even though Casseday had been a strict Methodist, many of her clients were poor Catholic women, and the priest was often called upon for various services, including baptisms and very often the administering of last rites. The last two times had been in the decade before World War II, when he had been called in to investigate various *disturbances* at the Sixth Street property. From research I did later, I was able to learn that in the 30s, the building had been turned in a neuropathy clinic to treat patients with various nervous conditions. Since then, Father Joe had hoped he wouldn't have to pay any more visits to the old clinic, but when he learned that Jack Conger was living in the building he was overcome with a sense of dread. As the two men strolled down the sunny streets, the priest shared more of the details.

Jack Conger, as it turned out, happened to be living in the part of the infirmary that used to serve as the maternity ward, an area that saw no small share of pain, suffering and death on the part of its patients. The priest could recall that on one weekend alone he gave the last rites to four women who died in childbirth, and he could still hear the torment of their screams in his ears, as if it were yesterday. Then there was the influenza epidemic in 1918; he couldn't even keep track of how many women perished that month. Although he was a sceptic, he wasn't at all surprised when rumors started surfacing about awful screams and strange visions when the place was completely empty. Jack's living room, he said, at one time had two beds in it, set aside especially for the most severe cases. As a consequence, quite a few women met their unfortunate ends in that very room. The odd occurrences seemed to be a result of that sad connection.

Both men stood and examined the room. Nothing looked out of the ordinary, save for a small puddle of water Jack had missed, on the floor directly in front of the floor lamp. Next to it, on a wooden end table, the radio sat in silence. The priest pointed to the wall behind it and said the two beds he mentioned usually stood perpendicular to the wall, in that very spot with their headboards touching it. Other than that area, he knew of no other part of the house where strange things were said to happen. Turning to look at Jack, he said "I still don't believe in ghosts and all that stuff, but I have to admit that I cannot logically explain any of the things I've witnessed in this room. I've seen some odd things, mind you, but in my entire career as a man of the cloth, this infirmary is the only time I couldn't explain it away. I saw things floating in the air, and then I saw one of the women who had died the day before. She was standing right in front of me, just as if she were alive." With a sigh, the priest set the leather valise on the couch and extracted the book of rites, turning it over in his hand as he stood next to the young man. "Granted, the church does teach us about the occult and things of that nature, but most of us nowadays think it's pretty old-fashioned. We live in the modern age now, don't we?"

Jack Conger stood and stared at the priest, shaking his head. He could hardly believe what he was hearing. Father Joe had known about the strange happenings in his apartment. He didn't know if he was more relieved that someone could actually vouch for his story or more concerned that the priest had not been able to eliminate the supernatural events. When he asked the older man what they should do, the priest replied that they would wait until dark and try to convince the strange force to leave – just as he had done on two separate occasions in the past. He hoped this time it would not return.

Several hours later the two men were standing in the same spot in the room as the last of the light outside gave way to the gray shadows creeping across the floor towards the lamp and the radio. The priest had laid out the crucifix and the holy water and he held the opened exorcism book in his hands. As he had already explained to Jack, priests usually used the rites of exorcism to cast demons and evil spirits from human bodies, but in this case some of the ancient rituals outlined in the book would serve to confront the entities present in the old infirmary. Father Joe started to read a liturgy in Latin and out of the corner of his eye he kept a close watch on the young man at his side.

Jack Conger recalls standing there and watching for what seemed like hours, but looking back, he figures it was probably more like an hour or forty-five minutes. He had started to relax a bit and began to wonder if anything would happen. No sooner had he let down his guard when the crucifix on the small end table next to him suddenly lifted a foot into the air and shot across the room as if hurled by an invisible hand. Although he had started to tremble, the young man noticed that the priest kept on with his liturgy as if nothing had happened. Several minutes after that, beads of moisture started to collect on the wall in front of the two men and then trickled slowly downwards as a faint rumble shook the ground beneath them.

As the vibration in the floor increased and spread to the walls and ceiling overhead, the light in the lamp started to flicker on and off and then buzzed into a bright glow. At the same time, a staticky crackle filled the room as the radio came to life and randomly switched from station to station. A misty fog started to rise from the floor, and the lamp and radio both simultaneously lifted off the ground and floated as a blanket of cool moisture seemed to envelope the two men. Water droplets fell from the ceiling, and the brass crucifix that had shot across the room before now reappeared in front of the priest, apparently suspended in mid air as it rotated on its vertical axis just inches from the man's nose. The walls seemed to shake, and a low wail surrounded the two men, barely audible at first, but then expanding into a powerful, pleading scream.

Apparently unperturbed, the priest continued his prayers as the moaning increased and sent reverberations through the floor and ceiling. The fog in the room seemed to become denser, and as he concentrated on the sounds about him, Jack realized that more than one voice could be heard. It sounded like multiple female voices, crying out in agony as the volume and pitch increased and threatened to drown out the voice of the priest. The light bulb in the lamp died, and it seemed that a dense shroud of blackness had been lowered. Only a small ball of hazy, pulsating, blue light hung in the air before the two men, its radiance fading to almost nothing then surging to blinding brilliance as the cross danced in the air around it.

As the intensity of the moans grew, so did the size of the ball of light, and within several minutes it had assumed the size of a human figure. Jack Conger and Father Joe looked on as the vague form of a woman materialized before them, flanked on either side by two other forms that appeared to be female as well. The light shimmered and flickered, and faint features became visible on the staring faces, eventually revealing mouths opened wide in a tortured scream. His heart pounding, Jack watched the three ghostly figures hover before him, the agony in their disembodied voices at a crescendo as the priest continued the methodical recitation of his prayers.

Horrified, Jack could only stand and stare as his brain attempted to process a barrage of information. Although he had never actually seen a ghost before, he was quite convinced that he was beholding the ghosts or spirits of three women, and they seemed to want to tell him something. Sadness overcame the young man as he watched the lifeless forms hovering and wailing before him, and although the eyes were nothing more than mere gray ovals, he sensed that they were looking to him for something, almost pleading, as it were. The priest finished his prayers and addressed the vague, silvery forms in English, telling them they were free to leave this realm and move on to the next. He repeated this several times, and when Jack realized it was not providing the desired effect, he added: "Your babies are fine. You can go on now. Your children are fine." With that, the awful moaning stopped, and the figures started to fade and then quickly vanished, leaving the two men standing alone in dark silence.

"I guess it hit me, all of a sudden, that they were worried about their babies," recalls Jack of that night. "All they needed to hear was that their children were fine. When they heard that, it released them, I guess." Jack Conger says he and his friend, Father Joe, retired to the kitchen after that and drank coffee and talked till the sun came up the next morning. After that day, Jack says he never had any problems with supernatural activity in the living room at 1412 South Sixth Street. There were no more strange mists inside his apartment, and the radio and floor lamp only came on when he turned them on.

The day after he shared his story, Jack and I met at the coffee shop again, so I could take better notes and record his account. He arrived, chipper as ever, and had a small sack of sugar cookies that he shared with the dogs as he retold his story. We were there for about three hours and afterward he gave me his phone number and we agreed to stay in touch. When the book with his story in it came out the following year, I called to invite him to the book signing, but he never showed up. I never saw him or heard from him again after that.

After that story came out, several individuals contacted me, all of them offering information that corroborated Father Joe's claim about multiple women dying over the years inside the old slate-covered building at 1412 Sixth Street. Several of them had family stories to share and some even had death certificates proving that their ancestors had died there. One of them, a lady by the name of Becky Bernheim, found me at a book signing and told me that she had lived in the old infirmary not too long after it was first converted into residential units. From the description she gave, it seemed that she had occupied the same part of the building once occupied by Jack Conger. Like Jack, she had experienced strange happenings that involved lights going on and off and unexplained moans and groans in the night, but her story differed in that she didn't see three apparitions. Instead, she had seen only one, "and it was a woman hanging from the ceiling." When I pressed for details, she explained that "it looked like she had hung herself. There she was, dangling up near the ceiling one minute, and then gone the next."

Bernheim claims that she saw the apparition only once in the three years she lived there, but that the strange sounds and activities were a regular occurrence.

Since none of the previous death reports from 1412 Sixth Street I had uncovered dealt with a suicide, I wasn't quite sure how much stock to put in Bernheim's story at first. But a short time later, I received an interesting email from someone else that made me sit up and take notice. Her name was Karen Marcroft and she was writing to see if I could provide her with some information about the history of the old infirmary at 1412 Sixth Street. The reason it interested her, she wrote, is because her great-aunt had hung herself there in the fall of 1926. As proof, she attached a copy of the death certificate. Marcroft was hoping that if she knew exactly what the building was used for at that time, she might better be able to understand the cause of her relative's suicide. The woman's name was Ida Ahlf.

What I was able to share is that after her death in 1893, Jennie Casseday's Free Infirmary for Women became known as McMurtry's Infirmary – probably in 1897 or thereabouts. Dr. McMurtry was a famous physician and a pioneer in gynecological medicine, so that might have had something to do with why Marcroft's great-aunt was a patient there. That is, if it was still McMurtry's Infirmary in 1926, because he died in 1925, I believe. However, I recalled seeing an old photograph of the building from the 1930s, and at that time it was The Louisville Neuropathy Clinic or something along those lines – so if was already a neuropathy clinic in 1926, Marcroft's great-aunt might have been a patient there for some nervous disorder and maybe had chosen to take her life because of the pain or suffering she was enduring. Marcroft wrote that Ida, who was married to her grandfather's brother and lived in nearby Tell City, was known to have "moods" so it might be that the woman had to deal with depression and that could be what landed her in Louisville for treatment. The sad part is that the treatment didn't work and that Ida chose to end her own life.

Does Ida's sad spirit haunt the bottom floor of the old Jennie Casseday's Infirmary in Old Louisville? Or could it be the ghost of one of the other women known to have suffered there? Little by little, this unique building on Sixth Street is offering up its secrets, but we might have to wait a bit longer to know the full story.

A death certificate from November 26, 1926 shows that Ida Ahlf, the great-aunt of Karen Marcroft, committed suicide at the former Jennie Casseday Free Infirmary for Women on Sixth Street.

An old family photo shows Ida Ahlf (second from the right) in happier days. Her suicide in 1926 at 44 years of age was one of many deaths associated with the building at 1412 Sixth Street in Old Louisville. Has her untimely passing contributed to the reported hauntings there? (Courtesy of Karen Marcroft, grand-niece of Ida Ahlf's husband)

According to reports, a tragic female spirit haunts the steps of the First Church of Christ, Scientist. Locals refer to her as "the lady of the stairs."

Chapter 14 – The Lady of the Stairs

At the corner of Third Street and Ormsby Avenue sits one of Old Louisville's most beloved and visually striking landmarks. Sheathed in white granite and marble that seem to glow at all hours of the day, it anchors that stretch of Third Street known as "Millionaires Row." An imposing structure originally begun around 1917, the austere exterior of the First Church of Christ, Scientist belies an interior noted for its understated elegance and beauty. Outside, observers see a long porch ensconced by a row of twelve monolithic columns towering along the front entrance, subtly balanced by nine sentinel-like wooden doors topped with mullioned transoms guarding the entrance. Inside, an enormous lighted boveda overhead commands attention and lends a sense of airiness to the solid surroundings. Brass torchieres flank several flights of stairs as they drop to the sidewalk below, and locals claim that the spirit of a young woman – also noted for her beauty and elegance – haunts these steps. They call her the Lady of the Stairs, and those who have seen her always remark on her singular grace and loveliness.

"She was very statuesque and seemed to be lost in thought, but I noticed right away that she was extremely beautiful. She had ivory white skin, her eyes and hair were jet black, and she was wearing a long, cream-colored gown with lace trim and a ruffled collar like they would have worn in the early 1900s. I saw her, and it literally took my breath away." Donald Spade reports that no woman had ever taken his breath away before his encounter with the Lady of the Stairs. A no-nonsense historian employed at the Filson Historical Society in the 1980s, his friends describe him as somebody who wouldn't make up stories, either. "If Don says he saw something, then I believe him," says a former co-worker. "He's probably one of the most reliable and trustworthy people I know." Everyone who knew him said the same thing: Don was not the kind of person to make up things.

"I thought I must have been seeing things, since I had just worked fourteen hours straight," he explains, "but the more I stared, the more I realized there was something standing in front of me on the stairs in front of the church. It was a woman, and I wasn't imagining anything at all." It was a cool fall night, and Don had been forced to park across the street from the historical society while workers repaved the parking lot. The spot he found sat directly in front of the stairs leading up to the church.

Housed across the street in the former Ferguson residence, a huge beaux-arts mansion built in 1905 and considered by many the largest home in Louisville for its day, the Filson Historical Society has amassed Kentucky's largest collection of genealogical records, local lore and historical documents since its founding in 1884. Reputedly a favorite haunt of neighborhood spirits itself, the sophisticated façade of the structure presents a nice counterbalance to the inherent simplicity of the church's design. For more than fifty years the Pearson family had used it as a funeral parlor, and several Filson workers claimed to hear strange noises or feel a strange presence late at night. Don, however, had always dismissed these accounts as the result of overactive imaginations. "Whenever anyone told me they heard steps overhead when no one was there, or that they sensed someone was watching them, I never took it seriously. I didn't think they were lying or anything, but I just didn't think they were looking for a logical explanation when there could have been one. I thought they were a little too eager to blame strange events on ghosts and spirits."

One chilly night in mid-October, however, Don reports that any skepticism he harbored regarding explanations for other people's strange happenings took quite a beating. Darkness had fallen several hours earlier, and he had decided to leave for home about 9 that evening. He turned off the lights in the stately mansion, set the alarm, and locked the door behind him before he dashed across the street to where he had left his car. The branches rustled uneasily in the trees overhead, and a brisk breeze swept along the sidewalk, scattering dried leaves and adding to the chill in the night air. "It was getting a bit cool, but it was still a nice night, and if I hadn't been so worn out, I'd have taken a walk around the neighborhood, like I very often did. This time I just decided to go home and get some sleep instead."

Stifling a yawn, he unlocked the car door, opened it and slid into the driver's side before putting the keys into the ignition. Enjoying the momentary relief after hours on his feet, he pushed his head back against the seat rest, stretched his legs and listened to the strains of classical music wafting from the radio.

"I started the car and was just about ready to pull away from the curb when I glanced out my window and noticed a strange light on the steps in front of the church. Mesmerized, I put the car in neutral and rolled the window down to get a better look." What he saw sent chills down his spine. Although he knew at an instant that something otherworldly stood before him, he couldn't but help notice how real the vision seemed. "I was looking at a woman from another era; I knew it right away. She looked like a lady from the turn of the century or something, and it was obvious that she felt out of place."

With the car engine gently humming and filling the interior with a comforting blanket of warm air, Don clutched the steering wheel and stared over his shoulder while the apparition slowly made its way down the flight of granite steps. Her figure bathed in a silvery glow, she had all the trappings of a turn-of-the-century Gibson Girl including the long-sleeved blouse ruffled at the neck and characteristic coiffure. She also wore a long skirt with a wasp waist and a lacy hem that hung over polished, black high-top shoes, however, her feet made no sound as she slowly came down the stairs.

"It was totally quiet and she seemed to float down the steps. But it looked like she had been pacing along the upper stair before she started to come down the stairs, waiting for somebody. There was a far-away look about her and she appeared reluctant to leave the steps. An overwhelming sense of sadness immediately came over me," says Don. "And then she reached the sidewalk and disappeared, just like that." The whole episode might have lasted ten or fifteen seconds at the most.

"I usually don't use the word melancholy, but that's exactly the word that came to mind when I saw her," explains the no-frills historian. "She was overcome with melancholy. I had such an overwhelming sense of sorrow that it made my eyes tear up. And that terrible feeling lasted the whole time I saw her slowly walk across the steps. When she reached the sidewalk and vanished, the feeling of dread I was experiencing vanished as well, just like that." He sat in the car and stared at the vacant steps for a moment, rubbing his tired eyes and not really sure if he hadn't imagined the whole scenario. Deciding he had indeed witnessed something very strange, he put the car in drive and headed to his condo downtown. After several hours of tossing and turning, he allowed himself to drift off to sleep, but visions of the woman on the stairs plagued his slumber throughout the night.

The next morning he could hardly contain himself at his desk in the Filson Historical Society. "Even though I was opening myself up to ridicule since I had always been so skeptical of other peoples' stories, I went ahead and told a coworker about the apparition from the night before." But instead of ridiculing him, Don's colleague seemed intrigued by the tale. "I had heard one or two stories about the lady on the stairs before, but I had no first-hand experience with her myself," she recalls. "I believe I might even have been witness to a strange sighting in the Ferguson mansion several years prior to that, but I really didn't have much to offer Don, other than an ear to listen with." Although she only lived several blocks down the road and usually walked by the church at least once a day, the middle-aged woman had never noticed anything strange there. Her mother, on the other hand, claimed that she had seen a similar ghost in the 1940s when she was a child, and she had always referred to her as "the lady on the steps."

The elderly woman had unfortunately passed away the year before, so Don decided to try and locate other possible eyewitnesses to the mysterious lady on the stairs. None of his coworkers at the historical society knew much about the supposed haunt, however, and Don found himself with little more than a huge craving to learn more about the woman who haunted the steps in front of the old church.

"For several weeks after that I spent hours rummaging through old documents in the library here, trying to find information about anyone associated with the church or about Old Louisville society in general," he says. "I did not find anything at all that might have shed some light on the haunting, but I did uncover a few other stories about ghost sightings in the neighborhood, and this time I wasn't so skeptical when I read them." Although the enthusiasm for his ghostly research gradually subsided, a year later Don still found himself squeezing in at least an hour or two of investigation every week. "I wasn't spending as much time looking for articles and such as I did the first week or two after I saw the spirit, but I was still looking. And to tell the truth, I was sort of miffed that I hadn't found anything to substantiate whatever it was that I had seen. I was starting to think I had imagined the whole thing, but every time I came outside the Filson, I couldn't help but stare at those steps in front of the church. When I remembered back to that night, I could recall almost every detail of the vision. I know what showed itself on those stairs had to be real."

A week later Don had his first bit of evidence to support his claims that the spirit of a beautiful young woman haunted the steps in front of the First Church of Christ, Scientist on Third Street. Involved in research for a series of articles meant to capture the colorful history and notable characters of Old Louisville, he needed to interview the relative of a neighbor who had worked for local culinary legend Miss Jennie Benedict at her downtown restaurant in the early 1900s.

A student of Fannie Farmer's cooking school in Boston, Jennie Benedict had made a name for herself in the catering business she ran out of a home on Third Street. After years of satisfying hungry Louisvillians' cravings for her popular beaten biscuits, chicken salad, pulled candy and devil's food cake, *Benedict's* thrived at its final location at 554 Fourth Avenue from 1911 to 1925. Even though the lady herself died in 1928, *benedictine*, her most endearing creation, lives on in the minds – and mouths – of many in the Bluegrass State to this day. Originally concocted of cucumbers and cream cheese, it served as the filling for her famous tea sandwiches. Today no true-blooded Louisvillian would ever consider hosting even the most meager of get-togethers without the obligatory plate of Benedictine finger sandwiches. With the passage of time, many variations in the original recipe had evolved, and Don now hoped he would get the low-down on Miss Jennie's authentic recipe.

"This lady's daughter lived in one of the large mansions near Central Park, a huge red brick building that had been in the family for many years. I found out that her mother had left behind a collection of original recipes from prominent families in Old Louisville from around the turn of the century, and she offered to let me have a look at them. Her offer included some personal recollections of Louisville's Fourth Avenue during its heyday in the '30s and '40s." After several minutes of waiting, a regal-looking woman in her late fifties answered the door and escorted Don to a large salon off the front reception hall.

"After I introduced myself, she apologized for the delay," says Don. "She said they didn't have servants anymore like they used to, so it took her a while to get from one end of the house to another. We sat down in a beautiful corner room with an amazing wood-coffered ceiling and walls covered in green silk. A roaring fire blazed in the focal point of the parlor, a gigantic oak fireplace with a lovely hearth done in very unique blue and green tiles." Noticing his fascination with the fireplace, the lady informed him that the Rookwood Pottery Company in Cincinnati had designed the unusual ceramic tiles especially for the house sometime around 1885 when an eminent Louisville businessman built the mansion for his wife. Looking around at the rich paneling that wainscoted the room and the delicate crystal chandeliers in the double parlor, Don remembers thinking to himself that the gentleman had spared no expense for his wife.

"I didn't get the grand tour or anything, but you could tell that this was definitely one of the grander mansions at the park. It had to have at least 10,000 square feet of living space, if that tells you anything." He considered the foyer and paneled grand stairway, with a beautiful curved staircase that gently wound its way up to the third floor, the crowning features. During the day, sunlight poured through art glass windows at various levels and accented the rich woods in dancing tones of green, amber, gold and peach.

Don and the woman talked for a bit about the history of the house she had lived in for the last twenty years, and then gradually got around to talking about her mother's recollections of working with Jennie Benedict. Delighted to find out that the two women actually knew each other as friends and not just employer and employee, he learned that the one lady would help her friend, Jennie, whenever she needed an extra hand with catering jobs. A half hour passed, and Don soon had more than enough information to finish his research, including substantiation that

Jennie Benedict herself insisted on adding a couple drops of green food coloring to give her Benedictine spread its characteristic green tint.

"I was talking about the Benedict residence on Third Street and I realized it had to be near the First Church of Christ, Scientist so I decided to ask if this woman – or her mother – had ever heard about the mysterious woman who haunted those steps." The woman paused for a moment, and then smiled before putting her teacup back on the saucer. "She looked at me with some surprise and said 'Oh, you must mean the Lady of the Stairs,' and then she started to tell her story."

Elizabeth, as she now insisted Don call her, had lived most of her life in the same few blocks that surrounded Central Park. Other than a few years in California while her husband brokered tobacco for various markets in Asia and the South Pacific, she boasted that they had never lived anywhere outside of Kentucky. She considered herself a fixture in Old Louisville, and knew quite a few stories as well. Apart from the expertise lent her by years of residency in the neighborhood, she felt herself especially qualified to share her own tales of supernatural phenomena and parapsychological experiences since she enjoyed what some called "psychic gifts." Elizabeth had been born with a caul over her face, a layer of membrane that occasionally covers the features of infants who often develop special clairvoyant powers and paranormal abilities later in life. And although her mother didn't tell her about this until she had started grade school, Elizabeth still knew she had certain powers that most did not.

For example, she could discern colored energy fields or auras surrounding most individuals and could therefore make judgments about their character and personality. Since Don radiated a pleasantly soft green and yellow aura to her eyes, she believed him to be someone worthy of her confidence. While out in the country on a family outing, a stranger had pointed out this gift to her as a girl in the '30s. The unknown man turned out to be none other than Edgar Cayce, someone who had already established himself as a pioneer in the field of paranormal studies. A native Kentuckian himself, he had spotted the young Elizabeth while motoring by a field of daisies and brought the car to a sudden halt. Taking note of the golden aura that mirrored the yellow of the daisies, he approached the child and informed her that a great gift had been given to her. To the amazement of her parents, Cayce asked if the girl had been born with a caul.

According to Elizabeth, her other great skill involved the capacity to see the spirits of deceased individuals. This happened for the first time at age four, shortly after the passing of her grandmother in a tragic accident. Although word of her death had not yet reached the family, Elizabeth announced to her mother that granny woke her up that morning and wanted everyone to know that she had to leave and would not see them again for a while. When a deputy sheriff showed up later that day with the sad news of the grandmother's death in a car crash in downtown Columbus, no one doubted that the young Elizabeth had the power to see into the next realm.

Her next sighting happened several months after that when her father took her out on a late-afternoon stroll through the neighborhood. Walking by the imposing Church of Christ, Scientist, she observed a shadowy figure in white as it slowly paced along the upper step, seemingly on the lookout for someone or something. When the diaphanous form noted the girl's gaze upon her, it slowly turned, smiled and then vanished. Somehow, Elizabeth always felt that these spirits were just as aware of her as she was of them.

"Elizabeth told me that she saw that woman on more than one occasion during her childhood, but the older she got, the fewer sightings she had. I guess that sort of thing is like practically any skill – you lose it if you don't keep in practice," Don says. "I read somewhere that younger people, especially adolescents, have so much pent-up energy that they make the best mediums and are more receptive to paranormal activity. It stands to reason then that Elizabeth would have seen fewer spirits as she got older," he says. Although much of her clairvoyance remained, Elizabeth readily admitted that she rarely saw spirits anymore. As for the ghostly female apparition on the stairs, she had little concrete evidence to share. She knew for certain that the lovely girl still waited for someone who never showed up, and this caused her great pain and anguish. What or who caused her such sorrow, she couldn't say exactly, only that her spirit still pined away on the lonely steps in front of the large church at the corner of Third and Ormsby.

Strangely enough, congregants of the First Church of Christ, Scientist have no knowledge of any ghostly activity in their midst. Nor can anyone recollect any stories or individuals that might tie in with the alleged haunting. All in all, Christian Scientists don't come across as the superstitious or frivolous types, either. In fact, after my first book came out and I started offering guided tours of the neighborhood and its famous haunts, I was told by an icy-voiced church member that "we do not believe in ghosts" when he saw me in front of the church one day and heard me talking about the alleged haunting there.

There is, however, someone who for a brief time attended services at this church, and he claims to be every bit a believer in the occult. Charlie Imorde says he experienced a rebellious phase in his twenties when he broke with the family's strong Catholic tradition and dabbled in various other religions, including Christian Science. He came from a family of grocers who for decades ran a small store at the northeast corner of Third and Ormsby – directly adjacent to the First Church of Christ, Scientist – and he frequently found himself sneaking away to listen to readings there. Within a year, however, he had decided that the teachings of Mary Baker Eddy didn't suit his preconceived notions of religion. He quickly moved on to a six-month period when he regularly attended synagogue downtown, however, not before he had an unsettling encounter with the phantom on the steps of the church.

"My uncle was always telling us stories of a strange woman in white he used to see walking up and down those steps late at night, but we all just teased him and told him he was crazy. He was old-world Italian, and very superstitious. Nobody else had ever said anything about a ghost, so we just figured he was a little cuckoo in the caboose." Charlie soon realized he might have judged his uncle too quickly. Late one spring evening he stood on the steps in front of the church, heatedly discussing politics with another young man after their weekly reading group had let out. A warm wind blew softly across the steps, and a cold chill suddenly ran down his spine.

"All of a sudden I stopped talking because I got this creepy feeling," he recalls. "We just stood there, and then out of nowhere this lady came walking towards us. But she wasn't any normal kind of lady, I tell you, she was all white, and you could see right through her." Charlie and his friend stood transfixed as the shadowy figure in white slowly approached them, and then walked right through them. "It was like she didn't even see us. She just kept coming and walked right through the both of us till she got to the other side of the steps and then just disappeared into thin air. It was the creepiest thing I had ever witnessed. And the worst part was, when she passed through us, we turned cold as ice, just as if we were standing in a winter wind."

Needless to say, that ended their argument over politics. The two quickly said their goodbyes, and Charlie ran back across the street to the family shop. "My uncle was restocking the shelves, and I just had to tell him what had happened. When I told him, he just laughed and asked if I still thought he was crazy, and he wouldn't go on until I apologized. He was like that, very proud and stubborn, and I guess I had really offended him. Well, I didn't have any problems with it, so I went ahead and said that I was sorry, and then we talked about what he had seen before." Just as the old man had said on many occasions, he had seen the same apparition of a beautiful young woman on the steps to the church, in the evening and usually around 8 or 9. Charlie looked at his watch. In five minutes it would be 8.

"He described the exact same woman that I had seen – to a tee. Hair, eyes, dress, even the way she seemed to float along instead of walk. It all matched what I described to him. The only thing was, he didn't know exactly who the woman was, or any details about her, just that she was waiting for someone. Well, I shouldn't say he didn't know anything about her, because he did have a couple interesting tidbits." According to his uncle, Charlie learned that the young woman had suffered the tragic loss of a lover, and that she too had died soon after, leaving only her spirit to pace the steps of the old church at the corner of Third and Ormsby. Although the uncle had no first-hand information about the sad love story, he claimed to know someone who did, and he promised his nephew he'd have the old gentleman tell his story the next time he stopped in at the grocery.

Charlie didn't have to wait very long, because the old man just happened to pay a visit the very next day. Charlie recognized him as one of the regulars and had grown used to seeing him all over the neighborhood, but he knew little else of the man, other than his friends used to call him "Red" because of his fiery auburn hair. Even though he had just turned 90, his hair had changed little with age, and despite his years, he still managed to stay active and get around the neighborhood. Charlie's family had a special fondness for the old man because he had worked for them at the counter. Apart from the family itself, Red knew as much as anyone about the grocery business and had been privy to most all of the goings-on in the family store. When the young man realized his uncle had been talking about Red, he quickly approached the old guy and soon had him sharing his own stories about the phantom woman on the church steps.

"Red had worked for my family for at least fifteen or twenty years, and he was real popular with the regulars. And he knew practically everyone in town, it seemed. A lot of people used to stop in just to say hello and have a chat with him, since he was so personable. That's where the mysterious woman comes in, see?" Although he didn't know the young lady's name, Red explained that locals used to call her 'Miss G' since she was somehow related to the Gathright family up the street. "He wasn't quite sure what her story was, but she was a relative or something and she was staying with them. He had heard that it was because she had a suitor who didn't meet with her parents' approval, and their way of dealing with it was to ship her off to a relative's." She made it a habit to stop in for a soda late in the evenings, and Red had grown used to – and truth be told, even looked forward to – her visits since she had the reputation for being quite a beauty. People often commented on her stunning jet-black hair, piercing yet demur dark eyes and ivory skin.

"The only thing Red mentioned that could be a negative was that she didn't come across as the most-friendly of sorts. Extremely lovely, yes, but not the outgoing type, I guess you'd say."

Given that she had an admirer already, Red conceded to the man that when he looked back on it all, the young lady probably didn't intend to be unfriendly or anything. "Times were really different back then, that's for sure, and respectable women had to act a certain way. If she had acted too nice and friendly, people might have said she was a floozy or something, and this was before the flappers and the Roaring Twenties, so people still had a very strong Victorian upbringing. I think Red was probably interested in her a little, too, and that might have been a way to put a little distance between them on her behalf. Like he said, she already had a boyfriend, so she probably wanted other guys to know she wasn't available."

Even though time had clouded some of his memory, Red could still place the time at 1918 or 1919. The Great War had just ended, and optimism filled the air. Granted, the United States had only participated in the last year of WWI, but a sense of national pride and accomplishment pervaded the country nonetheless. As with most other cities across the land, a patriotic fervor gripped Louisville, and men in uniform seemed to be especially popular. No wonder then that the young Miss G had become enamored of a dashing soldier who she met at a party in Bardstown. Barely a year out of high school, he had enlisted and planned on fighting in the Ardennes. Tall and handsome, observers described him as the perfect complement to the grace and beauty of the black-eyed woman he had fallen in love with. The two, it appeared, planned to settle down and marry after a period of courtship that would allow the gentleman to establish himself and put aside some money for his bride.

Fate, on the other hand, apparently had different plans for the couple. The young girl's parents had already chosen a husband for her, someone they thought more befitting of her social and economic standing. The oldest son and heir of a wealthy distilling family in Bardstown, the young gentlemen had one semester left at a prestigious university on the East Coast before he would return to Louisville and claim his betrothed. When the young lady's father and mother realized her emotions would not be so easily managed, they sent her away to Louisville, to live with wealthy relatives who happened to be friends of the family they wanted their daughter to marry into.

Unbeknownst to her parents, however, Miss G's handsome young suitor was stationed at nearby Camp Zachary Taylor. During WWI, this was the largest army camp in North America, with over 45,000 people there, and one of their most famous recruits was F. Scott Fitzgerald, who during his time in Louisville became inspired to write *The Great Gatsby*. Fortuitously enough, only a couple miles distance now separated the two lovers. And even though her relatives kept a close watch, as had been requested by her parents, Miss G hardly considered them tyrants. True, when she called on friends or attended concerts or plays, a chaperon always accompanied her, but they always allowed her an unsupervised evening constitutional stroll up and down "The Street" if she wished. This half hour of liberty she received every night soon evolved into regular rendezvous with her young army suitor.

According to some oral accounts, Miss G's suitor was one of the soldiers in this unit at Camp Zachary Taylor. (Courtesy of the Library of Congress, LC-USZ62-63662)

Red remembers that many people in the neighborhood realized the young woman was using this time to secretly meet her boyfriend, but most felt sympathy for her and said nothing about the affair. Some even went so far as to cover for her when her relatives became suspicious and inquired about her whereabouts. By all accounts, public opinion sided with the young soldier and the beautiful young woman he hoped to make his bride.

"Red said they used to meet practically every night right across the street where the First Church of Christ, Scientist was being built. They had laid the cornerstone the year before that, and it took them almost ten years to complete it, so there wasn't much there at the time. But they did have the foundations laid, and since it sat on a raised parcel of land, there were some hidden little nooks and crannies where they could sneak away and not be seen, I guess." For several weeks it went on like that. Red got used to seeing the young woman practically every night he was in the store. "She'd come in, order a soda, pay for it, and then leave to go meet up with her boyfriend."

One night, however, the young woman appeared visibly distressed when she left the store. She returned fifteen or twenty minutes later and asked Red if anyone had entered the grocery looking for her. When he replied that nobody had enquired after her, she lowered her head and made for the street. When Red closed up shop and walked to his own small house a half-mile away, he noticed that Miss G still stood at the top of the stairs. Waiting in the freezing night air as the wind whipped about her, she had little more than a thin satin shawl to guard against the cold. From her white skin, it appeared that she had already been chilled to the bone.

The next night the very same thing happened. She showed up at her normal time, looked around, and disappeared. A short time later, she returned and asked if someone had been looking for her. By then Red had heard through the grapevine that the two had made plans to elope because the young beauty's parents had discovered their secret meetings. They now planned on shipping their daughter off to stay with relatives in Saint Louis until the wedding, which was planned for her in the spring. Realizing the inherent difficulty in overcoming a separation of this magnitude, the young couple decided to elope and stay with relatives of his in Chicago while they dealt with her parents' anger and disapproval. He, after all, had very good prospects for the future and came from an upstanding family. Their plan had been to rendezvous at their usual spot and time, get a ride to the train station and then take a night train to Chicago where they could get married as they wished.

For another several nights, the same scenario played out in the small grocery at the corner of Third and Ormsby. The young lady would come in, leave, and then return a short time later looking for her beau. She hardly said a word and appeared highly agitated. The next afternoon as Red restocked shelves in the front of the store, he spotted a young servant girl who worked for one of the families living next to the Gathright house. He approached her, one of his best sources for neighborhood gossip, and asked if she had any word about the planned elopement that had generated such a curious buzz among busybodies in the back parlors and kitchens along Millionaires Row.

She seemed almost dumbstruck when he asked the question of her. "Haven't you heard?" she stammered, her eyes wide in amazement. Noting his confusion, she went on to tell more of what she knew. According to the young maid, there was a glitch with the couple's plans to elope the night they were supposed to meet. The soldier, as it turned out, never showed up that first night to take away his bride to be because he had been overcome with a terrible illness and lay on a cot in his barracks, delirious with fever. "He knew Miss G was waiting for him, and he tried to get dressed and leave to go and see her," explained the maid. "But he and a number of others in the barracks were so ill that they put them in quarantine." Knowing that his fiancé was waiting for him, the young soldier had even taken his suitcase and broken out a window so he could leave, but the person in charge stopped him and had him strapped to the bed so he couldn't escape. When the soldier tried to explain that he had to go and meet his girlfriend, no one could understand him in his disorientation, and word about what had happened never got back to the waiting woman. "Miss G just stood there and waited there all night, in the cold night air," said the maid, "and then finally she gave up and went home, thinking that she had been jilted."

Then came the tragic news Red had been expecting. "The poor soldier died the next day." But he wasn't anticipating the next part of the story. "And the worst part is, Miss G contracted the flu as well," said the young servant girl. "And she died the day after. Young Miss G and her handsome soldier are dead – both of them." The maid became more upset and between sobs revealed that the funerals had been planned for that very day. When Red claimed that to be impossible, since he had seen Miss G just the night before, the servant could only look at him and shake her head in horror. "Oh, no," she sobbed, "they died a couple of days ago. Both of them taken by the flu." That's when Red realized the two lovers would be going to their graves without ever knowing what happened to the other.

1918, for those who don't know, saw one of the worst influenza epidemics in the history of the United States. As the plague-like fever swept across the nation, few cities could withstand the tragedy and human devastation at hand. Louisville, like so many other cities of its

DICKSON.—On Saturday, Dec. 7, at Camp Zachary Taylor, Louisville, Ky., of pneumonia, Herbert Fullerton Dickson, aged 18 years, son of the late Howard and Almira Fullerton Dickson and ward of John Van Nostrand Dorr. Services at Winchester, Mass.

One of the sources interviewed for the story about Old Louisville's famous Lady of the Stairs has identified the young soldier in question as "being a Dickson from out east." This obituary from The New York Times *proves that a soldier with the last name of Dickson died of the flu around the time that matches up with the story, but other than this, no substantiation has been located that proves the existence of the young soldier or Miss G.*

size, lost hundreds of inhabitants to the flu. Reports say some four hundred souls succumbed to the illness in the city itself, and at nearby Camp Zachary Taylor over eight hundred enlisted men perished, the handsome young soldier who had courted Miss G. among them. On the night of their planned elopement, he lay overwhelmed by fever on a standard army cot only a couple miles from where his beloved waited dutifully in the freezing night air. Already chilled to the bone and overcome with anguish when she finally returned home several hours later, she quickly fell victim to the flu and took to her bed. As Red suspected, they both died without knowing the fate of the other.

Don now feels he has an answer to the mysterious riddle of the Lady of the Stairs. Although he no longer works at the Filson Historical Society, he admits to often craning his neck in front of the First Church of Christ, Scientist when he travels up Third Street to his new job at the University of Louisville. He figures he must have passed it hundreds of times in the evening already, and to this day he has yet to have another encounter with Old Louisville's legendary Lady of the Stairs.

GENERAL VIEW OF CAMP, AS SEEN FROM OVERHEAD BRIDGE.

Above: Postmarked October 29, 1918, a postcard depicts a daytime scene at Camp Zachary Taylor. The fall of 1918 saw the first outbreak of influenza at the camp. Below: Another view of Camp Zachary Taylor

STREET SCENE SHOWING LOCATION OF COMPANY BARRACKS.

U. S. NATIONAL ARMY CANTONMENT, CAMP ZACHARY TAYLOR, LOUISVILLE, KY.

Located across the street from the First Church of Christ, Scientist, the Filson Historical Society is housed in the 1905 Ferguson Mansion. The Beaux Arts structure is reportedly haunted by a book-throwing poltergeist named Sally.

Chapter 15 – Seven Ghosts, One House

One of the major thoroughfares in Old Louisville, Saint Catherine Street unfortunately lost much of its original residential charm in the years following World War II when an interstate highway sliced its way south from the downtown and destroyed scores of beautiful old homes. The stretch of street running west from Third to Sixth Streets has remained largely unchanged and affords visitors several picture-perfect vistas of the best Old Louisville has to offer. From west to east, two rows of tidy brick townhouses frame the lacy façade of the Methodist Church, a Victorian masterpiece built of limestone and brick in 1884. Looking back to the west one can see the spires of Saint Louis Bertrand Catholic Church, another Old Louisville landmark of stone and brick erected in 1869.

The street had gained such a favorable reputation as a comfortable residential enclave that by the late 1880s many of the master craftsmen and designers employed to work on the more prestigious mansions on Third, Fourth and Ormsby Avenues decided to construct their own homes there. Several famous architects of the time even made their homes on West Saint Catherine. Kenneth McDonald lived at 514, for example, and L. Pike Campbell lived at 517. Another one, Cornelius A. Curtin, built a large house for his family in 1885, one supposedly influenced by a large manor house he remembered from his childhood in Ireland. A solid three-story structure built of red brick with attractive stone trim and a unique wooden exterior pocket door, it still stands at 539 West Saint Catherine Street today. Although the years have obscured much of the history about the house at 539 West Saint Catherine Street, Jon Huffman and Barb Cullen believe these basic facts about their home and neighborhood to be true.

Barb and Jon purchased the 3,800-square-foot house in 2000 and set out to make it their home. Like many transplants to Old Louisville, the two had started with a smaller house and – after succumbing to the area's charm – decided to buy one of the grander homes in need of some attention. Not only would the house at 539 West Saint Catherine serve as a comfortable home where they could entertain their many friends and family members, it would also be a place they could ply their trades. Barb, a choreographer and dancer, could give lessons from a room she used as a studio, and Jon, an actor and screenwriter, could do his work from the home office on an upper floor. After some repairs and remodeling, they would move in and set up house. Little did they know that they would not be the only residents in their lovely brick home.

539 West St. Catherine Street – a house with more than one ghost?

Self-proclaimed skeptics of anything dealing with the paranormal, Jon and Barb never expected that they would one day come to believe their own house was haunted. They had heard plenty of local ghost stories and legends, but they always seemed, nonetheless, a bit far-fetched to their sensibilities. The idea of an otherworldly entity in their own house had never even entered their minds when they finally moved in. When items in their new house started disappearing and reappearing in strange locations, and when they heard loud, unexplained crashes, they chalked it up to overactive imaginations and nothing else. In addition, workers still hadn't finished the final touches on the interior, so it seemed that someone could always be blamed for the frequent loud crashes and strange noises.

One evening the two found themselves at home when the sound of shattering glass echoed somewhere in the house. Jon ran into the kitchen, and, seeing that Barb wore the same shocked look on her face, asked her if she had heard something. Nervously, they both searched the house, realizing that for the first time since they had moved in, they were truly alone. Finding nothing, they both agreed it had sounded like a large light fixture or chandelier falling from the ceiling and crashing to the floor. From that point forward, the two started to take more notice of the sounds in the house around them; however, the reoccurring, unexplainable rattling of glasses clinking together or the faintly audible moans and shouts they repeatedly heard hardly made them think they had disembodied spirits in their home. That didn't happen till they experienced more than just sounds.

Jon and Barb can each recall one distinct incident that stopped them both cold in their tracks at the realization that some paranormal activity might be at play at 539 West Saint Catherine. For Jon, the incident was a rather simple, albeit unnerving, one. He had just walked in from a morning of errands and placed a bag of fresh bagels from a corner bakery on a counter in the kitchen. He hung up his jacket, put away his keys and ran up to his office to get in a couple hours of work before lunch. When one o'clock rolled around, he went back down to the kitchen for a quick bite. Opening the door to the refrigerator, he sensed something wasn't quite right. Looking back over his shoulder, he realized someone had removed the bag of bagels from the counter. Scratching his head, he searched the kitchen from top to bottom but found nothing. He even returned to the car in the driveway, hoping that he had merely forgotten and left them inside, but still no bagels.

"For a half hour I searched up and down, and I just couldn't find that bag of bagels," he recalls. "I thought I had imagined the whole thing." Jon fixed himself a fast lunch, ate while he watched the news on

TV, and then ran back upstairs to finish his work. He busied himself in his office for a couple of hours and then decided to take a quick bathroom break and call it a day. Walking down the hall to the bathroom, he never expected the sight that awaited him in the bathroom. Jon pushed open the door, and there, in the middle of the white, tiled floor, he spied the six bagels that had gone missing. Now out of the white paper bakery bag he had carried them in, they had been stacked neatly one atop the other to form a little column of bread that stood perfectly straight before him.

"It was so creepy," he remembers, "all I could do was stand there and stare. It was obvious that someone had done this, and I started to think for the first time that something supernatural might be going on in our house."

Barb says those same thoughts ran through her head one day when she walked into her dance studio after a quick trip to the kitchen. Alone in the house, she had just given a dance lesson and wanted to tidy up a bit before her next pupil arrived. "I remember it very well," she explains, "because I had just picked up a small picture book and jump rope I keep in the studio for some of the younger kids and put it back in its spot under the TV. I was sort of irritated because I was always finding them in the middle of the floor and putting them back." When she went back into the studio, she froze, because the jump rope and book she had just placed under the TV once again lay in the middle of the floor. "That's when it hit me that something or someone was playing with me."

Whatever had caught Jon and Barb's attention this way seemed to them to be of a very mischievous nature, almost childlike or juvenile, and for this reason they claim they never really felt afraid or threatened – at first. "For the most part, it was little things like the book and jump rope moving around and stuff, and things disappearing. And it seemed that it happened most on the bottom floor, like in the kitchen and the studio," says Barb, adding that she even started to get a feel for it and knew when to expect its antics. "I finally realized that most of the stuff happened when I was in the kitchen, cleaning, or right afterwards. It was strange. I noticed at other times weird things would happen after children had come to the house."

Another incident that caught Jon off guard and really gave him the "creeps" happened one day while he sat at his writing table on a cool fall evening in October. He had just come in from an afternoon with Barb strolling around the neighborhood and admiring the brilliant fall foliage and needed to take care of some matters at his desk. Barb had run to the grocery to get a few items for dinner, and he hoped that they'd have the time to catch a movie afterwards. Somewhat thirsty after his long walk,

Jon decided to run to the kitchen for a cold drink. A minute or two later, he returned and stopped dead in his tracks as he approached the writing table. There, in the middle of the table, stood the pencil Jon had just put down. However, as he explains, "it was *literally* standing there, upright and perfectly straight, balancing on the eraser end." Although he admits that this stunt raised the hair on the back of his neck, he had to chuckle in spite of himself because he got the definite impression that someone had played a joke on him.

When the couple found themselves on the second floor, however, they got a completely different vibe, and according to Jon, it wasn't a good one. "There was a large linen closet across from the bedroom on the second floor, and we never really felt comfortable around it," he explains. A plant lover with a huge green thumb, Jon first sensed this when he started to notice that perfectly healthy houseplants he had placed near the window in the linen closet had the unfortunate tendency of dying there, sometimes overnight. All over the house, plants thrived and flourished, but in this one room, he couldn't manage to keep anything alive, no matter how hard he tried. "It was puzzling, that's for sure. That closet really started to worry me when I noticed the animals acting strange around it," adds Barb.

Barb and Jon have three pets – two cats and one dog – and they noticed right after moving in that their companions displayed a clear aversion to the linen closet. "You couldn't make them go inside," explains Barb, "no matter how hard you tried. They hated it. They even hated walking past it in the hallway." Rocky, their lovable dog, had even been seen to pivot his entire body as he passed the doorway so as to keep the interior of the closet in sight at all times, a low growl in his throat as he did so. The couple's two cats – the best of friends before the move to 539 West Saint Catherine – seemed to act strange around it as well, and according to Barb, she often heard them hissing and screeching at each other, something that had never happened before. All three of them seemed to get spooked now and then in the bottom part of the residence as well, but it didn't compare to the reactions they showed when they were near the second-floor linen closet.

As the accounts of the strange occurrences spread among their friends and family, someone suggested that Jon and Barb call in a psychic or medium to get a reading of the house. Still skeptical of all things paranormal, they hesitated at first, but acquiesced after some friends went ahead and scheduled a psychic visit without telling them. "She had a good reputation," says Barb, "and by the time they told us she was coming, it was too late anyway. She was coming the next evening." It was a cold January night, and the skeptical homeowners at 539 West

Saint Catherine could not have anticipated the shock they would soon receive.

The following evening the doorbell rang at 8 sharp. Barb answered the door and showed the visitor in, impressed both by her neat appearance and self-assurance. A lively woman in her 40s named Cheryl, she had come to do a "cold reading" where no prior information whatsoever about the house or the strange events had been given. They all said their hellos, and Cheryl then got down to work. Standing in the inviting foyer, she took a long look around her and seemed to admire the surroundings – a huge oak staircase, lovely sliding pocket doors and delicate inlay in the gleaming hardwood floors. After several moments of silence, the psychic turned her attention back to Barb and Jon and asked a question. "What was going on here last week that brought so many children together?"

Dumbfounded at first, the couple didn't know how to respond since they hadn't anticipated that type of question. When Cheryl rephrased the question, they realized she had to be asking about a party they had thrown on the first of January. Over the years Barb and Jon had always thrown a large New Year's Day party at their house for family and friends, and it had become an annual tradition that carried over to the new house on West Saint Catherine. As usual, a lot of children had been present at the latest gathering. When Barb shared this information with the psychic, she gave a simple reply: "Oh. That's why the little girl who lingers here was so happy."

The couple exchanged nervous glances and intently watched the psychic, who slowly closed her eyes, took a long, deep breath, and raised a hand to her neck. As if sensing the unspoken question that hung on their lips *What little girl?* she went on and told them she had made contact with a young girl who had lived in the house many years ago. Her parents had named her Rose, and she was eleven years old. She had red hair and blue eyes, and she loved to play, especially with other children her age. Cheryl informed them that when the house was full of kids the week before, the little girl was so happy to have someone to play with.

As they listened, Jon and Barb both realized that a fine rash of goose flesh had broken out over their bodies. "Jon," Barb said, in a hushed but excited voice. "The pictures! The pictures from the party!" Barb wanted to run to a nearby drawer and pull out the pictures from the last few parties they had thrown in the house, but the psychic calmly raised a hand with the palm facing out to let them know she needed silence and stillness. Barb stopped and stayed where she was, deciding she could get the photos after the lady had finished her reading, even though the suspense was unbearable. Jon's eyes widened as he realized what pictures she wanted to see. Although he had originally convinced himself that a paranormal investigation of any sort would be a waste of time, he now realized they needed to take this woman seriously.

Jon and Barb followed as Cheryl circled the foyer in a trance-like state and made her way to the parlor and then the dining room, making brief utterances now and then as she "received" information. In the dining room, she slowed her pace and cocked her head while the faintest hint of a smile spread across her face. "Yes, she likes to play, all right," remarked the psychic. Barb looked at Jon, and then they both looked under the television set in the corner of the room. The jump rope and picture book were still in place. Cheryl made for the door, but paused for a moment while she furrowed her eyebrows and appeared to listen while an unheard voice plied her with information. "She loves your pets and doesn't mean to scare them, she just wants to play with them," she commented. "Rose says she'll try not to scare them next time." Cheryl swept past Jon and Barb, unaware of the stunned looks on their faces, and entered the hallway leading into the kitchen.

She crossed the threshold into the kitchen and once again slowly canvassed the room in a relaxed, almost dreamlike state while getting a feel for the space and picking up whatever signals or vibes came her way. She stopped at the narrow stairs leading to the next floor and took a step, but then hesitated and stopped. She seemed to shake her head and back away, heading instead to the counter on the other side of the room. Stopping in front of the sink, the hand around her neck seemed to tighten, and her breath appeared to become shallow and labored. "Oh. It was *so hard* for her to breathe." Cheryl now wore a pained look on her face, and sadness could be heard in her voice. "She was a very sick little girl. There was something wrong with her lungs. Probably tuberculosis." She paused a moment, and seemed to concentrate before looking in Barb's direction. "She doesn't like it when you clean the sink. She says the cleaner you use hurts her lungs." Dumbfounded, Barb watched as the psychic opened her eyes and appeared to come out of her trance-like condition. "That's all I get from her. Rose is gone for now," she said, and then walked back down the hall to the foyer at the front of the house.

Barb and Jon followed, silently pondering the revelations they had just heard. Like so many residents in the area, they hailed from somewhere other than Louisville – Barb, from Cincinnati, and Jon, from North Carolina – and considered Louisville their *new* hometown. They had both spent half their lives in the Derby City, and this being the case, they had both heard many stories about the infamous TB sanatorium at nearby Waverly Hills, supposedly one of the, if not *the*, most haunted locations in the United States. Thousands of men, women and children died there in the first years alone after it was built in 1926. Jon wondered to himself if Rose had been one of those unfortunate victims and started to form a mental image of her in his mind. He could see a small child in an old-fashioned, summery dress, frail perhaps, but cheerful, her long red hair done up in ribbons.

Cheryl had reached the foyer and started to ascend the stairs to the second floor. When she reached the landing, she paused and looked back down over the entry hall, apparently resuming her trance. She cocked her head and listened to something unseen while Barb and Jon looked on. They had assumed the woman had completed her psychic investigation and hadn't expected her to continue her way through the house. Cheryl mounted the remaining flight of stairs to the floor above and informed the two of them that she had made contact with another spirit, that of an elderly lady who had lived in the house. Once again Barb and Jon exchanged glances. They hadn't bargained on *two* ghosts in their house.

Cheryl mentioned that the old woman moved around a lot inside the house, and that she frequently went in and out as well. "She's telling me something was not right with her medication," the psychic informed them. It seems that the unhappy woman suspected her grandson of changing pills around in her prescription bottles, or even poisoning her, because he wanted the old woman out of the picture. Her suspicions rose when she started to notice that various heirlooms and valuable antiques began disappearing. Once again, Jon and Barb exchanged surprised looks. They had both heard neighborhood stories about an old woman dying under mysterious circumstances, perhaps poisoned by her own grandson.

Cheryl continued her self-guided tour through the house, the two homeowners following in silence as she slowly and methodically made her way through one room after another. Every now and then she would stop and pause, her head turning as if she had heard something far off in the distance, her lips parting as if she wanted to speak, but then she would close her mouth and resume her wandering. A half hour later, they all stood together at the back of the hall on the second floor, still not a word having been spoken. Almost hesitant, Cheryl looked towards the only part of the house she hadn't visited – the linen closet – and then squinted her eyes before slowly making her way to the half-opened door. Although nothing had been said, Barb and Jon sensed that the psychic had deliberately avoided the small room until now. Trailing behind, they caught up with her as she stopped and pushed the door all the way open. She hesitated a minute and then cautiously stepped into the closet.

A small window on the back wall allowed a bit of light to shine in from the street, but other than that, there was no illumination. To the left, a shiny coat of beige paint shimmered softly on a smooth plaster wall. To the right, a tall bank of oak cupboards and drawers spanned the twelve feet of wall that rose from floor to ceiling. Enveloped in silence, Cheryl waited in the tiny space, unmoving and still. With Jon and Barb watching from the hallway, she lowered her head a bit and then twisted it to one side as if a loud noise had pierced her ears. She raised her head, turned and quickly exited the room with a shudder. Half way down the corridor, she stopped and turned to face the couple she had left standing outside the door.

"There are five *entities* in that room," she informed them, "and I'm getting some *very* negative vibes from them." She pivoted and then bolted down the stairs to the foyer. Glancing over her shoulder she added, "They're extremely hostile. I've asked them to leave, but they won't." Barb and Jon both cast a quick glimpse in the direction of the linen closet, and then bolted down the stairs after her. They found the psychic below, visibly shaken but in the process of regaining her composure.

Jon sat on the bottom stair and considered the situation. By the latest count he and his partner had seven disembodied spirits to contend with, and truth be told, he wasn't quite sure what one did in a situation like this, especially since he had gone from skeptic to believer in a matter of minutes. He looked at Barb, who in turn looked at Cheryl. "So, what should we do?" she inquired. The psychic studied the two of them for a moment and gave them a measured response.

"The energy in that room is very negative," she explained with a serious look. "It's very dark and very overpowering. I've never encountered such an overwhelming sense of animosity and anger before. You walk in and it's black and stifling, and it's like they're brooding about something. I've never had to deal with that before." As she spoke, her tone remained steady and severe, and she never took her eyes off of them. "They're very stubborn, as well," she added with a slight sigh. She relaxed a bit and then waited for them to speak.

The two, in turn, just stared at each other, but Jon did manage a feeble shrug of the shoulders in response. Still overwhelmed by the revelation of these new cohabitants, he found himself at a loss for words. Barb, torn between feelings of anxiety and dread at the sinister nature of the forces in her linen closet and a sense of relief because they had at least put a face – so to speak – on the powers responsible for the disturbances in their house, asked the psychic if they needed to worry about the entities *leaving* the small confines of the closet. She had the very distinct impression that they gravitated to that area for some reason and didn't bother with other areas of the house.

Cheryl informed them that they could say prayers and let the entities know that they could freely "leave" this realm if they so desired, but other than that, she could only offer one suggestion to keep the spirits at bay. And that was to get a potted sage plant and place it in the doorway to the linen closet. This would ensure that the negative energy stayed within the small space of the closet. Sage, she informed them, was a mystical plant with cleansing powers that had been used by many cultures throughout the centuries for rituals involving purification and exorcism. Sort of in the way garlic was rumored to ward off vampires, sage, especially when burned as incense, had the power to tame negative forms of energy.

"For some reason I don't get the impression they want to leave that space," she explained. "They're mad about something and don't want to come out. But if they *were* to leave that closet for some reason and enter other areas of your home, it wouldn't be a pretty sight. You'd have a real problem on your hands then." Observing the look of concern on their faces, Cheryl added: "Just put a sage plant in the doorway and you'll be fine." Realizing she hadn't quite assuaged their fears, the psychic quickly tried to change the subject from the five malevolent powers upstairs to the two kinder beings on the ground floor. "The old woman and the little girl down here are very happy," she added. "They feel very much at home, and they want you to feel that way, too. The little girl's presence is especially strong."

With a bit of a jolt, Jon suddenly regained his speech and looked at Barb. "Show her the pictures from the New Year's Day parties," he insisted. Without a word, Barb ran to a nearby drawer and returned with several stacks of 35mm color prints. As she rummaged through the bundle, Jon repeated the information he had shared earlier about their annual get-together on January 1, pointing out that something strange started to happen after they moved into 539 West Saint Catherine. "Look," Barb said, handing Cheryl one stack of photos, then another. "Remember what you said about the little girl liking the fact that she had so many children to play with? Look at these."

With Jon and Barb looking on, the psychic slowly sifted through both files of prints, a smile forming on her lips as she stared at the last of the pictures. "How unusual," she remarked, as she lay the two stacks down and then started to go through the first, and then the second. "As I said, Rose has a very strong presence here, and I think these photos make this quite clear. These pictures are from the first year you had this party in the house?" she inquired, setting the first pile down so she could devote her attention to the second pile in front of her.

"That's the thing," interjected Jon with an energetic nod of the head, "those are from two years in a row now! Every time we have the New Year's Day party here it happens. The first year it happened, we just thought there was something wrong with the film or the camera, but when it happened the second year, we started to wonder. We didn't really put two and two together till you made that comment about Rose liking all the kids in the house." He took a step towards her and started to sift through the photos himself.

One by one, he laid the pictures from the first stack down on the small table in the foyer, spreading them out as he did so. One had a young couple posed in front of a lovely carved wooden mantel draped in garland and ribbon; the next showed a middle-aged man with specs pushed down on his nose as he lifted a cup of holiday punch in a toast; another had several elderly adults sitting around the counter in the kitchen. All in all, nothing out of the ordinary could be seen, just random faces and bodies, groups of coworkers and friends, neighbors and couples, all in festive surroundings.

With the next stack of pictures, Jon started to sift through and spread them out on the wooden surface so they could all see; there was something different about these. One by one, he picked out a color print, held it up for examination and then put it down. In each one, it became obvious that a child or children had been the subject matter for the photographer. In some of them, children could be seen playing together on the throw rug in front of the cozy fireplace in the front parlor, or else darting around among the adults gathered in the kitchen. Some of the other photos showed individual infants, or smiling little boys or girls sitting on a parent's knee, posed in groups, standing next to the Christmas tree, or eating cookies.

Aside from the children present in each of the pictures, they all had something in common: oddities in the photos that appeared to be bright flashes of orange light, hazy yellow blurs and streaks of something small that seem to have been moving at speeds too high to be caught on ordinary film. When the two stacks are compared side by side, it becomes obvious that these anomalies can be seen in the pictures of little boys and girls only. In the pictures of the adults alone, not one of these strange manifestations can be observed. Only in cases where adults *and* children are present in the pictures can you spot these strange occurrences.

Two experts – one a photographic specialist, the other, an old hand in the investigation of psychic phenomena captured on film – have examined the original pictures and negatives from Jon and Barb's holiday parties, and both have come to the same conclusion. They cannot

Taken at Jon and Barb's annual New Year's Day party, this is one of many photographs displaying anomalies when children were present at 539 West Saint Catherine Street.

explain what caused the strange appearances in those pictures. Although one or two of the photos with the blinding yellow-orange flashes could technically be attributed to overexposure, the others definitely fall into that small category of rare, unexplained activity that paranormal investigators hope to catch on film when doing research of reputedly haunted houses. Theories abound as to what could possibly account for these odd blurs and streaks of light, but most specialists in the field claim that bona fide psychic events almost always involve a huge output of latent energy, something usually indiscernible to the human eye, yet susceptible to the magnetic properties of ordinary 35mm film.

Jon and Barb don't really care what scientific reasons might explain the weird lights and streaky blurs they caught on film. The strange pictures, coupled with the eerie revelations Cheryl made about the little girl named Rose, seemed to convince them that they live in a haunted house, something they wear as a badge of honor in their neighborhood.

As a matter of fact, Barb has confessed that she sometimes feels comforted, sensing that the spirits on the first floor want to protect her. She recalls one snowy evening in winter when quiet sobs and low moans from somewhere in the house caused her to get up and check the house. In the process she startled and scared off a would-be intruder at her back door. "I was frightened at first," she admits, "but when I realized that he might have come into the house if I hadn't gone looking for those strange moans, a sense of calm overcame me, because I had the feeling the old woman was trying to warn me about the danger."

Barb doesn't have the same positive outlook regarding the five entities in the linen closet on the second floor, however. She took the psychic's advice and placed a potted sage plant on the floor in the doorway of the small room, and since then, she and Jon haven't had any problems with it – or them. Their animals still seemed to be wary of that area, but the sense of uneasiness associated with the closet dissipated noticeably after Cheryl's visit. Once in a while, both Barb and Jon find themselves staring at the linen closet on the second floor, their uneasy sense of relief tempered with anxiety at the notion of what would happen should their efforts fail to keep the malevolent entities contained in the linen closet. Jon says they enter the small storage room as little as possible and that they make sure the sage is in its spot on the floor at all times. Barb keeps a spare pot in the kitchen, should something happen to the original plant they placed there.

On January 1, 2004, I attended Jon and Barb's annual New Year's Day party at 539 West Saint Catherine. Decorated with garland, colorful ribbons and festive lights, the interior of the house was cozy and inviting, despite the lively throng of guests wandering from room to room. Some nibbled on smoked salmon and cream cheese atop toast points, some demurely sipped champagne, others gulped cups of holiday punch; most everyone talked about the ghosts and wondered if this year's batch of pictures would produce more of the same strange streaks and blurs as in the previous years. With a 35mm camera around my neck, and a smaller, disposable one at my side, I wandered from room to room as well, snapping pictures between sips of red wine – all the while convinced that I would capture something on film.

While meandering about on the ground floor, I chit-chatted here, stopped for a bit of small talk there, all the while making sure to get shots of adults by themselves, children alone, and adults and kids together. I even devoted an entire roll of 36 exposures to the infamous linen closet on the second floor, mentally provoking the five entities as I boldly crossed the threshold and defied them to manifest themselves. For good measure, I also pounded on the wall and irreverently slammed one of the cupboard doors shut, hoping this might anger them and give them more reason to brood. (And, when no one was looking, I moved the potted herb off to one side and snapped a couple of daring shots *sans sage*.) I couldn't wait to get them developed. I thanked the hosts, finished my glass of wine and ran off to the one-hour photo place.

As was often the case, the one-hour photo service advertised actually turned out to be twenty-seven hour photo service, and I had to wait till the next evening before I could take a gander at the pictures from the party. One by one, I quickly scanned through each of the photos from the four rolls of film that had been developed. I'm sure the crestfallen look that had overcome me by the time I rifled through the last of the pictures and found absolutely nothing – for the second time – would have been priceless had anyone been present to take my picture, but other than that, it had been a waste of time and money. The party itself was enjoyable, but the pictures were a flop. As consolation, I asked if any of the other photographers present had captured anything, but as far as I know, no one had caught the slightest blur, blip or flash of light. Much to my chagrin, I had scared Rose away.

On a brighter note, I did have a strange occurrence regarding 539 West Saint Catherine several days after that. I had returned during the afternoon hours the next day to get some pictures of the exterior of the house and, in addition to some outside shots of Barb and Jon's house, I also took several photos of the neighboring houses, including one involved in the rumor about the old woman supposedly poisoned by her grandson. Some days later, I had the roll of film developed and found myself at my computer, nonchalantly perusing the pictures, looking for a good exterior shot to go along with this story, which appeared in my first book. I had them placed on a disk, and as I viewed the last of them, I was startled to find an old sepia print of what appeared to be a family portrait.

There in front of me, five unknown faces – four male, one female – stared back, their gazes severe and unmoving, as a creepy feeling spread over my body. A woman who could have been anywhere from twenty to forty years old sat on a lone chair with the four men standing behind her, their ages also in the twenty-to-forty-year range, I'd say. From the look of the hairstyles and outfits they wore, it appeared to be in the 1920s or 1930s, but other than that, it was hard to discern anything else concrete about the five somber figures assembled before me. From the dark hair, dark eyes and presumably olive-toned complexions that characterized each of their features, I got the impression that they were of Italian or Greek origin maybe, or definitely something Mediterranean. They had to be related, but I couldn't figure out the actual relationship – perhaps brothers and sister, or cousins? They all had heavy brows and almost brooding dispositions that made me think of the five entities in the linen closet.

Upon closer inspection I could see that the family portrait had frayed edges and a slight crack that wrinkled its way across the surface of the print. It looked like an old picture someone might have had restored, and somehow it ended up on my disk. I called the drug store where I had them developed and asked the manager of the photo desk about this possibility. He said he thought the chances were very slim – albeit not impossible – that something like that could happen. When I sent him a copy of the picture as an email attachment, he commented that he didn't recognize the picture and that, being the manager, he would have seen all restorations in the previous week.

The next strange thing happened when I was sorting through the pictures again, in search of a frontal shot for one of the neighboring houses to 539 West Saint Catherine. As I compared two photos, my eyes were drawn to the shadows in an upper right-hand window, and I realized I could discern several vague forms. Upon closer examination the photo revealed what appeared to be the shadowy figures of a young child leaning forward on the window sill and an old woman in a nightgown standing behind. The child appeared to be dressed in a shirt with a solid stripe across the chest, and the grandmotherly shape seemed to have her hair done up in a bun and had a hand resting on the child's shoulder. On the other shoulder rested another hand, however, from the angle and size, it appeared to belong to another, unseen, figure.

I tried a little experiment and showed that picture, along with several others, to about ten friends and asked if they could pick out anything odd about any of the shots. I made sure not to tell them what to look for, either. All ten were drawn to the photo where I had seen the strange figures in the shadows, and five of them quickly identified a child perched at the window ledge, and then, an older woman standing behind – and all without any prompting. The other five agreed they recognized the shapes after I pointed them out by tracing the edges with the tip of a pencil. For curiosity's sake, I had the picture enlarged, and printed in black and white as well. I was amazed to see that individual fingers and thumbs seemed visible on each of the hands, something that had gone unnoticed on the smaller prints. When most viewers study the enlargements, they usually point out the shapes of a young child and old woman right away. Whether or not these shapes come as nothing more than the coincidental result of odd shadows and reflections caught in the pane of glass, no one has told me. Nobody was able to say that they were lost spirits randomly caught on film, either. When I submitted the photos of the strange image caught in the window and the old family portrait with the five people to my publisher with the original manuscript, they didn't find the images interesting enough to print in the chapter about the house where Jon and Barb still live today. Of course, when I tried to locate the images ten years later so I could include them with this updated version of the story, the images were nowhere to be found, no doubt buried at the bottom of some box shuffled into oblivion during one of my subsequent moves. I have lots of witnesses who saw the images for themselves, however, and they'll attest to having seen them and having the same strange reaction I did when I first discovered them while writing this story back in 2004.

These two events relating to the pictures taken at 539 West Saint Catherine definitely made the story more interesting, although it was interesting enough as it was. Barb and Jon slowly accustomed themselves to the idea of living in a house with disembodied spirits and they claim it doesn't really bother them anymore. Although something strange and unexplained still happens from time to time, like the loud crash of breaking glass or quiet sobs emanating from somewhere in the house, they say the activity died down considerably after their last-minute visit from Cheryl. As time passes, Jon and Barb slowly dig up bits and pieces of the lives lived in 539 West Saint Catherine, but they have yet to uncover anything about a little girl with red hair named Rose, or any concrete details about the old woman whose grandson might have poisoned her, or any reasons why five brooding spirits might have a penchant for the confines of the linen closet on the second floor. Till then, they will wait patiently and see what they can unearth, always making sure the ceramic pot with the live sage plant is in its spot near the linen closet.

Chapter 16 – A Little Girl in a White Dress

Susan Shearer is part of that rare group of individuals that have decided to make a significant contribution to the preservation of American history. She – despite the inordinate amount of inconvenience, discomfort and expense – purchased a Victorian home in Old Louisville and dedicated all her money and energy to a historic structure that might have languished to nonexistence were it not for her passion for antiques. "I got my first antique years ago," she recalls, "and after I got my first piece, I was hooked." It seemed only natural, then, that she would purchase an antique home in which to house her collection of antiquities later on. Little did she know that the cozy 1891 Queen Anne house at 1439 South Sixth Street would come with its own odd assortment of paranormal occurrences.

Susan, an energetic insurance agent, says she purchased the house on a whim in 2003, after deciding to fulfill her lifelong dream of one day owning an old home with a fireplace. "I picked up the paper, and there wasn't anything interesting in the real estate section, so I decided to go and check out Old Louisville." She drove from her home in the south end of the city and found herself in front of the weathered frame structure that stood before her. White paint had started to peel away in strips, and it appeared that years had passed since a human hand had tended to the yard and front walkway. A compact, two-story structure, the dwelling had nonetheless retained much of its original charm despite the neglected appearance. An inviting porch welcomed visitors at the front door, and stained glass in a horseshoe-shaped window to the left and over the large picture window overlooking the yard hinted at the home's former grandeur. A picturesque turret at the roofline added an extra bit of enticement to the visage. Several weeks later, it belonged to her.

"I got a restoration loan," Susan explains, "and the bank had strict stipulations as to how much I would have to invest in the home's renovation. That's when the money started pouring out." The once grand lady had definitely seen better days, and Susan started to question her sanity as she took stock of the property she and her sister, Linda Gregory, had just acquired. "It had been divided into four apartments," she remembers, "and the back part of the building was actually crumbling apart." She knew a lot of hard work and patience would be required, but she had no idea just how much. A year later – just as her budget neared depletion – the house had been stabilized, and most of the major work like the replastering and the tearing down of walls that were added at a later date had been completed. "Then came the point where I

According to Susan Shearer, the ghost of a little girl in a white dress haunts her Sixth Street home.

could start decorating, and that was exciting," Susan says. "I couldn't wait to get started!"

The exterior now sports a fresh coat of paint that attractively accents the muted blues and creams that highlight the home's painted-lady charm, and all that remains is to put on the final touches. Susan doesn't think it will take much longer to return the quaint residence to its former splendor, and she feels fortunate that the old house has chosen her as its custodian. She also hopes that the ghost of the little girl on the stairs likes what they are doing to the place.

"I don't know if I was exaggerating at first," Susan says, "but odd things just kept happening, and I started to get the feeling that something was trying to let me know that I wasn't here alone. And I just couldn't explain it all away with coincidence. I could *sense* something." These feelings of unease had started to plague her months before the misty apparition of a young girl in a white dress showed itself on the front stairs. What started out as random strange noises and odd occurrences quickly established itself as a series of unexplainable events with a pattern. The first happenings that made Susan really take notice involved the strange knocks she would often hear at the front door. "Usually around dusk I would hear three or four knocks on the window glass in the front door; and at first I didn't think anything of it," she explains. "Then after it started happening often enough for me to pay attention, I started waiting for it. Whenever I went to the front door after I heard the knocks, there was never anything there."

Susan recalls how she – on several occasions – went to the front of the house just as night fell and waited patiently to see if unseen hands would produce a knock at the window in her front door. "And sure enough," she says, "I would hear distinct raps right on the glass in front of me, but I couldn't see where the sound was coming from, and I know nobody was outside." Susan had the windows checked, and they appeared to rest snuggly in their frames, so she claims there is no explanation for the series of odd knocks that she would hear only as sunlight faded at the end of each day.

The next strange occurrences centered around the radio she would listen to as she worked away on one of the many restoration projects that kept her occupied for the first year in the old house. "If I walked outside for something and left the radio on," she laughs, "it would be off when I came back in. And if I turned it off before I left, it would always be on when I came back." Susan says she would pay extra special attention to whether or not she turned the radio off as she left the house, and when she returned, the radio would invariably not be in the on or off state as when she had left it.

Susan then remembers how little things started disappearing every so often. "And it wasn't like I had misplaced anything, because I know that happens now and then, but it was different than that. It usually involved things I had more than one of," she explains. "For example, one day I had gone out and bought four new smoke detectors. I came home from the store and set them down, still in their bag, and when I went to get them later, there were only three." Susan distinctly remembers bringing four of the devices home, and she had the purchase receipt to prove that there had been four. She says the same thing happened when she went out shopping one day and came across two small crystal lamps for the downstairs powder room. "I got them home, and when it came time to put them out, there was only one there, and I had seen both of them a short time before." She also says no one who could have taken the items had entered the house, either. At least the house has a ghostly thief that is somewhat considerate because it could have taken *all* of Susan's items.

Another item to disappear, the picture of a young girl, made her stop and analyze her surroundings as well. "The workers found a small photograph of a young girl in white one day and they came and showed it to me. They discovered a secret compartment in the fireplace mantel in the dining room, and the picture was hidden away inside." Susan says she had never seen it before and had no idea who the little girl was. The black-and-white snapshot could have been taken anywhere from the 1920s to the 50s, she suspects, and the little girl – perhaps eight years of age or so – sported a simple white dress. "I took it and put it on the mantel shelf for safe keeping, but when I went to get it the next day, it was gone. It wasn't back in the secret compartment, either. I haven't seen it to this day and I have no idea what could have happened to it."

If Susan had already harbored some misgivings that her house might be haunted by this point, the strange episode with the picture of the little girl only served to strengthen her suspicions. However, something had happened only the day before that really made her question her skeptical beliefs in the supernatural. The incident involved her son and the previously unseen figure of a ghostly little girl in white on the stairs. It seems that Susan had lost the old photograph of the little girl, but acquired a bona fide apparition in its place.

Her son, Susan Shearer explains, "Is not the kind of guy who tends to invent things and make them up." She says he comes across to most as a no-nonsense type of individual, the type of fellow most would consider a skeptic. "So, if he says he saw something," Shearer clarifies, "I know he must have seen something. And he says he saw the ghost of a little girl on the stairs." She had chuckled nervously and tried to shrug it off

The fireplace mantel in the dining room, where the old photograph of the little girl in a white dress was discovered in a secret compartment (Photo courtesy of F&E Schmidt)

when her son had told her about an eerie encounter with a dark shadow that had mysteriously blocked the light streaming through the small square overhead where an ancient heating register had been removed for cleaning. But this time, she started to take it seriously. In remarkable detail, her son told her how he had been at the front door when the odd feeling of someone staring at him caused the hair on his arms to prickle. He turned around quickly and felt his blood turn cold as he stared at an unexpected form standing on the landing. A serene, disinterested gaze painted on her face, a young girl stood there and watched him, unmoving, while the rash of standing hairs spread up to the back of his neck with a shiver. A bow held her darkish hair up from her face, and she wore a plain white dress that might have served as a school outfit. A second later, the vision faded and vanished.

Although she herself has never seen this little girl, Susan speculates that her appearance on the stairs holds some connection to the other strange happenings in her home and that it might have something to do with the black-and-white photo that had been found in her house. Curious to see what other secrets the house held, she dug up the deeds at the Jefferson County courthouse and pored through pages and pages of aging script.

She discovered that the history of her home really started on July 8, 1890, when the owner of the land, Mr. W. Slaughter, sold the land to the newly formed Victoria Land Grant Company. This real estate venture had emerged when city developers acquired the site of the former grand Southern Exposition of 1883, dismantled the huge wooden exhibit hall that at one time covered the entire St. James Court area and then sold off plots of land in an attempt to develop Louisville's first suburb, in a part of town once known as the *Southern Extension*. In July of the following year, the Victoria Land Grant Company deeded the property to Mr. John W. Gernert, and he and his family had the house until 1923, when Joseph C. Chickering bought it. He lived there with his family until 1946, at which time the Tomerlins purchased the property and called it home for the next fifty years or so.

After rummaging through the public records of the local courthouse, she took a list of the various individuals who at one time had owned the Sixth Street property and spent an afternoon at the Louisville Free Public Library perusing the old *Caron's City Directories* in an effort to retrieve details about the home's prior inhabitants. An early precursor to today's telephone books, these useful tomes provided names and addresses of city dwellers according to street and intersection locations, as well as listed the occupations of those who resided there. Although she unearthed a trove of interesting information about the former occupants of the home, she came across nothing that might account for the ghostly apparition on the stairs. That would have to wait until she contacted me and I started interviewing people who used to live in the home.

Susan said she did receive some interesting information from local psychic Cheryl Glassner, however. I had put her in touch with the woman who had discovered the various "entities" that had provoked a rash of strange occurrences in Jon Huffman and Barb Cullen's house at 539 West Ormsby, and Cheryl reportedly picked up on some very positive female energy in the Sixth Street home. "She was able to tell me a lot of things I found very useful," says Shearer, "and she also picked up on a lot of different things about my personal life, which I thought was very interesting." The most interesting information by far came when Cheryl made her way down the stairs from the second floor to the foyer at the front of the house.

A cold winter day raged, and I had met Cheryl at Susan's house to watch her do a psychic reading of the premises. She came with no prior knowledge of the house, other than the fact that unexplainable incidents had been reported.

Susan had done an amazing amount of work in the several months since I had paid my first visit to the residence, and the place had an inviting feel. The floors had a high-polished gleam, and I couldn't keep my eyes off of the elaborate fireplace mantels with their ornate tile inserts and built-in curio shelves. Susan had recently refinished the fireplace mantel with the secret compartment in the dining room and couldn't wait to show me. The place was finally shaping up, and I could tell she was happy to be home.

After Susan passed around steaming mugs of herbal tea and got me up to date on all her recent projects, Cheryl took out a small package and quietly unwrapped it before making her way around the house. "This is a pendant," she explained, "and I use it, like a pendulum, to measure the energy around us." She walked to a nearby window and held the small, dangling pendant up in the air and waited to see what would happen. Suddenly, the suspended object seemed to start swinging on its own, back and forth, and then around in long, lazy arcs. Although Cheryl claimed that the pendant moved of its own accord and that she was not moving her hand, to me it seemed that she had indeed caused it to swing. Despite my suspicions, I decided to bite my tongue and not interfere with the investigation. "Oh yes," continued Cheryl, "there's a lot of good energy here." For half an hour, I followed as Cheryl and Susan slowly made their way through the house, Cheryl commenting the whole time on the antics of her pendulum while Susan listened eagerly to the reports of "strong, positive female energy" in the place. Every once in a while I would raise my camera and take a shot of the psychic at work. As they made their way down the front stairs, Susan sat on the steps and listened as Cheryl continued with her observations and impressions. As if suddenly distracted, the psychic stopped in mid-sentence and looked at Susan. "There's a little girl sitting next to you on the stairs, and she seems to be very happy."

For Susan Shearer, that was enough to convince her of the psychic's ability. "I think it's amazing that she picked up on all the female energy in the house," she says, "because I was getting those exact same impressions. And then when she said there was a little girl on the stairs, well, that was enough for me! I knew there had to be a reason for it all."

When I met Susan the next week, after having the photos developed, I told her that I suspected Cheryl of manipulating the crystal pendant and that she should perhaps take the psychic's findings with a grain of salt. As proof, I produced a snap shot of Cheryl using the pendant, and from the blurred lines of her hands, it clearly appeared that she had been swinging the pendant with her own hand. Susan, however, was undeterred and said that the psychic's impressive degree of accuracy was enough to convince her, moving hands or no.

Cheryl Glassner used a crystal pendant to detect psychic energies during her investigation of Susan Shearer's and Linda Gregory's Sixth Street home in Old Louisville. The psychic claims to have made contact with a young girl in a white dress.

About that time I also met Cheryl for coffee one day to discuss her thoughts about the house at 1439 South Sixth Street. It was a sunny day, and we sat in a front booth at D. Nalley's, a diner on Third Street. Outside, two black cats were chasing each other on the sidewalk. I stirred my coffee and listened as Cheryl explained that the strongest presence in Susan's house was a young girl, and one who had died tragically at a young age. When I showed the psychic several of the photos I had taken, I diplomatically pointed out that her hands appeared to be moving in one of the shots. Cheryl studied the photograph for a moment and then pointed to the blurred outline of her fingers and said: "Oh, that's just the White Ghost, the spirit who lives inside of me and reaches out to help me communicate."

After my conversation with Cheryl, I figured that would be the end of the story. But then I heard from someone who added another interesting twist. When I started doing research for my first book, I left notes on various online message boards and placed announcements in local newsletters informing people that I needed historical information of a ghostly nature pertaining to Old Louisville. Every once in a while someone would contact me with very useful leads. Sometimes I would receive random, unsigned postcards in the mail, kind letters, anonymous telephone messages and, more often than not, emails. I received an interesting email message one evening in early summer as I polished the glasses at the table I had just set for a dinner party I offered to host for some writer friends.

Wade Hall and Gregg Swem were the guests of honor, and since I had a break from teaching my regular load of classes, I decided to go all out and do a proper sit-down with enough courses to impress. Once again, I was testing recipes for a Kentucky-themed cookbook, and I was happy to have a table full of guinea pigs. In the front parlor we sipped sherry and nibbled chicken salad canapés before seating ourselves at the table. I popped the cork on a bottle of sparkling wine and served the first course, which was fried green tomatoes with cucumber remoulade. After that came a salad of dressed bitter greens with grilled fennel, sweet corn, and goat cheese. Once the salad plates had been cleared, I opened a nice pinot noir and served broiled salmon with creamed spinach and purple potatoes, followed by homemade lemon sorbet with large chunks of candied ginger. We switched to a heartier red wine and then tackled the main course: roast pork tenderloin with caper sauce. After half an hour of congenial conversation about a new play that my friend, Jerry Rodgers, had just written, we had our first dessert: rhubarb crisp with cinnamon whipped cream. After that, I passed around glasses of port, and we tucked into the evening's finale, bourbon chocolate crème with butter cookies and fresh cherries.

The guests – all of them contented – had left by midnight, and I decided to check my email after cleaning the kitchen. I had only one message, and it came from a woman named Mary Barton who explained that her relatives had at one time lived at 1439 South Sixth Street. She had read my first book and wanted to know if I had heard any tales about this particular house. She had some stories and was offering to share them with me. No one, as far as I knew, other than Susan's immediate family, had any inkling about the recent goings-on in the lovely Queen Anne home on Sixth, and I could barely contain my eagerness as I replied to Mary's message and made arrangements to meet her the next day.

A breeze rustled the bright green leaves overhead the following afternoon as I approached the fountain in the middle of St. James Court. Squirrels chattered in the branches overhead. Summer hadn't really arrived, as the oppressive humidity so typical of the warm months in Kentucky hadn't quite taken its stranglehold on the neighborhood yet, and the afternoon seemed unseasonably fresh. Mary hadn't showed up, and I walked to the railing around the fountain and leaned against it as I watched the water dance and sparkle.

A postcard shows the fountain on St. James Court during its early days. In the background is the turret of the Pink Palace.

An original fixture since the court's inception in the late 1800s, the "Central Fountain of St. James Court" marks the center of the old Southern Exposition of 1883, an early kind of world's fair that put Kentucky on the map and ultimately led to the development of Old Louisville. Across from it, to the east, sits tranquil Fountain Court, its opening flanked on both sides by early examples of elegant apartment and condo buildings. The swanky St. James Flats originally caused quite a bit of consternation when St. James Court resident Theophilus Conrad built it with six floors that towered over its neighbors. When a terrible fire destroyed the topmost floors in 1912, many could hardly contain their gloating at the news that they would finally get their way and have no disproportionate structures on the court.

On the other side of the fountain, to the west, sits the former home of Madison Julius Cawein, Kentucky's first, if unofficial, poet laureate. Built in 1901, the Georgian-Revival residence boasts a unique rounded entry portico with an enviable view of the fountain. Often referred to as the "Audubon of poetry" because of his many poems about nature, Cawein could often be seen wandering the pleasant walkways of St. James Court, stopping frequently to examine the wide variety of local flora on display there. Off in the distance, the turret from the Pink Palace appeared and disappeared as the leaves rustled and jostled back and forth and I tried to imagine what the neighborhood must have been like when Madison Cawein still lived there. I closed my eyes and inhaled the green, leafy fragrance when my ears caught the sound of a small voice drawing near. "Hello," she said.

I opened my eyes and pivoted. Mary Barton, a smallish woman with graying hair pulled up in the back, stood before me. We made our introductions and exchanged a bit of small talk before she suggested that we start strolling around St. James Court. As we strolled, she told me her story.

Mary Barton, a native of southern California, had come to Louisville in the 1940s when her husband decided to move back to the area to take care of an ailing mother and father. "My husband, John, was born in Bardstown, but his parents moved to Louisville when he was ten," she explained. "His mother's side of the family has roots that go all the way back to Daniel Boone and some other early pioneer names that settled the state. They were always really proud of that."

Within two years of their arrival in Louisville, said Mary, both her mother-in-law and father-in-law had died, as had been anticipated, and she and her young husband were able to enjoy their newfound freedom. "We lived with his parents on Zane Street," she commented, "and after they passed on, we inherited the house from them." The house, still standing today, counted as one of the more modest examples of residential architecture in the neighborhood, but Mary claims the staid brick structure felt "like a real mansion" to them once she and her husband had it all to themselves. "It was a large home with three floors, and we lived there for almost five years, and we had a great time," she says. "The house was really close to downtown, and some of our happiest memories came from there."

We strolled past the intricate limestone façade of the enormous Conrad-Caldwell House with all its Richardsonian Romanesque detail at the mouth of St. James Court and then past the whimsical Moorish arches of the Venetian Gothic masterpiece at 1412 where pottery legend Mary Alice Hadley had her original studio. As we walked, Mary Barton regaled me with interesting stories of life in Louisville in the 1950s, a time when the area started to go into decline. According to Mary, the Old Louisville neighborhood still occupied a place of honor among the city's various neighborhoods back then, and twice as many elegant mansions dotted the entire district. "It was a place with a very vibrant society life," she recalls, "and tradition was alive and well. Huge Victorian mansions were on the way out as people moved to the suburbs, but this was always a classy part of town."

At the southern end of St. James Court, we turned right on Belgravia Court and made our way down the narrow sidewalks while the constant flames in the gas lamps flickered and added a bit of needless illumination and romance to our stroll. At the Sixth Street exit, we turned right again and steered our way north towards Central Park, and when we came to an unexpected stop in front of the tidy little house at 1439, I had all but forgotten the reason I had arranged to meet Mrs. Barton in the first place.

Without looking at me, Mary raised her hand and pointed at the wooden structure with its neat splashes of blue and beige. "I have seen some *very* strange things in that house," she stated matter-of-factly, "things that I will never forget." When I coaxed her for more information she told me the story of the little girl in white on the front stairs.

"I'm kin to the Chickerings," she said, "and they used to own this house." My ears immediately perked up at the recognition of that last name. "When we lived in the house over on Zane Street, I'd spend a lot of time over here visiting my Aunt Viola. Taking care of two elderly people was hard," she recalls, "and it was nice to get out of the house whenever I could." But it seems that these visits weren't always pleasant, either.

"Aunt Viola's husband – Joe, or Uncle Chick as we used to call him – had a hard time of it the older he got, and towards the end of his life he suffered from dementia. My aunt had a horrible time taking care of him, and it really wore her out." When she realized she hadn't made any mention of the ghostly phenomena in the house that she had alluded to, Mary looked at me and explained. "He always talked about this little girl in white who used to come and talk to him. But there was no little girl in white who lived there. We all thought he was just out of his mind and ignored it. There were always different ghosts floating around the neighborhood, like one over at the corner of Twelfth and Zane Streets, but I never took those things too seriously."

That is, until Mary witnessed an apparition herself one day. "Back then nobody locked their doors – there was no need to – and I had just stopped by for a visit. It was a beautiful fall afternoon," she remembers. "I opened the door and walked inside and called out for my aunt, and I had just started to head down the hallway to the kitchen at the back of the house, when this strange sensation came over me." Mary says she stopped dead in her tracks and remained motionless while the hairs on her arms stood on end. "It was almost like I was paralyzed," she explains. "I couldn't move a muscle, just like in one of them dreams where you're scared and try to scream out and can't do anything at all."

Out of the corner of her eye, but well within her line of vision, she perceived something to the left, where the stairs went up to the next floor. "I moved my eyes a bit," she says, "and then I saw her. A little girl in a white dress as plain as day. Standing on the stairs looking right at me!" Mary says the vision appeared to look straight through her and had a translucent quality about it. "She just stood there and stared, but she wasn't looking at me – just *through* me. And, the funny thing is – I could see right through her, too." Transfixed, Mary remembers counting the steps she could see on the other side of the ghostly denizen on the staircase. "She was all shimmery-like, and I counted eight steps behind her before she vanished and was gone!" The front door then swung open and closed with a violent slam.

At that moment, Mary's aunt emerged from the kitchen and told the stunned woman to join her at the table for a cup of coffee, admonishing her for slamming the door in the process. "I was visibly shaken when I sat down," Mary says, "and the first thing my aunt says is 'Good grief, you look like you just saw a ghost!' Then she narrowed her eyes at me and asked if I had seen something in her house." By the time Mary replied that she had indeed seen something, her aunt had already guessed as much, and confessed that she had also seen the strange apparition. "We realized that Uncle Chick might not have been so crazy after all."

Mary Barton claims she saw the strange vision – always on the front steps – several more times during the next year or so. And she says other strange things happened in her aunt's home on South Sixth Street. "The doors and windows used to open and close by themselves," she recalls, "and on one occasion, I even saw a large skillet fly through the air and land in the sink with a terrible ruckus. It got to be that I became nervous whenever I had to go over there." It wasn't till later that Mary's Aunt Viola told her the reason for the haunting.

"At first she denied that there could be ghosts in her house," recalls Mary, "and whenever I pressed her for more information about the house, she always skirted the issue. One day, though, I just kept after her, and she finally broke down and told me about the accident."

According to her aunt, the Chickerings at one time had boarders in their house, two of them being a young, single mother and her eight-year-old daughter. "I guess they were hard up and needed cash," Mary speculates. "And this would have been during the Depression years, so it would stand to reason. Lots of people in the area had to take in boarders to make ends meet." It appears that the young girl had some behavioral problems, and her mother sometimes had a hard time keeping the young girl from running out the front door and into the street. One night, just as dusk was falling, a knock came at the front door and the young girl ran down the front stairs and outside as her mother washed up for the evening meal. "The mother wasn't quick enough, and the next thing people heard," says Mary Barton, "was a honking and the terrible screech of brakes. They all ran outside and found that the young girl had been hit and killed by a passing motorist. And the man just drove off and left her there." She had been wearing a simple, white dress. Not too long thereafter, Uncle Chick began complaining about the apparition of the little girl on the steps at the front of the house at 1439 South Sixth Street.

Had he really seen the ghostly apparition of the young girl who had lived in the house, or did this merely signal the onslaught of dementia? Mary Barton has convinced herself that her uncle witnessed the same strange manifestation that she herself had witnessed, and for her, it was enough to learn that a little girl had been tragically run down and killed in front of the house in the past. Her aunt and uncle eventually moved from South Sixth Street, and Mary Barton says she had never returned to the charming Queen Anne until the day she and I met at the fountain and strolled around the neighborhood. When I told her that current occupants had indeed reported strange sightings of a young girl in white in the very same location she had described, she smiled and suggested that we resume our stroll through the neighborhood.

Right around the corner from Susan Shearer's house on Sixth Street is the lovely fountain that marks the center of St. James Court, the residential heart of Old Louisville.

The ornamental fountain at the center of St. James Court – according to local legend, an apparition known as the Ice Boy is said to haunt this location during the coldest months of the year.

Chapter 17 – The Legend of the Ice Boy

Story, legend, myth – what's the difference when you're talking about folklore and accounts of the supernatural in America's most haunted neighborhood? In its most basic form, a story is nothing more than the recounting of a series of events. Many of the stories in this collection are considered to be true because they come from human sources whose veracity has been established or accepted at face value, something that would classify them as non-fiction. When you start dealing with fiction, however, things can get interesting in the story-telling world, especially when real events and characters are introduced into the narrative. Myths are pretty easy to define and understand in that most see them as entirely made-up stories, often with origins in the distant past, that try to explain how the world works. Legends, on the other hand, are a different kettle of fish. Depending on your sources, definitions might vary, but most agree that a legend is a semi-true story, one that has been passed down from person to person and holds special significance or symbolism for the culture where it arose. Most important, a legend usually is based on historic facts and includes some element of truth.

Several of tales in this book easily fall into the legend category because, although there may not be proof for certain individual details, they are firmly rooted in neighborhood lore and can be traced directly back to important historical events and characters. One such story involves the Ice Boy, a neighborhood ghost who is only spotted during the winter months. People who have seen the specter describe him as a sad ragamuffin covered in soot and ash, and they say he is usually running about or playing in the area around the fountain on St. James Court or in the adjacent walking court. One witness, Malcolm Satterwhite, claims to have seen this apparition late on a snowy night in February 1988. "It had just snowed and the neighborhood was covered in a white blanket that made it look really pretty. I had an apartment on Fountain Court and was returning from my sister's wedding," he recalls. "I parked half a block from the apartment, and as I walked down the sidewalk on the east side of St. James Court, something near the fountain caught my eye." Satterwhite says he then saw the shape of a small boy as it ran around the railing and disappeared around the other side. "He was just filthy," he recalls, "and it looked like his face had been blackened with something, and that made his sad eyes stand out all the more." Satterwhite claims that when he went to look for the boy, he couldn't find him. "At first, I thought it was a little boy who was lost or something, so I tried following him. But when I got to the side of the fountain where I thought he was, there was nobody in sight." Satterwhite says he initially assumed that the boy had just run away, but upon closer inspection, he found no footprints in the snow, other than his own. "If he had run away, I would have seen his tracks leading away from the fountain. He just disappeared." Later, after recounting the strange experience to some of his friends on St. James Court, Satterwhite heard about the legend of the Ice Boy for the first time.

On a bitterly cold morning in February 1912, throngs turned out to behold a spectacular sight at the Saint James Court entrance to Fountain Court. Looming before the onlookers, an eerie vision in ice and snow towered overhead, the remnants of a terrible fire from the night before. The Saint James Apartments – otherwise known as "Conrad's Folly" because of Theophilus Conrad's insistence on constructing a then-unheard-of-five-story apartment building – had caught fire, totally destroying the top two floors. As firemen battled the blaze in the frigid night air, water cascaded down the sides of the building and froze in place, leaving behind a magnificent sculpture of stalagmites and crystallized ash. Rather than rebuild the top floors, the then owner opted for the easiest route and had them removed entirely, leaving the three bottom stories, which still stand today. It seems that in the end, the residents on St. James Court got their wish and they no longer had to contend with an overly tall building looming over their elegant residential enclave. Although there was surely the temptation to gloat, most in the neighborhood expressed their concern and eventual relief when it was revealed that all the inhabitants of the apartment house had escaped the flames and made it to safety. It was reported that not a single life was lost.

Not too long thereafter, as the snow and ice still lay on the ground, residents began reporting strange sightings on St. James Court. A young boy, they said, was lurking around the fountain at night; and workers reported a similar apparition in the shadows of the large apartment building as repairs were underway. All of the descriptions were similar in that they involved what appeared to be a dirt-covered young boy in raggedy clothing. More often than not eyewitnesses reported hollow eyes staring out from a blackened face. Over the next several years, the sightings continued, but only during the frigid months when snow and ice covered St. James Court. It wasn't for another ten years that someone offered an explanation for the ghostly sightings of the poor ragamuffin, which locals had come to know as "the Ice Boy."

To commemorate the tenth anniversary of the terrible fire and the rebuilding of the apartment house, a party was held on St. James Court

A photograph shows the front and side of the St. James Apartments after a fire destroyed the top floors in February 1912. (Courtesy of the Caldwell family)

and the whole neighborhood was invited. Tables were set up for lemonade and picnic foods, and a marching band played from a wooden stand on Fountain Court. The festivities were in full swing when a local dignitary took the stand and addressed the crowd and thanked them for coming. As he stepped down, the attendees were ready to resume their celebrating, but an old gypsy woman supposedly took the stage and commanded their attention. Although official reports said no one perished in the fire ten years before, she told them all she knew better, adding fire to a rumor that had been circulating the city ever since. According to the woman, a young boy from the nearby, and much poorer, Cabbage Patch district – not wanting to return to the freezing temperatures outside – had supposedly fallen asleep while warming up on the top floor of the building after making a grocery delivery there the night of the fire. Firefighters found his body the next day, huddled in a corner and covered in soot and ash, but because the boy wasn't from one of the wealthy neighborhood families, they never reported his death to the authorities. When someone in the crowd called out to the gypsy woman and asked how she could know such a thing, the angry woman alleged to know it for a fact because she was the boy's own mother. She herself had come the day after the fire and taken away her son's body for burial. In roaming the area near the fire on icy nights, she warned them, her boy's spirit was seeking the recognition denied him in death.

Although reports of this casualty have never been substantiated, legend in Old Louisville has it that the fire at the St. James Apartments did indeed claim the life of a young errand boy in February 1912. Many residents of St. James Court and the environs have heard the story over the years, and a number even claim to have seen the ghost themselves. Wandering around the fountain in the wintertime, and between the houses on Fountain Court, his forlorn spirit has become part of neighborhood lore, whether he is real or not.

The St. James Apartments as they look today, more than a hundred years after a mysterious winter fire destroyed the top floor

Chapter 18 – Spirits at the Conrad-Caldwell House

What starts out as a leisurely fifteen-minute stroll through the streets and alleyways in Old Louisville, one of the country's largest Victorian neighborhoods, can easily turn into an adventure that lasts several hours or the whole day. For many people, this journey has become a permanent odyssey. For lifelong residents and first-time visitors alike, this colorful neighborhood offers a steady stream of surprises and secrets to those who take the time to explore it. A treasure trove of architectural splendor and forgotten history, Old Louisville stands out as something special in the nation and in the state of Kentucky. Although somewhat slowly perhaps, the inhabitants of the city of Louisville itself have also come to realize that no other place in the city can surpass this area for its wealth of charm, elegance and nostalgia. Within the boundaries of historic Old Louisville, however, Saint James Court stands out among all the other neighborhoods for its grassy, gas-lit boulevard, splashing fountain and picture-perfect homes. And on elegant Saint James Court, one magnificent mansion at 1402 stands out as the most impressive residence: the Conrad-Caldwell House.

Known as the finest home in the city for many years, this massive Bedford limestone construction in the Richardsonian Romanesque style still counts as one of the most stunning residences in Old Louisville. When Theophilus Conrad, a Frenchman from Alsace who made his Louisville fortune in the tanning business, hired famed local architect Arthur Loomis to design the mansion in the 1890s, the city had already established itself in the new "West" as a comfortable enclave noted for its lavish homes. In 1831, traveler Caleb Atewar commented on a recent trip to Louisville, then just barely in its fourth decade of existence, that "[t]here are probably more ease and affluence in this place, than in any other western town – their houses are splendid, substantial, and richly furnished; and I saw more large mirrors in their best rooms, than I saw anywhere else. Paintings and mirrors adorn the walls, and all the furniture is splendid and costly." With this in mind, Conrad set out to maintain the city's reputation and impress his neighbors.

The original construction price was set at $75,000, and within weeks all eyes in the city had turned to the large corner lot on Saint James Court where work on the "Castle" had begun. Within several months local workers and stone masons had erected a huge stone shell replete with gargoyles, floral swags, massive arches and elaborate decorative motifs that dominated everything else on the court. After another several months had passed, craftsmen started to embellish the interior with the finest appointments money could buy. Beautiful stained glass and elaborately carved woodwork in the balustrade and wainscoting along the stairway and balcony graced the magnificent front staircase. Throughout the interior, many lavishly carved details could be found, details such as the fleur-de-lis, the stylized iris from heraldry that is itself a symbol of Louisville. The most opulent room in the house, the parlor, featured woodwork of birds-eye maple, and in other rooms off the entry hall, ornate chandeliers, carved paneling, crown molding and intricate parquet floors offered just a glimpse of the abundant decoration yet to be discovered throughout the rest of the house.

The library at the Conrad-Caldwell House – one of several areas in the mansion where ghostly activity has been reported. (Courtesy of F&E Schmidt)

Although the house has been run as a museum since 1987, tour guides at the Conrad-Caldwell House don't recommend that you wander off and try to explore the sumptuous interiors unsupervised. It seems that a former resident of the stately home doesn't appreciate strangers snooping around unattended in *his* house – even if he died and left the premises over a century ago.

At the beautiful Conrad-Caldwell House there have been more than just a few reports of curious individuals getting more than they bargained for when trying to sneak off and explore by themselves. In the mid 1990s a lady visitor did just that; however, when she slipped away from her group and decided to poke her head through a door into a third-floor room that had been closed for restoration. Several moments later she ran screaming down the stairway past her friends and refused to go back up to the third floor. When asked what had upset her so, she would only reply that she had seen "a mean little man from the olden days, shaking his raised index finger" at her in admonition. The terrified woman also reported that she knew the man wasn't real because "he was see-though and diaphanous."

Theories abound as to the source of this ghostly figure seen on so many different occasions over the years, but many feel that some of the sightings involve none other than Theophilus Conrad himself. Reputedly a stern taskmaster, associates knew Conrad as a hard worker and no-nonsense kind of person, despite the wealth and prestige he had accumulated. While other mansions in the neighborhood usually employed an entire staff of live-in servants, the frugal Conrads supposedly made due with several "dailies" who came in every morning and took care of the cooking, cleaning and gardening. Although he wasn't a big man, he nonetheless carried himself like a giant and demanded the respect of his family and employees. By all accounts, Conrad was indeed the king of his castle.

Several other visitors have reported seeing a short man in the billiard room as well, and curiously enough, he always seems to manifest himself to those who wander off and try to explore the house on their own. "He looked like the man in the picture I saw," reported one tourist after an unsettling encounter with the little man in the billiard room in 1995. The man in the picture he referred to was none other than Theo Conrad himself.

On one occasion, two newlyweds had just held their wedding reception at the opulent mansion, and as they filed down the walkway through the throng of family and friends, they looked up and noticed a gentleman "in an old-fashioned tweed suit" smoking a cigar on a third floor balcony. Neither the new bride nor her groom recognized the little man, so the woman asked her mother about the unknown guest's identity. But when they looked up, he had already vanished, and a thorough search of the house turned up nothing but the faint aroma of cigar smoke in the former billiard room. Coincidentally enough, the balcony where the man had been spotted was known as the smoking balcony, a small outdoor area connected to the billiard room where gentlemen of the Gilded Age could enjoy their tobacco after a game of snooker.

Elizabeth Stith seems to think the descriptions of the gentleman in the third-floor pool room fit the description of Mr. Caldwell, the second king of the Castle, rather than Mr. Conrad, who died there in 1905, ten years after moving into the mansion. The Caldwell family purchased the huge house on Saint James Court and lived there for the next thirty-five years or so. After the Saint James Court Historic Foundation purchased the home in 1987 and restored it for use as a museum, Ms. Stith served as director of the house for a time. If anyone would know details of the former residents of the Conrad-Caldwell House, she would be the one. During her seven years as director, she conducted numerous hours of research and investigation about the house and the families who had resided there. "That description sounds like Mr. Caldwell," she explains. "He was a very stately man. And the billiard room wasn't added to the house until after he and his family moved in." She points out that Mr. Caldwell died in the house as well. He reportedly spent many hours with his gentlemen friends in his favorite room of the house, the billiard room on the third floor.

According to Elizabeth, Mrs. Caldwell designed the present-day billiards room and added the cabinets for the cue sticks and billiard balls in the early 1900s. "She really loved this house, and she put a lot of work into it. When the Caldwells moved in, it was Mrs. Caldwell who redecorated the mansion and gave it the feel it has today. She got many of the ideas while traveling abroad." Elizabeth points out that Mrs. Caldwell also died in the house, illness confining her to her second-floor bedroom for the last couple years of her life. Even though the prominent Louisville socialite died many years ago, there are those who feel she hasn't quite left the lovely house she adored on Saint James Court, Elizabeth Stith included.

"I get the impression she wants to make sure we're taking good care of her home," the former director explains, recalling a strange encounter she had one February evening. "It was six o'clock, so it was dark at that time already, and I was there alone." She needed to turn off the lights before leaving, and as she made her way down the grand stairway from the third floor, an odd shape appeared on the steps. "It was down by the grandfather clock, and I noticed a white, milky form, almost like a veil hanging there. I couldn't really make out a definite shape or anything. It was more like a patch of something foggy just hanging there." Not quite sure if her eyes were playing tricks on her, Elizabeth tried to maintain her composure as she made her way around the odd shape and down the stairs.

Taken a couple of years before 1910, this photo shows the elegant grand stairway in the Conrad-Caldwell House. Over the years, various phenomena such as misty apparitions and disembodied voices have been reported on the steps. (Courtesy of the Caldwell family)

"Somewhere in the back of my mind I remembered what someone had once told me," she recalls, "that when things manifest themselves like that, they just want to be acknowledged. So I tried to acknowledge it." Elizabeth then continued with her business and assured the strange form that everything in the house was fine and that she "was just turning out the lights." Elizabeth says the figure eventually faded and disappeared completely, but not without leaving behind an extremely cold spot on the steps. Hardly surprising, many people have reported a mysterious cold spot on that very portion of the stairs.

Deb Riall took over as the director of the Conrad-Caldwell House museum after Elizabeth left, and although she herself has not witnessed any apparitions or such, she has heard stories from other people who have. She can also recall one occurrence that "was definitely odd." Deb had gone to the kitchen to heat up her lunch in the microwave and found herself at the sink, waiting for the timer to go off. "I was standing near the sink," she explains, "when I looked down and noticed the little drain basket on the counter. It was rocking back and forth, from side to side, very slowly and deliberately. I just kept staring at it, waiting for it to eventually stop, but it just kept going back and forth." At that point she remembered the same thing that Elizabeth Stith had. *They just want to be acknowledged.* In a loud and clear voice, she said, "OK. I know you're here" and looked around the room. Although she didn't see anything, she looked down and noticed the drain basket as it stopped rocking back and forth. "I slammed the microwave door a couple times, I leaned on the counter," she explains, "but I was never able to get the drain basket to move like that again. I don't know what it was." Was Mrs. Caldwell trying to get her attention?

Some think that the former lady of the house can be very vociferous if she needs to. A housekeeper recollects an incident a number of years ago that made her think so. It was late summer, in the afternoon, and a storm had just blown in and darkened the neighborhood as she cleaned the stairs in the front of the house. It began to thunder loudly, and then large drops of rain started to fall and splash against the windows. "It happened so fast," the woman recalls, "that I didn't even notice anything till I looked up and saw how black it was outside." No sooner had she noticed the rain coming down in torrents, she claims, than a woman's voice frantically called from the third floor that *"the windows are open!"* The housekeeper ran up to the top floor of the house to discover that someone had indeed left the windows open, and she quickly closed them before more rain came in and did any serious damage. "I'm pretty sure it was Mrs. Caldwell," she remarked. "She's always watching out for her house."

Aside from on the grand stairway, some people sense that Mrs. Caldwell exerts a very strong presence in the butler's pantry as well. A small storage room off the dining room that connected to the pantry and the kitchen, this area was used originally to store the best china and serving items. A very typical feature in nicer Victorian homes, these small rooms served as the last stop for food on the way to the dinner table. After the cook prepared the dish in the kitchen, it would be brought to the butler's pantry where it could be kept warm and then arranged and formally presented for serving. Many of the homes in Old Louisville still have the original butler's pantries, and like most, the one at the Conrad-Caldwell House has various cabinets and drawers used to store tablecloths, napkins, cutlery and stemware in addition to a large table used for plating dishes between courses. The pantry in the Conrad-Caldwell House has one thing, however, that lets visitors know that they haven't entered just any run-of-the-mill butler's pantry. A tall, narrow, wooden door opens to reveal a tall, narrow, metal safe used to hide some of the most valuable silver in all of Old Louisville. This could explain why former employees say Mrs. Caldwell's presence has always been "exceptionally strong" in the butler's pantry.

Often described as a woman with impeccable taste, Mrs. Caldwell reportedly prided herself on setting a lovely table for family and friends. She often supervised the selection of courses for elegant meals and she always insisted on using the best table linens, bone ware, crystal and silver for her meals. She could often be seen in the butler's pantry, fussing about before meals, and she herself would unlock the safe and extract the choicest silver items to deck the table. Her neighbors reported that she could turn an ordinary afternoon tea into the most elegant of affairs. Maybe this is why an unexplained cold spot in the room has been experienced on numerous occasions, often right before elegant weddings or lavish meals are held on the premises.

"I hope she was just checking on things!" says a former bride who hosted her wedding reception in the house several years ago. "I was standing by myself in the little pantry room off the dining room, right in front of where the safe is, when all of a sudden I was surrounded by an ice-cold blast of air," she recalls. "I looked up and around me, because I thought the air-conditioning had just come on and was blowing at me through a vent, but I didn't see anything at all. Then I got this very strange feeling like someone was watching me or something, and I knew I was not alone in that room."

Perhaps one of the oddest encounters with the former Mrs. Caldwell – if that's indeed who it is – happened several years ago during preparations for another wedding at the house. The groom's sister, a self-described no-nonsense kind of woman from Salt Lake City, had just flown in, and she and some family friends had gone to the mansion to decorate for the ceremony the next afternoon. "It was about nine in the evening, and it was very dark outside," she explains. "It seemed like none of the streetlights were working. There were five of us all together, and we were decorating the grand stairway with flowers and ribbons. I was at the very bottom of the steps, and the others were on the second-floor landing." The woman says she looked up from what she was doing and noticed at eye level a spoon, not more than three feet in front of her. "It was just floating in the air!" she says. "A beautiful old-fashioned silver spoon, all ornate and stuff, just hanging in mid-air." As she watched, the woman claims the spoon sailed through the air and landed with a clatter on the floor of the butler's pantry. "I went and found it there, lying on the floor in front of the old safe. But the safe was wide open, and I don't think it had been open when I saw it before that. I noticed there were some matching pieces of silver in the vault, so I put the spoon with them and then closed the door. Maybe the lady of the house was trying to get my attention so I'd close the door to the safe," she says. "When I told the others what had happened, they just said I had to be going crazy, but I know what I saw."

It seems that peculiar occurrences at the Conrad-Caldwell House don't limit themselves to encounters involving former visitors or employees and the supposed ghosts of Mr. and Mrs. Caldwell, however. After the Caldwells sold the house, it passed to the Presbyterian Church and served for many years as a women's retirement home. Although the caretakers of the property took precautions to preserve the basic integrity of the structure, they did add on two wings that changed the original layout of the mansion. Some of this space can be rented as rooms and apartments today, and a former tenant got a little more than she bargained for one night when she and some friends pulled out a *Ouija* board.

"I lived in the back part, the new part that was built by the nursing home, and I had heard people say the old mansion had a lot of ghosts," reports Sue Larson, a former U of L student who lived there for two years. "One night I was in my room with a couple friends, just hanging out and stuff, and they convinced me to let them get a *Ouija* board and play around with it." Because she "didn't believe in things like the *Ouija* board," Sue says she didn't feel threatened by it. "I thought it was perfectly harmless," she recalls. "I'd heard scary things about people who used the *Ouija* board before, but I never believed it."

By the end of that night, she wouldn't be so skeptical of other people's stories about the *Ouija* board. "We started off with simple, goofy kinds of questions. *Is anyone there? Can you hear us? Are you a woman? Are you a man?* And we'd get simple answers like YES and NO on the board, but I just assumed that someone was manipulating the planchette, so it was no big deal." The girls started to get a strange feeling, however, when they began asking more specific questions of the board. "We found out it was a girl, and when I asked her name, we got G-R-A-C-E on the board. Her favorite color was P-I-N-K. Then someone asked her what color her hair was, and she spelled A-U-B-U-R-N." Sue says it went on and on like this for about a half an hour. When she asked the woman where she lived, the answer was H-E-R-E.

"We all got freaked out then," she says. "Especially me. I didn't want to do it anymore, but they were laughing and stuff, and not taking it too seriously, so I let them talk me into putting my hands back on the board." The girls decided to try a different vein of questioning from that point forward. "They all wanted to ask personal things about themselves, things that only they themselves could know, to see if the spirit knew the answers. *What did I have for breakfast this morning? Who did I talk to on the phone last night? Where does my father come from?* And most of the answers were dead on!" Sue realizes that the answers to some of questions could have been common knowledge to those assembled, but she got the distinct impression that several of the answers would have been known only to the ones who had asked the questions.

"Who made my bed this morning and yesterday?" asked Sue, resting her finger tips on the pointer as she looked at Sarah, a quasi roommate who lived down the hall. Two days in a row, Sue had walked into her bedroom after showering and dressing to find that someone had neatly made her bed. Although there was no reason for the other girl to make her bed, Sue could only assume that her friend down the hall had done it as an unanticipated act of kindness. She expected this to be borne out as she intently watched the pointer silently glide from one letter to the next. "It spelled out *I D-I-D!* Not *S-A-R-A-H* as I had anticipated!" Sue also says her shocked glance in Sarah's direction elicited nothing more than a quizzical look in return. "I asked her if she had made my bed, and she just looked at me like I was crazy and asked why she would start doing something she had never done before."

Sue Larson looked down at the *Ouija* board, suddenly overcome with a sense of uneasiness, and decided to ask one more question: *Why did you make my bed?* The pointer started moving slowly and spelled out this reply: B-E-C-A-U-S-E-Y-O-U-L-O-O-K-L-I-K-E-T-H-E-B-E-S-T-F-R-I-E-N-D-I-U-S-E-D-T-O-H-A-V-E-A-N-D-B-E-C-A-U-S-E-Y-O-U-A-R-E-N-I-C-E. *"Because you look like the best friend I used to have! And because you are nice!"* says Sue Larson. "That really spooked me and I made them put the board away right then and there. I haven't touched one since then, and I don't plan on it ever again. Especially after what I found out a couple of weeks after that episode."

Sue says her encounter with the spirit on the *Ouija* board was made all the more eerie several weeks later. "My family was in town and wanted to get a tour of the mansion. They wanted me to go with them since I had never even done the tour, if you can believe it," she says. "I had calmed down a bit, so I wasn't nervous anymore or anything." But when she arrived and started the guided tour with her family, she claims no more than a minute or two had passed when her sense of uneasiness returned. "The docent had just started her explanation of the formal parlor when one of the other people in the group pointed to a portrait of a young woman on the far wall. She's a young girl with brown hair done up, and she's dressed nicely, and there's lots of pink in the painting that matched the pink throughout the room." According to Larson, the elderly woman wanted to know who had painted the portrait and who had been the subject. When the tour guide answered, Sue says a chill ran down her spine and reminded her of the incident with the *Ouija* board. "Oh, that's *Grace*, the Caldwell's daughter," the woman had responded.

A photo of Grace Caldwell hangs in the front parlor of the Conrad-Caldwell House. Her ghost counts as just one the reported haunts in the magnificent Richardsonian-Romanesque mansion.

Sue Larson says she moved to an apartment in the Highlands and hasn't been back to the Conrad-Caldwell House since. "I don't know if we really made contact with Grace Caldwell's spirit for real or not," she explains, "but it was a really weird experience for me. I don't do *Ouija* boards anymore. And if I think a house is haunted, I don't go in it!"

In the meantime, there have been several new directors at the Conrad-Caldwell House and the stories of strange occurrences continue to surface as more and more people tour the mansion or rent it out for parties and weddings. Margaret Caldwell, a direct descendant of the second owners of the mansion, is very involved in the house today and she and her cousins have heard a number of stories themselves. Margaret is skeptical, however, that it was Grace Caldwell who made Sue Larson's bed. "That doesn't sound like Grace to me at all. She was sort of spoiled and I don't think she made a single bed in her entire life."

Descendants of Mr. Conrad, on the other hand, firmly believe that he could be one of the entities haunting his former residence. One day at a book signing, a woman who said she was a great-granddaughter of Mr. Conrad sought me out and introduced herself. We got to talking about her family and the things she knew about the big mansion. When we got around to the accounts of the apparition resembling Mr. Conrad, I asked her what she thought about the possibility of his ghost haunting the premises, and she said, "Sounds just like him! He was a terrible control freak and would hate to see people in his house." According to the Conrad descendant, her great grandfather was also somewhat of a cheapskate. "Back in the day, when they used to pay their skilled workers 50 cents to a dollar for a full day's work, he'd only pay them a quarter and brag about it to his business associates afterwards."

Is the Conrad-Caldwell House really haunted? And are the would-be specters members of the Conrad family or members of the Caldwell clan, or maybe both? Who can say, except the scores of people who have had unexplained encounters in the lovely stone mansion on the corner of Saint James Court and Magnolia in the heart of Old Louisville?

A local news crew interviews Ally Wroblewsi, the executive director of the Conrad-Caldwell House, about various reports of apparitions and other paranormal activity on the stairs and in other parts of the mansion. The residence is open five days a week for tours. Call (502) 636-5023 for more information.

Chapter 19 – The Ghost of Central Park

Like much of Old Louisville, there's more to Central Park than meets the eye. Scratch the thin veneer covering the past lives of this public green space, Louisville's old DuPont Square, and you might be surprised at what you find. To see it today, with its quiet paths, towering trees and shady walkways, visitors couldn't begin to imagine the long and colorful history behind the seventeen acres of land in the heart of the Old Louisville Preservation District that comprise Central Park. Most wouldn't suspect, either, that it is reputedly one of the most haunted locations in the city, a spot where local residents have caught fleeting glances of a shadowy figure clad in a black cape and top hat as it drifts along the lamp-lit walkways. Speculations vary as to who the spectral figure might be; however, most seem to believe the apparition is none other than a member of a well-known Louisville family who died under mysterious circumstances over a century ago. But, in order to understand the circumstances around his death, one first needs to understand a little of the history behind Central Park.

Although the city has grown considerably, when settlers to the region first arrived in the late 1700s, nothing but marshes and woodlands covered the entire Old Louisville area. It wasn't until 1837 that Cuthbert Bullitt built a small log cabin used as a hunting lodge on the gentle rise that now comprises the highest ground of Central Park. Although a farmhouse also occupied the little hill for a time after that, the land remained virtually unspoiled for years. Stuart Robinson, pastor of the affluent Second Presbyterian Church, bought the land that is now Central Park in 1859; however, the Civil War broke out before he could do much with the land. The Reverend Robinson, a strong and vocal supporter of the Confederacy in a city with considerably more pro-Union sentiment, fled to Canada and remained there until after the war ended. Upon his return to Louisville in the late 1860s, he began to focus his interests on his property south of town. He expanded his estate on the hill and included an Italianate country villa sometime thereafter.

The Reverend Robinson didn't spend much time in his new house in the woods, however, and sold it to one of the DuPonts in 1871. The famous DuPont family of Delaware had built a financial empire on gunpowder and chemicals and counted as one of the wealthiest families in the nation. One branch of the family, Alfred Victor DuPont and his younger brother Antoine Biederman, had settled in Louisville in the late 1850s, and it seems they eventually took a fancy to Robinson's mansion and grounds. They reportedly offered to buy it from him for an exorbitant amount, and Robinson took the money and built himself an even finer mansion just across the road. The Robinson-Landward House still stands today at the corner of Fourth and Magnolia and is recognized as one of the more impressive early homes of Old Louisville.

Alfred Victor, or "Uncle Fred" as he came to be known, acted as the patriarch of the Kentucky branch of the DuPonts. By all accounts, he cut a rather unkempt and disheveled figure, despite the large fortune under his control. Some claim this might be due to the fact that there was no Mrs. DuPont to help him maintain a neat appearance. In spite of his somewhat eccentric nature and gruff demeanor, he still had the reputation of being a dandy about town, and being an independent bachelor, Uncle Fred preferred to live in a hotel room at the old Galt House Hotel downtown. Although rumor has it that he built several of the grander Old Louisville mansions, he didn't live in any of them. It appears that Uncle Fred preferred certain downtown "amenities" that were harder to come by in the wilderness.

Photographs of Alfred Victor DuPont (left) and Biederman DuPont (right), as seen in a bound volume about the movers and shakers in the Louisville of the late 1800s

Uncle Fred's brother, Biederman, and his family lived in the former Robinson estate, and they eventually opened the front lawn to the public as a park and playground – due in no small part to the DuPonts' keen business sense. "Bid" realized that if they offered residents a green space with regular special events like concerts, fireworks, and balloon ascensions, people would most likely have to use the DuPont's mule-drawn Central Passenger Railroad to get there. As a result, the park became known as DuPont Square, although Central Park appeared as the preferred name in city atlases and the city directory.

Much of the development of Old Louisville can be attributed to the DuPonts and their proximity to today's Central Park. When the site for the grand Southern Exposition was chosen in 1883, many historians feel that it came as no coincidence that Biederman DuPont, chairman of the committee, chose a location just south of and adjacent to DuPont Square. And when the brothers realized there was a need for more skilled labor in the neighborhood, they took action and provided the major funding for a new high school, the DuPont Manual Training School, which opened at the corner of Brook and Oak Streets. Barely two weeks after attending the dedication ceremonies for the school in 1893, however, Uncle Fred suddenly died of a tragic heart attack on the porch of the Galt House Hotel. At least that's what the *Courier Journal* reported. Certain townspeople agreed, liking to point out with a snicker that Alfred DuPont had indeed suffered an "awful" little heart attack.

Although many years would pass before the "truth" surfaced, it seemed to be common knowledge at that time that Uncle Fred preferred downtown living because of the proximity to various "parlor houses" he frequented and the lovely *filles de joie* who provided him company. When the madame of a bordello at Eighth and York became pregnant, a significant problem developed, as she accused Alfred DuPont himself of being the father. The woman, Maggie Payne, confronted Alfred DuPont at the Galt House, but he refused to accept any responsibility and sent her away. When she pleaded with him to acknowledge the child or help pay for its upbringing, he refused again, and she – so the story goes – shot him straight through the heart.

A scandal of this magnitude would have rocked the DuPont family in modern times, so one can imagine the uproar it would have produced in the image-conscious Victorian society of late 19th-century Louisville, Kentucky. After a hurried family conference, one of Uncle Fred's nephews, Thomas Coleman DuPont, smuggled the body back to Wilmington under the cover of darkness, and after a pay-off, the police backed the heart-attack story, and the newspapers published a fictitious account of the death. (The fact that the editor of the Louisville paper was heavily in debt to Mr. DuPont might have played a part here.) Maggie Payne was never prosecuted, and DuPont family members managed to keep the truth behind Alfred's death hidden – at least locally – well into

WAS MILLIONAIRE DUPONT SHOT?

Rumors Afloat in Kentucky that He Met Death by Violence.

LOUISVILLE, Ky., May 18. — Startling news regarding the death of Albert V. Du Pont, millionaire and philanthropist, was disclosed to-day. Instead of dying of heart disease at Central Park, the home of his brother, it is now alleged that he expired in a disorderly house, and there are rumors that he was murdered.

Dr. T. L. McDermott, the physician who reported Mr. Du Pont's death, first stated that he died in the parlor of his brother's house. It is now affirmed that he died in the residence of a woman named Payne at Eighth and York Streets.

A shot was heard in the neighborhood on Monday night. It could not be traced, and nothing more was thought of it until the next day, about noon, when a wagon belonging to J. C. King's Sons, undertakers, drove up to the Payne house and a coffin was carried in. Shortly afterward the coffin was brought out and placed in the wagon, which was driven away rapidly.

The Payne people say that this coffin contained the remains of James G. Johnson, who had died there. Dr. McDermott signed a death certificate for James G. Johnson, and also issued a transit certificate to take the body of Johnson to Bowling Green, Ky.

The express agent and the baggage master at the Union Station, from which all trains for Bowling Green leave, say that no corpse was shipped to that city. In the official list of deaths of the day there is no record of James G. Johnson's death.

King's wagon was seen to go into Central Park shortly after noon Tuesday, and a few moments later the announcement of Mr. Dupont's death was made. To-day the Payne woman admits that Mr. Dupont was a visitor to her house, and she also admits that he died there, but says there was no violence.

Nevertheless it is whispered that Dupont was shot by the husband of a woman from Owensborough, who found her in company with the millionaire and who then knocked her down and whipped her. The body of Mr. Dupont was shipped to Wilmington, Del., yesterday morning for burial.

The New York Times
Published: May 19, 1893
Copyright © The New York Times

DUPONT WAS NOT MURDERED

HE DIED OF HEART FAILURE IN MAGGIE PAYNE'S HOME.

Becoming Ill in the Street, the Millionaire Philanthropist Sought Rest in the House of the Woman He Had Befriended—A Foolish Effort to Suppress the Facts Aroused Suspicion and Produced a Crop of Wild Rumors—Odd Adventures of a Distinguished Family.

LOUISVILLE, Ky., May 19.—Interest in the death of A. V. Dupont, the millionaire and philanthropist, which occurred under mysterious circumstances last Tuesday, grows instead of waning. The silence of the Louisville papers only tended to whet curiosity and furnish material for all kinds of sensational stories.

After sifting the matter from beginning to end, THE NEW-YORK TIMES's correspondent is able to state positively that no murder occurred.

Mr. Dupont did die in the house of Maggie Payne, at Eighth and York Streets. His body was hurried into a coffin and hauled in a wagon to his brother's home in Central Park before it was cold, and then, to avert suspicion, a bungling attempt to suppress the truth was made. The story of the millionaire's death and his connection with the Payne woman, as learned from Dr. T. L. McDermott, the attending physician, and from Mr. Dupont's brother, is here told for the first time.

Mr. Dupont left the Galt House, at First and Main Streets, at 8:30 o'clock Tuesday morning. He walked down to Seventh Street and Broadway, where he stopped for an hour, talking to some acquaintances. While standing on the corner he suddenly became ill and started along Seventh Street toward York, one block. He turned down York to Eighth Street, one block further, and entered the house of Maggie Payne. He told her he was cold, and she at once started to make a fire. Mr. Dupont sat down in a rocking chair and threw his head back.

Previous pages: **The New York Times** *was just one of the newspapers across the nation to publish conflicting accounts of the death of Alfred Victor DuPont, mistakenly referred to as "Albert" Victor DuPont. Excerpts of reports from May 19, 1893 and May 20, 1893, respectively, show this discrepancy.*

the 1930s when certain relatives allegedly started to acknowledge the details of the scandal. Two days after the death was announced in Louisville papers, the *Cincinnati Enquirer* ran a story revealing all the sordid details, but many Old Louisvillians conveniently chose not to accept that account of the story.

Alfred's brother Biederman continued to live in the country villa for several more years after the scandal, although he eventually returned to the family estate in Delaware, where he died in 1904. His seven children still had use of the estate after his departure, and DuPont Square still hosted many special events that drew large crowds of Louisvillians to its front lawn. After Bid's death, the city carried out its plans to use the grounds for a public park, and hired the famed Olmsted Brothers to do the design. Not too long thereafter, reports of a strange caped figure allegedly began to surface. Many people assumed it to be the ghost of Biederman DuPont himself, since he had loved his country estate so much and could often be seen strolling the grounds after dark. However, when details of the scandal surfaced some thirty years later, rumors started to circulate that Uncle Fred had returned from the grave to clear his name, even though it seemed that public sentiment clearly weighed in on the side of Maggie Payne.

Clancy Berger recalls many summer evenings when he and his brother would play stickball in Central Park, very often long into the night after darkness had fallen and his mother had sent their sister out to fetch them home. He remembers an eerie encounter on one occasion as he ran to retrieve a ball lost in the grass: "I had just stooped under a tree where I thought I would find the ball, when I noticed a strange figure approaching me. He was wearing a cape and big hat, but I couldn't make out much else because the light was behind him. And I remember that it must have been late summer, because you could feel a bit of the fall in the cool night air. And it was sort of humid and damp all around, and there was an unusual fog rising from the earth." As the young boy stared at the figure, the man supposedly stopped and held out his hand. "And he was holding the ball I was looking for! He just sort of half tossed it to me, and it rolled to my feet, and then he was gone. Like he hadn't even been there at all. The fog was pretty thick then, so I figure he disappeared into it. When I asked my friends about it, they said it was the ghost of

Uncle Fred looking for his illegitimate son."

Others have claimed to see a shadowy caped figure in the park after dark as well, and some old-timers refer to it as the Ghost of Uncle Fred. Although the apparition doesn't appear to frighten anyone, an encounter with Uncle Fred can be quite unsettling. When darkness falls over old DuPont Square, and a faint wind gently rustles the leaves overhead, some even claim they have heard the music of an organ grinder off in the distance, and on lazy summer evenings the happy voices of visitors from a forgotten time can be heard lilting in the air. So, although Alfred Victor DuPont is the most famous ghost associated with Central Park, he is by far not the only one.

Central Park's former life is inextricably linked to the world-famous Southern Exposition of 1883, a would-be world's fair of its day that put Louisville on the map and led to the development of today's Old Louisville neighborhood. Although the Derby City had entertained the notion of hosting a large exposition since the end of the Civil War, it began to seriously consider holding its own grand Southern Exposition after the successful Atlanta Cotton Expo of 1881. Biederman DuPont himself served as chairman of the expo committee, and many feel that this directly influenced his choice of the exposition location on the site of the present-day Saint James Court, and just steps from the family estate in DuPont Square. Although the Louisville city limits at that time had reached to within several blocks of today's Central Park, some locals still considered the area south of the park as wilderness. Laborers spent months draining the swamps and clearing land, and before long a magnificent exposition building – reputedly the largest wooden structure in the world – covered the thirteen acres of land.

The Southern Exposition with the theme "From Seed to Loom" opened amid much fanfare on August 1, 1883, with President Chester A. Arthur presiding and Thomas Edison supervising the first throw of the switch. Central Park became both midway and entrance to the fair, and almost 5,000 incandescent electric light bulbs illuminated the building and grounds, the largest concentration of the newfangled electric lights anywhere at that time, even more than in New York City. For this reason Old Louisville bragged for many years that it was one of the earliest neighborhoods lit by electricity in the nation.

Melville O. Briney nostalgically captured the feeling experienced by many visitors to the exposition in one of her many *Fond Recollection* articles from the late 1940s and '50s in the *Louisville Times*: "Ask anyone who was a child back in the '80s and he will tell you about that breath-taking experience. For no matter how often he saw it (and families went over and over again), the miracle was always the same." She wrote,

"There was a quiet that covered the waiting crowds. Then an amber glow began to seep through the dusk, brightening, brightening – until what had been familiar corridors of the big barn-like building became for him aisles of blinding light and beauty, touched with the gold of heaven."

An engraving of the main building of the Southern Exposition, as seen from the west and facing today's Fourth Street – the footprint of the disassembled structure became the site of St. James Court.

A reporter commented: "Mr. Edison's fabulous display of 4,800 incandescent lights of 16-candle power each comes on every evening to bedazzle the beholder. The contract with the Edison Company is the largest ever made for lighting a building with electric lights. The cost of the plant was $100,000 alone, and it is said to have taken 100 men working constantly for a month to string all the wires and to get the equipment in working order." Given the attention Mr. Edison received during his time in Louisville, does it come as any surprise that several residents of Saint James Court claim that his spirit still walks the grounds that he illuminated in such a revolutionary fashion so many years ago? Although it doesn't appear that the famous inventor actually made it to Louisville for the Southern Exposition, he worked very closely with the planners and developers to make it successful. And as a younger man Edison did in fact reside in downtown Louisville, where he worked for a while as a telegraph operator for Western Union. Perhaps his spirit has returned to check on the progress made in the city since then. According to a young couple who left their Belgravia Court townhouse in the early 1990s for an afternoon stroll, a "gentleman who looked just like Thomas Edison materialized out of nowhere, looked around as if lost, and then vanished."

Hardly surprising, the Southern Exposition was a phenomenal success, and hundreds of thousands of visitors showed up in the first season alone. Originally scheduled to last for only three months, the "expo" ended up closing four years later in 1887. For many, these would be the golden years for Central Park, a time when it served more as an amusement park than the quiet oasis it is today. A roller coaster, still a recent invention, joined the park grounds, and a racetrack hosted some of Louisville's earliest bicycle races. Laborers constructed a large bandstand, and some of the nation's leading musical acts and orchestras gave frequent concerts.

Park officials also had a man-made paddleboat lake installed and a fireproof art museum as well, where paintings and other works of art from the collections of J.P. Morgan, John Jacob Astor, Jay Gould, and the Smithsonian Institution – among others – could be viewed. An electric railway, designed by Edison, took visitors around the exposition grounds and all around Central Park. A few years later Louisville would have one of the best electric trolley systems in the country, and at least twice as many street railroads as any other city its size.

Central Park still attracted large crowds even after the closing of the Southern Exposition; however, it soon became apparent that the enormous Southern Exposition building would not be needed for long. Workers gradually dismantled the buildings and used many of the materials in other local construction projects such as the infirmary building still standing at 1412 South Sixth Street and the Fireworks Amphitheater & Auditorium that once stood at the southwest corner of Fourth and Hill. Developers took over the expo grounds and formed the Victoria Land Grant Company, deciding to go with an aristocratic-London-inspired theme. Centered around an elegant mall of landscaped green spaces and an impressive fountain, the streets would be named Saint James Court, Belgravia Court, Fountain Court and Victoria Place (now Magnolia). An added feature would be the unique "walking courts" that provided some extra green space and seclusion in an already tranquil neighborhood. As a result, the park-like layout of Saint James Court merged with the green space of Central Park, turning the whole area into one of the most desirable districts in the city. Before long, it would be home to Louisville's economic and intellectual elite, a favored spot for business magnates and a number of artists, writers, musicians, poets, and architects as well.

A small stone marker at the entrance to Saint James Court commemorates the Southern Exposition, and just steps from that, the lovely Conrad-Caldwell House towers over sidewalks that trace the paths of visitors from a hundred and thirty years ago. Even if recycled materials from the huge exhibit hall can be found throughout Old Louisville, not much else remains from the grand Southern Exposition of 1883, other than newspaper clippings, stories and memories. Every evening, just before night falls, the gas lanterns that line the walking courts and grassy boulevard of Louisville's most prestigious neighborhood hiss and bathe the area in a soft, nostalgic glow. Although the electric lights that debuted here so long ago still remain, gaslight has always been the preferred choice on Saint James Court and around Central Park.

Central Park at dusk – an old mission-style building in the center of the park is the location for an information center today. Call (502) 718-2764 to arrange a guided history and architecture walk of the neighborhood; or better yet, sign up for the evening's "America's Most Haunted Neighborhood" walk and see many of the sites described in this book.

Below: a vintage view shortly after the park's redesign by the firm of Frederick Law Olmsted in 1905.

Photos by Robert Pieroni

Chapter 20 – Strange Goings-On at the Spalding Mansion

Little by little, word is getting out about Old Louisville, this somewhat remote corner of the world with its grand mansions and stately homes in the heart of Kentucky's largest city, this Victorian time capsule with its stories and secrets. But, no matter how many books are penned about the colorful characters here, no matter how many years one resides here, it seems that new things can always be discovered. A hidden gargoyle of stone perched on a church tower, a unique turret hidden away behind a leafy canopy of maple, the tragic story of a prominent family's financial hardships, the sad tale of unrequited love. Old Louisville holds secrets inside and outside the walls of stone and brick that form the bodies of the staid homes here – and one only needs a curious attitude and a penchant for the undiscovered to get swept up in the past lives of this unique part of the world. But be forewarned: Old Louisville has been known to "swallow" people up.

A similar reference could be made about one of Louisville's nearby architectural treasures, the very lovely Thompkins-Buchanan-Rankin Mansion. One could say this lovely Victorian residence – also known as the Spalding Mansion or the 851 Mansion – has been swallowed up as well. Located just a block outside the official boundaries of Old Louisville, this important local landmark remains largely undiscovered to even the most intrepid of explorers – possibly because of its location slightly *outside* the Old Louisville Preservation District, but most likely because it remains totally invisible to passersby. Planners at Spalding University thoughtfully incorporated this elegant residence into the main building during the construction in 1941, and today the small liberal arts university envelopes it on all four sides. A fortunate twist of fate, it has preserved a rare glimpse into the Louisville of the 1800s, when so many other architecturally shortsighted ne'er-do-wells would have gone ahead and torn the building down.

Granted, the lavish residence does come a block or two short of falling in the confines of the modern-day designation of Old Louisville; however, given the fact that the impressive structure can be said to be more indicative of the typical upper-class city residences that in their heyday dotted the *real old* Louisville – that residential area between Broadway and Kentucky Street that housed wonderful examples of Federal and early Victorian domestic architecture – it certainly deserves inclusion in this book. It's also the location where I had one of my most eerie paranormal occurrences, so it's an exceptionally fitting way to end the book.

Most people passing by today wouldn't suspect that the 1941 administration building at Spalding University hides an architectural secret. An entire mansion from the 1870s has been incorporated in the newer structure.

Constructed in the Italianate Renaissance Revival style, the Spalding Mansion lays claim as one of the few remaining structures designed by architect Henry Whitestone, the preeminent regional architect of his day who left an indelible impression on the young architectural landscape of Louisville. Whitestone completed the mansion in 1871 for a local importer, Joseph T. Tompkins, who spared no expense when appointing the spacious interior rooms with the finest oriental carpets, hand-carved furniture, delicate porcelain vases and ornate light fixtures. In 1880, a local distiller, George Buchanan, purchased the property, and when he declared bankruptcy in 1884 and put the house up for auction, another distiller, Rhodes B. Rankin, purchased it. In 1918, the mansion fell into the hands of the Sisters of Charity of Nazareth, who opened Nazareth College, the school that later became Spalding University.

Today, the old residence forms the hidden heart of the university, tucked away in the entrails of a state-of-the-art institution yet offering a refined slice of the past where students can be found casually lounging on antique settees and davenports or where the teaching body gathers for frequent receptions or department meetings. How many of them stop and ponder the past lives of this gentle giant known as the Spalding Mansion? How many of them give a passing thought about the previous owners as they trudge up and down the original hand-carved walnut staircase while sunlight filters down through the beautiful stained glass skylight overhead and illuminates the intricate walnut rosettes, florets and leaves in a comforting shower of blue, gold and green? One day I decided to find out, and the student I subsequently met – and whose story I heard – lead me to believe that some experiences in the old mansion can be anything *but* comforting.

She called herself Amber and refused to give a last name, saying only that she had recently enrolled in the university's creative writing program and that she hailed from eastern Kentucky. Tall and thin, with jet black hair and ivory skin that hinted at her Goth leanings, Amber and I had met on a steamy day in early spring when I had walked over to the mansion to snap a couple of photos with my digital camera. As with other stories, I hadn't actually dug anything up at that point, but I had the distinct impression that I eventually would.

Despite the heat outside, the spacious interior had managed to stay somewhat cool, and only a few students could be found inside; the regular term had ended and summer classes had just begun. As I had done on previous occasions, I tried to strike up impromptu conversations with those who weren't bothered that a complete and total stranger had approached them. To the contrary, most displayed a look of pleasant surprise when I informed them of my intentions of documenting – in some form or other – the history of the 851 Mansion. All of them – to my dismay – had precious little information they could share regarding encounters of the otherworldly kind in the lavish interior of the stately mansion at the heart of Spalding University. All of them, that is, until I met Amber.

She came across as a pleasant girl, if not somewhat aloof, and when I told her about my project, she informed me that she had already read my first book, eager to add that she was looking forward to the next. "I

A side view shows part of the original mansion still visible at Spalding University today. According to numerous reports, the dining room of the mansion is a hotbed of paranormal activity. (Courtesy of F&E Schmidt)

was wondering when you were going to get around to mentioning this place," she interjected between dainty nips at a raspberry snow cone. "There's a *lot* of activity in this place. I can feel it." I asked her what she meant when she said she could *feel* it, and she gave me a bland retort: "I can *sense* those kinds of things, and I always have. I don't know how, but I just *feel* it, that's all. It's something you can't explain to someone who hasn't experienced it for herself."

We sat in the front parlor as we spoke, surrounded by high Victorian furniture. A long, rectangular room with a small bay to the north flanked by beautiful double fireplaces, its walls glimmer in gold-patterned paper, and an enormous brass light fixture with numerous large globes and countless crystal prisms hangs from the ceiling. A masterpiece in and of itself, the ceiling – with its hand-appliquéd geometrical designs of ivory, turquoise and gold – accents the Art Nouveau elements in the room and counts as a stunning example of the importance upper-class Victorians placed on all aspects of interior design.

Amber quickly tired at my ignorance of her extrasensory abilities and decided not to "beat around the bush. If you're interested," she informed me, "some friends and I have been holding séances down here, and we've made some *interesting* discoveries." She raised her eyebrows and lifted her head in the direction of the dining room next door and smiled. "We're having one this evening, if you're interested. Be at the side porch at midnight, and I'll let you in." She quickly gathered up her things and left, not so much as another single word having been said.

I stood and half-heartedly considered the invitation, trying to keep an open mind in defiance of my skepticism regarding séances. Walking through pocket doors into the adjacent dining room, I observed a monstrously large sideboy of intricately carved wood towering against walls done in green and red when a sudden chill ran down my backbone. Enjoying the brief shudder, I realized my curiosity had been piqued, and I decided to make an appearance at that evening's show. I cast a glance at the large dining room table with its ornate centerpiece and eight high-back chairs in red upholstery and then left.

Eight hours later, I seriously reconsidered the idea of joining the festivities as I let myself out the back door and made my way through the alley behind my house and then down Fourth Street to the corner with Breckenridge. However, I reminded myself that I sorely needed some good information for the story, and I let desperation lead the way. As I approached the intersection and the fortress-like, red-brick, turreted structure known as Presentation Academy, I caught a fleeting glimpse of a shadow lurking at the base of the baroque-inspired limestone of the Christian Church across the street. A homeless person? I hoped it was nothing more than that and made my way through a back alley and into a series of maze-like pathways at the back of the main building for Spalding University. I ducked under a small Gothic arch and exited into a secluded courtyard.

Although the façade has disappeared, the lateral exterior portions of the former Thompkins-Buchanan-Rankins residence still remain visible to observers, and the south side of the mansion loomed before me as the soft light of a solitary street lamp bathed the weathered brick and ivory trim in a soft sheen. I glanced at my watch and saw that midnight had just arrived, a fact echoed by the lone peal of a tinny church bell off in the distance. My left hand tightly grasping what appeared to be a wrought-iron railing, I walked up the sweeping steps of the galleried, side porch and came to stand in front of a wooden door. I hesitated a moment and decided to knock softly, but before I had the chance, the door opened silently. Amber stood before me. "Good. You came." She said it matter-of-factly and pulled me inside, the door closing without a sound behind me. I decided to forgo the questioning as to how she had gained entry to the building at such a late hour and followed her through the dim shadows of the hallway.

The double parlor at the Spalding Mansion retains many original fixtures and features from the 1870s. (Courtesy of F&E Schmidt)

We quickly entered the dining room, where four others sat at either side of the enormous table. In the center, a single large, ivory candle rested in a brass holder, while a bright orange flame flickered and danced about, its subdued light providing the only source of illumination for the assortment of somber faces in the cavernous room. "This is Peter, Marella, Christian and Jon," she said, pointing at the respective seats with a richly bejeweled index finger. Concluding her hasty introductions, she sat down at the head of the table and indicated that I should take the chair at the far end. I stammered a bit and tried to explain that I preferred to act as a spectator and not as a participant, to which she responded, "Suit yourself. You can still sit there and observe. This isn't the typical kind of séance, anyway, the kind where you hold hands and stuff." With an inaudible sigh of relief, I sat down and made myself comfortable.

As I looked on, it seemed that the group had gone through the same ritual many times before. Unprompted, they all closed their eyes and "cleared" their minds of negative thoughts for five minutes, upon which followed a sort of prayer in which Amber requested the spirits in their midst to cooperate or vacate the premises – or at least not interfere in their plans. She also assured them of her benign intentions and asked her "spirit guide" for protection during the séance. That completed, she stood and made her way around the table in a counter-clockwise motion, pausing as she passed each participant to gently rest a hand on top of each head. When she reached her own chair, she turned around and repeated the whole procedure in a clockwise motion, this time uttering a soft "amen" as she patted each head. After she rendered her last "blessing" and headed back to her chair, I noticed she had somehow acquired an object that she held out before her. She sat herself down – leaning forward in the process – and placed it on the table so it rested equidistantly from the five participants.

From what I could tell, it looked to be a large, etched crystal vase with a feather inside. I studied it a bit longer as she and the others seemed to pause and concentrate for a moment. The vase, an antique most likely, had a cylindrical shape and looked like it stood eight or ten inches tall. The white plume inside measured several inches taller than the vase so that the top portion of the billowy, downy mass stood visibly higher than the vase. Somewhat perplexed as to its significance, I studied the vase and feather a bit and then let my eyes wander about the rich appointments in the dining room as the others carried on with their ritual.

Overhead, the soft light of the solitary candle reflected off the glossy finish of the ceiling, painted in a light turquoise similar to that in the adjacent parlor. A band of pale yellow crown molding with dentils framed the space and skillfully merged it with the elegant wall covering, and lengths of carved wooden trim had been applied to the ceiling so as to create a pleasant geometrical design. Only the barest hint of light could be seen through the two large windows that flanked the wall behind Amber, and it seemed that the rich burgundy of the draperies melted into the darkness. The stately mantel of carved wood with tiered curio shelves towered over the table and seemed to anchor the room.

I returned my attention to the séance and heard Amber take a deep breath. "Are you here?" she enquired. "If you are present, please let us know." To my amazement, the feather in the crystal vase seemed to raise itself an inch or two from the base where it rested, and then hovered for a second or two before falling back into the container, almost as if a slight breeze had caught it and borne it aloft momentarily. I tried not to act surprised as I observed Christian, the man to Amber's right, ask the next question. "Are you the same being we communicated with the last time we met? If so, please let us know." Once again, I stared in disbelief as the feather lifted effortlessly out of the vase and hung, suspended by who knows what, before falling back inside. I tried to hide my discomfort as the others carried nonchalantly on. I paused for a moment and slowly turned my head both ways, trying to detect a draft in the room that might account for the feather's odd behavior. I could feel nothing except for the slow chill that ran up my spine.

Marella, the girl to my left, had the next question, and, like the others, she appeared to have her eyes closed. "Have you new information for us? If the answer is yes, please let us know." The feather moved a bit, then hesitated and danced an inch or two into the air before settling back into the vase. I slowly turned in my chair and tried to focus on the feather and its receptacle, curious to see if there were any discernible strings or wires or anything that could cause the plume to lift out of the vase the way it had done. I couldn't see anything at all.

To my right, Jon inhaled deeply, closed his eyes and said: "Will you tell us the year you departed this realm? If yes, please let us know." Almost as if on command, the feather quickly darted an inch or two upwards as the participants opened their eyes, and then it turned a graceful pirouette and dropped back into the vase. Peter, the one to the left of Amber, closed his eyes – almost in unison with the others – and then asked his question. "Did you leave after 1900?" If so, please indicate it to us." Unawares, I held my breath as I concentrated on the crystal vase. A few seconds passed, and nothing happened to the feather. Then Amber took over again. "Did you leave between 1870 and 1900? If the answer is yes, please let us know." The feather flew into the air higher than it had before, although it never came close to exiting the vase entirely, and then quickly fell back inside. I could feel my stomach churn a bit.

For the next five minutes, all the participants assembled at the table took turns asking what year the "date of departure" had occurred, starting with 1871 and patiently working their way up into the 1880s and then the 1890s. Throughout the entire procedure, the feather remained – motionless – in the vase. When Amber finally asked, "Did you leave in 1892?" and said, "If the answer is yes, please let us know," the feather quickly darted upwards several inches and landed horizontally on the table, next to the vase. "So, 1892 it is," affirmed Christian as he reached forward, picked up the feather, and deposited it back inside its container. I involuntarily tensed for a moment, my knuckles turning white in the process, and let my eyes scan the room for reactions. Other than Christian, no one had made even the slightest movement.

Suddenly, all heads turned at the sound of several long notes issuing from the baby grand piano in the far corner of the adjacent parlor. There were only three solitary tones, and it sounded as if an unseen hand had slowly pushed down on the same key three times in a row. Everyone hesitated, and I craned my neck to see if I could detect any movement in the shadows near the far-off piano. I could see nothing, save for the reflection of the candle light in a majestic, floor-length peer mirror trimmed with gilt that towered behind the piano. "It's doing it again," whispered one of the others. A knife of tense silence cut through the air. Again, three long, drawn-out notes resonated from the piano.

Instinctively, I got out of my chair and darted into the next room. Although darkness had largely shrouded the space, I could still discern the basic shapes and silhouettes of objects before me. In the second or two it took me to reach the piano, I saw nothing. At least ten or fifteen steps removed from the keyboard, the large doorway and adjacent hallway provided more light, but nothing could be seen there, either. Scratching my head, I returned to the séance table, only then coming to the realization that I might have upset the plans for the evening.

"Well, we might as well call it a night," said Amber somberly. "We won't get anything else now." She looked at me as she uttered this last sentence, but I couldn't tell if she was angry or not. I hoped I hadn't acted inappropriately. I mustered an apologetic gaze and glanced at the others. "Sorry," I said. "I hope I didn't ruin anything. I couldn't help myself, I guess."

Amber reached over and collected the vase and feather, while the others stood and pushed their chairs back into place. "No big deal," one of them said. "The same thing happened last time, anyway. It appears we have a jealous ghost or spirit on the premises." I knitted my eyebrows in confusion. "When we make contact with our regular spirit, it seems that another one always butts in and messes things up," he clarified. "We use the feather as our instrument," he added, "but there's obviously another spirit who prefers a different instrument. Whenever we make any headway with our normal friend here, the other one gets jealous and starts banging on the piano. It has happened the last three times now." With that, we all exited the dining room, sauntered down the hallway and out a back exit. Several minutes later, I was on my way home.

Fortunately, Amber didn't bar me from coming back for the next séance, and in the week leading up to it, I tried to do a little more research into the history of the lovely mansion at 851 South Fourth Street, which I discovered had originally been numbered 931. While rummaging through microfiched editions of *The Courier-Journal* at the Louisville Free Public Library one day, the past came alive as I stumbled across this interesting story from December 17, 1884 about the old house on the campus of Spalding University:

A big policeman stood at the door of No. 931 Fourth avenue [sic] yesterday and warned everybody who passed in to "keep your hands on your pocket-books." The entrance was to the palatine residence formerly occupied by the family of George C. Buchanan. The occasion was the trustee's sale, at the public auction, of the costly furniture and fixtures.

The crowd that gathered was notable for its elegance, large numbers and many ladies. Fully 500 thronged the hallways, blocked the staircases, and filled the parlors and reception-rooms, but the majority were present to satisfy an idle curiosity. It was a luxury to gaze upon the magnificent appointments. Nothing short of the most lavish outlay of means could have provided such a bewildering array of blended utility and artistic beauty.

Even the coverings on the walls have been made the subject of aesthetic study. This was shown in the new wallpapers, frequently designed to imitate metal, leather, majolica, delft and porcelain tiles. The wall ornaments, such as paintings, frames, plaques and statuettes, were in perfect keeping. The floors were richly carpeted, and variety, beauty and a perfection of finish was everywhere in the handsome polished wood appointments arranged in sections of various colored boards, yellow satin wood, white ash, yellow maple, buff oak and dark walnut. Holstery tapestries, damask curtains and portiers harmoniously contrasted with the wood finishings and wall-coverings.

The wall-coverings were made by Hegan Brothers, and are

said to be the most elaborate of any in the Southwest, the cost of this work alone having been over $14,000. The side walls are covered with French *delicante papeur* of elegant design, while the ceilings and friezes are particularly fine. The library is papered with red bronze, with broad, hand-painted frieze and ceiling to match. The side walls of the reception-room are in green and bronze foliage, and the ceiling is in embossed red velvet laid in gold and picked out in transparent colors. The side walls of the drawing-room are in solid embossed gold paper, and the ceiling is beautifully frescoed. The dining-room walls are made to represent old tapestry designs, with the ceiling paneled in black walnut moldings, brass rosettes and hand-painted ornaments. Taken as a whole, the decorations are something simply magnificent, and as a specimen of the decorator's art, reflect great on the Messrs. Hegan. The work attracted great attention from those present at the sale.

The crowd began to pour in before 9 o'clock. The hour and a half which intervened before the auctioneer commenced the sale was devoted to an inspection of the furniture and equipments. Back and side entrances were locked and policemen were stationed at convenient intervals through the building to see that nothing unpurchased and not paid for was removed. From the first floor to the third, the visitors elbowed their way, stopping frequently to admire some striking article or ornate work of art.

An item which attracted more than passing notice was a group of 28 paintings, thirteen being the creations of Mr. Carl C. Brenner. Another noteworthy collection embraced 26 handsome and valuable etchings in bronze, the work of the late John Williamson.

At 10:30 o'clock Auctioneer Sim Meddis erected himself on a table in the back parlor and commenced the sale. The auctioneer's outfit consisted of a huge pair of eye-glasses and a rolled gold watch chain. Mr. Meddis displayed a slight nervousness as he looked before him into an army of expectant faces. Almost every lady present wore diamonds and a sealskin sacque.

Among the bidders were: Mrs. R.A. Robinson, Mrs. John M. Robinson, Mrs. Garvin Bell, Mrs. Samuel B. Churchill, Mrs. Wesley Read, Miss Minnie Read, Mrs. Hampton Zane, Mrs. Henry McDowell, Mrs. Bland Ballard, Miss Walker, Mrs. Bonniecastle, Mr. M. Muldoon, Dr. and Mrs. E. D. Standiford,

Mrs. Wm. Cornwall, Mrs. M. L. Clark, Mr. and Mrs. J. G. Coldeway, Mr. John Hancock, Mr. John DeWitt, Mr. and Mrs. Henry Heath, Mr. and Mrs. J. T. Gathright, Bishop T. U. Dudley, Rev. J. G. Minnegerode, Mrs. James Barbour, Mr. and Mrs. John H. Weller, Mr. C Henry Dorn, Mrs. J. B. Alexander, Mr. Joseph Brown, Mr. and Mrs. Cochrane, Mr. Julius Winter, Mrs. Allen Houston, Mrs. F. D. Carley, Mr. and Mrs. William Bridgeford, Mr. and Mrs. Flyshaker, Mr. and Mrs. Goram, Mrs. Quigly, Mr. and Mrs. Dennis Miller, Mr. and Mrs. Muir Weissinger, Mr. and Mrs. Beckley, Miss Lettie Robinson, Judge William Lindsay, Miss Muir, Gov. and Mrs. Luke P. Blackburn, Mrs. R. H. Higgins, Mrs. W. C. Tyler, W. Chambers Taylor, Jr., Mr. John Stratton, Mrs. Hatton and Mrs. Eugene Elrod.

Just before the bidding began a sensation was created by the announcement that a lady had been robbed. Policeman Jacobs had a few minutes beforehand ejected two suspicious-looking characters from the residence. An investigation developed that the lady who had been robbed was Mrs. A. T. Smith of No. 636 Sixth street [sic]. The lady claimed that a pocket-book containing $15 and several valuable notes had been abstracted from inside the pocket of her cloak.

The bidding was not lively, but the prices realized were satisfactory, averaging about 40 per cent of the actual value of the original purchase money. It was amusing to note two diamond-decked ladies trying to outbid each other. Such sport was relished by no one so keenly as the auctioneer. He never missed an opportunity to excite the indignation of rival ladies, and make the winning bidder pay the highest price possible.

I also came across several photos of the Buchanan interior, and it appeared that little had changed since the splendid auction that had marked the decline of the Buchanan fortune. I could almost hear the auctioneer's gavel as it came down one last time in the opulent downtown mansion. I wondered if this sad departure from the family home had somehow triggered the paranormal activity that Amber and her entourage had tapped into.

Although my research had yielded no satisfactory explanations as to who or what could be paying supernatural visits to the elegant mansion on Fourth Street, I was looking forward to our next meeting, nonetheless. Once again, I met Amber and her friends at midnight on a Friday in June, and it would prove to be an experience that I would never forget.

As before, Amber met me at the side door and let me in. She wore black again, but this time a large, gold amulet hung around her neck. I followed her through the dark corridor, and after exchanging cursory greetings with the others from the night before, I took the same seat I had previously occupied. The darkened room basked in the soft light of a single candle, and I realized how little must have changed in the house since the sad auction so many years ago. Amber commenced with her ritual, and I closed my eyes and envisioned the chamber full of elegantly dressed Victorians as they secretly gloated over the misfortunes of another.

A cool breeze on the cheek jolted me from my reverie, and my eyes popped open. The room had suddenly cooled, and I could see my breath as I exhaled. Gooseflesh appeared on my arms and spread to my neck and legs. I glanced at the others and noticed that Amber was the only one who had managed to maintain her composure. From the startled expressions painted on Marella and Christian, and their rigid bearings, I could tell that this had never happened before.

Despite the uneasiness around the table, I could discern a faint smile on Amber's lips that gradually expanded to a complacent grin. She took a breath and then said, "Good. You are here. Are you the same as we met last time we were here? If the answer is yes, please let us know." All eyes stared at the vase and feather, and we waited, focused. After what seemed an eternity, the feather stirred slightly and raised itself over the rim of the crystal vase. "Good," she replied with a nod of the head that indicated that Christian was to resume the questioning.

"Will you tell us your name?" the young man enquired. "If the answer is yes, please let us know." The feather shifted a bit, hesitated, and then catapulted into the air. One by one, the others took turns asking questions as they tried to discern the name of the entity present.

"Is your last name Thompkins? If the answer is yes, please let us know." There was no movement from the feather.

"Is your last name Buchanan? If the answer is yes, please let us know." The feather teetered back and forth a bit and then lifted slightly. I wondered to myself if Mr. Buchanan really was paying a visit after all these years.

"Does your first name begin with an A? If the answer is yes, please let us know." The feather did not stir.

"Does your first name begin with a B? If the answer is yes, please let us know." The feather did not stir. "Does your first name begin with a C? If the answer is yes, please let us know." The feather did not stir. It wasn't until someone asked if the name began with a J that the feather lifted itself from the vase in the middle of the table. Then they started all

The dining room at the Spalding Mansion – the sight of séances and other eerie events

over from the beginning of the alphabet till they hit on the correct second letter of the first name. It was O. In another half an hour, they had worked their way through the tedious process of ferreting out the letters that would spell the individual's first and middle names.

Amber looked down at the notepad where she had jotted the letters and read the name aloud: "Joseph Rhodes Buchanan." She continued with a question: "Mr. Buchanan, did you use to live in this house? If the answer is yes, please let us know."

We all stared at the feather and vase, and nothing happened. Peter had just opened his mouth to ask the next question, when a sudden wind swept in from the drawing room. All heads turned and once again, the sound of several long notes issued from the baby grand piano in the far-off corner of the adjacent parlor. Again, only three solitary tones could be heard, and it sounded as if an unseen hand had slowly pushed down on the same key three times in a row. Everyone hesitated, and I craned my neck to see if I could detect any movement in the shadows near the far-off piano. Once again, I could see nothing, save for the reflection of the candle light in a majestic, floor-length gilded peer mirror that towered behind the piano. "What should we do?" whispered one of the others as the silence swirled about us. Again, three long, drawn-out notes resonated from the piano. This time, however, I made sure not to budge from my chair.

Amber kept her composure and asked another question. "If there is someone else here, would you like to communicate with us? If the answer is yes, please come to the table and let us know." In the silence, a clock could be heard ticking somewhere off in the distance, and all eyes trained on the crystal vase with the feather in it. Seconds passed and nothing happened. "I don't think it wants to talk to us," said Jon in a whisper. "Maybe we should just leave now." From the tone in his voice, it appeared that Jon had become genuinely nervous, a trait I hadn't noticed in him before.

Amber ignored his comments and sat, her eyes focused on the crystal vase. The candle sputtered a bit and sent a shower of shadows dancing across the wall behind her head. "Once again, will you communicate with us?" she demanded. "If you desire to communicate, please let us know." The candle flame continued its waxy dance as we rested our gazes on the vase and feather. It seemed that about half a minute passed, and then, the feather shot gingerly out of the vase and then settled back in. The temperature in the room seemed to drop, and we could all see our breath around the table.

"Will you tell us your name?" someone asked. "If the answer is yes, please let us know." Moments passed and nothing happed to the feather.

"He's obviously very stubborn," muttered Jon under his breath. "I don't like this at all."

"Will you tell us your name?" repeated Amber in a stronger tone. "If the answer is yes, please let us know." Nothing happened to the feather. "Do you still want to communicate with those assembled? If the answer is yes, please let us know." The feather stirred a bit and lifted out of the vase. Puzzled glances passed around the table.

"OK," resumed Amber, "Do you want to tell us something?" Before she had a chance to continue, the feather flew out of the vase and landed on the table in front of her. She reached over to pick it up, and then put it back in the vase. She looked at the others. "Let's do the alphabet thing, then."

Marella started. "We will each say a letter of the alphabet. If the letter is one you want to use please let us know." The feather did not move.

"Is the letter a B? If the answer is yes, please let us know." The feather did not stir.

They continued down the alphabet but it wasn't until someone asked if the name began with an M that the feather lifted itself from the vase. Then, as before, they started from the beginning of the alphabet till they hit on the next letter. It was Y. Amber jotted each letter down, and they eventually worked their way through the monotonous task of spelling out the message.

Even before Amber looked down at her notepad and read the result, we had all managed to decipher the message. She read it aloud as we silently mouthed the words in unison: "MY NAME IS DARKNESS."

We all got up and left quickly without saying a word.

Amber invited me back to another séance at the 851 Mansion, but I decided I had seen enough. Still a skeptic, I've given up on trying to come up with rational explanations for the strange things I witnessed there, and have chalked it up to the 'unknown.' I'll forego any investigation dealing with the "My-Name-Is-Darkness" element from that night, but the very next day after the séance, I started researching possible connections with a Joseph Rhodes Buchanan who died in 1899. I was very startled with the information I found.

Searches at the Filson Historical Society and the Louisville Free Public Library revealed very little about the Buchanan family, and even less about the Thompkins and Rankin families. What family material I was able to unearth about the Buchanans made no mention of Joseph Rhodes Buchanan, and the trail quickly grew cold. I found it interesting to learn that the family home reportedly had been at one time a favorite gathering spot for neighborhood séances, many of them taking place at the large table in the dining room. Not only that, the Buchanan residence supposedly had been the scene of an authentic mummy unwrapping in the late 1800s as well. As a last resort, I decided to rummage through the clippings files at the library and see what I could find.

From what I could tell, it appears that the clippings files came into being in the 30s and 40s when an attempt was made to organize various newspaper articles dealing with the same people and topics. Hundreds of green cardboard file holders filled with brittle pages pasted with yellowing clippings line the shelves, and pulling out their contents is not for those with an aversion to dust or musty smells. I located a box with clippings from BRU to BY and delved into its dusty contents. About halfway through I pulled out a single, typewritten entry that had been pasted on a brittle piece of black construction paper. It appeared to be an annotation from the *National Encyclopedia for American Biographies* about "Dr. Joseph Rhodes Buchanan, the noted writer upon medical and occult topics." The clunky letters of an old-fashioned typewriter also said that he had been born in Louisville in 1814, and died in California in 1899. One final bit of information noted that after his death, his brain was weighed (a common practice, I learned) and found to weigh considerably more that the average human male's.

Intrigued, I went to the Internet for more research and found out that Dr. Joseph Rhodes Buchanan, a respected American scientist, enjoyed some level of renown for coining the term "psychometry" or "the measuring of the soul" in 1842. He had strong Kentucky connections, but as for his relationship to the Buchanans at 851 South Fourth Street, that's not quite as clear. I decided to leave that to Amber and her friends, assuming it would be something they'd have to find that out at a future séance.

Although I've been back to the Spalding Mansion many times since, I never ran into Amber or her séance cohorts again. In short, I don't know if they ever made any further discoveries, much less ever had another séance in the dining room after the ones I attended. As I continued to do research on the old house, I encountered a number of people who reported strange goings-on there. Although the reports varied from person to person, one thing they all had in common was the fact that the dining room was always involved. Shadowy figures during the day and full-body apparitions after dark, disembodied conversations around the table when the room was empty, unexplainably loud crashes and thumps – these are just some of the things that eyewitnesses have reported.

And as it turns out, the strange goings-on at the Spalding Mansion account for only a small fraction of the purported paranormal activity in the Old Louisville neighborhood. It seems that you cannot walk more than half a block in the neighborhood without coming across a house or an old church or a secluded corner that is believed by locals to be haunted. In the ten years I've been writing about the neighborhood, I've researched over a hundred cases of supposed hauntings myself, so it's not very surprising that word about the wealth of paranormal activity and spooky legends has started to spread. Nor is it surprising that Old Louisville is gaining a reputation as the most haunted neighborhood in the nation. People who love ghost stories and old houses are discovering that this is a neighborhood worth checking out for themselves.

Much of the year, Old Louisville sits safely tucked away beneath a leafy canopy of green and gold that fades in the fall and disappears all together in the winter. While brick and mortar crumble off buildings in other parts of town, Old Louisvillians paint their shutters and prune the azalea bushes in preparation for autumn. When the first parched leaf lets go and silently cascades to the sidewalk below, something unseen in the ground starts to pulsate, and a signal runs quietly through the neighborhood. People feel the vibration in their feet and on the tips of their fingers when they notice the first bristle of chill fall air about them. Somewhere off in the distance, as a milky pall of gray creeps up over the horizon, something clicks and hisses. A tiny spark ignites and flickers, and then mellows into a soft, orange glow as the panes of crystal in the old gas lamps gratefully accept the warmth.

Day is gone. It is just before dark. It is the time ghosts start to wander the streets in Old Louisville.

Seasonal Views of Old Louisville

Spring   *(Photos by F&E Schmidt)*

Seasonal Views of Old Louisville

Summer

Seasonal Views of Old Louisville

Fall

Seasonal Views of Old Louisville

Winter

*Looking for a place to stay during your trip to Old Louisville?
Contact one of these comfortable bed and breakfast inns.*

1888 Rocking Horse Manor	*(502) 583-0408*
Austin's Inn Place	*(502) 585-8855*
Campion House	*(502) 212-7500*
The Columbine	*(502) 635-5000*
Central Park Inn	*(502) 638-1505*
Dupont Mansion	*(502) 638-0045*
Inn at the Park	*(502) 638-0045*
Samuel Culbertson Mansion	*(502) 634-3100*

*For more information about neighborhood events or to arrange for a
history tour or ghost walk, call (502) 718-2764*

For more stunning images of Old Louisville, inside and out, check out this book by David Dominé which features the stunning photography of Franklin and Esther Schmidt. Available at amazon.com and in your local bookstore.

About the Author

A native of Wisconsin, David Dominé has called Kentucky home since moving to Louisville in 1993. Over the years, his adopted state has provided him an unending supply of artistic inspiration, so it's not surprising that - from local hauntings to bourbon recipes - Kentucky spirits frequently come alive in his narratives. In addition to writing travel pieces for local and national publications, he has also published books on Victorian architecture, regional cooking, folklore, and haunted history. David has an MA in German Literature from the University of California at Santa Barbara and an MA in Spanish Literature from the University of Louisville. He also completed studies in literary translation at the Karl-Franzens Universität in Graz, Austria, and received an MFA in Writing from Spalding University. When he's not writing, he teaches language and literature classes at the university. When he's not writing or teaching, he's usually cooking or eating or exploring. Learn more at daviddomine.com/ Read on to learn about his most recent project.

Find out more at: www.facebook.com/TheHouseInOldLouisville

THE HOUSE IN OLD LOUISVILLE

A sledgehammer. A body in the basement. A bizarre love triangle. Kinky sex, illicit drugs, counterfeit money, female impersonators - and a spooky old house. You couldn't make this stuff up.

On June 17, 2010 at 9:30 p.m. police were called to break up a domestic dispute at 1435 South Fourth Street in the historic Old Louisville neighborhood. Patrol officers responded within minutes and they found the caller, Jeffery Mundt, unharmed, in a locked bedroom. They arrested his boyfriend, Joseph Banis, and took him to the station. On the way, however, Banis made a startling claim. A man, he said, had been murdered the year before, sometime around Thanksgiving, and was buried in the basement of the 8000-square-foot house.

When officers returned later that night, they found a large plastic storage container under several feet of dirt in the basement. In it was the body of James Carroll, who had been shot and stabbed. Known as Jamie to many of his friends, Carroll was a hairdresser from eastern Kentucky who also performed as a drag queen by the name of Ronicka Reed.

Banis and Mundt were charged with the murder of James Carroll, but both insisted that the other was responsible. They stood trial in 2013 and the result was one of the most bizarre cases ever seen in the Derby City. In the end, Banis was convicted of the murder and Mundt was acquitted, although he was found guilty of lesser charges. Today, they are both in prison, but people are still wondering about what really happened that night in The House in Old Louisville.

18507206R00173

Printed in Great Britain
by Amazon